AN EXTRAORDINARY DESTINY

AN EXTRAORDINARY
DESTINY

SHEKHAR PALEJA

BRINDLE
& GLASS

Brindle & Glass
An Imprint of TouchWood Editions

Edited by Colin Thomas
Cover design by Tree Abraham
Interior design by Pete Kohut
Author photo by Emily Cooper

LIBRARY AND ARCHIVES CANADA CATALOGUING IN PUBLICATION
Paleja, Shekhar, author
An extraordinary destiny : a novel / Shekhar Paleja.

Issued in print and electronic formats.
ISBN 978-1-927366-59-2

I. Title.

PS8631.A43E98 2017   C813'.6   C2016-908157-5

We acknowledge the financial support of the Government of Canada through the Canada Book Fund and the Canada Council for the Arts, and of the province of British Columbia through the British Columbia Arts Council and the Book Publishing Tax Credit.

The interior pages of this book have been printed on 100% post-consumer recycled paper, processed chlorine free, and printed with vegetable-based inks.

PRINTED IN CANADA AT FRIESENS

17 18 19 20 21   5 4 3 2 1

To my father, Natvar Jamnadas Paleja

1942–2015

"Long years ago we made a tryst with destiny, and now the time comes when we shall redeem our pledge, not wholly or in full measure, but very substantially. At the stroke of the midnight hour, when the world sleeps, India will awake to life and freedom. A moment comes, which comes but rarely in history, when we step out from the old to the new, when an age ends, and when the soul of a nation, long suppressed, finds utterance."

—Jawaharlal Nehru, 1947

PROLOGUE
1947

V AROON WAS HALF ASLEEP WHEN his mother scooped him up in her arms and whisked him to her bedroom, where his father was frantically packing a suitcase. Varoon could hear crickets chirping outside the window and smelled smoke in the air. His mother began to help with the luggage.

"Pack all the jewelry. No clothes," his father said.

"But we should take some clothes. How long will we be gone?" said his mother.

"There's no time, *jaan*. If the Muslim League is behind this—we have to leave now!"

Varoon wondered where they were going in the middle of the night. He was about to point out that he was starting school soon. They'd bought him a school uniform, sent it to be laundered and starched. But Varoon was bleary-eyed and yawned while he watched his parents pack. A distant scream made his parents straighten immediately. His father slammed the suitcase shut while his mother scooped Varoon up in her arms again and they ran down the stairs in the dark.

Outside, Varoon could smell smouldering wood. His mother gripped him tight. His father led them to the gardener's carriage, then whispered, "Wait under here. I'm going to the Desais'. I'll be right back."

Varoon had no idea what was happening and began to cry. His mother cupped her hand over his mouth and shushed him. They hid under the gardener's carriage, behind a wheel with wooden spokes. The red earth they were crouching on smelled chalky. Varoon heard fires crackling. A nearby bungalow was ablaze and its amber flames were sending plumes of smoke billowing into the air.

His mother clutched him closer to her while praying quietly as they hid under the carriage. *Om tát savitúr várenyam bhárgo devásya dhīmahi dhíyo yó nah pracodáyāt Om.* It was the *gayatri* mantra she'd been trying to teach Varoon, which all adolescent Hindu boys are required to learn by rote before their sacred *janoi* ceremony. Since Varoon was only five years old, he hadn't yet memorized the entire mantra. His mother had taken the time to explain some of the ancient Sanskrit: *Giver of life, Remover of pain and sorrows, Creator of the universe, Thou art most Luminous; We meditate upon thee* . . . Varoon couldn't remember the rest and as he watched his mother pray with her eyes shut he wondered if God could hear her prayers. They were so closely huddled together that Varoon could feel his mother's heart racing. It was beating so strong he thought it would surely tear through her chest like the goat-skin drum he'd accidentally ruptured a few days ago. His father had warned him several times, "It's a valuable piece of history—a beautiful heirloom." Varoon didn't have the nerve to tell his father how he'd broken it. Instead, he hid the broken drum among dozens of other items his father collected in the shop attached to their large bungalow, where he made fine chairs from local walnut and rosewood.

Under the carriage now, Varoon could hear distant shouts and screams. He was scared and cold and asked, "Can we get my sweater?"

Just then, a Jeep full of men approached and parked. His mother put a finger to her lips to remain quiet. As the men climbed out of the Jeep, she covered Varoon's eyes. He tried to peer through a tiny chink between his mother's fingers. It was dark but the fire provided some light. Varoon could make out that the group of men had sticks and machetes. About fifty feet away, they pulled the *dhobi walla* who worked by the river out of his hut.

Varoon would often meander down to the riverbank, looking for stones to throw into the water. He liked the ripples. He would go to the river where the dhobi walla and his wife laundered clothes by wringing, scrubbing, and beating them against rocks. Just earlier that week the dhobi walla had asked Varoon, "Want to learn a secret trick?"

Varoon had said yes.

The dhobi walla had scoured the riverbank for smooth, flat stones and told Varoon to do the same. The dhobi walla threw a stone into the river, and it did something incredible—it skipped several times over the water. Varoon asked, "Is it magic?"

The dhobi walla had laughed, flashing his white teeth against his dark skin. He taught Varoon how to hold a flat stone and throw it. After half a dozen tries, Varoon was able to make a stone skip.

The dhobi walla's wife had said, "You're a clever boy. I can tell you're going to be a powerful *zamindar* one day." Varoon had blushed at the compliment. His family owned a bit of land and employed some farmers.

Now the dhobi walla was kicking and screaming while Varoon and his mother hid quietly, waiting for his father. The men pulled the dhobi walla's wife from the hut. She fell to her knees, begging, pleading. The dhobi walla was shouting and struggling to get free. Then one of the men stabbed the dhobi walla in the stomach with a knife. His wife shrieked. The man plunged his knife into the dhobi walla again. And again. The wife's cries pierced the night and made Varoon's mother's hand tremble. Varoon only caught glimpses of what happened next. He heard the wife continue to scream while the group of men gathered tightly around her and stripped her of her clothes. She shrieked and with each cry Varoon felt as though he were being kicked in the stomach. The men threw her in the Jeep and her cries faded as the vehicle sped off.

Varoon's mother was crying now, holding Varoon tightly. She released her grip when she realized that he too was crying silently. Keeping him close to her, she shushed him and kissed him in apology. He could taste salt in her hot tears. The faint scent of white jasmine flowers that she put in her hair every morning after her bath calmed him.

His father returned soon after, breathing hard. He crouched down to speak to Varoon's mother under the carriage. "Mr. Desai says the Muslim League have paid off the police. No Hindu is safe. There's a five-thirty train to Amritsar. The Desais have agreed to give us a ride."

Varoon's mother said, "What about my parents and sister? I can't leave without them."

"But they're the opposite direction from the train station."

Even though Varoon was shivering, he noticed his father's *kurta* was drenched with sweat. It was the same kurta that the dhobi walla washed every week. He wanted to tell his father about what had just happened to the dhobi walla. What would happen to his wife? But before Varoon could get his thoughts together, his father pulled him out from under the carriage and relented, saying to Varoon's mother, "Come, let's get your parents."

Taking Varoon in his arms, his father ran along with his mother. Over his father's shoulder Varoon saw the dhobi walla's lifeless body lying on the ground, his white kurta stained with patches of crimson blood.

When they reached the Desai home, all five Desais were already in the car, ready to leave. Varoon and his parents squeezed into the back seat with the three Desai children, who seemed instantly resentful of the Sharmas. They were all packed together tighter than matchsticks in a new matchbox. With the headlights turned off, they drove in silence. Fires were burning, glowing in the night sky, and the air was permeated with a smoky haze that stung Varoon's eyes.

When they reached his grandparents' home, Varoon's mother ran in and returned quickly, saying to Varoon's father, "We should go in my parents' car. They have more room. They just need some time to pack."

"No," Varoon's father said. "They can meet us at the station."

"But it'll just take a few minutes."

"It's too dangerous," Varoon's father said.

Suddenly a car pulled up behind and honked, which immediately startled everyone, especially Mr. Desai, who was in the driver's seat and jumped half a foot in the air.

"It's just the neighbours," Varoon's mother reassured him and everyone breathed a sigh of relief.

Mr. Desai put the car in gear, turned to Varoon's father, and said, "We're leaving now. You choose."

Varoon's father hesitated and before he could speak, Mr. Desai began driving.

Varoon's mother kept up with the car for a few yards, long enough to touch Varoon's hand through the window, and said, "I'll be right behind you."

Varoon's father leaned out the window and called to his wife, "See you at the station."

It all happened so quickly. No one had asked Varoon if he'd rather go with his mother and he began to cry. His father held him tight. "Mama will be right behind us. I promise."

The drive to the station was dark, quiet. Varoon sat on his father's lap, looking up at the stars and tried to think of the gayatri mantra. *Om tát savitúr*—but the rest of it escaped him. He tried several times but couldn't recall any more. Looking at the stars made him think of his *kundali*, his destiny prediction that a Vedic astrologer had rendered. His mother had tried to explain how wise men could read the position of the stars in the sky at the moment of one's birth to determine a child's destiny, but Varoon didn't understand it. While sitting on his father's lap now he asked, "Are those the stars that the *panditji* saw when he made my kundali?"

"Well, yes. But not everyone believes in kundalis. Some people think it's just silly superstition. I don't think that the stars all the way up there can tell you what your life will be like. You have the choice to make your life however you want, by your actions."

At the train station, they scanned the chaotic platform where hundreds of people had either just arrived or were about to depart.

While passengers boarded the train, Varoon and his father remained on the platform. Eventually, the train blew a sharp whistle. Varoon felt a pit begin to form in his stomach. The train lurched into motion. His father picked him up in his arms. The iron wheels crunched the rails underneath. Varoon kicked and screamed in his father's arms. "Mama! Mama!" They boarded. The train gathered torque and began to accelerate. Varoon kept kicking and screaming while the train chugged out of Lahore Station without his mother. His father held him tight while saying, "She'll be on the next train," and then repeated it again, trying to assure himself as much as his son. "She'll be on the next train."

PART I

ANUSH
FIRST LIGHT

- 1 -

1983

SUNLIGHT FILLED ANUSH'S ROOM AS his mother, Anju, pulled the curtains open and said, "Wake up, wake up, my morning star. It's a special day today."

Anush moaned, "But it's summer holidays. No school today." He and his cousin Paresh had been playing till late in the night with Anush's new football in the back courtyard.

His mother yanked at the soft cotton sheets but Anush resisted. Eventually his mother relented the tug-of-war and lay next to him. She began to trace circles on his back, then letters that spelled his name. It was a long-established ritual from Anush's childhood that had somehow lingered and even though Anush was now nearly ten years old, he savoured this habit. On school days, there was never enough time in the mornings to indulge like this. When he was younger and had nightmares or couldn't sleep, his mother sang him a song from a popular romance, *Kabhie Kabhie*, starring Amitabh, Anush's favourite Bollywood hero. As he lay on his stomach she'd lightly trace his name on his back with her fingertip while reciting verses. But last year he'd overheard his father complain to his mother, "A nine-year-old boy needing his mother *every* time he wakes up in the night?" Anush was aware of the insinuation that he lacked courage, but he liked the way his mother's hair smelled faintly of coconut oil—it never failed to soothe him. Her voice was so tranquil and sweet when she sang quietly to him:

> *Kabhi kabhi, mere dil mein, khayaal aata hai* . . .
> Sometimes, in my heart a feeling emanates
> As though you've been created just for me;
> Before this, you existed among the stars somewhere,
> And now, you've been called down to earth only
> for me . . .

The song had a special meaning because she'd explained to him when he was younger, "Your name, Anush, means beautiful morning star."

After humming a verse now, Anju whispered in her son's ear, "Remember, your father is expecting you to be on your best behaviour today for the guests this evening."

All of a sudden, Anush was reminded of the report card that he'd kept hidden from his father, who had warned that if better grades were not achieved, Anush would be sent to a boarding school. Anush was waiting to give him the report card later that evening, when he would be in a good mood from the whisky with his friends.

Later, after breakfast, when Anush was playing with his new football in the drawing room, he heard his mother from the kitchen. "Anush! Don't play football in the house!"

He was forbidden to play indoors, but he also knew his mother was busy in the kitchen making preparations for the big dinner that evening with Colonel Advani and other important guests. Anush had just smuggled a few ice cubes from the freezer into his water glass—something he was also forbidden to do this late in the afternoon as the ice was reserved for the guests' drinks that evening and because of the summer heat it took a full eight hours for the water to freeze solid. His mother was sitting cross-legged on the kitchen floor, cutting slits into small eggplants, which Chottu, the head servant, stuffed with a dry mixture of tamarind, red chilli, turmeric, cumin, coriander, and poppy seeds before they would be sautéed in oil with garlic, ginger, and onions.

The ceiling fan above provided little comfort from the summer heat—the fan only swirled around the heavy, humid air, which was why Anush preferred playing in the breezy drawing room by the large bay window.

"Anush, will you please come help? There's lots to be done before the guests arrive."

"But, Ma, I'm practicing for the game in the back courtyard this afternoon," Anush said from the drawing room, trying to keep the football in the air using only his knees.

"*No but-ma fut-ma.* No football in the house."

Anush had broken two glasses earlier that week, but now he was on a roll. Once he got past his old record of fourteen he got excited and lost count. Each consequent knee bump was slightly less controlled, sending the football into higher and wider arcs, making Anush follow the ball around the drawing room. It was sheer luck that he kept going as long as he did, but somewhere in the early twenties the football butted against a plate of tomatoes on the dining table and sent it smashing to the floor.

"Anush!" his mother cried.

Anush was already sprinting to the front door, keen to make a quick escape. In the outer hall, he buzzed for the lift.

The lift at Sea Face Terraces, like most residential buildings in Bombay, wasn't automated and required an operator. On each floor, you could see through the slits in the collapsible iron gate and hear the buzzer as it rang in the lift and reverberated through the shaft.

The morning lift boy was new. A few years older than Anush, he was in his teens—a thin, dark-skinned boy trying to grow a moustache. No one knew him by name; everyone simply referred to him as "Lift Boy."

Anush rang the buzzer, but the lift boy didn't come right away so Anush kept the buzzer ringing. The bell echoed up the long shaft. There was no reason the minion should be taking this long, Anush thought, and kept the buzzer ringing even after the lift arrived to the ninth floor. It was a standoff: Anush would not stop ringing the buzzer until the lift boy opened the gate, and the lift boy would not open the gate until Anush stopped ringing the buzzer. The lift boy said, "The lift doesn't go faster if you keep pressing the buzzer."

Anush hated being condescended to. Didn't the lift boy know Anush lived on the top floor in the largest flat? That his father was Varoon Sharma? The building president? The richest man in the building? And how dare this peasant imply that Anush was stupid?

Anush gave the collapsible iron gate a swift kick to put the lift boy in his place and said, "Open it, *gandu*!"

Just at that moment, Anush's mother opened the door to hear him call the lift boy an asshole. She glared at Anush before walking to the lift with the football. "For you," she said to the lift boy.

"But, Ma!" Anush cried. It was unfair punishment; the football was brand new, barely broken in. How could she just give it away?

The lift boy opened the gate but was perplexed and didn't accept the gift until Anush's mother threw the football at him and he had no choice but to catch it. Anush's mother shot her son a look of disappointment before returning to their flat and slamming the door shut.

Entering the lift, Anush turned his back to the lift boy and made a show of checking his hair in the mirror. He didn't want to let the lift boy see how upset he was about losing his football.

Maybe he could talk to his father later and get the football back. His mother had been entirely unfair. Sure, he might have lost his temper, but it wasn't as though it was unwarranted. The stupid lift boy had provoked him, and Anush was certain his mother hadn't witnessed that. So he kept his cool—not an easy thing to do in a tiny lift in the middle of summer with nothing but a minuscule overhead fan, which rotated so slowly you could watch a full revolution if your eyes went around fast enough.

Anush nonchalantly flicked at his hair, trying to make it look like Amitabh's. (Even though the only available tickets to his new film, *Coolie*, were on the black market for four times the original price, he'd begged his mother for tickets and seen the film three times already at the Regal Cinema.) As they stood with their backs to each other, Anush noticed in the mirror that the lift boy was silently laughing to himself and realized he'd have to endure the bastard's tacit smirk every day. The smirk that said, I got your football! He wanted to wallop the lift boy but he knew he'd be unjustified and be reprimanded by his father, who'd just become building president. His muscles stiffened and he clenched his fists. As soon as the lift boy opened the door on the ground floor, Anush fled through the marbled corridor to the back courtyard to meet his cousin Paresh.

All the boys from Sea Face Terraces and the building behind it, where Paresh lived, took advantage of the shade at this time of morning to play cricket on the grassy lawn of the courtyard. Some of the boys were sitting on the concrete ledge now, trying to pick teams, while intermittently punching each other in the arm, arguing over which cricket player on the national team was the best. A few other boys were warming up with cricket bats and balls, hurling insults at one another. A kind of game had begun—whoever could invent the best insult got a round of cheers. As Anush walked towards them, he heard one of them say, "You've got a donkey's dick up your ass and you're braying because you like it!" There was laughter with some applause.

One of the boys spotted Anush and said, "Where's your football, Anush?" which led to a few of the others repeating the question like a poorly rehearsed chorus.

Anush wanted to thrash the boy and yell a line from his and Paresh's favourite film, *Sholay* (also starring Amitabh): *Kuttay! Kamineh! Mein tera khoon pi jaaonga!* Dog! Scoundrel! I'll drink your blood! But there was nothing to gain from showing his frustration. The boys in the courtyard would only revel in the idea of the spoiled, rich only child who lived in the largest penthouse flat in the building losing his brand-new football to a lowly lift boy—it was a whole summer's worth of teasing. Anush kept his distance from the boys and kept looking for Paresh. While walking to the other side of the courtyard, Anush said, "Get your own football." By the swing set there was a thicket of bushes with wild flowers, at the centre of which grew three large palm trees. It was a spot where Paresh and Anush often met.

Anush bent down and made his way through the purple and pink hydrangeas to his cousin and said, "What are you hiding here for? You got a skin mag or something?" One of the boys from Sea Face Terraces had recently visited America and had brought back a *Playboy* magazine, which he'd smuggled down to the courtyard to show some of the other boys, charging them half a rupee each.

Paresh didn't answer. Anush grew irritated as he worked his way through the thicket of green, continuing into the thorny part of the garden, where he found Paresh holding a large brown paper bag.

"Don't tell me I got all scratched up for nothing," Anush said.

Paresh smiled, pulling out a large stash of fireworks from the bag. Anush's eyes widened as he saw strings of lady fingers, aerial shells, fountains, ground spinners, and Roman candles. It was the motherlode. Anush and Paresh had never lit fireworks this big, which were deemed too dangerous for children.

"My uncle gave me these as a going-away present," Paresh said. He was moving to Canada soon. Neither of them knew anything about Canada, except that it was big and cold and on top of America on the map. They were best friends and not being able to see each other every day was too strange, so they avoided talking about it.

Some of the boys from the other end of the courtyard became curious and began to make their way towards the bushes. Not wanting to share their stash, Anush and Paresh quickly stuffed the fireworks back into the bag. As they emerged, one of the boys started singing, "Anush and Paresh sitting in a tree, K-I-S-S-I-N-G . . ." It drew raucous laughter and applause. Anush wanted to punch him in the face, but the boy was bigger than him. Sensing that it might escalate into a quarrel and risk exposing the fireworks, Anush restrained himself and kept walking, his fists clenched.

- 2 -

1983

AFTER DINNER, *SHRIKAND* WAS SERVED. It was Anush's favourite dessert, creamy and sweet with hints of saffron and cardamom. As it was a special occasion, the dish arrived topped with freshly slivered pistachios rather than the usual almonds. The VIP guests bestowed compliments on the meal while Anush's mother and father smiled graciously. Apart from the colonel—an old friend of his father, Anush had no idea who the guests were, but by the way his father had fretted over everything from what the servants would wear to how the furniture was to be arranged—things he usually paid little attention to—Anush knew they were, indeed, very important people.

While the adults talked and laughed at the table, Anush couldn't stop thinking how he'd have to endure the lift boy's stupid smirk all summer. It galled him that someone of no consequence, a minion, a menial attendant, would have the upper hand on him.

To calm himself, Anush thought of the fireworks he and Paresh would soon set off. Would they be caught? Large fireworks were banned in the courtyard, except at Diwali. His father had warned Anush that bad behaviour would not be tolerated, that he'd have to set a good example for the other boys. "No more fights, no more broken windows with cricket balls, no more mischief in the courtyard. Along with the privilege of living in the largest flat in the building and being the son of the building president comes responsibility . . ." Anush could see, sitting at the dinner table with the VIPs, that the rumours and jealous whispers around the building about his father becoming a richer and more important man might be true.

More than once, Anush had overheard his father say, "Anju, you're spoiling him."

Anush finished his shrikand quickly as he was afraid one of the other boys from the building might find Paresh (who was a bit of a pushover) and convince him to set off the fireworks without Anush.

Running down the long corridor to the front entrance, Anush surreptitiously took his father's lighter from the front hall table. It would be easier, safer, to light the fireworks with it rather than matches. His father wouldn't even notice it was gone. Anush would return it within ten minutes.

Not wanting the lift boy to ruin his evening, Anush decided to take the stairs. At this time of the evening the servants of Sea Face Terraces were setting up their bedding for the night on the middle landings in between floors. Anush did his best to avoid stepping on their mattresses and sheets, but he was in a hurry and couldn't avoid every single one. A washer woman between the sixth and fifth floors cursed at Anush as he stepped on the edge of her thin mattress. He stopped on the next floor landing and considered going back to apologize but realized he was wasting precious time.

Anush had never lit a real firework before. He was only allowed to light mini ground shells and small firecrackers, like the impressive-sounding but measly Black Cobra, which was nothing more than a small button that, when lit, sprouted into a paltry black worm. During Diwali he'd watched the older boys from the building light rows of lady fingers and throw them so they exploded like machine-gun fire, or stick an aerial rocket in an empty Thums Up cola bottle, light it, and scamper away before the lit wick reached the main charge and detonated the rocket into flight, sending it upwards at a breakneck speed so that all you could see was a thin, straight streak of lightning zip into the air, fizzle, and disappear into the darkness. It was incredible to have the power to put into motion something so exhilarating. To make the impossible possible. It seemed magical.

When Anush reached the ground floor, he could hear the ocean waves crashing on the black rocks. There was a slight breeze, making the air seem not quite as heavy with humidity as earlier in the day. Anush ran across the grass of the back court-yard, towards the garden with its hydrangeas and blue dawns, which seemed to emit a stronger scent after sunset.

Paresh hissed, "Where the hell have you been?"

"Sorry, *yaar*, couldn't get away."

The two courtyard lights weren't bright enough to illuminate the entire garden and it was dark where the boys were standing, where the palm trees and bushes kept them concealed. Anush stole a glance at the kitchen window nine floors above to make sure it was dark. His parents and the guests would be in the drawing room by the balcony on the front side of the building, with the ocean view. He reassured himself that they wouldn't be able to hear the fireworks. But some of the children who'd laughed at Anush and Paresh earlier that day had windows that faced the back courtyard—they'd be in for a show. They wouldn't dare laugh at Anush or tease him about the lift boy getting his football.

But Anush and Paresh only had two, maybe three minutes to detonate as many fireworks as they could before an adult from the rear of the building would notice and beckon the night watchman. Somewhere in the back of his mind, Anush was aware that if he were to be caught it'd be a huge embarrassment for his father. He might be sent to bed early for a few nights. But his father might secretly be pleased that Anush had taken the initiative to light fireworks usually reserved for the older boys. Wasn't it a sign of maturity? Exactly the kind of thing he said his son lacked?

Anush and Paresh discussed their plan several times, making sure there wasn't a flaw. If the night watchman came, they would make a quick escape into the building directly behind Sea Face Terraces, where Paresh lived. His parents were out for the evening so they'd retreat there.

The boys started setting up the empty Thums Up cola bottles that Paresh had brought for the aerial rockets.

"I'll light the first three," Paresh said, putting three in a group.

"No," Anush said, spacing them apart. "It'll look better if they're farther apart."

They argued about how and where to set the ground fountains and spinners, which would supply the brightest spectacle. Lastly they set up the long string of lady fingers. It was the longest they'd seen. This row of red sticks would be detonated at the end and make the most noise. All those watching would get a show they'd never forget.

Back at the base of the palm trees they went over the whole sequence of lighting the fireworks before beginning.

"I'll light the first shell," said Paresh.

"No way, I'll do it. I'm older," Anush said.

"I found them."

"I got my father's lighter," Anush said, implying that his courage in stealing it should be justly rewarded.

They continued arguing. Paresh could be such a little whiner. He kept pointing out that he'd soon be moving away to Canada and therefore should have the honour.

Wanting to get things underway, Anush passed the lighter to his younger cousin. "You better be careful your dick doesn't freeze and fall off in Canada."

The ground fountain shimmered brilliantly, spewing showers of sparks ten feet high. The boys were impressed. The fireworks were of good quality, not shoddily made as was the case sometimes at Diwali, when high volumes of product were sold and the quality suffered. They took turns lighting spinners, which whirred and whizzed in circles as incandescent sparks flew out from every opening. Anush lit his aerial rockets and made it back to their home base by the palm trees just in time to watch them take off with a quiet *whizzz*. They flew up sixty feet simultaneously, and as quickly as they'd lit up the night sky around them they disappeared. Anush and Paresh lit a few more fountains and spinners, laughing at themselves for jumping at the unexpected sound the spinners made. Anush's heart raced. They were both elated, giggling with delight, running out whenever a fountain or spinner was dying down to light a fresh one. Anush lit his three aerial rockets and sprinted back to the base of the palm trees to see them soar up in beautiful arcs. Three flashes of blue lightning in a dark sky. He noticed his forearms were scratched and bleeding a little from the thorns in the bushes, but he was so euphoric he felt no pain. After Paresh lit his aerials, they were both back at their base, ready for the finale—the two massive Roman candles.

Anush didn't admit to Paresh that he was nervous about lighting the Roman candles. They'd seen older boys light them, and it seemed that the courage of a boy was truly tested when he was holding a Roman candle. Some boys who acted tough ended up being cowards when they lit Roman candles in their hands, dropping them and scurrying away as the charges detonated and the sparked stars shot out from the tube lying on the ground. Some were so afraid that they would place them in bottles and run away to watch from a distance. But the bravest ones held the tube firmly in their hands while the stars propelled from it like bullets.

Both Anush and Paresh had their Roman candles pointed away from them towards the opposite end of the courtyard. Paresh lit his first. For five long seconds nothing happened. And then the first star fired out: a red comet, and then the next, and on and on. Anush gingerly lit his, holding the Roman candle out as far away from his body as he could. Paresh lit the long wick of the lady fingers on the ground after his Roman candle had emptied. Anush's hand was still outstretched, holding the Roman candle, his body knotted tight. The first star from his Roman candle seemed to take an eternity. Maybe it was defective. When it finally fired, the first star took off with a screaming hiss and reached the other end of the courtyard with reckless speed, sparkling against the cement wall. These candles, especially Anush's, were the best they'd seen, packed with plenty of powder, giving the stars incredible velocity. The string of lady fingers went off like intermittent machine-gun fire while the courtyard was ablaze with shimmering sparks from the ground fountains and the Roman candles. As the second star detonated from Anush's Roman candle, he noticed something shift in his peripheral vision. It was the lift boy coming towards them. Anush pointed the Roman candle at the lift boy and another star fired.

Through the noise of the exploding lady fingers, Anush could barely hear the lift boy's cries of pain, but he did see him on the ground, writhing, clutching his face. The night watchman from the building yelled at Anush and Paresh. Anush dropped his Roman candle, which continued firing. Paresh went the route they'd discussed, but Anush became flustered, and by habit found himself dashing into Sea Face Terraces through the back entrance and up the stairs, running quicker than he ever had, his heart racing as fast as the rupturing row of lady fingers that were still going off in the courtyard. On the ninth floor Anush stopped to catch his breath, doubling over for air. What had happened to the lift boy?

I just wanted to scare him, he kept thinking. *It was an accident.* He kept rewinding to moments earlier. *How could I have aimed the Roman candle from so far and hit him?* But he had aimed it. No matter how many times he went over it he couldn't go back in time, and as his desperation grew, he realized what was done couldn't be undone. As he heaved for breath, he knew something, somehow, had irrevocably changed.

- 3 -

1983

THE PILLOW AND SHEETS ON the bed that Reza was lying in were so white that he thought he was dreaming at first. The sterile smell of medicine was foreign and slightly discomforting. A curtain hung to his right. He had never been in a room like this before, let alone on a proper bed raised off the ground.

Where was he? Why was he here? His head hurt and his stomach rumbled. He was ravenous.

A lady carrying a tray and wearing a white nurse's cap pulled the curtain open. Reza sat up, thinking she would berate him. Beds like this were for rich people. He noticed a tube attached to his arm. The lady said, "Lie down, lie down," easing him back down, making sure the tube remained in his arm.

"Where am I?" he asked.

She looked at him as though he'd just asked the stupidest question. "In the hospital," she said, adjusting his bedsheet and then giving him a glass of water and two pills. "Take these."

He put the yellow pills in his mouth and began to chew. They were the foulest thing he'd ever tasted. Worse than the time he and his brother found old *jalebis* behind a sweet shop.

"Don't chew them!" she said. "Just swallow with water."

He did. She left, annoyed.

He wished he were home. Reza hadn't been to his village in nearly a year. Since he could barely read or write, every month he would pay Akil, a night watchman at Sea Face Terraces, to write a letter, dictating his thoughts. Reza imagined his mother and his brothers and sister all huddled outside their hut while his uncle, Nabil *chacha*, read the letter out loud. Despite having to work six, sometimes seven days a week, the job wasn't too difficult, Reza said. He left out the part about having to adjust his sleep schedule to the night shift every second or third week. He also didn't mention how most of the residents paid no attention to him, carrying on conversations in the lift as though he were invisible. Over the months, Reza had picked up some Marathi, Punjabi, even a bit of Bengali. When the residents spoke of private affairs in the lift, they whispered in English, a language foreign to Reza.

In his letters he described being a lift boy for the wealthy as a thing of privilege. *The sea is just a hundred feet away with gardens full of colourful flowers I never knew existed. There is nothing like the cool sea breeze at night—it sings me to sleep. The marble-lined walls and floors of the main hall in Sea Face Terraces are so magnificent, so smooth . . .* He left out the part about where the lift boys lived, which was essentially next to a garbage pit. The residents of the building dropped their refuse in the tiny inner courtyard that was next to where the three lift boys slept. Rats were a problem. The senior employees, such as the custodians and watchmen, had much nicer accommodation—they stayed in the back of the building, sharing a small, old garage space.

In his letters, despite his efforts to not mention his loneliness, his longing for home, Reza wondered if his mother was able to sense it.

He was looking forward to his full month off. All three lift boys took a month off yearly to visit their villages, and Reza's turn was coming up. He would return with a brand-new football.

The football. The ninth floor. Anush Sharma.

His heartbeat quickened and Reza sat up. There was something he was not remembering. But what was it? Something just out of reach—like reaching for a low-hanging mango that he could barely graze. He'd just been given a brand-new football, which he kept hidden near his bedding. Where was it now? Had the other two lift boys found it? If so, they would claim it as theirs. They were both older than Reza.

It occurred to him he had not missed a day of work till now. What would happen? Would he be sacked? Be out on the streets? Forced to return to the village? There was no work there except seasonal farm work, which was dangerous and paid little. His father could help him with that. But Reza had sworn never to speak to him again.

The curtain opened. It was Akil, the night watchman.

"How are you?" he asked.

"Alright."

"Listen," he whispered, "the *sahib* is on his way. He will most likely offer you some money. The more you act in pain, the more you'll get."

Reza didn't know what Akil was talking about. But the idea of getting money was important enough not to interrupt.

Akil sat on the edge of Reza's bed and leaned closer. He reeked of beedis and whispered, "Your father's debt isn't paid off yet. Whatever you get from the sahib, I will take half."

"But the debt is almost paid in full," Reza said. The whole reason Reza had gotten the job at Sea Face Terraces was because his father had got drunk one night and gambled away the family savings to Akil, who was home on vacation. Reza's father couldn't pay the debt so Akil had suggested that Reza work at Sea Face Terraces for a year and pay it back. After that, he'd be able to keep his full income. It seemed like a fair deal to all: Reza got a job in the city at a beautiful building by the ocean, Akil collected his debt, and Reza's father could keep drinking.

"I will take half," Akil said, squeezing Reza's arm. "I got you the job. Do you know how lucky you are? Do you know how many poor Muslim boys like you would slit your throat to be in your shoes?"

They heard the footsteps of fine shoes clacking down the hall. Reza could tell by the confident but slow gait that it was someone important. Akil stood up in deference, like a soldier. The curtain opened and Sharma sahib stood there.

"Leave us," he said to Akil.

"I am like the boy's uncle. We are from the same village," Akil said meekly, looking at the floor.

Sharma sahib said nothing and Akil quickly did as he was told.

Sharma sahib looked at Reza for a while. Reza made sure never to raise his gaze.

"You alright?"

"*Ha, ji,* yes, sir." Very rarely did the residents speak to the lift boys. When they did it was usually to ask if the vegetable walla or milk walla or post walla had come that day. A sahib had never asked him a question about himself. It felt strange, unnatural. Reza wanted to ask, *What am I doing here? What happened?* But to ask a sahib questions like that was too impertinent. Especially a Hindu sahib.

He remembered what had happened a couple of years ago to his father's friend who'd spoken up against a nearby zamindar. No one was sure exactly what the friend had done or said to this landowner. He was reported missing, his body found days later in a ditch. Reza and his cousins got a quick look before being shooed away by local police. The man's face was unrecognizable. Stomped out. Obliterated. The rest of his body was similarly trampled. As though he were a cockroach. Bits of maroon and brown from his insides spewed out of his decomposing body and mixed into the dirt and mud while flies droned. The man was only discernible by his yellow paisley-patterned head scarf. Reza remembered the policemen stood smoking, talking, shooing the children away, as though it was nothing more than a dead rat. Rumours abounded in the village that the local police, who were all fed by the zamindar, had ordered the police to murder the man. Some said the man had tried to rape the zamindar's daughter, or just brazenly looked at her too many times; a few had suspicions that the zamindar had gotten the man's sister pregnant, and the man wanted some money from the zamindar. Reza's father maintained his friend's innocence. Not long after the body was found, Reza's father was drunk for a solid month. It was the beginning of his long stretches of being away from home, drinking to excess, and abusing his wife and family.

Reza was only ten at the time but never forgot how easily blood and flesh could disintegrate into the earth. It made him queasy, and unlike some of his friends, he didn't stick around for more glimpses of the corpse.

Varoon Sharma sahib said, "It was a senseless accident. Would you like a new job? Learn a new skill? Earn more money?"

What accident? Reza didn't know what to say and kept his gaze on the floor. To be able to send more money home, have a real job, and not live next to the garbage pit might be a good thing. He nodded his head.

"Good," said Sharma sahib, giving Reza an envelope. "This is for you and your family. You can start working whenever you feel better." Then he left.

Reza opened the envelope to find a wad of hundred-rupee notes. More money than he'd ever seen.

Akil returned, sat on the bed, looked in the envelope, and began counting. He smiled like a street dog at a king's feast and said to Reza, "Well done."

Reza was about to tell Akil about his good fortune in receiving a better job but then decided against it as Akil might claim some of that income too.

Akil licked a finger, recounted his half of the bills, and said, "The doctor says you should be feeling better in a few days. I'm going to buy some cigarettes. You want a sweet *paan* or something?"

Reza shook his head. Akil left with a spring in his step.

Reza felt an itch near his left eye and went to scratch it but was surprised to find the eye bandaged. He looked around the room and spotted a small mirror. His reflection confirmed it, Reza thought the bandage made him look like a criminal bandit. When he pressed the white padding there was a sting of pain.

It all came rushing back to him. The courtyard. The fireworks. The Roman candle. Anush Sharma.

What had happened to his eye? It would be fine. Wouldn't it? He pressed at the bandage again, gently, but it was still painful.

He understood at once what the money was for. His left eye. It was gone.

- 4 -
1984

MORNING FOG SAT HEAVY ON the hills as a lone pond heron waded in a creek. It was so focused on fishing that it failed to hear a rustle thirty feet away. A small rock whizzed by, grazing its neck, and the heron took flight.

The group of boys standing behind Anush groaned with disappointment, but a part of Anush was secretly relieved that the rock had missed its target. Slingshots were contraband on the boarding school grounds, but the fifty-two acres of Bharat Academy provided plenty of hiding places. Anush and the other boys had spent the morning searching for rocks along the creek. Each rock they spotted was evaluated for its size, shape, and weight; the smoother and denser the rock, the better the aim.

There were a good deal of woodpeckers, thrushes, orioles,

herons, nightjars, owls, and hawks on the grounds that the boys used for target practice, which was strictly forbidden. The penalty for being caught was a lashing by the headmaster: a tall, menacing man with thick glasses who seemed to trawl the school grounds for no other reason than to find boys breaking the Bharat Academy rules of conduct so he could administer punishment.

It was a cool and misty Sunday morning and the five hills of Panchgani, the area the town was named after, collected thick mists in the morning at this time of year. At night, the temperature dipped so low that the boys had to wear double sweaters to bed and even then they could hear each other shivering in their bunks. Sometimes you could see your breath, especially after drinking a hot cup of chai, or soup—which wasn't often; the soup was frequently stone cold, while the chai was hot but with only a hint of sugar, making it undrinkable.

Being a new student, Anush had had his share of hazing when he first arrived a few months ago. The worst was the bullshit sandwich: two pieces of bread with a thin layer of buffalo dung. But to earn the respect of the older boys, or at least keep them off his back, he knew he couldn't show he was intimidated. He'd noticed a handful of boys at Bharat Academy who were continually bullied and he didn't want to end up being lumped with them. Scrunching up his eyes he took a bite as the crowd of boys around him cheered. After a few chews, one of the older boys commanded, "Swallow it, *bhain chod!*" Anush had never been called a sister fucker before. His impulse was to retaliate; that's what his father would have done. Varoon Sharma didn't let anyone intimidate him. But Anush was the newcomer with no friends. Many of the boys were older than him. As he continued eating the bullshit sandwich, the crowd erupted with wild hoots and hollers and applause. He passed the test, ensured his place among the boys, but for days after, no matter how much water he gargled with, he could still taste dung at the back of his throat.

Even though it was only a half-day's journey by train, the heat of Bombay seemed an eternity away. Panchgani was a hill station that the British had used in the summers to retreat from the torridity; over the past forty years it had become a quaint town with a number of well-regarded boarding schools, a few hotels, and little else. The lush landscape was home to a wide variety of flora, including some alien species brought by the British. Silver oaks and poinsettias were a common sight, as were a plenitude of wild birds and animals.

A few boys had ventured ahead and were calling, "We hit it! We hit it!"

Anush and the others ran to see. A small black-and-gold oriole was lying on the ground, feebly flapping its wings. The boys gathered around it, pushing and shoving each other, arguing over what to do. Some wanted to give it room to fly; a few wanted to step on it, either to put it out of its misery or to satisfy an adolescent barbaric curiosity. Eventually, after one last haphazard twitch of its wings, the bird died.

Even though he hadn't hit the bird, Anush felt somewhat culpable. An older boy patted the back of the boy who shot the oriole, congratulating him. Not wanting another bullshit sandwich, Anush did the same.

He hated Bharat Academy most of the time. His father had said, "You will grow to like it. I promise." With his less than stellar report card and the fireworks incident, Anush had had little choice but to go. He often thought of the night of the fireworks. After bidding an early farewell to his VIP guests, Anush's father had called Paresh over. Anush had hoped his cousin would share the blame with him, but after both boys received a few stinging slaps to the face, Paresh cried and pissed his pants, confessing, "Anush's Roman candle hit the lift boy." Anush said, "But it was an accident" so many times he almost believed the lie himself.

Paresh was sent home and Anush was given a few more burning slaps to the face before the ambulance arrived. By then, half the building had already gone downstairs to see what the fuss was about. Anush remained upstairs, crying in the arms of his mother while his father and the colonel dealt with everything downstairs. Paresh had joined the crowd, and the next day, before flying to Canada, he told Anush how tense it had been when the ambulance came. Some were saying it looked like the lift boy might not even live. Rumours and gossip spread quickly among the crowd. It didn't take long for the truth to be contorted. All kinds of stories were being bandied about as the lift boy was put onto a stretcher. The next day Anush even overheard a boy in the courtyard tell another: "Anush Sharma gouged the lift boy's eye with a broken bottle!" People in the building were clucking their tongues and shaking their heads. "What a tragedy," they said. Someone pointed out, "The lift boy is barely thirteen. What will happen to the poor child? Become a beggar in the streets?"

Anush overheard his parents discussing various boarding schools. At night, when his mother would tuck him into bed, Anush would clutch her and plead, "Please, please, please don't send me away." For the rest of the summer Anush could feel people in the building looking at him with disdain behind his back. He hated it. He could tell what they thought: a spoiled only child who lived in the largest flat on the top floor at Sea Face Terraces, who took delight in blinding poor, defenceless, loyal workers. Paresh, the little bhain chod, had fucked off to Canada, and Anush was left to bear the guilt and humiliation by himself. One night, his mother finally said to him while lying in his bed and tracing circles on his back, "Bharat Academy is a lovely place. If you behave and work diligently, your father will let you come home. He loves you more than you know." Anush was glad he was facing away from her and that the room was dark—she hadn't noticed his tears. His father had not spoken to him since the fireworks incident. It was a silence that Anush knew was imbued with much disappointment. When the time came, Anush was relieved to be sent to Bharat Academy.

While the rest of the boys now made their way into a dense patch of oak and mango trees, Anush stayed, looking at the dead bird. Above its eye there was a small wound where the rock had hit.

A large hand clasped Anush's shoulder from behind. He knew instantly it was the headmaster.

"Come with me," said the towering headmaster. His thick glasses magnified his eyes, making him seem almost deranged.

"But I didn't do it, I swear!"

The headmaster said nothing but tightened his grip on Anush's shoulder as he led him towards the school.

What would happen now? A rap on the knuckles? A lashing with the cane? Expulsion? If that was the case, his father would go ballistic and send him to a stricter boarding school, even farther away. Maybe a lashing would be fine. Maybe he'd be lucky and get away with being grounded to the residence hall on Sundays for the rest of the year.

The headmaster led Anush into his office. It smelled of leather and tobacco. Apart from a portrait of the recently assassinated prime minister hanging on the wall with a fresh garland of marigolds, there were also a few framed black-and-white photographs on the walls, most depicting the history of Bharat Academy. According to the photos, at one time it had had a British name and a pleasantly plump British headmaster who seemed much friendlier than the current one. Anush was left standing in the middle of the office. He dared not take a seat without being told to.

Anush was breathing quickly. His heart raced, reminding him of the row of lady fingers rupturing in steady synch.

The headmaster walked briskly back to his chair. "Please, have a seat," he said without looking at Anush. He took off his glasses and spoke softly, "I'm so sorry to have to inform you of tragic news. Your mother has expired—"

Anush's first thought was that this was some kind of test, to see how new students dealt with adversity. But he realized that was less likely as the headmaster went on with some difficulty. "Your mother, she—expired in the hospital rather suddenly from a tumour. You will be leaving tomorrow morning on the first train for the funeral."

This couldn't be possible. Old people died, sick people died—his mother was neither. Part of him was waiting for boys to jump out from behind the desk and shout, *Surprise, just kidding!*

Was he somehow responsible for this? If he hadn't pointed the Roman candle at the lift boy, he wouldn't be here, he'd still be at home with his mother, and this would surely never have happened. The trickle of guilt quickly turned into a torrent.

Your mother has expired kept echoing in his head. He

thought of the oriole, how it jerked its wings before it stopped moving, and even though it was completely absurd he couldn't stop thinking of his mother doing the same with her arms. He felt as though someone had just kicked him in the stomach. The floor seemed to vanish beneath his feet. The earth swallowed him whole as he plunged into darkness.

- 5 -

1984

IN HINDU CREMATION CEREMONIES, THE eldest son becomes the chief mourner when a parent dies. While some Hindus bestow that duty on the youngest son when the mother dies, in Anush's case it didn't matter, since he was the only child; the onus to lead the cremation ceremony fell on him. But never having been to a cremation, Anush was unfamiliar with the rites and rituals he had to perform.

When he arrived home from boarding school, he barely recognized his home. There were nearly a hundred people packed shoulder to shoulder, mostly distant relatives from his mother's side, half of whom he didn't even know. His father—to whom he hadn't spoken since the fireworks incident—was an only child too, and had no living relatives in Bombay. And Anush's *dadaji*, his grandfather, had died when Anush was a baby. A small photograph of him hung in the *mandir* room where his mother had prayed. It made Anush anxious to think that all he had of his mother now were photos as well. Worse was the vague notion that the emptiness he felt now might grow bigger than he could imagine, that it might eventually engulf him.

A bald priest draped with an orange cloth sat next to Anush. As he nasally recited Sanskrit verses, giving the ancient words a tinny sound that reverberated throughout the house, he sprinkled rice and flower petals over the body, prompting Anush to do the same. They were seated around a small copper cauldron in which a fire was lit. Immediate family sat on the floor with the priest, while relatives and friends sat surrounding them, some chanting along with the priest. Anush tried not to stare at his mother's body, at her sunken face. She didn't seem dead, just thinner and asleep while dressed in a white sari. The priest instructed Anush to place a few sprigs of basil on her lips, which Anush did obediently. Then his aunt applied a strip of turmeric paste on his mother's forehead and tied her two big toes together with a piece of white string. The priest leaned over and instructed Anush to circle a clay pot of water over his mother's head, which he did, but the priest stopped him immediately to point out he was going in the wrong direction. Mortified, Anush corrected himself and circled clockwise. He didn't understand Sanskrit or the reason for any of the rituals, but considering the amount of time his mother had spent praying at the temple and meditating in her mandir room, he wanted to do everything right and not be the one responsible for barring her from being reborn—if that's what happened.

After the ceremony his mother's body was placed on a wooden stretcher. Since it couldn't fit in the tiny lift, a handful of men had to carry it carefully down the stairs. On the ground floor she was loaded onto an open-bed truck full of flowers. Anush rode silently in a car with his father, the priest, and the colonel, who drove, while other family members and friends followed in slow procession.

Anush still wasn't entirely convinced that his mother was dead. In the back of his mind he was sure he'd see her on his next visit from boarding school. The idea of life without his mother was too nebulous to comprehend. But the fact that her body was now going to be burned made him anxious. It all seemed so surreal. At home, people had been praying, crying, shuddering, and leaning on one another for support and now he was on his way to light his own mother on fire.

Everything at home over the past day had reminded Anush of his mother: her plants on the balcony were still alive and well, scores of relatives were paying visits, talking of her, and his aunt's cooking was exactly like hers, which annoyed Anush. He'd always assumed that the small strips of cinnamon bark, cloves, and cardamom pods in the basmati rice were his mother's secret signature and so he was disappointed when he found out that his aunt, his mother's sister who now lived in Canada and came halfway around the world for the funeral, made rice the exact same way. He was glad that her son, his idiot-snitch cousin Paresh, hadn't come too. Had Paresh not snitched on Anush over who had injured the lift boy, Anush would not have been sent to Bharat Academy, and had he not been sent away, his mother would not have died. He was aware the logic made little sense but he felt in his bones there was a truth to it, something he could not put into words.

Stepping out of the car, the priest said, "Come, my son—it

is your duty to help release your mother's soul from this world. She was a pious woman who will be at one with God."

They made their way inside the cremation chamber. Looking at his mother's body, covered in the white cotton shroud, Anush began to feel queasy. It dawned on him that this really was the end of his mother's life, and that his life, every life, would end, that there was nothing more. Despite all the talk of his mother being reborn or being with God, Anush wondered if she really would. He was old enough to know that people lied about a lot of things. Even to themselves. Did people really become reborn? Come back as ants or insects? She'd never return, at least not as herself. She was gone forever, and if she did exist somehow, her soul might be up in the ether, among the stars, floating around as cosmic dust, unavailable to him, at least in this life.

As the men placed the body on the pyre, the priest chanted more Sanskrit. A tiny part of Anush was still hoping his mother would somehow, miraculously wake up. The priest asked him to place more flowers and sandalwood incense sticks on top of his mother's body, followed by tablespoons of rosewater and ghee. The fragrance from all the garlands of marigolds and hundreds and hundreds of flower petals that surrounded his mother's body now was so overwhelming it almost seemed sickly sweet. Then he was handed a clay pot filled with water, and he had to walk around the body three times while slowly pouring.

The priest explained, "This signifies the soul leaving the body. When you're done, smash it on the ground."

Anush did as instructed. The clay pot broke with a quiet thud. His mother was no longer the person who loved going to Chinese restaurants, talked excitedly about going to the salon once a month to get her hair done, ate pistachio *kulfi* with her son on Sundays. All that remained now was a body, a shell, a vessel, a clay pot that was easily broken. Why had his mother died when all his friends' mothers hadn't? They would all be alive for decades. It was too much to make sense of. A wooden torch was lit and after the priest said a few more Sanskrit verses in his nasal voice, he passed it to Anush, keeping one hand on it as it was rather large for an eleven-year-old boy. Lighting his mother's body on fire seemed wrong, against every instinct Anush had. The priest, while chanting *Om Shanti Om . . .* , guided the torch towards her body but Anush resisted. However, the priest was stronger, and as the torch's flames licked a few pieces of dry wood, they crackled and the fire spread quickly.

Later that night, lying awake in his bed, Anush listened to the waves from the Arabian Sea break rhythmically on the black rocks. His bedroom on the ninth floor faced the ocean and, as always, the large bay window was open. It was late, past his bedtime, but he couldn't sleep. In the darkness, the ceiling fan overhead whirred faintly. From his bed, through the window, Anush could see a portion of the night sky littered with stars.

He wondered if the eagles that circled during the day for fish left behind in shallow pools by the waning sea would be out now. He remembered him and Paresh throwing pieces of *roti* out his window and how the eagles would tuck their wings, plunging to try to catch the falling pieces of bread.

In the hall, the last of the extended family were finally leaving. Anush could faintly hear them exchanging solemn farewells and best wishes with his father. He'd managed to keep at bay the anxiety of living the rest of his life without his mother—maybe that's what the constant presence of the extended family had done; with all of them around he hadn't had time to be alone with his thoughts. But now Anush could keenly feel a void, an emptiness, take root.

Closing his eyes, Anush imagined himself as an eagle flying away over the shimmering sea, without destination.

After bidding the final guests goodbye, Anush could hear his father shuffling down the long entrance corridor to the drawing room, where he opened a mahogany *almirah* in which the whisky was kept. After some time, his father opened Anush's bedroom door and whispered, "Anush?"

Anush's first instinct was to feign sleep, but he reasoned he wasn't going to be in trouble for being awake. Not tonight. So he opened his eyes as his father sat on the edge of his bed without turning on the light. A patch of moonlight illuminated the ceiling and provided just enough light to make out his father's outline.

His broad-shouldered father, who always had the most upright of postures, was now slouched. Until now, Anush had never thought of his father as an old man, like some of his friends' fathers seemed. Varoon Sharma, the building president, the successful business magnate, the man who lived in the largest flat at Sea Face Terraces, was stalwart not only in stature but also in character. People sought his opinion and were careful to stay on his good side. His sighs were usually laced with exasperation or annoyance, but now Anush spotted in them a sense of defeat.

His father sat on the bed for a while. Anush wanted nothing but his mother to sing him "Kabhie Kabhie " and trace his name on his back. He thought about asking his father to sing the song for him but was afraid that he would think him too effeminate.

His father stared at Anush for some time, tousled his son's

hair, and said, "You have your mother's eyes." He lay next to Anush—something he hadn't done since Anush was a young child. The smell of whisky reminded Anush of the sweet violet jacarandas and pink orchid balsam flowers in the back courtyard of the building.

"You know I lost my mother, your *dadima*, when I was young too."

Despite Anush asking many times about his paternal grandparents, whom he had never met, his father never spoke of them, but his mother had told Anush that his father's mother was lost when his father's family fled Lahore, right after India gained independence from Britain. "Millions of people had to flee from one newly created country into another."

Anush gathered the courage now to ask his father, "How was she lost?"

His father continued to lie next to him, breathing, staring at the ceiling, and finally answered, "Many people were lost that night. It was chaos. But your dadaji and I made it to Bombay. We stayed together and thrived. Just like you and I will."

His father sat up to sip his drink and then said, "Your mother and I were going to tell you something special when you were a bit older. Do you want to know what it is?"

Anush nodded and sat up, intrigued.

"A monsoon storm gathered offshore the night your mother went into labour."

Anush imagined his mother telling this to him now. If he closed his eyes he could almost smell the coconut oil in her hair.

"The wind was tossing branches and spraying dust in all directions. We made it to the hospital just before the rains began. After you were born, I ran through the raging storm to the astrologer to find out your kundali. Even though it's customary to wait for the seventh day after a child is born, I went—I was too excited. With sheets of rain flying sideways into my face I ran to the astrologer to find out your destiny."

Anush asked, "How is a kundali made?"

"God lives in the stars and only God knows everyone's destiny. But over thousands of years, wise men, Vedic astrologers, studied the stars and planets—they learned to read parts or aspects of people's destinies, and yours was read by one of the very best."

A lot of things about God and reincarnation that his mother had told him seemed implausible to Anush. But he remembered her saying, "There are so many things we don't understand or can't see, *behta*. You must have faith, son."

But it provided little comfort now. He tried to convince himself that her soul was free and that she was in a better place—it was what uncles and aunts had said. Anush imagined his mother up in the stars and thought that maybe somehow she might be a part of his destiny now.

But he couldn't help think it was all a lie. He'd burned her body on a pile of dry wood and she was gone forever. Maybe a mistake had been made up in the stars. His mother wasn't supposed to have died so young. Was Anush somehow responsible? The void he'd felt all day began to gnaw its way deeper into his stomach and grow. Would the abyss he was lost in keep him forever?

His father continued the story. "That night the panditji made your chart, then shook his head. He checked it over, and then checked it again. He couldn't believe his eyes and finally said, 'This boy is extraordinary.' When I came back to hospital to tell your mother the good news, she wasn't surprised. She held you in her arms and was so happy. You see, we'd been trying to have a baby for nearly seven years. The doctors had said your mother would probably never be able to. She was so happy holding you in her arms. She said she didn't need a panditji to tell her that you were very special."

AFTER A FEW days, Anush's father returned to work. Anush wondered if it was because he had already forgotten his wife. Was it possible? Could the old man be so cold? What had happened to the affectionate father who shared the story of his son's special kundali a few nights ago?

After coming home from work, Anush's father lit a Marlboro and asked Anush, "So when will you be returning to the academy?"

Anush had assumed he'd return to his old school in the city. "But, I don't—"

His father put his hand on Anush's shoulder and said, "I know you miss her, behta. I miss her too. But we have to carry on. She would have wanted that."

No—she wouldn't have, he'd wanted to yell but couldn't find his voice. Later that night, Anush snuck out and slept in the small single garage downstairs where their driver slept. There was barely enough room for the driver with his bedding unrolled between the car and the wall, but he was accommodating and let Anush sleep there. Anush wasn't sure why, but he didn't want to be in the same place as his father. How could his father return to work and pretend as though everything was fine? Nothing was fine.

The next morning Anush awoke to the garage door being opened by his father, still dressed in his pyjamas. As father approached son, Anush feared being slapped, but his father embraced him and broke into sobs. Anush understood then that his father missed his mother just as much as he did, but in order to not let the weight of the loss crush him, his father had to carry on, and returning to work was the only way he knew how. Anush thought of his mother tracing his name on his back, of her being pregnant with him, of the night he was born, his father running through the storm, the special kundali. If he pleased his father and returned to Bharat Academy, everything would be alright. There were extraordinary things in store for him.

- 6 -

1993

ANUSH WAS PARCHED WHEN HE woke up, hungover, in his queen-sized bed. He reached for a glass of water on the bedside table. Major refurbishments were ongoing since the old man had bought the flat next door and the Sharma residence was expanding. The hammering and sawing and drilling could be muffled with a pillow over his ears, but Anush couldn't escape the battering inside his own head from all the cheap whisky the night before. Every heartbeat felt like an assault in his cranium. He regretted getting so drunk last night with his friends—if you could call them that; Anush was aware most of them only hung out with him because he was one of the very few in college with his own car. The old man had bought him an aged Fiat, hinting that if he did well in school, a better car was in his future. Now that he was only a couple of years away from finishing college and being in the real world, Anush wanted to prove to his old man that like him, he'd make a fine leader and take over the successful family business one day. A large part of that meant making tough decisions by yourself and being able to hold your whisky.

Last night, Anush had taken a few of his friends to the outskirts of Mahim, where for over a month, Hindu and Muslim mobs had taken to the streets in riots—at least a thousand citizens were dead. The city had been on lockdown, and now with the military deployed in some areas, it was starting to become safe to venture outdoors again. Anush and his friends had gotten a thrill out of seeing the carnage of arson and riot aftermath.

As Anush drained his water glass, he could hear the din of morning traffic nine floors below while the overhead fan whirled above his bed. The shirt he'd passed out in now clung to his perspiring back and wrapped around his torso—like some kind of python trying to suffocate its prey, reminding Anush of the nature documentary he'd seen late last night on a new satellite channel, Discovery. He wrestled it off now, ripping a few buttons, and flung it to the floor. Chottu or one of the other servants would mend the shirt. The clock on his bedside table said it was just half past ten, but since it was the middle of summer, the heat was already fierce.

Lighting a Marlboro, Anush walked over to the large bay window. The sea shimmered brilliantly, making Anush squint as he exhaled smoke. All those years at boarding school had made him forget how unbearable the city heat could be. Anush had asked the old man for an air conditioner in his room several times. Everyone was getting them these days. But his father's response was always the same. "It's a luxury," he would snap, implying that it was for spoiled, lazy people. Never mind he had one in his own room, but of course, the great Varoon Sharma had earned it. According to the old man, he didn't have air conditioning when he was young so he didn't see why Anush should. Keeping with this logic, progress would never be permitted, all kinds of technology would be denied to the next generation. Bullshit sandwich. He was punishing Anush for not being a perfect student at college. Anush was fed up with the old man always insinuating that he'd made his mark in the world on his own, and that Anush was a spoiled layabout. But deep down, the old man had a soft spot for his son. The Fiat was proof of his love.

Anush wondered if his father had always been so self-righteous or if it was something that happened after Anush's mother died. As far as Anush could remember, the old man seemed different then. However strict at times, he was also happy, capable of spontaneity and mirth, certainly not as aloof as he'd become, but Anush wasn't sure if that was an accurate memory; it'd been too long. Sometimes Anush thought the old man was happy being alone. Maybe it was the environment he thrived in. Sharma Shipping had grown immensely after his mother's death.

Varoon was an early riser while Anush was a night owl, so they barely saw each other. By the time Varoon was off to work, Anush was just waking up. If Anush or Varoon needed to relay something to each other, they did it via Chottu.

Anush was sitting in bed, flipping through the *Bombay Times*, when the banging began again, louder this time. He yelled, "*Arre*, stop the work!" but the drilling and hammering were so loud he could barely hear himself. He leaned over to pour himself another glass of water but the jug was empty.

Anush bellowed for water, *"Pani!"* but it was useless. He heaved himself out of bed, drenched in sweat. It was almost as though the workers had planned it all. He'd instructed them several times now, in strict terms, that loud work was not to begin until he left for college. But some mornings he wondered if they started the hammering early on purpose, knowing full well that he was still asleep. Getting their laughs on the spoiled, rich only child. The epithet had followed Anush for years. No one ever actually said it to his face, but it was implied in their condescending smirks. Even the sea seemed as though it was in on the conspiracy that morning, providing minimal breeze.

Anush stood in his underwear at the foot of the bed, admiring his physique in the full-length mirror. He dropped to the floor, did forty pushups, and then jumped back up, flexing his thin but muscled torso and biceps, and then with his hairbrush began to preen the thick, jet-black hair that he carefully styled every day. He was already late for college, but it was only a maths class he was missing. Nothing he was learning now would ever be of use and so Anush kept brushing his hair, even though he'd soon be showering and restyling it. Now that he'd started playing with it he couldn't stop. The front had to be a little wavy with a bounce to it, suggesting a kind of heroic vivaciousness. After finally getting the last few tufts just so, he picked up his cigarette from the ashtray, still looking at himself in the mirror, pleased with the ab muscles he could faintly make out under his smooth brown skin, and muttered at his own reflection, *"Kitne aadmi thhe?"*—a famous line from *Sholay* in which the villain, Gabbar Singh, asks his top bandits, who've been duped by the two heroes out of all their loot, how large the crew of men was that foiled them. The bandits respond meekly, in terror, "Two—there were only two," and Gabbar Singh begins to snicker, then laugh riotously, maniacally, for a long minute before shooting his men dead with his pistol. It was an infamous bit that he and Paresh used to re-enact as children, taking turns being Gabbar Singh.

Anush hadn't seen Paresh since he left nearly ten years ago, but Anush was going to visit him in Canada soon. Once or twice a year Anush and the old man spoke to Paresh and his parents. The phone line was echoey and often got cut. They talked over one another and asked banal questions with enthusiasm: "How's the weather?" "Oh my god, two feet of snow! How's the weather there?" "Are the mangos good this season?" The calls became less frequent as the years passed. The old man was courteous but brief with Anush's aunt and uncle; perhaps speaking with his dead wife's sister brought back too many memories.

Anush did another forty pushups before taking off his underwear to shower. He was about to go into his bathroom when he caught himself in the mirror at an attractive angle and started to flex his arms again. He wondered what exercises would broaden his shoulders so he'd look more like his father. Just then, two construction workers came into his room carrying tools and buckets. They didn't notice Anush at first, but stopped abruptly as soon as they did.

Anush was instantly enraged. He yelled, "*Chale jao!* Get out!"

They backed out of the room, apologizing profusely. "Please, beg your pardon, sahib. We thought you'd already gone . . ."

But Anush was too angry for excuses. Kicking at their buckets, he shouted, "You're stupider than a fly that sits on a whore's ass! You're worth less than the semen of a street dog!"

He was outside his room now, near the dining area, shouting

at the top of his lungs at two dozen workers, until he realized he was naked. Covering his penis with a cupped hand, he retreated back into his bedroom and slammed the door shut. His heart was pounding nearly out of his chest. The construction had stopped altogether and everything was silent. Through the door he was sure he could hear a few of them trying to stifle their snickering.

His face went red. He'd never been so embarrassed. He looked down angrily at his penis for choosing such a time to become so flaccid. Of course now he'd have to endure them all, every day, looking at him with the knowledge that he'd been posing and flexing in front of his mirror, naked. They wouldn't dare snicker in front of him, but it'd be tacit. He could imagine them during their lunch break, mocking him, cackling with laughter as they did impressions of him flexing his arms. He tried to reassure himself that it wasn't a big deal; at least it wasn't his friends, his peers, mocking him behind his back, but that provided little comfort.

Slamming his bathroom door shut, he stepped into the shower, imagining himself as Gabbar Singh, shooting the workers like bandits with his pistol. Eventually the cold water from the shower nozzle quelled his exasperation somewhat as it cooled his hot skin.

- 7 -
1995

AFTER GRADUATING FROM COLLEGE, ANUSH was put to work at Sharma Shipping, but instead of working alongside his father in the plush, air-conditioned office, he was given a small desk alongside the accounting peons to go over ledgers, inventory, revenue, expenditures. Bullshit sandwich. He didn't see why the boss's son should have to suffer that type of boring minutiae. Sharma Shipping exported fabrics, leather bags, purses, belts, shoes, etc. But the big money was quietly being made in construction, real estate, and whatever else the old man was always on the phone about in his private office. If the old man wouldn't let him play in the big leagues right away, that meant there was more money involved in the real estate ventures than he first thought, and so Anush prepared himself to work in the shipping side of the business for a while, eventually earning his father's trust in order to one day advance to construction and real estate. For years now, he'd imagined himself being a bigwig at Sharma Shipping, taking clients out for seafood lunches at Trishna, hobnobbing over drinks at exclusive clubs like the Bombay Gymkhana—not working alongside lowly clerks and making a paltry salary.

It was humiliating that with all his father's success, Anush still drove a Jurassic Fiat that wheezed and sputtered. Most of Anush's friends had nicer cars now that they were all out of college. One even had an imported American left-hand drive, limited-edition Ford Mustang (despite the fact that it was a killer ride, the loser was chauffeured by a driver).

After a few weeks at the same desk with an onion-smelling account peon, Anush began to wonder if the old man would ever want to promote Anush. Was middle management the best he could hope for? No. Life had better things in store for him. Or did it? He hadn't thought about his kundali for a while. He wasn't sure exactly when, but sometime after coming to Bharat Academy he'd begun to wonder if astrology was nothing but a bullshit sandwich. Did destinies even exist? If so, did he truly have a special destiny? Perhaps getting it read by a panditji was the answer. If it was all bogus, then was this as much loyalty, mentoring, and generosity as the old man was capable of? Maybe it was part of his plan to make Anush feel unwelcome, hoping Anush would just quit, disappear.

Often in the old man's presence, Anush bore the weight of being a failure, and so he couldn't help daydream what it'd be like if his father were no longer around. In this fantasy, the old man wasn't dead per se—just absent—and for the briefest of moments, the weight dissipated and Anush felt as though he could finally breathe, that he was no longer a disappointment, and an effervescence buoyed him. The more he felt this way, the more he indulged in the fantasy.

But after a few months Anush was fed up. It had occurred to him perhaps this was all a test. A real leader wouldn't put up with this kind of humiliation. A real leader would speak up for himself and demand to be taken seriously. One day he finally strode into his father's office and said, "I can't work out there any longer. I'm not—I'm not a low-level accountant."

The old man was on the phone and said into the mouthpiece, "Let me call you right back," and hung up.

"So, you think you're better than everyone else. Is that it?" he said, lighting a cigarette.

"Well, no, not exactly—"

"How many times did you promise to do better in school, huh? I bought you the Fiat for receiving passing grades—not even a single A. But I thought rewarding success, no matter how little, would encourage you to work harder. But you never did. And how the hell do you think you managed to get your degree, let alone not get kicked out, even though you failed so many of your damn classes? Because I kept making sizeable donations every year!" He was yelling loud enough now that the entire office could hear. His words stung harder than any slap.

As Anush left the old man's office, he wished he was anyone else's son, and almost said it out loud but knew better. Instead, he stepped out for a Marlboro.

It was lunchtime in the Fort District and throngs of people passed by on the crowded footpath. As they bumped and nudged their way past Anush, he realized that his father had no faith in him, in his kundali even. Maybe the old man was jealous.

After his cigarette, he walked back into his father's office and said, "Why don't I sell the furniture shop? You're always complaining how it hasn't made a profit in years."

The furniture shop had been languishing for over two decades, since Anush's grandfather had passed away. Anush's father had intended to sell it but didn't have time to deal with the ludicrous amounts of bureaucracy involved, so he ignored it. Over the years most of the three dozen workers had been let go; only about a dozen remained.

The old man finally agreed to Anush's plan, instructed him which lawyers to talk to, and warned that he'd need a mountain of patience as there were decades of old paperwork to clear up for the sale of a building bought nearly fifty years ago. He'd have to go to court and sit with lawyers for hours on end, figuring out which officials to bribe. It wouldn't be an easy task, but Anush agreed. He understood that getting through all the red tape was a kind of test, one that the old man thought Anush would likely abandon and fail, but Anush would prove him wrong, and so he left the office, without saying goodbye to the onion-smelling accountant, got into the Jurassic Fiat, and drove to the other side of Marine Drive.

Anush hadn't been to the shop in over a decade, since he was about eight years old. One of the older workers recognized him and said, "Anush sahib, welcome, welcome." In the office, Anush drew open curtains that had been shut for decades. The air was stale, with dust settled thick on the tables and chairs. Inside a large glass cabinet there were at least a hundred miniatures of chairs and tables. On the wall was an old black-and-white framed photograph of Anush's dadaji. The grandfather had gone mad and jumped out the window at Sea Face Terraces when Anush was a baby. No one knew why. Anush had no memory of it but when he was older he'd overheard boys in the courtyard: "The old man lost his marbles and jumped!" "Splat! Like a watermelon all over the pavement!"

Although Anush never knew his dadaji, now as he stood staring at the dust-laden photograph, he couldn't help but wonder what his last moments were like. Did his life flash before him in that split second he flew? Was there pain? Or just nothing? Anush wondered if the swooping eagles fell faster than a human body when they tucked their wings and dove. He still threw them bits of roti when he was bored, curious to see if an eagle would ever miss unfolding its wings at the last split second. He wanted to see what he'd missed, what no one had seen—his grandfather falling to his death in the middle of the night twenty years ago.

Opening the curtains to another window, Anush took in the view. Marine Drive could partially be seen through the verdant trees. The long, curving road separated the city from the sea, which sparkled under the midday sun. There was a rustle in the trees outside, followed by a screech that startled Anush.

"It's just the monkeys, sahib," a voice said.

Anush turned around to find a small man standing in the darkness of the doorway. "Don't mind them, sahib. They're just quarrelling for fruit."

"You're one of the workers here?"

"Yes, sahib," the man replied. He remained in the doorway, his face hidden by shadow.

"I want everything cleaned up in here. Dusted and mopped. Shining like new," Anush said. He'd learned from his time at Sharma Shipping the error in befriending workers. In lowering himself to their status it had given them permission to snicker at him when he made a mistake or asked a question he should've known the answer to. From now on, he would be in charge.

"Of course, sahib," the man said, continuing to stand there.

Was the idiot awaiting further instructions on how to clean? Anush snapped his fingers and said, "*Chal*, clean the whole place. Tell the others. Top to bottom."

"Yes, sahib. Is the shop opening again?" the man asked, stepping into the light of the office. He was so thin that Anush wondered if the men at the shop were getting enough to eat. Just then he noticed the man's eye patch—the lift boy. The night of the fireworks came back to him. The ground spinners, the rockets, the Roman candle. Anush had lied and said it was an accident, repeated it so much that he nearly believed it himself. But deep down, he knew he'd wanted to hurt the lift boy, that he'd aimed the Roman candle at him. The long-dormant guilt in him began to bubble up.

The lift boy wasn't a boy anymore, and yet except for the patch on his eye he was nearly unchanged. The same thin, angular face and dark skin. Even though he was in his mid-twenties, he'd barely grown and was dressed like a boy years younger, wearing shorts and a threadbare shirt.

As he squatted low to the floor and began sweeping, Anush wondered if the lift boy recognized him. A number of things occurred to Anush rather quickly. He realized the old man must have given the lift boy a job when the shop was fully functional all those years ago, providing the appearance of giving the boy a better future, teaching him a skilled trade, while the old man's real motives were more selfish. Having the lift boy stay at Sea Face Terraces with his eye patch would have been a constant reminder of Anush's delinquency, humiliating Varoon Sharma.

It was the same reason Anush was sent to boarding school—having him around would only remind people of the horrible accident, jeopardizing Varoon Sharma's position as president of one of the most sought-after properties in the area. With Anush at boarding school, and the lift boy working in some godown, people forgot about the ugly incident and the old man not only kept his post but sat on other boards, and as land became rarer on the island of Bombay and real estate prices surged, massive chunks of earth were dug up and reallocated by large bulldozers to make new foundations for new high-rises, and fortunes were made by those in power, by those who brushed unwanted things under the rug.

As Anush watched the lift boy sweep, he realized they weren't that different. They'd both been discarded because their presence was a disgrace. An anger began to stir inside Anush, like tectonic plates deep underground, slowly shifting.

- 8 -

1996

WHILE SANDING OUT A FEW scratches from an old sandalwood and teak jewelry box, Reza made sure to apply equal pressure throughout his stroke, and with only a few passes the surface was smooth. Despite having received little training when he'd begun working about thirteen years earlier in the lower godown as an apprentice, Reza found he had a natural talent with wood and had risen to the upper-level godown where he now worked among the higher ranks of the builders. The men in the shop were all Maharashtrians, mostly Hindu, from villages east of the city, and had grown up together, unlike Reza, who was Muslim and whose village was in the north, in Gujarat. Even though he'd learned to speak Marathi, earned their respect and trust over the years, he still felt somewhat of an outsider at times.

Switching to a finer grit of sandpaper, Reza continued sanding the jewelry box. Wood was unpredictable. Some types of wood seemed to accept coarser grits at first, while others required finer ones. It also depended whether the wood was cut by a sharp or dull blade. What type of finish had last been used on the wood? How many layers? How many years ago had it been stained? An adept sander could even a surface in half the amount of passes that a competent one could. Running his fingers along the jewelry box, Reza assessed the consistency. Were the teak edges equally smooth? The corners abutted snugly?

One of the sanders, a friend of Reza, was joining the rest of the workers in the courtyard for their midday meal, and walking past Reza, he said, "*Chal yaar*, you'll sand that entire thing into sawdust if you keep working on it any longer."

Reza took the box with him into the courtyard. Someone handed him a bowl of red lentils and rice. Now that Anush sahib was at the shop, they were eating a bit better. For years they'd been eating the same *dhal bhat* every day. But now they'd sometimes get red lentils, or a Maharastrian spicy chickpea dhal. If they were lucky, there'd be fenugreek with fresh tomatoes and onions. Reza sat in a shady spot under a guava tree and kept sanding.

From under another tree nearby, one of the workers said, "You practising the back and forth, back and forth, for your wedding night?" which drew a round of laughter from the others.

Reza was getting married in a week. He hadn't met the girl yet, but a few weeks ago, while in his village, he'd seen a photo in which four girls stood, all sisters. They were close in age and dressed in matching yellow and red *salwar kameez* and *dupattas* covering their heads. Reza couldn't tell them apart.

"You'll be married to the one on the left," his mother had said, excited, proud.

"Her name is Shareen," Nabil chacha had said, lying in his bed. He was ill, and it was his last wish to see his favourite nephew get married. So it was all quickly arranged with a family in a neighbouring village. Reza just had to show up for the wedding.

What was Shareen like? How old was she? Sixteen? Twenty-five? It was difficult to tell from the photo. What kind of movies did she like? Had she seen many? If she didn't have a brother to chaperone her, she wouldn't likely have been taken to the cinema in the nearest town. Did she like music? Ghazals? Qawwalis? Had she heard Nusrat Fateh Ali Khan's soul-piercing voice or Bandanawazi's sublime lyrics? Would they get a chance to be alone on their wedding night? Having never been with a woman, he was just as eager as he was nervous.

Before leaving the village, Reza had asked Nabil chacha, "Has she seen a photo of me?"

Nabil chacha looked at Reza, knowing exactly what he meant. Did the girl know she was going to be married to a one-eyed man who wore an eye patch? "I didn't have a photo to send, but I told them what a good boy you are, that you have a respectable job in the big city, how you send money home every month..."

As soon as he returned to Bombay, Reza had a passport-sized photo taken and sent to his village, to his younger brother, with instructions to take it to the girl's family. Even if she knew about him only having one eye, he didn't want to frighten or repulse her on their wedding day. He only hoped the photo would get there in time.

Now as Reza sanded the jewelry box, a present for Shareen,

he considered how many days' leave from work he would ask for. Since the shop wasn't busy, Anush sahib might allow him to take as much leave as he wanted, but of course that would mean less pay. Nearly ninety percent of his salary was sent home every month, and every paisa was well used for everything from feeding his younger brothers and sister to paying for their schooling to buying medicine for Nabil chacha. The little bit he kept for himself he used for seeing old films on Sundays. The new releases were too expensive.

Reza hoped Shareen would get along with his mother, that they'd be able to raise a few more chickens and goats. Would Shareen be happy in her new home? Did she know that Reza only came home for one month a year? Most of the older men in the shop who had wives and families back in their villages barely spoke of them, while a few talked about theirs longingly, non-stop. As Reza ate his lunch in the courtyard, he wondered what marriage would be like.

AT THE *NIKAH*, Reza sat behind Nabil chacha, while his bride-to-be, Shareen, sat behind her father. An imam led the ceremony in which Shareen's father gave her away and Nabil chacha accepted her into his family. The whole while, Reza was trying to spot Shareen, who was sitting among her mother and sisters. All the women's heads were covered by their dupattas and the sisters all looked alike, as they had in the photo. The girls stole quick glances of Reza and his family. Eventually Reza deduced that Shareen was the one who kept her gaze down the whole time and never once glanced at him. Had the photo of him reached her in time? Did she find him repulsive?

When it was time to bid goodbye to her family, Shareen

clutched her mother and sisters and father and they cried together in embrace. While Reza's mother and sisters received Shareen into their family, Shareen's eyes remained downcast, never once wanting to glimpse Reza.

Just as they were all about to begin the small but festive dinner, a loud commotion was heard not far away. Reza saw his brothers getting involved and ran towards the fight.

"How dare you not invite me? My eldest son's marriage—" It was Reza's father. Drunk. Reza hadn't seen him in nearly ten years.

Spotting Reza, his father said, "Ah, there he is. Let me see you, behta."

Reza's two younger brothers couldn't keep their father back and he stumbled towards Reza.

"What are you doing here?" Reza asked, full of shame and anger. Word was that his father was working periodically in neighbouring villages, tilling fields, picking garbage, whatever he could to buy *tharra*—a potent moonshine made of sugarcane, rotting fruit, and other chemicals. It had blinded a neighbour and induced liver failure in another, but the lethal side effects didn't stop poor villagers from drinking it. Before Reza began working in Bombay, his father often stumbled home late at night, drunk, shoving and slapping Reza's mother for keeping money from him that he'd earned so he could go buy more alcohol or gamble. He would rage at the top of his lungs, then cry for forgiveness. With tears in her eyes and a croak in her voice, wielding a knife, she'd say, "If you ever come back here again, I will take your life, by Allah, I swear!" It would keep him away for a few days, sometimes a couple of weeks. Then he would sober up and everything seemed a bit better until he started drinking again. It continued like that until Nabil chacha, Reza's maternal uncle, came to live with them. Reza had no idea what Nabil chacha had said or done to his father, but he hadn't returned since. Reza felt useless for not being able to protect his mother all those years ago as a young teenager while he worked in the furniture shop, not knowing if she and his siblings were safe. The shame still clung to him.

"I came to give you my blessings," his father said, with tears in his bloodshot eyes. Reza could smell the tharra on his breath. It reminded him of the same antispetic hospital smell all those years ago when he was blinded.

People were beginning to gather.

"You have to go," Reza said calmly.

"My eldest son gets married and I don't get invited?"

Reza's mother hissed, "Get him out of here now, before the bride's family sees!"

Nabil chacha was sick and no longer able to protect the family. Reza realized he was the man of the house now. Grabbing his father's collar, he pushed him back. His father's thin frame was light. It took much less physical force than Reza imagined to keep pushing his father, but inside the weight multiplied as his father's eyes welled up with tears. They were out of sight now from the main wedding party. His father fell to the ground. Reza grabbed his foot and twisted till the man began to scream in pain. Reza realized his father was no longer the menace capable of torment. He was just a frail man, fading away. Through tears, Reza said, "Don't *ever* come back."

AFTER DINNER, ONCE everyone had gone home, Nabil chacha said to Reza, "Your brothers put him on a bus to Surat. Don't worry, I doubt he'll return."

They listened to the crickets begin chirping and after some time, Nabil chacha said, "Your brothers helped me make a bamboo screen for you, so you and your wife can have some privacy."

Reza blushed and said, "Thank you." He set it up so that his bed with Shareen in the corner was enclosed. Nabil chacha, his mother, and sister would sleep at the other end of the hut while his brothers slept outside, as they always did, except during the monsoons.

Shareen continued to avoid Reza and went to help his mother and sisters in the kitchen. It was ridiculous, they still had not spoken to each other and at this rate they never would as Reza was due back to Bombay soon. Anush sahib had only permitted Reza a few days' leave.

Reza went outside and sat with Nabil chacha, who was smoking a beedi. The crickets in the lemon trees chirped loudly. The air was wonderful out here away from the city. No oils or lacquers or musty sawdust. No rickshaw diesel fumes, no cars and buses honking.

"What's on your mind, behta?" Nabil chacha asked, blowing smoke at the stars.

An owl screeched in the distance, at which the crickets' chirping subsided for just a moment and then resumed. Reza said, "I'm tired. I think I'll go to bed now. Good night."

"Good night, behta."

Inside, behind the bamboo screen, Shareen was already in bed, turned away, facing the wall. Reza undressed to his underwear and got into bed. He could see her torso rising and falling with each breath, and it quickened as he settled himself under the thin cotton sheet. They lay for a while in silence, trying to breathe normally. Although she was thin, the curve of her hips was exquisite. It reminded Reza of a Victorian chaise longue he'd been working on.

"Are you alright?" Reza asked.

"Ha, ji," she said, using the respectful suffix for addressing an older or higher status person.

"You don't have to be scared of me," he said.

Remembering the jewelry box, he got out of bed, found it in his bag, and returned. "I made this for you," he said. As he reached over her back so he could offer it to her, he caught a scent of jasmine flowers near her neck. It was the most divine thing he'd ever smelled. He'd never been this close to a woman before.

With her back to him, she accepted it, saying, "Thank you."

"It's empty. But I hope you'll be able to fill it one day," he said.

She said nothing more, leaving him to listen to the crickets until he fell asleep.

- 9 -

1996

O NE DAY, DURING THE PROCESS of cleaning the shop
in order to sell the property, while he was overseeing the
workers cleaning the first godown level, Anush turned on an old
band saw and grabbed a piece of wood to feed it, mostly to pass
the time. Just as the spinning blade was about to slice the wood,
Reza leaped over a worker to press the emergency stop button.

"*Arre!* What do you think you're doing?" Anush said, rebuk-
ing his employee.

Reza showed Anush that the safety latch wasn't properly
secure and explained, "Sahib, the wood might have snapped
back into your face. Very dangerous."

Without thanking Reza, Anush retreated into the office and
lit a cigarette. Showing gratitude to Reza in front of all the other

employees wasn't in keeping with Anush's plans of preserving a separation between him and the workers. And yet the guilt from the night of the fireworks all those years ago still swirled heavily in him. He willed himself to contain it. He wasn't going to let an accident from a long time ago cloud his judgment. Cleaning up the shop and selling the property to prove to the old man that he was dependable was his main purpose.

While the workers continued to clean, Anush explored the glass cabinet that housed all his grandfather's miniatures and after wiping away the cobwebs, he was surprised to find they were exquisite in detail—some were made with multiple types of wood: all kinds of chairs and tables, carved, sanded, and elegantly finished with stain. There were also old furniture design books with handwritten notes in the margins. Over the next few weeks, Anush had to meet with lawyers and various city officials every now and then in order to get the paperwork going on selling the property, but he much preferred being at the shop, in the office, leafing through furniture books, matching the pictures to his grandfather's miniatures. He began reading about various unique styles: straight high fiddlebacks, intricate Chippendales, majestic federal ovals, regal Hepplewhite shields, proud Sheraton parlours, graceful renaissance revivals, sweeping rococos. In the collection of miniatures, Anush came to see that his grandfather had taken some of the designs from the books and added his own touches. It seemed the old man had a fondness for curves, sweeping arches, gibbous circles, a preference for subtle S lines.

Anush kept playing with various pieces of wood, cutting, sawing, chiselling, even learning how to use the lathe. Apart from the satisfaction of cutting something in two, Anush liked working with his hands. For several more weeks he studied his grandfather's notebooks, learning about mahogany, teak, sandalwood, shesham, walnut. He'd had no idea that different woods could have such individual properties, that there existed nearly two hundred and fifty types of oak alone, that the grains of wood were all unique. He began to identify the different types of wood in his grandfather's miniatures and slowly began to take an interest in the stockpiles of antiques in the godowns. Some pieces weren't even intact, but the shop had a sizeable, albeit disorganized, collection of antique and heirloom pieces in the godowns: parts of dressers, backs of chairs, legs from tables, stacks of old wood lying in dusty piles, covered with cobwebs.

Then one day Anush had a flash of inspiration. He descended into the godowns and once he had all the workers' attention, he said, "We are going to organize everything in the godowns and start making vintage furniture again."

On the ground floor, Anush began to construct the first of his grandfather's miniatures to scale—a simple chair with spade-tapered legs. After a few unsuccessful attempts, Anush called Reza up and said, "I'd like to make one of my grandfather's miniatures come to life. Can you help?"

Reza nodded. "Yes, sahib."

Reza spent a couple of hours a day on the ground floor with Anush and the rest of his day in the godowns with the other workers. Even with Reza as his assistant, it took Anush weeks to get the chair to look anything like the miniature, and even then it was crude, but he had a natural inclination for the work. After a couple of months the shop was clean and organized, but the workers were bickering among themselves as to how and what sorts of pieces to make. The godowns needed a supervisor but Anush didn't want that role. He was happy to work on the ground floor. He liked working with wood, yet he knew very well he couldn't tell his father that. He wondered if the old man even knew that Reza was still at the shop. It was unlikely. He had probably long forgotten the half-blind lift boy who was surprisingly skilled at woodwork. The plan all along had been for Anush to sell the place, so he eventually telephoned the old man and explained. "There's quite a market now for antique Indian furniture, especially with all the Europeans and Americans travelling here these days. There's profit still to be made from the all wood in the godowns."

"I'll give you one year," his father said and hung up.

Anush was elated not only to keep making furniture but also to no longer have to meet with lawyers in court and bribe various city officials to obtain the mountains of paperwork for the sale of the building. Aware that he was deviating from the original plan of seeing this task through to prove to the old man that he was determined, trustworthy, Anush no longer liked the idea of parting with the shop, despite the fact that the money from the sale of the property would be considerable as developers would likely raze the current building and replace it with a residential tower. However, Anush reasoned, the Sharma empire was growing, and they weren't in dire need of money from the sale of one tiny old building.

The more he worked on the miniatures, the more he realized there was to consider. He experimented etching with different chisels and files while referring to his grandfather's notebooks that held countless sketches and scribbled notes. Each time he worked with a different type of wood, he learned something new about its texture, its malleability, its weight, its durability, its resistance to moisture.

"It's all in the grain," Reza explained.

Some of his grandfather's notes were indecipherable. The faded ink and slanted letters at times left Anush scratching his head, wondering how demented his grandfather's mind must have become before he jumped off the balcony. But between the cryptic mess of words, a line or two would become legible: "... *this season's shipment of cedar absorbs stain quickly, like a dry desert, unlike last season's teak, which repels rainwater like green banana tree leaves.*"

When Anush was uncertain how to cut or sand or join a piece, Reza would teach him, and Reza's status among the workers quickly rose as he became Anush's assistant. In the godowns below, despite their disagreements and squabbles, the workers began to make some lovely furniture.

On smoke breaks, Anush would sometimes stare at the old black-and-white framed photograph of his grandfather on the wall. Dressed in a Nehru cap and wire-rim glasses, Praveen Sharma had a docile countenance. Anush began to notice the physical similarities he shared with his grandfather: the thick, jet-black hair, the square jaw. It was the calm look on his grandfather's face that drew Anush into the photo. Was his grandfather really as serene and undisturbed as his face suggested? Or was there an invisible storm raging inside that led to his madness? Anush's mother had told him his grandmother had been lost during Partition. Anush's father had been barely five years old at the time and, apart from the time around his mother's funeral, they never spoke about it. Over the years, as his father busied himself with business, he and Anush had drifted apart. And now for Anush to ask his father something so personal seemed inappropriate, even outlandish.

While scanning through his grandfather's notes, Anush tried to search for clues as to how or why or when his grandfather had gone mad, but it was difficult to tell. It was funny, Anush thought, how a split-second decision like jumping off a balcony could change everything, irrevocably. It was a morbid curiosity Anush found difficult to let go of. Some evenings, while driving home after a couple of drinks, he thought about how steering the Fiat just a few inches to the right into oncoming traffic could change everything permanently. The passing *zooms* of the trucks held a macabre thrill that made him steer a bit closer towards them. One more inch to the right and what would happen? Would he die and be reborn? Become an ant? An insect? Another person? Would his soul float into the empty darkness of space and meet his mother's? Or would there be a desolate void of nothing forever? He knew his musings were more pedestrian than profound and tried to veer away from such thoughts. The more he focused on wood, the happier he found himself. He now received a bullshit-sandwich monthly allowance (that he had to beg the old man to increase). Even though his budget didn't always afford him the best nightclubs, now he was out on the town most nights. The proliferation of pubs, restaurants, hotels, and nightclubs in the city was relatively new, and like all wealthy Bombayites, Anush enjoyed their novelty and quickly built a name for himself in the burgeoning party scene. During the day, Anush was content working with wood and in the evenings his schedule was rarely empty.

Recently, after a night of partying, he'd come home and watched a show on Discovery channel about genes and decoding human DNA, how things like depression and madness and mental dementia could be inherited through genes. In his slightly drunken state, Anush wondered if he would, one day, eventually fall prey to one of the billions of spirals of DNA trapped inside him and succumb to his grandfather's fate—going mad and plunging to his death.

At the shop, customers—mostly Indian expats and foreign collectors—began popping by every now and then, interested in seeing the furniture that the workers were making. Since Anush was never a pushy salesman—a refreshing experience for foreigners visiting India—word had spread about the quaint heirloom furniture shop. Soon they had sold a few of the items that the workers had made.

In the evenings, Reza joined the other workers in the courtyard for dinner, leaving Anush alone in the office. Anush had gotten used to Reza's presence in the office through large swaths of the day and felt lonely by himself in the evenings. Since he wanted to avoid the old man at home, Anush began going to the gym in the early evenings, where he'd put on a bit of muscle.

One evening there was bickering in the godowns and Anush went down. The sanders and lacquerers were quarrelling. "Reza is in charge of the godowns," Anush said, and strode back upstairs. Promoting Reza ameliorated Anush's remorse, if only for a short moment. As he climbed the stairs, instead of feeling benevolent, compassionate, this little gift to Reza made Anush's guilt flourish. He remembered the night of the fireworks vividly, in slow motion, his Roman candle shooting star that smashed into the other end of the courtyard cement wall with such great velocity that sparks showered everywhere. Anush remembered spotting Reza in the courtyard, and then aiming the Roman candle at him, the lift boy's face being hit, him clutching his face and writhing on the ground. Anush's culpability, for so long buried ocean-deep, began to float to the surface. Maybe he'd made a mistake in promoting Reza. Maybe he should have promoted another worker. Maybe he ought to have thought this through.

In the office, Anush lit a cigarette as he began to gather his things, getting ready to go to the gym. There was knock at the door. He expected it to be Reza or one of the workers but a woman with a German accent said, "Hello. Is the shop still open?" She was a blond, stout but attractive lady in her thirties.

Stubbing out his cigarette, Anush said, "Of course. How may I help?"

Her name was Ebba. She said, *Namaste. Guten Tag,* he replied. They both laughed. Anush turned on the lights in the little showroom on the ground floor and showed her various pieces that the workers had recently made.

She said, "This is my first time in India. My girlfriend and I are going to Rajasthan tomorrow, the Taj Mahal and Varanasi." Anush tried to act surprised by her conventional itinerary. He'd been there on boarding school trips and like most teenagers had been bored.

While Anush showed her tables and chairs, he couldn't help but notice the ample cleavage her blouse revealed. He said, "The walls of the Taj Mahal are inlaid with intricate, priceless jewels. The king who had it built ordered the architect's hands to be cut off after it was finished because he didn't want anything else so beautiful in the world ever to be built." It was one of the few things Anush remembered from his visit there.

"Oh my goodness," Ebba said, covering her mouth, floored by the brutal romance. As they continued walking around the show pieces, one of her sizeable breasts brushed against Anush's arm.

He tried to conceal his erection while they talked about furniture. Ebba hung on Anush's every word as he explained, "Cedar absorbs stain quickly, like a dry desert, but teak repels it like a green tree banana leaf. It's all in the grain."

He'd been somewhat popular in college with the girls, even kissed one of them, which was more than most of his college friends could say. After their second year, Anush and his friends had gone out to celebrate. A few drinks in, someone in the group accused someone else of being a virgin (which they all were) but the boy denied it. Someone suggested they go to a brothel, and once the dare had been put forth it could not be rescinded. A few of the boys were too afraid and slinked away with excuses but Anush was one of the three who remained. It was kind of a test. One thing Anush had learned at boarding school was not to back down. Among the whorehouses on Falkland Road, a boy said he knew one that was clean, safe—his older brother frequented it. The three boys went and sat in a dark drawing room on couches while girls their age, maybe younger, came and stood on display in front of them for their choosing. The boys were nervous and ordered drinks and smoked cigarettes, delaying the inevitable. Anush finally chose a pretty Nepalese girl with long straight hair. They went to her tiny bedroom, which was no bigger than a cell. She undressed for him but when it came time for Anush to put the condom on, he couldn't go through with it. But he also couldn't chicken out so soon—his friends might spot him leaving early—so he remained in the room, got the girl to fetch him a drink, and smoked a couple of cigarettes before leaving half an hour later with his reputation intact.

Ebba noticed a chair in the corner, away from the display pieces, and said, "Oh my, that's lovely. I must have it." It was a chair Anush had made. He'd tried to copy one of his grandfather's miniatures but had messed up the eighteenth-century banister high back so he'd tried an experiment and turned it into an art deco back made from teak and dark walnut while keeping the fluted legs. Reza was perplexed with the mix of styles but helped with the dovetail joints. It had taken Anush months. He'd unwittingly inherited his grandfather's sense of perfection. When it was done, Anush had stepped back and cocked his head a bit, unsure of what he'd made. It was an odd chair. The straight high back was not proportionate in size or style to the short, fluted legs, but he'd worked on it for so long, and it was the first thing he'd made that hadn't turned out deformed. A small triangular piece of midnight ebony was added as an accent to the dark walnut, which contrasted the tan teak well. One side of the high back was purposefully taller than the other, resulting in a thirty-degree slant, lending the chair a unique and aesthetic air. As he looked at his first finished piece, for the first time in a long while Anush had felt a swell of pride.

Ebba asked, "How much?"

His first sale. He was euphoric. Although he didn't like the idea of parting with the chair, he said, "Twenty thousand rupees—five hundred American."

"If that includes delivery, you have a deal," she said, and they shook hands. They continued the tour and ended up upstairs in the tiny flat that his father and grandfather had once lived in. After being abandoned for nearly two decades, it had recently been cleaned by the shop workers.

Anush got Reza to fetch him a bottle of whisky, ice, and two glasses. Once they were all alone upstairs, Ebba and Anush talked, drank, and flirted through the evening. He noticed a faint tan line around the base of her wedding finger, where a ring had once been. Was she divorced? Or just promiscuous? He wondered if she could discern his virginity. Ever since the brothel, all his college mates had looked up to him as an experienced man. He was so cocksure around them that he nearly believed the lie himself, but now his heart pounded as Ebba undressed him and then herself. Their bodies entwined on the cool slate-tiled floor. Eventually, she climbed on top of him and fucked him with a wild abandon that even a virgin like Anush understood was only possible because they would never see each other again—and also because she had paid him.

- 10 -

1997

AFTER FINISHING SANDING THE LEG of a mahogany chair, Anush browsed through the list of contacts on his mobile phone. It was nearly six o'clock. He was trying to find someone, anyone, to have a drink with. One hundred and fifty-nine people and not a single close friend. A wave of melancholy overcame him. At this rate he'd soon be a depressed, lonely bachelor like his old man.

On nights he didn't have plans, like tonight, Anush could usually wrangle old acquaintances from college, or even old boarding school friends, out for a drink. Some were flattered to be called by Anush Sharma, who'd appeared in the society pages in the *Bombay Times* recently, photographed next to a former Miss India and other minor celebrities at a five-star hotel party. He'd made a bit of a name for himself as an artisan furniture maker using heirloom woods. New restaurants and hip nightclubs continued to sprout all over the city. There were more exclusive parties Anush hadn't yet gained access to, but the cool indifference that the photograph had captured seemed to suggest he might be on his way to achieving this soon. However, tonight he either couldn't get ahold of people or the ones he did weren't interested. "It's a Tuesday evening," most of them complained, lamely.

Anush was about to step out to get a fresh pack of Marlboro Lights when the phone rang. The call display flashed HOME.

"Anush bhai," Chottu said. Even though he was twenty years older than Anush, he referred to Anush with the respectful suffix of older brother. "Your father wants you to come home for dinner."

Enduring dinner with the old man was the last thing Anush wanted. Anush had come home earlier than usual a couple of months ago and the old man had berated him for not selling the furniture shop. Later, Anush noticed him pop a few pills into his mouth while sitting on the balcony, staring out at the ocean, sipping whisky. The next morning, after the old man left for work, Anush rooted through his medicine cabinet and found several vials of Calmpose, valium. Anush wondered how long he'd been taking the sleeping pills. They hadn't dined together since then.

"No, I can't. I have customers coming," Anush lied to Chottu.

Reza, who was on the floor sweeping, looked up with his good eye to correct Anush, but Anush put a finger to his lips to quiet him.

Chottu pleaded, "Your father says you must come home, Anush bhai. VIPs expected for dinner, and also don't forget your cousin from Canada is arriving later this evening."

Anush had visited Paresh—or *Parry* as he now went by in Canada—a year ago. Even though they didn't have a lot in common, they got along, and so Anush was relieved to have found a drinking buddy for the evening.

After going to the gym for a short workout, Anush walked through Priyadarshini Park, where he spotted three vultures circling overhead, most likely from the Towers of Silence nearby in Malabar Hill, the sacred place where Parsi people left their dead. It made Anush thankful to be a Hindu, for even though over the years he'd had nightmares about lighting his mother's body on the funeral pyre, he couldn't imagine her being torn apart and eaten by vultures. The idea of it brought bile up his throat and he spat it onto the red dirt track.

The palm trees swayed almost in time with the waves that crashed on the shore nearby.

Thinking about his mother made him realize how lucky he was the old man hadn't remarried. A stepmother, no matter how ingratiating, would be intolerable. Then again, maybe the old man would be happier remarried, and not spend so much time disappointed with Anush. Either way, Anush and the old man reminded each other of Anush's mother. She was gone but always there. Anush wondered if his father, deep down, blamed him for her death. If only Anush had never been born, the old man maybe thought, if only Anush had never been in his mother's womb, then she might never have developed cervical cancer. Did he subconsciously think Anush was some-how responsible for killing his wife? Did he think of Anush as the cancer? A cancer than had remained in her womb after Anush's birth? Was that his extraordinary destiny? Killing his own mother?

As Anush got into his car, he reminded himself that the destiny stuff was a bullshit sandwich. The sun was setting as he drove along Nepean Sea Road. He was ready for a whisky. The first one always tasted the best.

There was a cavalcade of expensive cars in the front courtyard of Sea Face Terraces, so Anush had to park his Fiat on the street. His father could afford to buy him a dozen new cars but hadn't yet. Anush knew it was a type of punishment for abandoning the plan to sell the furniture shop. The shop was making some sales, but Sharma Shipping still kept it afloat. After finding a spot Anush got out and slammed the door shut. It'd become increasingly embarrassing to show up to fancy parties and five-star hotels with this car.

At home, in the front hallway entrance, Anush could hear half a dozen men talking in the drawing room. He caught bits of the conversation, something about "A new civic manifesto . . ." "A saffron alliance . . ." Anush tried to sneak into his room for a quick drink but the colonel spotted him. "Anush, come join us!"

He had no choice but to be introduced to them all. One was a bigwig from the Shiv Sena, another from the BJP—right-wing Hindu nationalist parties. Another was a construction mogul, and one was the chief state minister. They all shook hands with Anush, including the colonel, who wrung Anush's hand and slapped his back. Anush winced and laughed obligingly, taking a seat. The men all smoked cigarettes, but like any good Indian son, Anush didn't smoke in front of his father or elders as a sign of respect.

"The slum dwellers need to be re-housed."

"Yes, new accommodations and infrastructure is what's needed."

"The congress government is inept, corrupt!"

Anush nodded, trying to appear as though he cared, agreed. He could've gladly slit someone's throat for a glass of the one-hundred-and-eighty-US-dollar-a-bottle Blue Label Reserve whisky the old man was serving.

The men spoke enthusiastically: "We need to open up the economy more." "We will take the next federal election." "With a majority." "To the BJP!"

They raised their glasses while Anush alternated from sitting on his hands, to folding them, to plunging them into his armpits. He was dying for a cigarette.

"So, Anush, what is it you do?" one of them asked.

"I make vintage furniture, some of it with a modern twist, at my grandfather's old furniture shop."

The men seemed intrigued, even impressed with that, except of course his father, who grimaced and said, "Anush will be working at Sharma Shipping soon."

Anush glanced at his father, and for the first time in months they locked eyes, staring at each other with equal intensity, a fierce fury. Anush could tell exactly what the old man was thinking, how he'd had enough of his only son dallying with furniture and partying every night. Anush should have been working under the old man's thumb at Sharma Shipping, but all Anush did was shirk his duties, his responsibilities. He should've considered himself lucky that he enjoyed an allowance every month, an allowance that he didn't earn, an allowance that the benevolent Varoon Sharma provided, hoping that Anush would come to his senses, but alas, what a shameful and ungrateful child Varoon Sharma had become burdened with.

Anush returned his father's glare. The old man hadn't even set foot in the shop to see Anush's work, which had recently been featured in the local papers. They were mostly heartwarming stories, buried near the rear of the entertainment section, but Anush was stung that the old man had not said a thing about it, let alone come see his work.

Anush had learned how to handle a band saw, how to cut and measure and sand different types of wood, how to seamlessly join two pieces of wood by intricate dovetail joints, how to half-blind dovetails, how to do box joints and sliding dovetails. For the first time in his life, Anush felt as though he was reasonably good at something. Apart from adding his own twists to some of his grandfather's models, he was now making originals. The process was slow, but you couldn't rush these things. And besides, success wasn't measured by sales, not right away. Didn't that lunatic Dutch painter who sliced off his own ear die penniless without having sold a painting? Not that he was comparing himself to artists like that, but you had to admit that creating unique pieces of furniture was a skill not everyone possessed.

One of the men asked, "Anush, would you like a drink?"

But before Anush could accept, the old man said, "Anush doesn't drink."

A couple of years ago, a policeman had woken Varoon Sharma up in the middle of the night. Anush had been caught speeding. Anush had only had two drinks, but once the policeman saw the penthouse flat at Sea Face Terraces, in order to receive a larger bribe he'd lied and said, "Sir, your son was out-of-control drunk, driving like a wild man." Varoon Sharma had paid the policeman and all was forgotten.

Father and son exchanged an icy look. The gloves were off.

"We can improve civic life for the city's residents by adding new infrastructure, bridges, hospitals, roads."

"Yes, it's time for India to come into its own and show the world that we aren't some backwater."

"Absolutely. We need to address the needs of the poor, their votes are critical."

"Yes, we can promise new housing to slum dwellers . . ."

It went on. Anush feigned attention. He was looking forward to picking up Paresh from the airport and having a drink. The old man stood up and everyone stopped talking as he presented a small duffle bag to the chief minister. "A humble contribution."

Anush caught a glimpse of the stacks of cash inside. The chief minister said, "Varoon, you've done good work and you'll do much more. We only need a few more Hindus like you and this country's problems will be solved. Here is a token of my appreciation," and tossed a set of keys on a Mercedes-Benz keychain to Varoon.

Anush's eyes almost popped out of his head.

"I can't accept a gift so generous," the old man said.

"You've earned it. A toast!"

The men filled their glasses and Anush filled a crystal tumbler as well. The old man shot Anush a look that meant *Absolutely not*, but it was too late. The amber liquor swirling around in Anush's glass tasted like honey with the most potent but velvety venom.

- 11 -

1997

FOR HIS YEARLY MONTH-LONG VACATION, Reza took the train from Bombay Central to Rajkot, which took fourteen hours, followed by a two-hour bumpy bus ride to Gondal, and from there he'd have to hitch rides on bullock carts to his village, Jamkandorna, or it was about a five-hour walk. Luckily, today from Gondal he was able to get a ride most of the way and only had to walk for the last two hours. It was nearly dusk when Reza reached the outskirts of his village.

The balmy red earth filled Reza's lungs as he made his way through the fields of wild Persian lilac shrubs where he'd seen male peacocks do their majestic mating dance.

The village had grown since he'd left nearly fifteen years ago. Now there were nearly five dozen dwellings, mostly made from mud and corrugated tin, scattered throughout the grove of lemon, walnut, and rosewood trees.

Outside his family's hut, his mother and younger sister, Mona, were crouched on their haunches, making rotis on a small stove fuelled by cow dung patties. When Mona saw him, she ran to embrace him, yelling, "He's here! Reza bhai is here!"

His mother stood up as Reza bent down to touch her feet and she said with tears of joy in her eyes, "May Allah bless you a thousand times, behta."

"Where's Shareen?" he asked. He hadn't seen his wife in eleven months.

"Fetching water from the pump. She'll be back soon," his mother said. "Your brothers are both working in Rajkot and come home on the weekends."

"But I thought Parvez was going to finish school," Reza said.

His mother said, "School fees have risen. Everything is more expensive these days." Reza's salary hadn't kept up with soaring inflation rates.

A few of the neighbour's children were playing hopscotch outside their hut and Reza waved to them. They ran over to Reza, who gave them a few confectionaries. The children were elated.

Reza went inside to see Nabil chacha, who'd been bedridden for nearly two years. He was asleep now. Reza knelt next to him and touched his feet.

The old man opened his eyes and spoke. "Welcome home, behta."

Reza held his fragile, wrinkled hand. "Sorry to wake you."

"I lie here all day waiting to be awoken. Luckily it's by you today."

His eyes had become even more yellow and sunken than the last time.

Reza said, "Is there anything I can get you?"

"Just stay here a while," he said, fighting to keep his eyes open. Since they couldn't afford morphine, he was sometimes given *bhang*, a drink made with the cannabis plant, milk, and honey. Reza remained by his side and soon they both fell asleep.

Half an hour later, Shareen returned and tapped Reza awake. Despite being exhausted, he perked up instantly at the sight of his beautiful wife. They'd been married a year and a half, and in that time had spent a total of two months together. Reza squeezed her hands but before they could speak, Mona called from outside, "Dinner's ready."

The gujarati dhal smelled wonderful and tasted slightly sweet with its jaggery and cinnamon. It was a welcome change from the eleven months of spicy maharashtrian tomato dhal. The *bajree* millet *rotlas* were thick, and Reza ate half a dozen of them, along with the salted, creamy buttermilk and rice.

After dinner, Reza wanted to retreat inside and be with his wife but neighbours stopped by, eager to say hello. He chatted with the men for what seemed like an eternity. In the past most of them had looked up to Reza with a certain amount of reverence for being one of the lucky few to live and work in a metropolitan city like Bombay, but the prestige of it had begun to fade as more of the men were finding jobs in nearby cities.

Reza finally yawned and excused himself after nearly an hour of small talk—anything less would have been rude. Shareen, Mona, and his mother had finished cleaning up. Outside, Reza splashed his face with some water from a clay *matka* and chewed on a *bavel* twig to clean his teeth. The bark had natural antiseptic properties and villagers had been using it for generations. Before going inside he noticed the little Ganesha idol near the entrance to the hut. After the Babri Masjid riots in 1992, many Muslims in nearby cities and towns had been dragged from their homes, beaten and burned by Hindu mobs seeking revenge, so the Hindu idol, although a blasphemy, served as protection, to fool angry Hindu mobs. Over the years of living in Bombay with many Hindus, Reza had come to the conclusion that there was little difference between Hindu and Muslim. People were just people. He took one last look at the crescent moon and stars in the sky. So many more here than in the city. Anush had said, "There are other solar systems and galaxies with billions and billions of stars out there we can't even see," but Reza wasn't sure even after Anush had shown him pictures of it on his new computer in the office.

Retreating inside, Reza bid his mother and sister and Nabil chacha goodnight and made his way to bed, which lay behind the bamboo screen. Shareen was there, lying down, facing away from him. He took off his clothes and lay next to her. Through the small window near their bed, the crickets chirped loudly, creating the perfect type of white noise that could drown out quiet conversations inside the hut.

One night last year they'd discovered a mutual love for a local folk song in which the hero and heroine reunite after a long separation. That night, Reza had put his hand on Shareen's belly and started whispering the song.

> Farmers search the skies for rains that are late,
> But, my lover, you have yet not returned,
> Without you, I'll not touch a fig from a Queen's plate,
> Your name from my soul shall never be burned.

Shareen had closed her eyes, tilted her head back, and responded,

> Peacocks in the dry fields do dance and sway,
> But, my lover, you have yet not returned,
> I will drip streams of blood if my skin they flay,
> Your scent from my soul shall never be burned.

Reza had cupped one of her breasts while kissing her neck. She had writhed against him, breathing deeply,

> Heaven and its stars finally entreat us with
>   monsoon,
> But, my lover, you have yet not returned,
> Street urchins laugh, but from their mockery I am
>   immune,
> Your eyes from my soul shall never be burned.

Reza had restrained himself, but continued to kiss her neck. She'd bitten his lower lip, drawing a trace of blood. They'd breathed in synch and moved as one. She'd guided him into her.

> Orange blossoms in the orchard are flowering,
> But, my lover, you have yet not returned,
> My entire body yearns for you, can you hear it sing?
> Your lips from my soul shall never be burned.

Tonight, while they lay together, Reza began the poem "Farmers Search the Skies for Rains," but Shareen didn't respond.

"Are you asleep?" he whispered.

"Of course not," she replied, still keeping her back to him.

Are all women impossible to figure out, or just my wife? Reza wondered. Had he done something wrong? He gently touched her hip but she flinched.

Too tired to continue this game, Reza whispered, "What's wrong? Tell me."

"I don't see you for a whole year, and then you expect me to lick your face like a dog?"

"I'm sorry. I wish I could home more often. Jaan, I've missed you so much."

He caressed her back, and she allowed him.

"How's it been? You happy?" he asked.

"It's lonely. Your brothers are gone. Your uncle is in bed all day. All I do is cook and clean, like a servant."

He slid himself closer to her and said, "One day I'll return home and start a furniture shop of my own."

"How? How will you be able to do that?"

"I've been promoted at the shop. I'm now the assistant to the new sahib. I no longer sleep in the musty godowns with the rats. Now I have a cot, upstairs by the office."

"Really?"

"Yes," he said, gently pulling her warm body towards his. "I've been teaching him how to cut and sand and join wood, helping him make furniture. A newspaper even came with a photographer to take pictures of the furniture we made." He could smell her musk and it aroused him instantly.

"Seriously?"

"Yes," he said, cupping one of her breasts. "The sahib is a mediocre furniture maker, at best. I have to help him with his joinery, detail his sanding, remind him all the time which woods to lacquer once, which ones need multiple coats. I could make much nicer furniture. If I opened a shop in Gondal or Surat, we could maybe live in a flat there, send my sister to a proper school, give Nabil chacha better medical care."

"Did this new sahib buy the shop?" she said, closing her eyes, undulating her hips into him.

"No, he's the son of the owner," Reza said, almost near ecstasy, breathing deep to make sure he didn't come right away.

"That's great. So did you get a raise?" she said, getting undressed while they lay together.

"Well, no. Not yet." His erection was rock hard against the small of her back.

"Why not? You're doing all this extra work. You're important to him." Their lips touched as they whispered.

"Yes, I know but—" He was finally inside her.

"You said a photographer came and took pictures of your furniture," she said, pulsating and breathing in synch with him.

"Yes, just give it time. I'm sure when the time is right, he'll pay me more."

"Wait," she said, stopping her hips from gyrating. "The son? The son of the sahib who owns the shop? You mean the one who blinded you?"

"Yes," Reza sighed. "But it was an accident. We were children."

It was complicated. At first he had been angry when Anush turned up at the shop, acting like a spoiled brat. But things had changed. Reza didn't know how to explain the nuances of his relationship with Anush. A camaraderie had developed between them. Anush no longer talked down to Reza, the way he did to the other workers. Sometimes they even joked about things.

Recently a fat white lady had come to the shop for a coffee table, her hair parted in the middle and curled up at the sides, and Anush had joked to Reza in Hindi, "She looks like a water buffalo," which Reza had to stifle his laughter at. After she left, they'd both howled.

Shareen pulled herself apart from Reza and turned away. Reza kissed Shareen's neck but she recoiled. He whispered in her ear, "Please, jaan, I'm sorry. It's not the right time to ask for a raise. They might be selling the shop."

"Then what will you do?"

This had been on Reza's mind a lot. If the shop were to close, would he be able to find work elsewhere? A one-eyed carpenter? No matter how good he was or how glowing a recommendation he'd get from Anush, it wouldn't be easy.

Shareen pulled the sheet over her head and turned away from her husband.

He lay looking at the cracks in the mud ceiling. Maybe she was right. Maybe he was nothing more than a coward who was helping the selfish brat who'd blinded him. Maybe he was nothing more than Anush's loyal dog, licking his master's heels.

Rather than becoming soothing white noise to fall asleep to, the crickets chirping outside grew louder as Reza lay awake.

- 12 -

1998

AT INTERNATIONAL ARRIVALS, ANUSH SCOURED
the crowd for his cousin. Paresh lived in Calgary, where,
depending on the time of year, there was an eternal sea of snow
or dead brown grass. Paresh had come home from university
when Anush visited. Despite not having seen each other for
over a decade they got along, playing ping-pong and video
games in the basement of Paresh's parents' suburban home.
They never spoke of the night of the fireworks, or how Paresh
played ice hockey with white friends now and wore baseball
hats with sports team logos that Anush didn't recognize, or
how Paresh listened to bands like Nirvana that Anush thought
dressed like beggars. Despite their differences, they had fun
night-bowling and drinking beer in parks around campfires.

Paresh's friends got a kick out of Anush's Indian accent and designer dress shirts; meanwhile, Anush pointed out that Paresh was the one who sounded funny with his Canadian accent and looked like a *bhikari*, a vagrant, with his beard and long hair and rumpled T-shirts.

Life in Canada wasn't that great. Apart from the climate being inhospitable, his aunt and uncle worked like dogs at jobs they constantly complained about, and of course they didn't have servants to cook or clean. Despite having a large home there was something altogether sad about their lives. Perhaps it was the lack of people. Anush and Paresh would drive in Paresh's mother's Toyota Corolla for miles sometimes without seeing a soul. A couple of weeks later when the time came for Anush to go home, he was happy not to extend his open return ticket, which the old man had bought, hoping Anush would fall in love with the place and attend a university there.

Now, at the airport, Paresh didn't spot Anush and was caught off guard when Anush embraced him. For flinching, Anush gave his cousin two swift punches to the shoulder.

"Fuck, it's hot!" Paresh said, letting Anush carry his gigantic backpack.

"Bhain chod, it's January—the coldest month," Anush said under the weight of the bag.

When Anush put the bag in the trunk of the Fiat, Paresh said, "Dude, vintage car!"

Anush wasn't sure if that was a compliment or an insult. Even though in Canada it'd struck Anush as odd that Paresh spoke with a Canadian accent, Anush had assumed that in India Paresh would revert back to his natural Indian accent. The fact that he didn't made Anush realize that the Canadian accent wasn't put on; it was how Paresh spoke—or, rather, how Parry spoke—and forever would. Dude was a full blown coconut, brown on the outside . . .

Paresh wiped the sweat off his brow as he rolled down his window. "Holy shit, I forgot how hot it was."

A few beggar children came up to Paresh's window with matted hair and open palms. Instead of telling them to buzz off, Paresh pulled a bill out of his pocket and gave it to one of them. Anush couldn't believe it. Paresh was acting like the most moronic of tourists, giving money to beggars while other beggars watched. Before they knew it, a small crowd had surrounded the car, and Anush said, trying not to show his irritation, "Paresh, don't be fooled by their puppy dog eyes, yaar. They'll make dog food out of us." He honked the horn several times, but it had no effect on the children. Fearing that even more beggars would notice and join in, Anush revved the engine, which made the beggars leap away.

A hundred yards later, the Fiat sputtered and died. Anush restarted it and continued to drive. He'd taken his father's Mercedes-Benz for a short test drive and fallen in love with the soft leather seats; the clutch and gears were sturdy with just the right amount of give. The old man could easily afford to buy Anush a dozen Mercedeses but Anush knew that would never happen. Not as long as he continued making furniture.

Before long they were racing south, towards the city, whizzing past poor neighbourhoods, makeshift huts made from scraps of corrugated tin and steel.

"So, my old man says you're travelling around?" Anush said. His father had told him nothing. Anush made an educated guess from the gigantic backpack.

"Yeah, dude. Goa, Delhi, Rajasthan, Kashmir, Varanasi, maybe Nepal," Paresh said, looking out his window, absorbing the foreign surroundings.

"So you finished uni?" Anush asked.

"Well, not really. You got a smoke?"

Anush tossed his pack of Marlboro Lights at Paresh. "Light me one too."

After lighting two cigarettes, Paresh explained, "I finished pre-med but didn't get into med school."

"So now what?"

"Fuck, I dunno. The 'rents want me to apply to law school," Paresh said, handing Anush a cigarette. "I'm just glad I don't haveta be an intern and work thirty-hour shifts at an ER and haveta put my finger up some fat fucker's ass to check his prostate, ya know? I just wanna travel and experience life and and not be in school, ya know? Maybe even write a book about it all, ya know?"

Anush nodded but wasn't sure if he did know. Despite being best friends once, Paresh now seemed from another planet. Anush considered how much he himself had changed. Even though it was a fraction of Paresh's transformation, Anush reasoned that he must have morphed somewhat. How different he was he couldn't say for sure. He cared less about things that many people talked about: politics, current events, sports—maybe at this rate he'd stop caring about everything by the time he was thirty. He wasn't sure why or when he'd become so indifferent. Sometimes it came in waves. Perhaps he was susceptible to his grandfather's depression or madness.

There had been a show on Discovery the other night about how each human cell dies and is replaced by a new one every seven years. So, technically, after seven years we all become completely different people. No matter how enthusiastic the host of the show had been in explaining how we, literally, became new people every seven years, suggesting that there was something profoundly exhilarating, rejuvenating in the process, it only made Anush wistful. There was something inherently despairing about it because the thing we lost was ourselves, and we had no control over it.

A huge truck zoomed past in the opposite direction so close that Anush could feel its displaced air.

"Whoa! You OK, dude?"

"Yeah, fine," Anush said, sitting up a bit, rolling his window down all the way for some fresh air. As they got near Worli Sea Face, Anush stopped near a shop and whistled for the shop boy, who came running to the car. Anush gave the boy some money and seconds later the boy returned with a plastic bag and some change that Anush told the boy to keep.

Anush could tell that Paresh was curious, so he explained, "Indian drive-thru," while opening the bag to reveal a quarter bottle of whisky.

The two of them laughed. Anush said, "Welcome home, *Kuttay! Kaminay!*" their favourite childhood defamation, while offering the bottle to Paresh, who took a swig and coughed a bit, trying not to pull a face though the whisky was too strong for him. Anush laughed, remembering how Paresh and all his friends in Canada only drank beer. He took a healthy swig for himself before putting the rest of the bottle in the glove box.

"So you have a girlfriend in Canada?"

Paresh pulled out a wallet-sized picture. "I'm seeing this dancer chick, Jenny. Smokin' hot bod, dude."

Jenny was a pretty, thin blonde. Anush couldn't help but

feel a little jealous because even though Paresh was two years younger, he was probably more experienced than Anush. The German woman that one time above the shop was the only notch Anush had on his bedpost.

As they drove towards the heart of the city, it struck Anush as odd that Paresh had yet to ask Anush a single question about himself. Wasn't Paresh at all curious as to what Anush was up to? Was Paresh jet-lagged or just self-involved? Not that Anush had done much with his life. When the two of them had last met, Anush had finished college. Apart from making a few chairs he'd accomplished nothing. Maybe his old man was right—he had pissed away the last few years.

Perhaps he was incapable of being extraordinary. That was the thought that lingered more often lately. That he'd never be able to live up to his kundali. He wished these thoughts were cricket balls he could bat out of his head with a resounding wallop, driving them into the sky in grand arcs to finally plop into the middle of the Arabian Sea, never to be found again.

Somewhere on Marine Drive, Anush was lost in thought when Paresh yelled, "Anush, slow down!" That's when Anush noticed a policeman just thirty feet ahead on the road, waving for them to stop. But Anush noticed him so late that he had to slam on the brakes. The Fiat screeched to a halt only inches from the police officer.

It was the same moustachioed police officer who had caught him speeding before. He whacked the ground with a cane that all Bombay Traffic Police carried.

Paresh was petrified. Between gulping deep breaths he managed to say, "Just do as he says. There's no fucking way I'm going to an Indian jail."

The officer thrust himself in Anush's face and shouted, "I remember you! Do you know how fast you were going? I can smell liquor!"

Anush was nearly paralyzed with fear but he knew he couldn't let it show, otherwise the officer would know he had the upper hand and could do whatever he wanted—throw them in jail, torment them for hours, or god knows what else, and milk them or, rather, the old man, for an exorbitant amount of bribe money for their release. Remaining calm, Anush said, "Sorry, brother, a thousand pardons."

"You two are coming to the station!" the officer said, clearly in no mood to be magnanimous, and whacked the pavement again with his cane for the boys to get out of the car. Once they were in a police station they'd be held all night and thrown in a maggot-infested cell with street criminals. Paresh begged for forgiveness in English, tried to convince the officer that it was Anush's first time driving, but the officer, if he understood much English, wasn't falling for that. If anything, Anush suspected it only offended him that Paresh was speaking English. The officer was an indigenous Maharastrian and there'd been such a hubbub in the city of late to repatriate street names and signage from English to Hindi. Maharastrians already referred to the city as *Mumbai*, the original name before the Portuguese and British had colonized. While the legacy of colonial rule was mostly unwanted, Hindu nationalist organizations such as the Shiv Sena used it as political leverage and some felt the name change was steeped in blood from the riots just a few years ago. The city was in an identity crisis.

Anush thought about fleeing but noticed the officer had his Honda 500 parked just a few feet away. Even though Anush knew the streets well, the officer could probably outmanoeuvre them on his motorbike.

"Driving recklessly, endangering the life of a police officer, driving under the influence of alcohol—these are serious charges," the officer said.

With tears in his eyes, Paresh put his palms together and begged for grace in broken Hindi with an English accent, which only made the officer snicker. Anush wasn't sure what was more pathetic: the fact that Paresh could no longer speak Hindi without sounding like a foreigner or the fact that he didn't realize he was only making their predicament worse by speaking in his coconut Anglo-accented Hindi. Either way, it only proved to the officer they were spoiled rich kids who could be used as leverage to milk more bribe money. They'd be thrown in jail and the old man would be woken up with a phone call in the middle of the night to collect them from the station with a hefty fine. Even if the newspapers didn't catch a whiff of it, this would be the end of Anush's life. The shop, the car—the old man would take it all away in a second. A scandal in the papers was the last thing Varoon wanted since he was in deep with the BJP and the election was near.

The officer rapped on the hood of the car, "Come on, this is your last warning. Out of the car!"

Anush could feel all the muscles in his arms contract as he clenched his fists. He couldn't get enough air into his lungs and his breathing became shallower.

"The police wagon is on its way," the officer said with a smile that showed his crimson betel-nut-stained teeth.

With each moment that passed, jail became an inevitability, which made Paresh plea with more intensity. "Please, sir, I beg you, please—"

The officer slapped the pavement with his cane again and rapped on the hood of the car harder with his knuckles. "Failure to comply with a police officer is also a separate charge," the officer said. A large wave broke on the seawall, sending a spray of water high into the air before it dispersed into the humid breeze.

Suddenly a memory Anush had long forgotten came rushing to him. He was five years old, with his parents. They were taking a horse carriage ride on a Sunday night along this very stretch of Marine Drive. The waves were high that evening and broke over the seawall with more force each time, sending up larger and larger sprays of mist that showered over the three of them in the open carriage. He remembered the *clip-clop* of the horse, of feeling anxious but also comforted because he was safely wedged between his parents. He remembered thinking what if the next wave would be much larger, crest above the seawall, and swallow them back into the sea with it? He remembered clutching his mother, she pulling him close to her, the scent of coconut oil in her hair. He imagined her giving birth to him the night of the storm, his father returning drenched with the good news of their son's kundali—it all allayed his anxiety.

The officer said, "Yes, enjoy the sea breeze now. In jail the only fresh thing you'll smell is the shit inside the open hole in the ground with the flies that buzz around it all day. Or maybe the commanding officer will be unavailable to process you at the station, in which case I'll have to take you to the Arthur Road jail for the night. Some of the country's best criminals are housed there, you know. You two cute birds would make them very happy tonight!" He broke into laughter.

Anush wanted to knock out the officer's teeth, but instead he pulled a few hundred rupees from his pants pocket and discreetly offered it to the officer. "We'll pay the fine to you right now."

But the officer shook his head, saying, "The police wagon will be here shortly."

A police wagon passed by the other side of the road. It would soon be making a U-turn several hundred feet up at the next break in the road and come to collect them. Anush hissed at Paresh for any money he had and Paresh pulled out a few American bills that the officer noticed with wide eyes and quickly snatched.

They heard the police wagon squeal its brakes and come to a stop fifteen yards behind them. In the rear-view mirror they saw a couple of officers open their doors and saunter out with canes as another wave broke onto the breakwater, spraying the air with fine mist.

The officer leaned into the Fiat window and whispered, "I think it's in your fate to see the inside of a jail," pocketing the American money before the two officers from the wagon got closer. Then he whispered, "But not tonight."

The moustachioed officer told the other two officers, "Everything's fine. Just giving these two kids a warning." Both Anush and Paresh breathed a sigh of relief. The two policemen got back into their wagon and the moustachioed officer sauntered back to his bike and sped away.

Anush reached into the glove compartment and gulped a healthy swig of whisky before starting the car.

- 13 -

1998

ANUSH LAUGHED AT PARESH. "BHAIN chod, you've only been in the country two hours and you've nearly shit yourself!"

Paresh surreptitiously wiped a tear away and then punched Anush in the arm. "We were almost thrown in jail. You were just as scared!"

Even though he was, Anush denied it by laughing louder at Paresh. "Too funny, yaar. You should see the look on your face!"

As they drove down Marine Drive, Paresh tried to light a cigarette but his hands were too shaky.

Anush had been relieved when the other two policemen arrived as it had cut short the first policeman's time to extort more money from him and Paresh. It wasn't a secret that men desperate for work were bribing their way into the city's police force so they in turn could collect bribes from the public. In some neighbourhoods it could be very lucrative. "If I come across that policeman again, I'll slap the *maadar chod*'s face clean off," Anush said.

"Yeah, right," said Paresh.

Anush would never have the nerve, but he instinctively went on the offensive whenever he felt threatened—a habit from boarding school.

It was nearly ten o'clock. A few beggars on the footpath were beginning to unfurl their sheets of cardboard to sleep on. A street dog scampered towards scraps of discarded food.

Anush grabbed the whisky bottle from the glove compartment and took a swig before yelling, "Kuttay! Kaminay!" out the window at the street mutt, who flinched. Anush expected Paresh to join him in their favourite line from *Sholay*, their favourite film. It was what they'd yelled before dropping water balloons from the roof of Sea Face Terraces onto unsuspecting boys in the back courtyard. It'd been fifteen years but surely Paresh would remember the classic Bollywood line.

Anush offered the whisky to Paresh, but he didn't take a drink. Giving Paresh a friendly jab, Anush said, "Come on, yaar, have some fun." But Paresh didn't say anything. Anush couldn't tell if he was just shaken up or if he had simply forgotten the film, forgotten they'd grown up best friends, playing together every day. Maybe Paresh had cast all that from his mind after moving to Canada. While he befriended white kids, maybe his childhood memories of India were replaced by the rules to ice hockey and grunge band lyrics.

No, it was impossible to forget certain things. *Kuttay!*

Kaminay! had been their motto, their catchphrase. Was it possible that Paresh had become so Canadian, so politically correct, that shouting at street dogs was offensive all of a sudden? He did go by Parry now. People changed. Completely, after seven years. Maybe Paresh would embrace his roots by the end of his travels. Isn't that why everyone came to India? To find themselves? Bullshit sandwich.

Anush parked the car outside the Taj Hotel and Paresh followed him in through the posh marble lobby to the central outdoor courtyard, past the swimming pool and to the entrance of the 1900s nightclub where a queue of well-dressed young people stood.

A sign was posted beside the large bouncer: *Couples only. No single men. No Exceptions.* Luckily, Anush knew the bouncer, who unhooked the velvet rope and let them in after Anush cupped him a hundred-rupee note. The nightclub had recently been renovated. It was impressively large, with centralized air conditioning, and was located in the city's most expensive hotel, making it one of the most exclusive nightclubs. The dance floor was full while the circumference of the club was packed with beautiful people sipping exotic cocktails and European beers in booths.

Anush was certain this was better than any nightclub in Calgary. Bombay had undergone enormous change since Paresh had left. Now there were world-class restaurants, nightclubs, and hotels popping up all over the place. The old India that Paresh supposedly didn't remember and was hesitant of identifying with was now a vibrant, sexy place to be proud of.

The DJ played a Spice Girls song, which brought even more people to the dance floor. Paresh followed Anush to the bar, where they ordered beer. The music was too loud to carry on a conversation, so they sipped their drinks with a seeming amount of indifference while casually checking everyone out. It was a skill that Anush had honed over the past few years at clubs like this, but lately the pretense of it was getting old. Young people trying to outdo each other with designer clothing while getting drunk and high, or *blown*, as the rich kids called it. Anush knew he wasn't entirely above their vanity. He enjoyed some of the finer things in life, but he wanted interesting conversations rather than just gossip or vapid small talk, like when the new Versace cologne would be coming out.

A stunning young woman on the dance floor caught Anush's eye. She was wearing a black dress that clung to her curvaceous body, with her hair up. She had the most mesmerizing deep brown eyes. A game began between the two of them wherein they would catch each other's eye and hold their gaze for a fraction of a second longer each time. She was dancing with a tall, broad-shouldered man who had his back to Anush, so she was able to continue flirting with Anush without the man noticing. Each time they locked eyes, Anush felt a surge of electricity.

"Hey, Anush!" Two young men Anush had met recently were walking over. One was a popular VJ on MTV India and the other was a son of a famous Bollywood actor. They were sharply dressed and surrounded by a gaggle of college girls.

The VJ said, "We just came from a party in a suite upstairs. Totally blown!"

Anush sipped his beer and pretended to listen while making eyes with the stunning girl on the dance floor. The actor's son said something amusing that made the college girls giggle. Paresh nudged Anush in the ribs for an introduction. Anush said, "This is my cousin, Paresh. From Canada."

"Parry," he corrected Anush and shook hands with them all. "I just landed, like two hours ago."

"Your accent is so sweet," one of the girls giggled.

Anush still had his eyes on the girl on the dance floor while the two jackasses ordered a round of drinks for them all. The college girls demurred coyly, but after some playful encouragement from the two jackasses, and even *Parry*, they accepted.

Anush whispered in the VJ's ear, "Do you know that girl in the black dress on the dance floor?" But instead of keeping the conversation discreet, the VJ's eyes went wide and he reported to the actor's son, "Anush has the hots for Nasreen!" The two of them laughed in a way that suggested she was way out of his league.

Anush wanted to reverse the clock ten seconds and not say anything.

"I can talk to her for you," the VJ said.

"No no no," Anush said. "Don't say anything."

The VJ said something to the actor's son, who laughed.

Anush tried to excuse himself, but the VJ grabbed Anush's arm and said, "Wait, yaar. Have a tequila shot."

Anush tried to break free of the seemingly friendly grip, but the VJ was strong. Reminding himself to spend more time at the gym lifting weights rather than in the eucalyptus-scented spa, Anush shot the VJ a hostile look. But the threat only made the VJ tighten his grip around Anush's arm, and he taunted, "If you like her, tell her. Or are you chicken?"

The actor's son clinked his shot glass of tequila with Parry and the college girls and said, "Yeah, Anush."

Even Paresh agreed. "Yeah, dude."

The VJ had Anush's arm in a vise-like grip. Anush could tell from the gleam in the VJ's eye that he'd always been a bully. Being a bit short for his age, Anush had had to deal with his fair share of bullies, but he'd never had the guts to punch one in the face. Maybe the VJ was a good place to start. And so Anush swung hard.

But the VJ was swift and dodged Anush's punch.

"Take it easy, yaar," he laughed and tried to grab both of Anush's arms. But Anush broke free.

As he stormed off, he could hear the college girls giggling at something the VJ said, but Anush was already out of earshot.

The marble-floored restroom was empty except for the attendant who stood by the sinks with clean linens. Anush splashed his face with cold water. Looking at himself in the mirror, he mouthed her name. Nasreen. Just his luck—a Muslim. The most beautiful girl he'd laid eyes on and she was Muslim. He mouthed it again. Nasreen. It flowed off the tongue gracefully like a waterfall. It sounded like a sublime invocation to a divine goddess. Nasreen.

- 14 -

1998

ANUSH DECIDED TO SLINK OUTSIDE for a smoke while
Paresh was getting on with his new friends and their swell-
ing entourage at the bar.

During the day the courtyard was full of hotel guests
swimming in the pool or lounging on deck chairs, being served
cocktails by waiters. But now it was deserted, dark. Green and
blue underwater lights from the swimming pool made the courtyard seem otherworldly, almost celestial.

The bass from the club thumped faintly as Anush lit a cigarette
and looked up at the night sky. Barely a star could be seen because
of the city lights—unlike his boarding school days when the sky
was filled with them. Even though during those first few years
at Bharat Academy he spent a large chunk of his time feeling

homesick, on sleepless nights Anush would look out the window from his top bunk at the stars with a vague sense of comfort, thinking they knew his destiny. He'd hear his mother singing:

Kabhi kabhi, mere dil mein, khayaal aata hai . . .
Sometimes, in my heart a feeling emanates . . .

As he grew older he began to realize the song was more corny than esoteric, and began to doubt if stars millions of miles away had anything whatsoever to do with people on earth and how their lives unfolded, but he couldn't quite shake the idea of his destiny being written up there. He imagined his mother existing up in the heavens, convinced she'd lived through enough incarnations as ants and insects and whatever else and achieved *moksha*, believing he'd liberated her soul at her cremation ceremony, ending her suffering and the repeated cycle of life and death that all Hindus were bound to. After his mother's death he began to question reincarnation. Wasn't it all just smoke and mirrors? A bunch of lies? Stupid superstition? A set of rules designed by the ones at the top to keep the lower castes in their place—with the only reward being in the next life? Wasn't kundali rendering, like pagan priests gutting the bowels of a sacrificial animal to see which way the entrails would flow out to choose a new king? Or witches burning hair to select an augury from whatever direction the smoke blew? Was there actually any scientific proof that the stars shimmering above affected people on earth? It seemed too preposterous. However, on sleepless nights it still gave him some solace to think of her up there, ensconced permanently, instead of having burned her body on a pile of wood all those years ago to char and ashes.

Standing by the pool now, Anush wondered if maybe she hadn't achieved moksha, if she'd been reincarnated into another human being, if her soul or consciousness was still somewhere on earth. But then he quickly shook his head for being so sentimental. How many drinks had he had? A shot of Blue Label Reserve at home, a swig or two of whisky in the car, half a beer in the club. The altercation with the police officer had been too close. He reminded himself not to be so careless again. As Anush exhaled cigarette smoke at the night sky he wondered what he was doing with his life. And why had he been feeling so lonely? If he truly was extraordinary, he'd surely have a lot more friends, feel like he belonged in the world. Even at parties full of people he often felt detached. It didn't help that most of the people at these parties were idiots like the jackasses at the bar who Paresh had befriended.

In the sky above Anush spotted a couple of stars shining meagrely. Why did we think we were special enough that the universe arranged itself and aligned the cosmos in a way that the stars, millions of light-years away, would shine and sparkle elusively for us to decipher? Wasn't predicting the future just a myth?

But then again, weren't all the great myths rooted in reality? Bethlehem? Ayodhya, the birthplace of Rama? Hadn't they excavated archeological evidence of Troy? He'd seen something about that on Discovery the other night but couldn't remember as he'd passed out with an empty tumbler of whisky and woken up the next morning with the TV still on.

"Do you have a light?" a voice behind him asked, making him flinch. Nasreen. Anush fished his pockets for his lighter and lit her cigarette.

"Thanks," she said. Her hair was pulled back tightly into a bun and it accentuated the long nape of her neck. The elegant curvature of it reminded Anush of a gracefully designed Victorian cabriole leg from one of his grandfather's miniatures. Anush was trying to build it to scale but he couldn't get the curve right. In his grandfather's notes, there was a lot written about the cyma curve, the elusive line of beauty, concave at one end and convex at the other. *A graceful cyma curve can be any shape or size, but an exquisite one is rare—like a slightly swollen pregnant belly, glimpsed at the right angle, it cares not for the rules of arithmetic for it has its own geometry and can inspire much* . . . Anush made a mental note to sketch the long elegant line of Nasreen's neck on a paper napkin in the bar before forgetting it. A fusion of modern and Victorian—it might be the perfect back to a chair he had in mind.

"I didn't mean to startle you," she said.

"I'm Anush."

"Nasreen."

They shook hands.

Not expecting her to have a firm grip, he offered a half-slack hand and immediately regretted it, feeling emasculated. He'd blown the ever-so-important first impression, first by being startled at the sound of her voice and then offering a dainty handshake. Again, he wanted to rewind ten seconds and have a do-over. Rewind his whole life, not point that stupid Roman candle at Reza so he wouldn't be sent to boarding school so he could remain with his mother so she wouldn't get cancer and die.

"You know Saurav?" Nasreen said, gesturing towards the club with her cigarette. It took Anush a moment to realize that she was referring to the jackass VJ.

"Yes, of course. Saurav is—"

"Annoying," she said.

He'd never met an Indian woman bold enough to start a

conversation with a stranger. There was something electric about her audacity. He couldn't help but notice how full her lips were. Anush smiled in agreement and looked down at his shoes for something witty to say but came up empty-handed.

They stood there and smoked for a while in silence. From the corner of his eye he stole furtive glances of her profile, her long eyelashes, her small nose, her perfectly shaped chin, her exquisite neck, the few tiny beads of sweat on her light brown skin. The night air was humid and he could faintly smell her perfume, which had a trace of orange blossom mixed with her perspiration. He'd never been so drawn to a scent.

"Thirsty?" she said matter-of-factly. "My sister has a suite upstairs for her birthday party. We could get a drink."

THE SUITE WAS on the fourth floor of the old wing of the Taj. It was luxurious, with a magnificent view of the Gateway of India and the sea. A few people were chatting on the couch, slightly drunk. Anush noticed the furniture right away. Most of it was late nineteenth century, Victorian. Much of it like the stuff that was made in the shop. As he fingered the edge of an end table he noticed the workmanship was decent but not perfect and wondered where it'd been done.

Nasreen opened the fridge, asking, "What can I get you?"

"Whatever you're having."

She dropped a few ice cubes into fine-sounding crystal tumblers that she then poured whisky into.

As she handed him a glass they locked eyes, and in that moment Anush felt a thunderbolt surge through him. She had the biggest, deepest, brownest eyes, and he felt her gaze on him as stepped out onto the balcony.

"Where's your sister?" he asked, trying not to think of the rather firm nipples that he could vaguely make out through Nasreen's black dress.

"Oh, Ameena's at the club downstairs with her friends. She's back from America for a visit."

"She lives there?"

"Doing her master's at Princeton. She thinks about staying there but I know she'll be back. Eventually."

"How can you be so sure?"

"I graduated from there and just moved back. Too damn cold."

Anush told her about his visit to Calgary. "It was so cold and dry there that it literally hurt to breathe."

Before long they were finishing each other's sentences. They talked about coconuts like Paresh. "My cousin and all his Canadian friends play ice hockey in the winter on a frozen lake in thirty below." They both snickered at the absurdity of it. What they didn't have to say, what was implicit, was that while there were scores of middle-class Indians who went for a better life, luckily the two of them belonged to a socio-economic class that enjoyed a very comfortable life. They didn't need to flee elsewhere to work like dogs and drive Toyota Corollas.

Nasreen said, "I liked Princeton but I never totally felt at home in New Jersey. The white ladies working the checkouts at supermarkets were always a bit friendlier with the white customers."

Anush said, "Yeah, no matter how successful my uncle and aunt become in Canada, I think they secretly long to come back here, to feel at home."

It turned out they had a lot in common and knew some of

the same people in the Bombay party scene. Nasreen, with a master's in communications from Princeton, was working as an entertainment reporter for the *Times of India*, covering stories on fashion shows and hot new trends. "It's not my dream job. I hate how people always judge me to be a vain and privileged socialite." But Anush could see how people put her in that box. She was patrician, and she carried herself with a confidence that most women could only fantasize about.

"So what is your dream job?" Anush asked.

"Journalist. Maybe even work with the UN or an NGO one day," she said with a shrug. "I don't know. Maybe I should just count myself lucky to be a socialite gossip columnist."

She was the most charming person he'd ever met. Intelligent yet sensitive, confident but self-effacing.

"And how about you?" she asked.

"I make a bit of furniture," he said. "Vintage stuff with a modern twist."

She was fascinated and asked many questions. He answered honestly, admitting, "I kind of stumbled into it. Actually, I have a very helpful assistant. I'm just learning as I go along." It was the first time anyone had taken a genuine interest in his work. When she listened to him, she gave him her full attention, staring into his eyes. He tried to look away but couldn't and found himself rambling. "Well, I'm taking my grandfather's old designs and putting a modern spin on them, using heirloom woods like mahogany, teak, walnut . . ." He nervously jabbered on, but she kept listening, eventually making him feel assured. They talked on the balcony for nearly three hours. It was one of those rare times when he didn't feel like a disappointment, that he might actually be capable of something.

- 15 -

1998

ANUSH AND NASREEN HAD GONE to several posh parties together over the past couple of weeks, but tonight they were going to the party of the year. Kulshand Malwani, the city's hottest restaurateur, was throwing a lavish party at the Taj Hotel in the presidential suite. Only fifty invites had been sent out. The beautiful Khan sisters, Nasreen and Ameena, having recently returned from America and frequently in the society pages of the *Bombay Times*, were invited. Anush and Ameena's friend Taran were their dates.

The party was in full swing by the time the four of them arrived. A stately chandelier hung in the centre of the generous drawing room where catering staff served silver trays of champagne and hors d'oeuvres.

People were mingling. Nasreen, Anush, Ameena, and Taran were among the youngest. Nasreen seemed to know everyone. She kissed people on the cheek like a Parisian while introducing them to Anush. He couldn't help but blush when he overheard a woman whisper to Nasreen, "What a dashing couple the two of you make."

Despite the fact that the shop was being cleaned up to be sold soon, Anush had never felt so content. The past two weeks with Nasreen had been sublime. During the days, he'd be at the shop, working on his furniture, and in the evening he'd meet up with Nasreen and they'd go out for dinner or drinks or dancing. They'd talked of a trip to Goa.

Nasreen wasn't just glamorous or beautiful or witty or charming, she was also generous, graceful, modest. At the parties she'd taken him to, Anush saw that she could debate anyone on politics, fashion, sports, self-effacing at times, and, if need be, virulent at others. Then there were her deep brown eyes, her luscious lips, her full round breasts. They'd done everything besides have sex. She wasn't a virgin, and he was aroused by her sexual prowess.

When he was with Nasreen, nothing else mattered. The entire world could collapse but with Nasreen by his side, he was inoculated from the disappointments, the calamities of life, the viciousness of the world. With Nasreen, his destiny didn't seem like a ridiculous omen. With Nasreen, anything seemed possible.

Kulshand Malwani, the gregariously gay host, squealed like a little girl when he saw Nasreen and Ameena. When Nasreen introduced Anush, Kulshand said, "So this is your scrumptious boy toy? Even more handsome than you said. Only kidding!" and leaned in to kiss Anush. Anush uncomfortably offered his cheek for a kiss, but Kulshand kissed Anush on the lips, which everyone found funny except Anush.

Kulshand gave the four of them a tour of the suite. The balcony had an incredible view of the harbour and the Gateway of India, an iconic local monument erected for some English king, Anush couldn't remember which. Kulshand casually mentioned, "Cindy Crawford stayed in this suite last weekend, while she was here doing a publicity tour for Rolex, and next weekend the suite is booked for the president of Switzerland."

The four of them oohed and aahed as Kulshand took them to the master bedroom to show them the four-poster king-sized bed and the opulent marble ensuite bathroom. There was even an adjoining bedroom nearby for the bodyguard. Kulshand winked at Anush. "You can be my bodyguard anytime, Anush," which again everyone found funny except Anush, who forced a laugh while trying to think of a curt comeback. Nothing came to mind except *Kuttay! Kaminay!* and he had enough sense not to say that. As Kulshand took them back to the kitchen and they joined the rest of the party, Anush had a loss of faith. It occurred to him that maybe he wasn't quick enough, smart enough for Nasreen. What was a clever girl like her doing with an untalented loser like him? Her friends were diplomats, writers, fashion photographers; they held doctorate degrees in comparative post-modern literature from Ivy League schools. Anush had barely finished college. If not for his father, he would have failed. He didn't even have any real friends, had never travelled anywhere except to visit his stupid coconut-Canadian cousin who was now backpacking around India. Up till now, he'd always managed to allay such fears and shortcomings, reassuring himself that he was just as worthy as any of Nasreen's circle of overachievers and well-borns. But it wasn't so easy to convince himself with this crowd in the most expensive suite in the poshest hotel in the city, possibly the country, that he was deserving of Nasreen.

As Kulshand led the group away, Nasreen held Anush back for a moment, kissed him, and whispered, "Don't mind Kulshand—he's a horny, drunk teenager trapped in an adult's body." She always knew what to say to make him feel better. He wanted to hold her tightly and never let go.

Nasreen and Anush were hand in hand as she introduced him to a variety of people. Catering staff walked around with trays. "Miniature crab cake and asparagus royale with stone ground mustard and lemon aioli?" "Fennel and blood orange chèvre butter?" "Mushroom cap stuffed with fontina cheese?" What the appetizers lacked in taste they made up for in title and presentation. Anush had to inconspicuously spit part of a lobster crepe back into a serviette.

A small entourage had formed nearby and there was a hubbub as to who had just arrived.

Ameena said, "It's that politician, Premtesh Malwalkar."

Taran whispered, "Isn't he the one who wants to ban rock concerts?"

"Yes. He says public displays of affection between young men and women are grossly indecent, un-Indian."

"A right-wing conservative at a party like this?" Nasreen tried to restrain a laugh while Ameena and Taran chuckled.

Anush, who didn't keep up with the news, joined in, not wanting to be left out. "What an idiot."

The four of them shushed themselves as the small constellation of people around the man came their way. At the centre of the orb was a short, middle-aged man with a large grin, shaking hands with everyone. Nasreen had to poke her sister in the ribs to stop her from tittering with laughter as they were introduced to the man. Anush thought he looked familiar. When the man shook Anush's hand, he asked, "How are you? Give my regards to your father."

It was one of the men his father had entertained not long ago with the Blue Label Reserve whisky. "Of course. Nice to see you, sir."

The politician grinned with a wink and pumped Anush's hand.

A photographer from the *Times of India* noticed the familiarity between the two and asked them to pose, along with Nasreen. The three of them stood together and smiled for a photo before the politician continued making his rounds.

Nasreen, Ameena, and Taran all turned their attention to Anush, curious.

"I think my father is friends with him," Anush shrugged, and they all laughed.

"Too many old people at this party," Ameena moaned just before her friend Priya showed up. Priya was a semi-famous model who did toothpaste ads. The five of them had smoked hash and danced till four in the morning at a party recently. Priya surreptitiously pulled out a small plastic bag of white powder and whispered, "Follow me," and the five of them slipped into the bodyguard's room.

With the edge of a credit card, Priya separated the cocaine into five lines. Anush had seen enough Hollywood movies to know what to do. When his turn came, he put the rolled-up hundred-rupee note up his nose and thought of Al Pacino in *Scarface* as he sniffed a line. There was an immediate taste of metal at the back of his throat that he couldn't get rid of, not even by draining his beer. It was only after Nasreen kissed him deeply that it subsided.

Ameena and Taran rolled their eyes at Anush and Nasreen making out. Ameena said, "Be careful the BJP politician doesn't see your orgy."

Taran teased, "Maybe Anush has a 'get out of jail free' card from him."

As they left the room and joined the party, Anush wondered if the coke was real. People were routinely swindled by Africans at the Leopold Cafe who sold fake pot and coke. He also wondered about his father's connections with the BJP. He knew that the colonel and his old man were supporters of the BJP, but he had no idea what they did apart from raising money for the upcoming general election. He wondered what his father had done to earn that Mercedes-Benz—a rather sizeable kickback.

Anush told himself to stop thinking of his father. He'd been catching himself daydreaming of a world without his father and felt horrible for having such malignant thoughts. But with the old man alive, Anush would probably never be allowed to continue making furniture or marry Nasreen. However, if the old man died, Anush would appoint the right people to keep Sharma Shipping functioning, be able to continue working at the shop with Reza, and spend the rest of his life with Nasreen.

He wanted to kick himself in the face. What kind of son was incapable of loving his own father? Much less wished his father dead?

A waiter with a champagne tray passed by and Anush helped himself. Soon, his anxieties about his father, about not being intelligent enough for Nasreen and her friends, melted away. As he put his arm around Nasreen's waist, he noticed how smooth the silk of her dress felt. The tips of his fingers found their way to the part of her back exposed by the dress. Her skin felt like velvet rose petals. For an instant he was transported back to his mother's funeral, where he'd thrown hundreds upon hundreds of flower petals on her body. Anush told himself to snap out of it. Nasreen looked devastatingly gorgeous in her black party dress, which clung taut to her perfect curves. Maybe the cocaine was real.

Nasreen introduced him to a few middle-aged people who were telling lame Monica Lewinsky jokes. "How many interns does it take to screw in a lightbulb? None. They're busy screwing the president!" "What does Monica Lewinsky have in common with a soda machine? They both say insert Bill here!"

Nasreen rolled her eyes. She'd mentioned to Anush how sexist she thought everyone was being about the whole affair, how unfair it was.

Anush said, "Well, it takes two to tango."

"What do you mean, young man?" said one of the men.

Anush said, "What's the difference between Bill Clinton and government bonds? One of them will mature one day."

The men laughed. Nasreen squeezed his hand surreptitiously and smiled to thank him. Anush felt more confident than he ever had. Is this what cocaine did? Made you feel confident without being cocky? Maybe it was just being around Nasreen that was his drug.

In his mind's eye he saw the two of them together for the rest of their lives in fast forward: a large, festive wedding celebration followed by a romantic honeymoon where they'd travel the world, followed by children whom they'd lovingly raise at Sea Face Terraces, they'd throw the best dinner parties, and even as they grew old they'd know how to have a good time, they'd be the couple whom everyone envied, the couple who lived life to its fullest. The old man was nowhere in this hypersonic daydream and a part of Anush knew that the chances of any of it coming true were unlikely. But he fought that with every ounce of his being and pushed those apprehensions away because the optimist in him was blooming, assuring him that everything would turn out well. Maybe it was the presidential suite. Maybe it was the cocaine. Maybe it was his destiny.

Clutching Nasreen's waist, he whispered in her ear, "Wanna get out of here? Just the two of us?"

It was barely ten thirty; the party was in full swing. She looked at him, a little surprised, and held his firm gaze for a moment. "Sure." They snuck out before anyone could spot them.

Downstairs, a valet brought the Jurassic Fiat. Although Nasreen hadn't said anything about it, Anush hoped she wasn't embarrassed to be seen in the old car.

Once they were both in, Nasreen said, "I'm famished. That food was so bland."

"Me too," Anush said, relieved. "What was that squishy thing on the Japanese rice cake?" They both laughed.

Anush drove around to the back of the Taj, to Bade Mia's outdoor eatery where a couple of chefs made everything fresh to order on a large portable coal stove. A boy came running up to the Fiat to take their order.

Nasreen ordered. "Four mutton kebabs with extra green chutney, two *baida rotis*, and a couple of ice cold Thums Up colas." Bade Mia's was Bombay street food at its best: inexpensive with bold flavour and spice. And they didn't even have to get out of the car to eat. When the hot food came, they devoured it with relish.

"Do you like paan?" she asked.

Eaten as a traditional after-dinner digestive, paans were filled with fennel seeds and areca nut, wrapped in betel leaf. Anush hadn't had one in ages and said, "Sure."

"I'll take you to the best *paanwalla* in the city," Nasreen said, ordering a few baida rotis to go before they left. She directed Anush to a paanwalla stand not far away on Marine Drive. There was hardly any traffic, and with the windows down the winter sea air felt deliciously cool.

She asked Anush to stop the car by a few beggars and gave them the extra baida rotis. He rarely did charitable acts like that and hated himself for it now. Nasreen's generous spirit was infectious and he promised himself to be more like her. Maybe give Reza a raise. But if the shop closed, what would happen to Reza? Maybe Anush could keep him on somehow as his assistant at Sharma Shipping. The thought of losing the shop and working at Sharma Shipping wasn't something he wanted to think about right then.

When they reached the paanwalla, Nasreen said, "How are you?"

"I'm well, *memsahib*, and you?"

"Well, thanks. Two special paans, please."

Most Indian women let the man speak to the working class as it was considered unbecoming, unladylike, but Nasreen was nothing like most women. If Anush had to construct an imaginary woman to be his soulmate, he wouldn't have been able to dream up one better than Nasreen.

Just as Anush was about to bite into his paan, Nasreen said, "Wait, let's take them home."

Nasreen's parents were still away vacationing in Alibag as

they had been the past couple of weeks. At Nasreen's place, the servants were asleep. Daisy, the senile Irish terrier, greeted them at the door. She had a habit of biting strangers if they got too close, but Anush had been over a few times now and Daisy had gotten to know his scent so she didn't bite him when he scratched her behind the ear. Nasreen led him directly into her bedroom, where she shut the door and pushed Anush onto the bed. They began to undress each other in the dark while a chunk of moonlight lit the room. Anush unzipped Nasreen from her dress. When they were both naked, she fed Anush the paan and he did the same to her. The sweet coconut jaggery melted in the warmth of Anush's mouth and slid down his throat. He couldn't remember the last time he'd had a paan. As Anush chewed he could smell and taste the cardamom, aniseed, fennel, coriander, rose, jasmine, lime, coconut, and then the pungent areca nut, which quickened the heart almost immediately, like nicotine. Exhilarating, satiating, divine.

They made love on the bed, on the floor, and on Nasreen's covered balcony, crowded with plants and creepers that ran thick up the iron grates—it was a little like a private forest. There was no air conditioning on the balcony and soon they were drenched in sweat from the humidity, their bodies writhing in ecstasy. Sex with the German woman had been pleasurable, but making love to Nasreen was an altogether enlightening experience. This was a deep connection. Every cell in his body reveled in bliss. As they lay in each other's embrace, panting, looking into each other's eyes, he knew the cocaine had worn off, and that it was Nasreen that was the most real thing in his life, the extraordinary thing in his destiny.

- 16 -

1998

REZA AND ANUSH WERE BOTH at work in Anush's office, creating a prototype of a dresser to show to a new five-star hotel manager. If it was constructed well, the hotel would purchase an order of over a hundred dressers from the shop. Although Anush had become reasonably adept with the tools, he still needed Reza's help. Most of the complex joining, for example, was done by Reza. And even though a couple of articles had been written in the newspaper about Anush's chairs, Reza wasn't jealous. In fact, he was a bit curious as to why people seemed to like the strange chairs that Anush had made by taking his grandfather's miniatures and putting his own, modern spin on them. Anush called it art, and on his new computer in the office, he showed Reza some examples of what he meant but most of the pictures of furniture seemed just as bizarre-looking, obviously for people who had too much money and time on their hands. There was one style Reza liked, called art deco, but Anush was always diluting it with other styles, making the end result peculiar. While the workers in the godowns below laboured ten hours a day or more making furniture for the hotels, Reza kept it to himself that some of the creations that Anush was toying around with in the office were just plain ugly. He was happy to not be working in the godowns. Working with Anush wasn't even tiring, Reza rarely broke a sweat. They even had some fun—when Anush was in a bad mood, or uninspired to work, they'd play cards together in the office.

As the day wrapped up, Reza squatted on his haunches to sweep the floor and Anush lit a cigarette.

The phone on the desk rang. Anush picked up and after a while said, "Sorry to hear that. I'll let him know." Hanging up the phone, Anush said to Reza, "That was your brother. Sorry, but your uncle passed away."

Reza had just seen his Nabil chacha two months ago when he was home for his yearly vacation. Despite being ill for a few years, Nabil chacha wasn't even fifty years old. "He hasn't got a single grey hair," villagers said. "He'll live to a hundred and one."

Reza stopped sweeping for a moment to steady himself. After taking a breath he said, "He was sick," and was about to add, *He was like a father to me*, but it seemed inappropriate, because despite the rapport they had built, Anush and Reza weren't real friends. They didn't share personal information like that. And yet they spent at least eight hours a day together, six, sometimes seven days a week—much more time than Reza spent with his wife, Shareen. Reza wasn't obligated to work on Sundays but

Anush would often show up on Sunday afternoons for a few hours, hungover, and Reza would help him with whatever he needed or just play cards.

"You should go for the funeral," Anush said.

"Are you sure?"

"Of course."

"Thank you, Anush bhai," Reza said.

When it was time to go to the train station the next morning, Reza touched Anush's feet as a sign of respect and for his blessing, as all the workers did before making the journey home. When Reza stood up, Anush pressed an envelope of bills into his hands.

"I can't accept this. It's too generous," Reza said.

"It's not nearly enough. Thank you for helping me," Anush said, embracing Reza.

It was entirely inappropriate for a sahib to embrace his employee. Reza didn't know what to do with his arms so he didn't return the embrace and left quickly.

The cold air stung Reza's lungs as he ran to his village, but running was the only way to keep warm on early winter mornings like this. The train from Surat had arrived at Rajkot in the dead of night. From there, he was lucky to find a night bus to Gondal, but it was standing room only. He'd been travelling for over twenty four hours by the time he reached Gondal. From there, he jogged about twenty kilometres and got a ride on a farmer's bullock cart for the last ten. Near his village, while he walked through the Persian lilacs, he could hear the roosters begin to crow. When he reached home, his brothers had just woken up and were outside the hut, washing their faces.

Reza embraced them. Parvez said, "We thought you were coming yesterday. The funeral was supposed to be at sunset. You're lucky Shareen *didi* asked us to wait for you. Come, we've got to prepare the body before it spoils."

Reza barely had time to greet his mother, sister, and Shareen, whom he held hands with briefly before having to undertake the duties of cleaning Nabil chacha's body. With the help of a village elder, Reza and his brothers disrobed the body, wiped it clean from top to bottom and from left to right.

"In the name of Allah," the elder repeated quietly as he rocked back and forth.

Reza choked back his tears. The small dark maroon oil stain on Nabil chacha's right thumb, from a lifetime of smoking beedis, couldn't be wiped clean. He was so much smaller now than the brawny man with powerful forearms who had first come to live with them years ago. Both his brothers were too young to remember how Nabil chacha had stepped in when their father disappeared for days on end and then stumbled home only to abuse their mother. She'd had no one to turn to. The other villagers could only sympathize. She needed a man at home to protect her and the children so she had turned to her brother, a bachelor, who agreed to live with them for a short while. That short while had turned into nearly twenty years. The reason Reza and his family were still alive and well was because of Nabil chacha. Without him, who knows what might have happened. Reza remembered one night when his father had tried to attack his mother with a knife. It was only because he was blind drunk that he stumbled, hit the floor, and passed out. The law provided little protection to villagers. Not all men in the village beat their wives, but it happened. One night after Nabil chacha moved in with them, Reza's father returned and Nabil chacha beat him to the ground and made him promise never to return. After showing up at Reza's wedding, word was that he took odd jobs in nearby villages or on farms. But it'd been many months now since anyone had even heard from him. Maybe he was dead and lying in a ditch, Reza sometimes thought, like the villager he'd once seen years ago, when he was a boy—the body stomped and trampled into the earth.

When the boys were done cleaning the body, the elder instructed, "Place his hands on his chest. Right over left. And wrap him in three white sheets. Then tie one rope around his head, one around his feet, and two around his body."

The three brothers did as instructed and carried their shrouded uncle's body on their shoulders out of their home and towards the cemetery, near the lemon trees. Reza's stomach was rumbling, he hadn't eaten and was beyond exhausted. After lowering the body into the ground, Reza, with his brothers and some of the other village men, stood in front, quietly reciting the *Fatihah*, while children and women did the same behind them.

"*Bismillah, Rahman, ar-Rahim . . .*" In the name of God, the merciful, the compassionate . . . guide us to the straight path . . .

The words washed over Reza. He wished Shareen was next to him. He felt like collapsing and wanted to fall asleep next to his wife, nuzzle with her. But as the patriarch of the family now he had to stand up straight. If his father returned, Reza wondered if he'd be as effective a threat as Nabil chacha had once been to Reza's father, keeping him away for years. After the prayers, Reza and his brothers lowered Nabil chacha into the ground so that his body would face west, towards Mecca. Reza noticed both his brothers wept as they did this, and Reza felt ashamed that he had no tears. The long journey home had drained him.

As Reza and his brothers filled the grave with dry earth, Reza was reminded of how Nabil chacha, years ago, had taught him to slaughter a goat, in the humane halal way. While Reza tied the goat by its hind legs and hung it upside down from a thick tamarind tree branch, Nabil chacha invoked the Prophet, "*Bismillah Allah hu Akbhar*," then with a knife that he'd sharpened with a whetstone, Nabil chacha pierced the goat's neck, from the front, and in one quick stroke sliced through the animal's windpipe, food tract, and jugular vein. The blood spilled quickly down onto the dry earth while Nabil chacha explained, "The neck of the animal should not be disjoined, nor should the bone marrow be cut as it's cruel and causes unnecessary suffering." Soon the blood was drained from the animal and with it, its life.

Reza and his brothers now patted down the last remaining bits of earth onto Nabil chacha's grave and Reza remained on the ground, wanting to shed tears onto the earth for Nabil chacha, but he had none. His mother handed him a handful of wild purple jacarandas and creamy yellow tamarind flowers that he lay instead.

LATER THAT NIGHT, as he lay in bed next to Shareen, he could see in her eyes that she was fretful.

"What is it?" he asked.

"I'm with child now for the last two months."

Joy bloomed in his heart. They'd been trying for three years.

He knew Shareen was apprehensive in telling him as this was a time of mourning, but the news was too important to conceal. He couldn't help but smile.

Shareen nuzzled closer to Reza and said, "I'm scared. My mother had four miscarriages, and my grandmother died giving birth to my mother."

"You'll be fine," he whispered as they lay in the dark hut together. "The sahib gave me five thousand rupees. Look," he said, fishing the envelope out of his pocket. "Our baby will be born in a hospital." As he opened the envelope to show Shareen, he noticed a small folded note he had somehow missed before. He read it and tears flooded his eyes.

"What? What is it?" Shareen asked. "Did he fire you?"

He showed her the note.

> Reza,
> The flat above the shop is yours. Bring your family to live with you as soon as you like.
> Anush

Reza understood Anush's embrace. It was an apology that had been padlocked away for fifteen years. Shareen held Reza while he cried silently. Then she took his face in her hands and for the first time removed his eye patch. As she touched her forehead to his, she whispered

> Farmers search the skies for rains that are late,
> But, my lover, you have yet not returned,
> Without you, I'll not touch a fig from a Queen's plate,
> Your name from my soul shall never be burned.

Their limbs entwined and he could feel the heat between her legs.

He kissed her neck as he spoke, cupped one of her breasts in his hand, and pressed himself against her.

> Peacocks in the dry fields do dance and sway,
> But, my lover, you have yet not returned,
> I will drip streams of blood if my skin they flay,
> Your scent from my soul shall never be burned.

She let him inside her as they whispered verses back and forth.

> Heaven and its stars finally entreat us with
>   monsoon,
> But, my lover, you have yet not returned,
> Street urchins laugh, but from their mockery I am
>   immune,
> Your eyes from my soul shall never be burned.

Being inside Shareen while holding her warm body next to his felt intoxicating, and yet there was an equal measure of agony in Reza's heart, for he felt the void of Nabil chacha now. But the knowledge of a new life in a flat in the city with his family filled him with euphoria. He was unaccustomed to such generosity.

> Orange blossoms in the orchard are flowering,
> But, my lover, you have yet not returned,
> My entire body yearns for you, can you hear it sing?
> Your lips from my soul shall never be burned.

- 17 -

1998

SOON AFTER NASREEN HAD INTRODUCED Anush to a manager of a five-star hotel, Anush approached him about replacing some of the furniture in their suites with pieces from his shop. The manager came for a tour of the shop. The workers had made a few sample tables and dressers. Reza was in charge of the workers, coordinating everything with Anush. The manager was impressed with the quality of the work and a large contract was signed. Anush couldn't believe his luck. Another contract with a different hotel was signed not long after and to celebrate, Anush bought himself his very own black Mercedes-Benz, just like his father's, which he drove straight to Sharma Shipping to show the old man.

"Is it your friend's car?"

"It's mine," Anush said, handing his father the furniture contracts. Anush feared another dressing down in front of the whole office, but the old man finally shook his son's hand and said, "Congrats." Anush had to hold back the tears as he heard his mother's voice, something she'd said just before he was sent to Bharat Academy: *He loves you more than you know.*

Feeling better than he had in years, later that evening Anush drove Nasreen, Ameena, and Taran out to Juhu Beach. There were no parties that night so they were happy just to hang out in the car, chatting and drinking and listening to music.

"The world's going to the dogs," Taran said.

"You're always so cheery," said Ameena, sitting next to him in the back seat.

Nasreen was in the front with Anush. The black leather seats felt plush.

"I'm sick of the news networks covering the Lewinsky affair 24/7," Taran said, opening a beer. "It was just a fucking blowjob!"

Anush felt a little out of place when they got into these sorts of discussions about politics, and the inevitable historical or philosophical references. He usually agreed with Taran, who was as friendly as he was smart. Taran came from money but was unemployed and said he'd probably never be able to get a job with his MA in English Lit. At first, Anush had liked Taran mostly because Taran was a skinny Sikh whose turban made his head look larger than it already did on his scrawny torso, making Anush the more handsome of the two. Recently, though, Anush had begun to appreciate Taran's sarcasm and quick wit. In college, Anush made fun of guys like Taran, but now Anush enjoyed Taran's perspective, his insights, and was even a bit jealous of Taran's ability to communicate complex ideas with ease.

Far up along the north side of Juhu Beach, Anush parked the Benz at the end of a deserted road with a view of the ocean. In the back seat, Ameena opened another bottle of Kingfisher and filled everyone's plastic cups.

Taran handed Anush a CD, saying, "Dude, play this advance bootleg of the new Lauryn Hill I got from a friend in London. His uncle's a record producer."

The waves were less than a hundred feet away, lapping at the shore.

As the music started, Anush examined the CD cover in his hand. Taran and Ameena talked politics in the back seat while Anush and Nasreen listened to the music. *The Miseducation of Lauryn Hill* was reminiscent of the Fugees, the band Hill had fronted, but this new album had much more soul, without losing any of the swagger that the Fugees were known for. It sounded amazing in the stereo system. The bass was deep, the highs crisp and clear.

Taran said, "I don't buy this bullshit about India being on the cusp of change."

"What do you mean? Everything is changing," Ameena said.

"Yeah, OK, lots is changing," Taran said, "but I hate the fucking CNN sound bites of India or China being compared to sleeping giants, or oversized elephants or dragons or whatever the fuck. The real story is the money—how it will change us, but not necessarily for the better."

Ameena said, "But if more Indians are lifted out of poverty, isn't that good?"

"On the surface, yes. But on a deeper level, no fucking way. As soon as the average Indian has the ability to buy more shit, avarice will eventually become the new religion."

Anush reminded himself to look up what avarice meant.

Taran continued, "Humans are too fucking gluttonous, selfish. Look at America. That is our destiny."

"You're so bleak," Ameena said. "Thank god there are people more optimistic."

"Optimistic or blind?" Taran said.

The two of them bickered often, serving as each other's devil's advocate. It was their way of flirting.

In the front seat, Anush and Nasreen sipped their beers while listening to the music. The lyrics on this album weren't just political but also private confessions. Hill's voice encompassed pain and longing and strength and joy all at once. *You're just too good to be true, can't take my eyes off of you . . .*

Nasreen said, "Lauryn makes Frankie Valli's original sound so delicate, so impotent."

Taran said, "I think our apathy and greed will turn everyone bourgeois and only pollute the planet more. We're already over-populating the fuck out of it."

"So we should just let all the poor suffer? Or better yet, nuke them?" Ameena said.

"That's exactly what the Western world wants," Taran said, and then in an American accent, "Nuke them Middle East sand niggers! Yee haw!" After opening another beer, he continued, "And don't get me started on Pakistan developing nukes."

Ameena said, "If we're trying to develop nukes, why shouldn't they be allowed? It's hypocritical for the West to ban us from making our own nuclear weapons when they have enough to blow the whole world up a hundred times over."

"Of course, it's totally hypocritical. I said, specifically, Pakistan should not be allowed. Secular democracy is in jeopardy there—actually, it's up for debate if it ever even existed there."

"We have a right to develop nukes, but the responsibility not to," Ameena said.

Anush and Nasreen were holding hands in the front seat. Lauryn Hill's vocals were like honey, Anush thought.

> You're just too good to be true,
> Can't take my eyes off of you,
> You'd be like heaven to touch,
> I wanna hold you so much,
> At long last love has arrived,
> And I thank God I'm alive . . .

Nasreen's parents were still on vacation in Alibag, and so Anush was at Nasreen's most evenings. He was wondering how he'd bring her home to Sea Face Terraces and introduce her to his father. Would the old man go ballistic because Nasreen was Muslim? It wasn't an issue for Anush or Nasreen, so why should the old man care? But of course, it wasn't that simple for people from the old man's generation. Like all young Indians, Nasreen and Ameena didn't align themselves with Pakistan just because they were Muslim. They were proud Indians. India was their home as much as anyone's. Anush reasoned that as the old man got to know Nasreen, her charm, her beauty, her intelligence would eventually win him over.

> Pardon the way that I stare,
> There's nothing else to compare,
> The sight of you leaves me weak,
> There are no words left to speak,

But if you feel like I feel,
Please let me know that it's real,
You're just too good to be true,
Can't take my eyes off of you . . .

Despite the old man's contempt towards Muslims he would eventually come around and see Nasreen for who she was. He'd have to. The world was changing.

Anush and Nasreen hadn't yet mentioned meeting each other's parents. After all, they'd only known each other a month. But Anush couldn't stop daydreaming about spending the rest of his life with her.

I need you baby, if it's quite alright,
I need you baby to warm the lonely nights.

The tide went out slowly as the night passed and they emptied a few bottles of Kingfisher, arguing over the world's problems. No one complained about the CD repeating. At some point, when the beer was all drunk, and Taran and Ameena ceased their faux hostilities, Taran asked Ameena, "In a perfect world, where do you see yourself in five years?"

Ameena said, "Working at an NGO that helps women in the Third World."

Taran said, "I'd love to write poetry, drink good booze, have a flat in Paris and one in Bombay, never get married, but have many mistresses and concubines in both cities."

Anush wasn't sure what to say. Whenever he got drunk with his friends in college they mostly talked about fast cars, argued over which actresses were sexier, and called each other fags.

He'd never earnestly confessed anything personal. But he felt different tonight and admitted, "I've been so busy supplying the hotels lately I haven't had time to work on my own designs. But maybe one day, I'd love to make all my grandfather's miniatures come to life—chairs and tables made of heirloom wood only with my own modern take. Maybe even show my stuff in a gallery one day."

"Wow, that's cool." "Brilliant."

They'd been to the shop and seen some of his work. Anush had given Nasreen one of his grandfather's miniatures—a mahogany and teak chair with a high ebony back fashioned in a type of Queen Anne style.

"You're so talented. You should do it," Nasreen said.

"I don't know. I'm not gifted like my grandfather was," Anush said.

"No way." "That's crazy." "You must do it."

Anush wasn't sure what to make of the encouragement and praise. Opening his door, he said, "Excuse me, I've got to go to the loo."

Taran followed. They walked to a wall thirty yards away and urinated on the side of it.

Taran said, "Remorse is the poison of life."

"What?"

"I think that's Charlotte Brontë. Or maybe Emily Brontë. I can never remember. They're kinda the same. Don't tell Ameena I said that. Basically it means, if you don't go for what you really want, you'll only regret it."

The February night air was cool. When Anush and Taran returned to the car, Anush noticed Nasreen shivering and gave her his sweater. Taran and Ameena teased them for the clichéd gesture, but Anush saw the way Nasreen's eyes lit up.

They sat for another hour in the Benz, sipping a quarter bottle of whisky Anush had in the glove box, talking about religion, the Lewinsky scandal, nuclear proliferation between India and Pakistan—things that Anush cared little about, but he couldn't remember a time he'd felt so content. In the front seat, Nasreen privately squeezed his hand every now and then.

At around four in the morning, after they'd finished all the liquor and couldn't stop yawning, Anush drove them home.

In the empty Benz, he drove past Sea Face Terraces on Warden Road, to the Mahalakshmi temple. He hadn't been there in years but ever since he met Nasreen, the temple had been at the back of his mind and yet he'd not gone.

The roads were deserted and dawn was hinting at materializing, marking one edge of the night sky with an imperceptible light. The roads were empty apart from a milk delivery boy who raced past on his bicycle with his milk canisters rattling on his rear carrier, getting ready to start his day of deliveries. Anush heard a lone bird twitter and warble as he pulled up to the temple, where two priests were pulling open the gates.

"Namaste," he said. "I wasn't sure if the temple would be open."

"We're opening early today for the Maha Shivratri preparations," one of the priests explained.

Slipping off his shoes, Anush went up the cool marble steps and into the dark temple. The smell of yesterday's incense clung in the air. It instantly reminded him of the incense sticks he'd laid on his mother's funeral pyre, but instead of feeling anxious or melancholy, he felt calm now. At the back of the temple he could just barely make out the sea that was lapping the black rocks nearby. On the veranda, the air was salty and moist. He scanned the sky for a morning star but couldn't spot one. Tiny beads of condensation formed on his face while Lauryn Hill echoed in his head.

> You're just too good to be true.
> Can't take my eyes off of you.
> You'd be like heaven to touch.
> I wanna hold you so much.
> At long last love has arrived.
> And I thank God I'm alive.
> You're just too good to be true.
> Can't take my eyes off of you . . .

EARLY IN THE morning, when he arrived home, Anush was barely through the door before his father charged at him and threw him to the ground. With the *Bombay Times* in his hand, he stood over top of Anush and yelled, "What is the meaning of this!?" It was a photo of Nasreen, him, and the BJP man at the party, with their names in the caption. "Your arm around the waist of a Muslim girl, standing right next to Premtesh Malwalkar? Have you no shame? Do you have *any* idea how hard I've worked? The sacrifices I've had to make in order for you to enjoy your comfy, easy life?"

"But she's not—"

"She's not Muslim? She has a Muslim name!"

"Yes, she's Muslim, but—"

With Anush still on the floor, the old man put his foot down on Anush's chest and said, "Listen to me. You will stop all this furniture nonsense, and you will stop seeing that girl. I've let you run around too long. It's my own fault. I'm selling that damn furniture shop like I should have years ago. Developers are desperate to buy that land and build a tall tower. I've arranged for you to meet with a nice Gujarati girl and her family. Her name is Jyoti Patik. It's time for you to get married."

"But, you don't understand—"

Applying pressure with his foot to Anush's chest, the old man spoke quietly. "No, it's you who doesn't understand. If you don't agree, you will never get another rupee from me. Ever. Choose wisely."

PART II
JYOTI
CELESTIAL GLOW

- 18 -

1997

WALKING UP KING'S ROAD TOWARDS Sloane Square, Jyoti picked up her pace, tightening the Kashmiri pashmina scarf around her neck. It was one of the items in a care package her mother had expedited after Jyoti had complained in a letter about the bitter wind that slapped and stung her face and felt as if it cut right through her bones. It was true what people said about the winters in England. She wondered if she'd be able to endure the remainder of her time alone in London, where most of the people were about as warm as the climate.

Jyoti was staying in a posh, but small, furnished flat in Chelsea, the walls of which were peppered with photos of sunny Spanish beaches. However, the photos failed to provide any comfort because even indoors, despite central heating, it was frigid and no match for Bombay heat.

It would have been more affordable to stay elsewhere in London, but it was her first time away from home and so her mother—the one who ultimately made these decisions—wanted to make sure her precious Jyoti baby was in a safe neighbourhood. It slightly irritated Jyoti that her parents still called her their Jyoti baby even though she was twenty-three.

Jyoti's mother was never keen on letting Jyoti go to London. It was something her parents regularly argued about. When they learned that the dormitory was co-ed, that was the final straw. Luckily, Jyoti's father had reminded her mother how prestigious the London School of Economics was. Jyoti and her younger brother had snickered at their mother's antiquated sense of propriety, but now Jyoti regretted it, realizing she'd been an ungrateful child. Her mother had only wanted to protect her. Now, Jyoti sorely missed home. She'd always taken it for granted. Everything had always been at her disposal in Bombay: the servants, the driver, the food, the hospitable climate.

Once they'd decided to send her, they searched through a letting agent in London for a modest flat, but the acceptable choices were all exorbitant. It was through a friend of a friend at her father's hospital where he worked as a physician that they heard of a retired Indian doctor who'd lived in London most of his life and was looking to sublet his flat in Chelsea while he retired to Spain.

"It's still much too expensive," her mother had argued.

"But it's an investment," her father said more than once, convincing her mother it would be a feather in her cap for finding a suitable boy when it came time for marriage. Her mother softened at that somewhat, but was still unconvinced until they learned that the doctor's flat was across the street from where Margaret Thatcher once lived. Jyoti and her father shared a private smile over the fact that her mother knew nothing of British politics, and yet approved of Jyoti going since living across the street from a famous, or infamous, ex-prime minister might be another feather in her cap. Regardless, Jyoti was excited at the chance to live abroad for the first time in her life.

Now, spring in London was around the corner. Or so everyone said. The air was brisk but the sun was out in full force, making a rare appearance. As Jyoti made her way to Sloane Square tube station, she thought back to the early days of fall, when she'd first arrived, how instead of taking the tube to school, she'd sometimes walk through St. James's Park, dazzled by the autumn colours. She couldn't walk past the ponds without stopping to feed the ducks, or the odd pelican or swan. But she hadn't been through the park in months now. Winter had made her somewhat of a hermit. Jyoti had begun to despise the outdoors. The city she'd begun to fall in love with in the autumn had now become anathema to her. In the fall, after classes in the afternoon, she'd go down every street in Covent Garden, work her way up to the Seven Dials, back down through Chinatown to Leicester Square, then nip into the fringes of Soho, working up enough courage to go a little farther into its heart every time, ignoring the panhandlers, the homeless, the mentally ill, and finally be rewarded when she reached the centre of Soho—the beautiful Soho Square garden, where she'd sit on a bench and take in the buildings surrounding the square, eating a piece of carrot cake she'd saved from lunch. How she longed for those warm afternoons. Nowadays you couldn't sit on a park bench for longer than a minute without shivering.

· Jyoti pulled out her travel card from her purse at just the right distance from the entrance to Sloane Square tube station and fed it into one of the ticket machines without breaking her stride, without holding up anybody behind her in the queue—it was what separated a tourist from a Londoner. There were so many damn tourists in the city lollygagging at entranceways and blocking the flow of pedestrians. She especially hated it when they were inconsiderate at the turnstiles, fishing in their pockets or jackets or bags for their travel cards, making people behind them wait. As she walked down the stairs it occurred to her that she was no longer the wide-eyed, ingenuous girl who'd first arrived six months ago, standing on the wrong side of the escalator and doing all the touristy things that annoyed her now. The timid and studious little Jyoti Patik, who always got the best grades and never dared to even look at a boy, let alone speak to one, was now an independent young woman, navigating her way through a foreign city. For the first couple of months she'd barely even spoken to her female classmates, let alone to the boys, but now she was finding the confidence to say hello and make small talk with a few of her peers, boys included. Her parents and friends in Bombay would've been shocked to see her wandering around the British Museum on a Saturday afternoon, talking to an elderly gentleman about the Rosetta Stone, or sharing her table with a Polish girl at the Natural History Museum café, having coffee and scones with clotted cream as they chatted about which Spice Girl was the least annoying.

As she made her way to the platform, Jyoti's heart began to race. Over the past few weeks, there had been a young man who'd often been catching the same train from Sloane Square with her in the mornings. He had dirty-blond hair and striking green eyes. There was something unpolished about his appearance and yet he seemed kind. More and more often, she found herself getting on the same compartment as him. Despite being taller than her by nearly a foot he didn't seem intimidating. Yesterday he sat facing her, a couple of seats away. Every now and then she sensed him glancing up at her from his book, or looking in her general direction, but she kept her face buried in her textbook, not able to summon the strength to look at him directly. She only had enough courage to steal a glimpse of him whenever he had his back to her. Even from that angle he aroused something sensual in her. On days when the train was full and they'd have to stand, even the way he gripped the overhead railing was seductive. The sinewy veins that spread across his knuckles were just one of the few details she found herself unable to forget, and these bits of him would linger with her, sometimes into bed. The other day on the tube, the thought of his hands running through her hair nearly caused her knees to buckle and made her blush, and she castigated herself all morning through class for such lewd thoughts.

A train squealed into the station. As it came to a stop and opened its doors, she paused, and instead of boarding right away, she surreptitiously scanned the dense platform, but amid the crowd she couldn't see him, and boarded before the doors closed, reprimanding herself for looking for a man like some floozy. *A respectable girl would never do such a thing,* she heard her mother's voice in her head as the train departed. The compartment was packed and she had to wedge herself between two hefty American tourists. She couldn't wait to reach Westminster Station, three stops away, where the annoying tourists would exit eagerly to take pictures of Big Ben and the houses of Parliament. As they approached the station, one of the Americans asked Jyoti in a southern drawl, "Excuse me, miss, is Westminister Station next?"

Jyoti took a breath before replying, "Yes, West*min*ster Station is the next stop." The Americans happily got off, thanking Jyoti, not realizing she was correcting their pronunciation.

As most of the train emptied, Jyoti found a seat. She saw the young man with the sinewy hands and striking green eyes come towards her from the other end of the compartment. He took a seat directly across from her, and she pretended to lose herself in a textbook. It was a chapter the class had yet to cover. Jyoti was trying to stay ahead. Her courses this semester were becoming more difficult to keep up with. The chapter was titled "Pricing Asset Derivatives, Options: how Theta (time) and Vega & Rho values change intrinsic values boldly." With her peripheral vision, she could see he was wearing a navy peacoat and flipping through a book himself. She looked out the window and saw that they were already at the next station, Embankment. Her stop was next. She wondered if he went to school somewhere in East London or if he worked in the financial district. From the few quick glances she stole of him she guessed he was about her age. She looked out the window again, considering whether to look at him directly. She was no longer in India; looking at a boy couldn't possibly carry all the implications it would back home. But every time she screwed up enough courage to lift her gaze from her textbook, she peered out the window instead at the last moment, as if looking at something in particular. The train was beginning to slow down, the recording of the tube lady's voice began. *The next stop is Temple, this is a Circle Line train* . . . She closed her textbook and as she gathered her things, she finally mustered up the courage to look at him. They held eye contact for a second, maybe two. It was filled with energy, licentiousness, the possibility of anything.

"That's a lovely scarf," he said with an Irish lilt.

"Thank you" was all she could manage. She said it so softly that she barely heard it herself.

After exiting the train, she gathered herself on the platform and brazenly glimpsed at him again through the window. As the train began to pull away, he gave her a small smile and she returned it.

Walking past Embankment Gardens and up Arundel Street towards the LSE, Jyoti felt exhilarated. She barely noticed the sting of the cool, wet air from the Thames.

- 19 -

1997

AFTER DELIBERATING FOR THREE DAYS over what to
wear on her date, Jyoti went shopping on Oxford Street for a
new top. Even though she'd never gone on a date, she was aware
that a delicate balance had to be struck: not too promiscuous,
not too prudish. After trying on over a dozen sweaters and tops
(a dress was out of the question—too suggestive), she chose a
smart black turtleneck sweater that clung to her petite frame.

Standing at the top of the front steps of the National Gallery
she felt unlike herself with her hair down, no ponytail. Tucking
a few strands of hair behind one ear, Jyoti scanned the square for
Gavin. She checked her watch again. He was only a few minutes
late. She thought about going for a walk around Trafalgar Square
but the hundreds of pigeons and tourists were off-putting.

Perhaps she could go around back, take a stroll through Leicester Square, and return shortly. She didn't want to be the one waiting, appearing desperate.

She inched her way from the top steps of the gallery facade to the bottom step, reconsidering this whole thing. With the hundreds of people milling about the square, she had a lingering sense of anxiety that someone would spot her with Gavin and inform her mother thousands of miles away. It was ridiculous, and she hated herself for being so irrational, but nevertheless she couldn't shake the idea of her mother's disapproval.

It wasn't too late to just go home. Sure, she would see him again on the tube next week, but it'd be easy to come up with an excuse. *I'm so sorry, I wasn't feeling well, or I totally forgot I had a group assignment with classmates.* He'd get the hint.

What was she thinking? Going on a date?! In Bombay, no self-respecting single girl would ever think of going out alone with a boy; it just wasn't done. She'd been out with girlfriends several times, meeting up with boys they knew from college, but nothing ever happened during those evenings apart from a walk in the gardens on Malabar Hill, followed by a coffee at the rooftop cafeteria with the view of Marine Drive below. If things got really rowdy, the boys would order cold Kingfisher beers and sometimes an adventurous girl or two would allow the boys to pour her a small glass (Jyoti never did). If her friends could see her now they'd be astonished that Jyoti Patik was on a date! With a boy she just met on the train! She heard her mother's voice again. *How scandalous! What would people say?*

It was only now, after having lived in London for six months, that Jyoti realized how entirely consumed her mother and her mother's friends were with gossip. She'd always rolled her eyes at them when they gathered for tea in the afternoons, clucking like hens. *Did you see the Shah's daughter talking with the Patels' driver from the seventh floor on the street? The fellow looks like a mawali. So shameful!* But now that she lived in London—where no one had that kind of idle time for chit-chat, at least not the people she knew—that kind of gossip seemed even more ridiculous, a remnant of the Victorian era. Exactly how or why it was still rampant in India in the post-colonial age was a mystery Jyoti found herself trying to unravel. And it nettled her even more whenever she caught herself thinking like her mother, silently judging other girls in class for flirting with boys, for wearing short skirts. She despised herself, or at least her instincts, for being so old-fashioned. Was she just jealous of the other girls? No, there was something definitely vulgar about some of them. Of course not all of them were so forward; some of them were focused on their studies, and those were the ones whom Jyoti kept near.

On Friday afternoons, many of her classmates went for drinks. Despite turning down several invitations from the girls, Jyoti had joined them last week. She couldn't help but feel a little out of place, sipping her ginger-ale as the other girls had glasses of wine or shandies. When the topic of pop music came up she chimed in. A debate was sparked over who was the better singer: Mariah Carey or Whitney Houston. Jyoti spoke in Whitney's defence, the less popular camp, and she enjoyed being part of the conversation until it took a tangential turn—probably from all the alcohol—to sex. She sipped her ginger-ale quietly while the other girls giggled over who was the cutest boy in their class. Allusions were made about a Welsh boy who had large hands, which made the girls cackle. Jyoti was sure she was the only virgin at the table and wondered if her silence gave her away. Feeling uncomfortable, she excused herself. "Sorry, I'm looking after the neighbour's cat and he needs to be fed," she said, slinking out of the large booth.

Checking her watch again on the gallery steps now, Jyoti thought about how in college a couple of boys had had crushes on her but she'd failed to see it. It was her best friends, Chaya and Kiran, who had to point out that the boys who were asking her to tutor them in maths weren't interested in algebra. Maybe she was naive, or maybe she just didn't want to disappoint her parents, who always insisted that she focus on her studies. She'd been perfect since she was a child always at the top of her class. At eight years old, her parents had had her take an IQ test. When it turned out she was as brilliant as they'd claimed, the option of being skipped a year ahead at school was presented, and before Jyoti could even think about it her parents decided for her. "Our Jyoti baby isn't being challenged enough," they said. So in the middle of the school year she was advanced from the third standard to the fourth. Looking back, she couldn't say that she had to leave all her old friends behind as she didn't really have many, but making friends in her new class was even more difficult. They viewed Jyoti from afar, as though she were a strange animal behind a cage in the zoo. As it was, she was small for her age, but as an eight-year-old in the new class of nine-year-olds she was even shorter. This hindered her self-confidence and when she realized she was smarter than all of them, it made her feel even more of an outcast.

Her new teacher thought to remedy the situation by making Jyoti his aide. He asked her to help some of the other children in the class who were behind, thinking she would benefit from the social interaction, but it only made matters worse. The nine-year-olds thought of her as the teacher's pet. She was never publicly ostracized, just ignored, and even though she brought home perfect grades, which her parents celebrated, she felt like an outsider at school. It wasn't until college, when she befriended Kiran and Chaya, that she felt somewhat normal. But by then the die had already been cast. Jyoti lacked the confidence and social proficiency that seemed to come naturally to girls like Chaya and Kiran, and she was never able to fully shake that feeling of being a little peculiar. She wondered if she was missing out on something and considered if her life would've been different if she hadn't been pulled ahead that year in school. Would she have more confidence? Instead of immersing herself in homework and textbooks after school every day, would she have had more friends? Had more fun? Felt less anxious? Would she be a little more social now? More normal? Or at least not hear her mother's nagging voice in her head all the time?

As beautiful and clean as London was, compared to Bombay it was a lonely place. She walked past hundreds of people every day on the tube and on the street who all looked right through her as though she was invisible. After crying herself to sleep during her first few days in London, she stopped. She hated feeling sorry for herself, unlike her mother, who was fond of playing the martyr. Whenever Jyoti's younger brother, Rahul, got into trouble at school, her mother would bawl, and before the tears had a chance to streak down her cheeks and onto the floor she would shake her fists skyward and plead, *God, why have you forsaken me so?*

Deciding to give Gavin one more minute, Jyoti continued waiting on the bottom step of the gallery and thought back to her first two weeks in London. She'd picked up the phone several times in the middle of the night to tell her parents how miserable the food was, how the people in the building always said hello to each other but barely looked at her, how school wasn't much better. She wanted desperately to return home but she wouldn't have been able to live with herself for disappointing them. They were so proud of their Jyoti baby for gaining admission to the LSE, and she knew that tuition for international students was a small fortune. Apart from the school being one of the best for Jyoti to receive her graduate degree from, both her parents had long planned for the eventuality of being daughter-less for an entire year. Since Jyoti had never been away from home alone not even for a single night her parents fortified them selves for it, her mother repeating, "It's a sacrifice we have to make in order for Jyoti to fulfill her destiny," before sobbing for her future-self who would be daughter-less for twelve months. Both parents assuaged themselves by telling each other that the LSE was only borrowing their daughter for a year before it made her into a great prize-winning economist, like one of the many world leaders who'd walked its famed halls. On the night before Jyoti left, the Patiks had some family friends over and her father, after having a few whiskies, said, "Jyoti already has something in common with one of the school's founders, the prodigious and eminent George Bernard Shaw. Any guesses as to why?" His guests were all stumped. "They're both vegetari-ans!" he finally revealed. It was a jump in logic and a joke that only a slightly drunk and very adoring parent could make. It was memories like this that kept her from dialling the last digit of her parents' telephone number in the middle of the night during those first weeks.

But over the months she'd grown to like London, and now that spring was here, an optimism or at least a buoyancy had crept in, which she chalked up to her having survived in a foreign city on her own. The mere fact that she'd withstood the winter gave her strength.

Just as she was about to abandon the gallery steps and go home, she spotted Gavin running towards her from the edge of Trafalgar Square. He smiled and waved as he ran. She felt the inklings of a new sensation in her stomach, something she couldn't clearly identify. Was it confidence? Is this what being independent, totally on your own, without worrying about disappointing other people felt like?

"So sorry I'm late . . ."

While Gavin apologized, she couldn't help notice how striking his green eyes were. He smelled like crisp mountain air. She realized the new sensation wasn't in her stomach—there was an ardent heat between her legs she'd never experienced.

- 20 -
1997

"I'M T-T-TRULY SORRY FOR BEING late," Gavin said, blushing. Jyoti knew his stutter came out when he was nervous. Over the past couple of weeks they'd chatted on the tube in the mornings, during which he'd stuttered less each time. At first she'd found his Irish accent difficult to understand but she was soon charmed by its lilt.

"It's alright," Jyoti said, feeling a little blush herself. As they walked, she tried to keep her distance from him, to keep her desire at bay. "I was just enjoying watching all the silly tourists feed the filthy pigeons."

"Flying rats," he said.

"You mean the pigeons or the tourists?" she asked with a smile. Making fun of the American tourists who disembarked at Westminster Station was a large portion of their banter. Just the other day they'd cracked each other up with impressions of overly amicable Americans who mispronounced other station names. "Beg yer pardon, miss, is Glou*cesester* Station the next stop?" "Do y'all know if Lie*chester* Square's on this line?"

Now, as they climbed the stairs and made their way into the gallery, Jyoti still couldn't completely shake the thought of her mother finding out that she was on a date. Taking a deep breath, she reminded herself: It's impossible, you're not in Bombay, stop being so anxious.

Inside the gallery, among the grey stone walls, the high ceilings, and the subdued voices of patrons she felt a bit more at ease. This being a Saturday, the gallery was considerably busy, but as it was less than an hour until closing, the crowds were beginning to thin.

"So, do you have a favourite painting in here?" Gavin asked when they arrived at the Central Hall. He wore his navy peacoat with a sea-green scarf that matched his eyes.

"Not really," she said, hoping he wasn't an art snob type.

They ambled through the Sunley Room and then ended up in one of the larger rooms of seventeenth-century paintings that Jyoti had been in before many times.

"I'll show you one of my favourites. It's awesome," Gavin said and smiled at Jyoti as he led her farther into the gallery. Jyoti had mentioned just the other day that one of her pet peeves was when people overused words like *awesome*, words they didn't know the meaning of. He turned back to her now, winked, and said, "Seriously, it's awe-inspiring."

Jyoti followed, trying not to let her smile show.

He led her to a seventeenth-century painting where in the

foreground, a naked man lay asleep on top of a bare-breasted woman. She read the plaque: "SAMSON AND DELILAH" BY PETER PAUL RUBENS 1577–1640. She'd seen most of the paintings in the gallery since she often came to use the restrooms while out on her walks through the West End and Soho. Though she made an effort to see different sections of the gallery, she rarely spent much time considering specific paintings. Usually Jyoti sat on one of the benches to give her feet a rest, briefly took in whatever paintings happened to be there, and then carried on. But clearly Gavin knew a thing or two, and Jyoti hoped he wasn't going to be annoyingly clever and lecture her on the merits of great art. But for now, all she could do was make an effort to come across as amenable. Maybe the only thing they both had in common was making fun of Americans. She considered making an excuse and going home. Maybe she'd have to stop seeing him altogether. Take an earlier train to school every morning for the next five months. Perhaps he'd stalk her. Perhaps it was what she deserved for agreeing to go out with a boy she barely knew. Her mother's voice began: *What if he's mentally unstable? A rapist?* Flicking at a few strands of hair on her shoulder, Jyoti tried to dislodge her mother from her head. She took a deep breath and decided that the sooner she found whatever it was that Gavin was pointing out about the painting, the sooner the date would be over. She continued looking straight ahead at the painting, partly taking it in, and partly thinking about getting home soon, relaxing on the couch, watching *Blind Date* with a grilled cheese sandwich and a cup of tea, forgetting about ever having gone on this silly date.

Gavin said, "See how he lets the light from different sources spill into the room and light the scene?"

Maybe he was right. She nodded while taking another look at the painting. He gave off a faint scent of tobacco mingled with what she could only describe as a fresh forest musk, which made her lean imperceptibly towards him. Jyoti wasn't sure why she found his smell so alluring.

She scrutinized the painting as if she were a discerning art dealer, trying to disprove or find fault with what he said. A handful of Japanese tourists had noticed Gavin going on like a curator and had gathered nearby, listening to his every word. Gavin was so wrapped up in the painting that he didn't even notice them and continued pointing to different parts of the large canvas.

"The flame in the candle stand on the far left lights the foreground. Look at how white Delilah's skin is."

Jyoti blushed at Delilah's bare breasts, but she thought there was something serene about the painting, about the way the bearded, muscled, nearly naked Samson had fallen asleep on Delilah's lap.

Gavin continued with enthusiasm. "And see how Rubens c-c-contrasts Delilah's alabaster skin with Samson's dark back, rippled with shadows? And standing behind Delilah is an old maid holding a small candle, which also helps illuminate the scene, but because it's behind the plane of the large candle stand, it gives us more depth. And at the far back," Gavin spoke faster, with more excitement, "one of the eager Philistine soldiers in the background is also holding a candle, giving the scene even more of a three-dimensional aspect."

They were standing side by side. Gavin's arm grazed Jyoti's every now and then as he pointed. He was enthralled. The Japanese tourists were impressed, nodding their heads. Jyoti found herself being drawn into the painting even more.

He was right. Jyoti started to see things in the painting she hadn't noticed before—it was subtle but dramatic and three-dimensional. Not wanting to completely accede (isn't that what coquettish girls did?), she asked, with some doubt, "So he was the first to start painting this way?"

"Well, I think Caravaggio was a big influence. He played with contrasting light and dark. The Italian word for it is *chiaroscuro*, which gives more depth." Taking a step closer to Jyoti, he continued, "See how Rubens uses shadows? Sometimes he uses light from a single source to light the scene, but he makes the scene really come alive with his use of contrasting light and dark. At the time it was really innovative."

He'd never spoken so passionately, so earnestly. Their conversations on the tube were always casual, jokey.

After a while, Gavin whispered, "Take a close look at Samson's back. See something?"

She looked but couldn't see anything unusual, so she took a step closer and squinted.

And then she saw it. She realized what he was talking about. A different light source. There were subtle shades of dark red and coral on the contours of Samson's back and on the sole of his foot, reflecting from what must be a fireplace off to the right side that was not actually in the painting—the fourth and off-canvas light source. Gavin was right: it was a beautiful painting with depth and dimension, but she wouldn't have known why or how to appreciate its beauty if he hadn't shown her.

He said, "One of my art college professors thinks this is a fake. She's actually been banned from the gallery."

"Really? Why does she think it's a fake?" Jyoti asked.

"Lots of reasons. The brush strokes in details like the carpet, the statues, the soldiers, are all rushed and not as precise like in most of his other works. Also the saturation is turned way up. A master knows when to stop, when to hold back. A forger, allured by the alchemy, isn't as self-restrained. Anyway, if it's a fake, it's a great study in chiaroscuro."

"How do you know all this? I didn't know you were an artist. I thought you worked in the Square Mile," Jyoti said.

"I'm not an artist. And I do work in the Square Mile. I work in the kitchen of a restaurant. I did three years of art college in Dublin and realized I was, at best, an ungifted amateur." Gavin shrugged with a self-effacing smirk, then went back to talking about how Caravaggio was frequently in duels, breaking out of prisons, fleeing Rome.

But all Jyoti could think about was that Gavin worked in a kitchen. A part of her felt betrayed because she'd assumed he was a young professional, an intern working his way up in an office or bank. But as he went on about Caravaggio with rockstar reverence, she reasoned that he hadn't set out to deceive her. During one of their conversations on the tube, he'd simply said, "I work in the Square Mile," and Jyoti had assumed it was in one of the many financial institutions or law firms there. When she realized that she'd never entertained the idea of him working in a kitchen, she hated herself for being such an elitist. After all, he was intelligent, funny, unlike anyone she'd ever met, and not to mention those gorgeous green eyes. A tug-of-war began inside her. She told herself that back home, of course, someone from her socio-economic background would never dream of talking to a kitchen worker, let alone go out on a date with one. But that provided little comfort, and she hated herself for being so old-fashioned, so judgmental, so like her mother.

She could just see her mother's jaw drop in horror to learn that her daughter was on a date, unaccompanied, with a *gora*, a white. Not even a professional gora, but a dropout! And not just any kind of dropout—if he'd failed at med school or law school that would've maybe been somewhat tolerable—but an art college dropout? Who now worked as a cook or dishwasher? (Please let it not be a dishwasher!)

And yet, as he went on about other paintings in the gallery, she found herself drawn to him. He was so passionate about how Caravaggio directly influenced Velasquez who influenced Rubens who influenced Rembrandt. Jyoti noticed how unaware he became, how earnest and passionate he was, how his stutter disappeared. He was the opposite of her. Unguarded, exposed, and unafraid. And maybe even a bit awesome.

They moved on to modern paintings, elbowing each other now and then when they disagreed.

"My neighbour's five-year-old could have done that."

"Yeah, but I doubt you could have."

It was the first time anyone had physically flirted with Jyoti. She found it electrifying.

If anyone were to describe Gavin's passion for art, it might seem as though he was pompous, arrogant. But Gavin was so thoroughly earnest and unaware of himself, of his own nerdiness, that it was charming. It made her heart quicken. The possibility that someone could open doors she never knew existed thrilled her, and yet her complete inexperience with romance made her feel inadequate, awkward. She continued to follow him like a giddy schoolgirl, tingling with the possibility of their arms grazing again.

As they left the museum, Jyoti couldn't help but notice how

nice his bum looked. The fabric of his jeans cupped his cheeks perfectly. *Snap out of it! Have you no shame?* Was her attraction to Gavin so strong that it had made her lose her senses? Where was her self-restraint? Where was this desire, fervour coming from? Had it been lying dormant inside her all this time?

They spent three hours in the Café in the Crypt, under St Martin-in-the-Fields Church, drinking tea and eating scones with clotted cream and strawberry jam. By eight o'clock, most of the patrons had left to see shows in the West End, but Jyoti and Gavin ordered more scones and tea and kept talking.

"After three years of arts college in Dublin I realized I'd never gone anywhere in the world. I have an uncle who lives near Sloane Square—he's a diplomat's aide and travels a lot for work. He needed a cat-sitter so I figured I'd start in London."

He rolled his own cigarettes and Jyoti enjoyed watching him make them. She'd never seen anyone do that before. He was masterful, rolling the loose Drum tobacco and giving the thin strip of velum at the end of the rolling paper a quick and precise lick before binding it effortlessly between his fingers. It took him mere seconds to make a perfectly symmetrical cigarette.

She said, "So what type of things do you like to paint?"

He laughed, exhaling a puff of smoke. "Not sure if I'll ever paint again. The more time I spend away from art college, the more I realize how truly ungifted I am. I do sketches once in a while, just doodling. What I really want to do is travel."

"Where?"

"Egypt. Turkey. Iran. Maybe I'll continue eastward on land and visit you in India!"

She smiled, overwhelmed by his enthusiasm, his audacity, and wondered if he knew his geography. Even if he were to get as far as Afghanistan, getting to Pakistan would be nearly impossible as he'd have to take the Khyber Pass, one of the world's highest and most treacherous roads. But there was such an air of optimism about Gavin that to point out a detail like that would've been cruel. She let him talk of his travel plans uninterrupted and enjoyed his fervour, not to mention the aroma of his hand-rolled tobacco, which she much preferred to the stench of regular cigarettes.

They caught the tube home together. It was past ten o'clock and there were a few young revellers in their compartment, young men and women like Jyoti and Gavin in their twenties, drinking cans of beer, presumably on their way to a party. One couple was so inebriated that they were fighting one minute and passionately kissing the next.

Jyoti and Gavin restrained their laughter at the couple. But this public display of affection was also unsettling for Jyoti. Would Gavin be expecting a kiss from her at the end of the night? She'd never kissed a boy before.

"What's it like riding a train in India?" Gavin asked. "Is it really people hanging out the doors and windows and sitting on the roofs?"

Jyoti had never been on a local train in Bombay in her life. She'd never really needed to as she lived in the heart of the city and her parents insisted that their driver take her everywhere. The only train travel she'd experienced was long overnight journeys with her mother to cities of religious worship in Gujarat, in first-class, air-conditioned sleeper compartments. But she didn't want to come across as a spoiled brat. Having never been to India, Gavin wouldn't understand. She found herself replying, "Well, it's crowded, but I don't take the train often."

"I'd *love* to visit India," Gavin said, which made Jyoti smile. Many of her classmates had said exactly the same thing. So many Westerners wanted to travel to India, as though the country existed solely as some rite of passage for them.

But Gavin seemed different from the students at school. Jyoti doubted he'd be one of those travellers who took photos of poor people and of cows roaming the streets only to return home and hang the photos on their walls as proof they'd survived a mystical, heathen land. She could picture Gavin travelling in a third-class train compartment and talking to locals. He was generous, curious. She found herself jealous of his independence, of his ability to quit school, drop everything, and travel aimlessly around the world. She could never in a million years entertain anything like that. Her mother would have a heart attack and drop dead before Jyoti could even begin to explain herself.

As they emerged from the station at Sloane Square, Gavin said, "Fancy a drink?"

In the gallery and the underground and in the café, Jyoti had felt enshrouded and therefore somehow free to flirt with Gavin, at least furtively, but now that they were standing in the street, out in the open, she felt as though her mother's eyes were somehow on her. It was ridiculous; she was aware of her paranoia, but couldn't shake her mother's voice. *Who is this Gavin-Favin? How do you even know if that's the boy's real name? What if the dropout cook is some kind of pervert, or murderer or rapist?*

But he's intelligent, interesting, and funny, Jyoti reasoned, and despite their differences, they'd made a connection. What was wrong in pursuing a friendship with him? Of course there was more than friendship on her mind. And probably his. She couldn't ignore that no matter how hard she tried. Every time she looked into his eyes there was an electric current and she had to dart her eyes away to muster enough strength to look at him again.

"I should be getting home," she said, fidgeting with her purse.

"Can I walk you?"

Even though she'd never walked down King's Road this late, she shook her head. "Thank you, but I'll be alright."

"I had a good time," Gavin said, leaning in to give her a peck on the cheek, but she pulled away and stuck her hand out for him to shake, which he did, a bit awkwardly.

Walking quickly up King's Road, feeling like a complete idiot, Jyoti couldn't stop thinking how immature she must have seemed, how prudish. Not allowing Gavin to kiss her on the cheek was quite possibly the stupidest thing she'd ever done.

- 21 -

1997

JYOTI STOOD UNDER AN AWNING of the LSE bookshop, sheltered from a late-afternoon drizzle, waiting for Gavin, whom she hadn't seen since the handshake fiasco at the end of their first date. Jyoti had expected to bump into him at Sloane Square Station in the mornings, but there'd been no sign of him. Was he going to work early to avoid her? She had his phone number, but it wasn't the irrational fear of her mother finding out that kept her from calling; she mostly felt like an imbecile for being so frigid, for not allowing him to kiss her on the cheek. She was convinced that he could discern her level of experience, or rather inexperience, and the fact that she didn't possess the skill to hide her lack of sophistication only compounded her fears. She thought calling him might seem too forward, desperate.

She didn't know any of the girls at school well enough to confide in and ask for advice.

It was ridiculous how much of her spare time was now hijacked with thoughts of Gavin. She'd catch herself thinking of him in the middle of a lecture, of his sandy ruffled hair and green eyes, his sinewy hands. One moment she'd be on the tube, surrounded by dozens of rain-soaked commuters, and then she'd close her eyes and suddenly be in a completely deserted room in the National Gallery with him. Simply thinking of his singsong Irish accent made her smile—at which point she'd remind herself she wasn't here to flirt with boys, that her parents were spending a small fortune on her, and then a ghostly image of her mother would pop up with a wagging finger: *Going around the town with a boy? With a gora?! What decent boy in Bombay will want to marry you if he comes to know? Just think of the shame!*

In Bombay, before Jyoti had left for London, her mother and aunts had dropped hints that a single girl in her mid-twenties in the Gujarati community was considered by many to be an old maid. "I don't hold that old-fashioned point of view myself," they often liked to remind Jyoti, "but it's what the rest of society thinks," implying that they had to comply, conveniently displacing any responsibility and guilt from themselves and onto society in general.

Jyoti understood that her mother was proud of her for gaining admission to the LSE not just because of the career opportunities but also because it would parlay well into a match with a top-notch Gujarati boy. Her father didn't see why there was any rush to get Jyoti married, but Jyoti knew her mother wasn't one to waste a ripe opportunity such as a graduate degree from the

LSE. She'd want to strike while the iron was hot. An arranged marriage wasn't far off in the future.

Yesterday—a week after their first date—Gavin had finally called and asked her to a movie, but she lied about having an assignment due and proposed that they meet in the afternoon for a coffee. The truth was that she was afraid to go out with him in the evening, when there was more possibility of romance.

Gavin now came running towards Jyoti, who was waiting under the bookshop awning. He was drenched. "Bad day to forget the brolly," he said with a smile. Even though he'd been running, he was barely out of breath. Jyoti wondered if he'd been an athlete in high school, a runner perhaps. She could see him in shorts with muscular legs that rippled with every stride. *Stop it! Where's your shame?*

"You're soaked," Jyoti said. The rain had begun to let up. The clouds were low and moving fast. They both looked out from under the awning and were surprised to find a bit of sun shining down now.

"Well, looks like Mother Nature's clearing the way for us," Gavin said. "Come on, I know a place where they make a deadly cappuccino."

They walked for a few minutes before the skies clouded over and it began to drizzle again, forcing them both to huddle under Jyoti's umbrella. She liked the faint scent of tobacco that clung to his coat. They got as far as Holburn before the rain came pouring down so hard they had to run into the British Museum for shelter. In the main foyer, they took refuge along with a couple of dozen tourists and passersby, stomping and wiping their feet on a mat while looking out the window at the deluge.

Her mother's voice began: *The rain is a bad omen. You're*

not destined to be together. But then Gavin smiled at her with his big green eyes and Jyoti decided being superstitious was her mother's thing, not hers. She returned his smile and said, "Reminds me of the monsoons in Bombay" while depositing her umbrella into an umbrella stand.

"It rains like this in Bombay?"

Jyoti laughed at the thought of Gavin walking down a monsoon-flooded road with rickshaws and cows. "Yes, even more. Sometimes it feels as though the rain will never stop."

"Well, looks like we've got a bit of London monsoon right now," Gavin said.

Jyoti had a flash of inspiration and said, "Follow me."

She led him away from the crowded foyer entrance towards the grand, sky-blue-domed reading room. Gavin said, "But isn't the reading room closed to the public?"

A sign by the door said: Reserved for researchers and students with special access only.

She whispered, "Just follow me."

When they reached the entrance, Jyoti showed her LSE graduate student card and said to the lady at the desk, "This is my research assistant from the University of Dublin. He's applied for his card but they're in the process of sending it to him in the post. Would it be alright if he accompanied me this one time?"

Gavin smiled innocently while the lady eyed him for a moment. She frowned and let them in.

The massive circular library was nearly empty. As Gavin followed Jyoti, she noticed him take in the surroundings as she had her first time there, gawking in wonder at the pale blue, 160-foot-high dome with white and golden columns that spread down from the centre oculus like long octopus tentacles.

She wondered if he felt as cozy as she did surrounded by all the books that lined the circumference of the room.

She led him to her favourite place there—a cubicle against the north wall, a quiet, almost private nook. It was empty now and they sat in two chairs, closely snug. The rain on the domed roof was no more than a distant murmur.

"Wow," Gavin whispered, looking up at the huge dome.

"Sometimes I come here just to read," she said. "It's much nicer than the library we have on campus."

"So what exactly is it that you're studying?" Gavin asked. "I know you said you were some kind of maths genius—"

"I said no such thing," she said, swatting Gavin. "I'm studying derivatives pricing."

"What the bloody hell is that?"

"It's about how stocks, or options on stocks, are priced. It's complicated. Not nearly as interesting as Caravaggio or Rembrandt."

She pictured herself travelling around the world with him. He inspired her to be more like him and less like herself, less introverted, less restrained, less afraid. She saw herself happy with him. *Are you mad? You should be ashamed! What kind of boy will want to marry you, just think!?* Before she was even aware of it, her eyes began to well up.

Gavin sat up straight. "Oh, I'm sorry, I was just having a go—"

She shook her head. "It's alright," she said, wiping a tear. "I guess—" She searched for the right words and could only come up with, "School's been really stressful." It was partly true. The workload this semester had been challenging, but the real reason she was anxious was because all her life she'd been dutiful and perfect, and now she was veering off the script her parents had written. Perfect Jyoti baby wasn't being so perfect anymore.

Gavin said, "Sorry if I said something I shouldn't have—"

Jyoti shook her head while wiping away a tear. "No, no, you didn't." The whole arranged marriage thing had never bothered her before. She'd accepted it, even looked forward to it in a general kind of way. Her girlfriends Chaya and Kiran had both written to her that they were recently engaged. At first, Jyoti had been a little jealous of their wedding plans, honeymoons, and new lives. But lately she wasn't so sure. She'd be returning to Bombay in five months, and then getting married to a boy she didn't even know. This was a simple fact she'd accepted blindly, without question, about how her life would unfold. After all it was what happened to nearly everyone she knew in Bombay. But now her whole body was almost rigid at the thought of going back and getting married, her face glowing hot because as much as she tried to fight it, she knew that the reason for her anxiety was sitting inches away from her.

But that didn't make sense. She barely knew him. They'd only been out on one date. Had only shaken hands, for god's sake.

Gavin touched her arm. "You alright?"

She considered telling him but she didn't know where to begin. She could tell him about how she was expected to get an arranged marriage soon. He would try to understand, but he wouldn't be able to really, and she couldn't fault him for that. They were from different worlds. He would probably think it all ridiculous. She didn't know what to do.

"Sorry, you must think I'm a lunatic," she said, wiping at another tear with her sleeve.

"No, just the cutest economist I've ever seen," he said and kissed her on the mouth.

Her teeth knocked against his. She wasn't sure what to do with her tongue and her heart hammered in her chest. Jyoti pulled away and was about to apologize for being so clumsy, but Gavin touched her arm gently. It assured her that he didn't need an apology or explanation. And so she kissed him back.

- 22 -
1997

JYOTI WAS TRYING TO DECIDE what to wear while
Gavin waited for her in the drawing room. It was sunny, and
on opening her bedroom window, Jyoti was surprised to find
the temperature outside teetering on hot, at least by English
standards. Perfect for her new pair of shorts, she thought, before
realizing she'd have to shave her legs.

Gavin leafed through a magazine in the drawing room while
the tub filled. As Jyoti settled into the warm water, she hoped
he'd picked up an *Economist* rather than one of the trashy
Bollywood gossip rags she treated herself to every month at the
international newsstand in Covent Garden.

"Isn't it annoying how the entire country is enraptured with
this election?" Gavin asked from the drawing room. It was all
Londoners spoke of these days.

"I know," Jyoti said from the bathroom with the door slightly ajar. The fact that she was naked and a boy was in the next room would have made her mother go into convulsions, but Jyoti did her best to play it cool.

"So have you decided when you're going to travel?" Jyoti asked, hoping he wouldn't go anywhere until after she returned home in the autumn.

"Well, it's up to my mates. One of them has an uncle with a boat we can work on in Turkey. Not sure if David and Tim want to carry on with me to Egypt or Morocco," Gavin said. "I think they prefer Ibiza."

She'd met David and Tim once. Carmen, a Spanish classmate she'd befriended, and a couple of friends of hers from the LSE had gone to a movie with them. Like Gavin, his mates were from working-class families in Dublin. They wore their blue collars proudly and seemed friendly but she could tell that they privately snickered at her and her academic friends and she wondered how disappointed they were in Gavin for fraternizing with white-collar nerds. Gavin was different from David and Tim. They'd grown up together and over the years as Gavin went to art college they'd lost touch but reconnected in London the way many foreigners in a foreign land coagulate (just as she had mildly befriended an acne-ridden, overweight boy from Delhi in her program, with whom she had next to nothing in common).

"Maybe I should just go by myself," Gavin said.

She didn't like the idea of him travelling to countries in the Middle East or Africa alone. He was sure to get fleeced, or worse. They'd mostly avoided talking about when he was going and what was implied by this evasion was that they were only together for a short time. After a few months they'd never see each other again, the significance of which was too nebulous, and yet Jyoti had an inkling it was something she wouldn't be able to handle so effortlessly as she let on.

While she began shaving her legs, Gavin said, "I really want to check out Algiers, Beirut, maybe Timbuktu."

Jyoti said, "I'd like to see Paris."

"Beirut was once the Paris of the Middle East."

But now it's completely ravaged from civil war, she wanted to say but was too polite to do so. He liked Radiohead. She liked Whitney Houston. They were just too far apart. It would never work. So why was she allowing daydreams of remaining in London with Gavin to play out in her head? What sort of life would that be for her? Away from her family? Her mother would have a heart attack at the first mention of it.

But wasn't the point of having children to give them something better? Wouldn't her parents be happier for her, in the long run, if she were to thrive in London? Her father might be able to adjust, but her mother would forever suffer paroxysms. Nevertheless, how would she be able to remain after her student visa expired? She would have to marry—she nearly slapped herself for getting so carried away and took a deep breath.

Gavin found the Bollywood magazines and asked who was who in the Bollywood scene. Jyoti answered all his questions from the bathtub, caught him up on all the recent gossip while shaving her legs. Who was going to marry who, who had made the longest string of flops, who was making the hits, whose father was part of the mafia, or the government, who had been caught poaching big game wildlife but evaded jail time, etc.

Gavin said, "Let's go see one of these films one day."

Jyoti couldn't help but laugh out loud and said, "You wouldn't understand a word."

She heard him tinker with the CD player and the soundtrack to a hit Bollywood movie, *Pardes*, began to play. Perhaps a Bollywood film with Gavin would be fun. She imagined the two of them sitting next to each other in the dark theatre, her leaning close to him to translate everything. But her day-dreaming came to a sudden halt when Gavin flung open the bathroom door.

She yelped and covered herself with her hands even though she was mostly submerged in soapy water. With his back to her the whole time, Gavin did his best impression of a Bollywood dance so outrageous that it was offensive at first as he gyrated his hips and moved his hands and head spastically to the music. But it was more merry than facetious, which is why she laughed and then cried, "Get out!"

After one last quick hip thrust he leapt out and closed the door.

Part of her was furious with him for barging in on her. But he'd kept his back to her the whole time, there was no attempt on his part to ogle her. After a few breaths, she settled herself and then laughed out loud again.

She wanted to tell him to forget about his friends and travel-ling the world. She was only here for a few more months. Didn't he want to spend that time with her? But that would be selfish, desperate. Instead, she watched beads of moisture trickle down the foggy bathroom mirror.

Jyoti emerged from the bedroom with her hair down. She always wore it tied back, but since this was the first time she'd be wearing shorts in London, why not go all the way? Her bare legs made her self-conscious. She hadn't worn shorts in public since she was ten or eleven years old.

"You look great," Gavin said.

Unsure of how to respond to the compliment, she ignored it and made a show of searching for something in her purse.

"It's your lucky day, Jyoti Patik," Gavin said, mispronouncing her last name like just about everyone else she knew in London (*Patick* rather than *Patuk*). Another reason they were incompatible—he couldn't even say her name correctly. Jyoti decided not to correct him as it had taken him several tries to get her first name right.

"I'm going to take you to one of my favourite spots in London," he said while putting his shoes on.

"Where?"

"It's a surprise."

"I hate surprises," Jyoti said, doing her best to hide her excitement.

By the time they left the flat it was nearly seven o'clock and as they began walking down King's Road, the warm spring air felt glorious on her legs. *You've made your choice now, you lascivious girl. Look at you, walking down the road in shorts like a common tramp with a guru for the public to gawk at!*

She couldn't believe she'd wasted almost the entire day inside trying to study and hadn't even finished a chapter. What was wrong with her? She could barely concentrate these days.

Even though it was nearing the end of rush hour, traffic was calmer than usual and there were fewer people on the street as it was election day. Each pub they walked past was packed with people drinking, awaiting results. There was an excitement in the air across the city. The Tories were fearing a loss for the first time in two decades; it was all the British students at the LSE had talked about. Even in Chelsea and South Kensington— conservative bastions—young people were campaigning for the Labour Party.

Gavin said, "I think the Labour Party might actually win tonight."

"I've never really followed politics. All Indian politicians are crooked."

"It isn't that different in the UK."

Jyoti seriously doubted that corruption in the UK was as endemic and systemic as it was in India but she didn't want to start an argument.

As they entered St James's Park she thought perhaps he'd gotten tickets to a West End show; she'd always wanted to see a big musical. But Gavin led her to a secluded spot by a few plane trees and shrubs near the duck pond. It was almost the exact same spot Jyoti came to feed the ducks on her way back from school when she walked home—a little quiet corner, a cove almost, that few people frequented. She smiled at the coincidence.

"What's so funny?" Gavin asked as he unpacked some food from his bag.

But she didn't want to ruin his surprise by telling him that she'd been there dozens of times. She was touched by his thoughtfulness.

Gavin said, "Shit, I forgot the wineglasses."

"It's alright, it's perfect," she said, touching his arm and sitting next to him on the blanket he'd unfurled. Gavin was trawling his bag for a Swiss Army knife that he finally found and used to uncork the wine.

Plane trees had begun to bloom a few weeks ago across the city and now in the park along with the scarlet oak and black mulberry trees they were just as verdant. The air was intoxicating with the fragrance of tulips, daisies, and daffodils.

With the Swiss Army knife, Jyoti spread cheese onto chunks of bread that Gavin tore from the baguette. The grapes were deliciously sweet, the olives delectable. She even had a few sips of the wine and drank it straight out of the bottle like Gavin.

He was trying to be a vegetarian. At first when she informed him she'd never eaten meat, he thought she was pulling his leg. But after Jyoti explained that it wasn't just her religion but how she objected to animals being mistreated in factory farms and slaughterhouses, Gavin couldn't find a reason to argue so he thought he'd give it a try. Growing up in Ireland, he said he'd never even heard of half the vegetables she knew. She was proud of the fact she'd made him a falafel and palak paneer addict. He'd meet her every Wednesday at the LSE campus where Hare Krishnas handed out free rice and curry. The food was a bit bland but vegetarian.

The warm evening air gave a hint of cooling as the sun began to set and Gavin rolled a cigarette. In addition to the tobacco, there was another scent to Gavin, something that gave him a pleasing fragrance. The other day, she'd stood next to a man at a bus stop who was rolling Drum tobacco and surreptitiously inched her way towards him to see if he smelled like Gavin. He hadn't.

Jyoti asked Gavin now, "What kind of cologne do you wear?"

"None," Gavin said, throwing a bit of crusty baguette into the water for the ducks.

Jyoti didn't believe him. While giving him a shove, she said in her best American accent, "Get outta here."

"It's true," Gavin said, shoving her back gently, "Never worn cologne. I wear Speed Stick, that's all."

"Speed Stick?"

"Yeah, Mountain Moss scent."

She stared at him and laughed. Partly at him but mostly at herself for being so pompous in thinking that only an expensive cologne could smell so alluring.

"They should rename it," Jyoti said. "Mountain Moss sounds like a fungus." She nestled closer to him as they watched the ducks dawdle in the water while the sky above began to shift into shades of dusk. A brood of ducklings swam behind their mother, creating ripples in the still water. She couldn't remember the last time she'd felt so calm.

Jyoti noticed that Gavin's face and arms were flushed a faint pink. She asked, "You feeling alright?"

"Yeah, I'm brill. Why?"

"Your face—it's red," she pointed but couldn't describe it.

"Oh, my skin burns quickly. I must be a bit red from my time in the sun earlier in the day. I turn into a lobster on the beach in half an hour. Guess you don't have that problem, eh?"

She felt foolish for not realizing sooner and then answered, "Well, if I stay in the sun for too long my skin turns darker. Most girls in India don't stay out in the midday sun."

"Why not?"

"Because no one will want to marry them," she said matter-of-factly. As soon as she said it, she regretted it.

"Really?" Gavin said, puzzled. "Why wouldn't anyone want to marry them?"

She shook her head, wanted to rewind and take it back, but it was too late. "Well, uh—I guess—some people in India regard people with dark skin as something—lower—I don't know. It's ridiculous, right? But there are people who think like that." She could feel her forehead bead with sweat. Her mother was one of those people. *Don't play outside in the afternoon sun, it will suck the beauty from your skin and leave you black. Who will marry you then?*

The self-loathing of dark skin was largely a by-product from hundreds of years of colonialism but no one seemed to question it. And every girl Jyoti knew in Bombay followed these rules deeply ingrained in Indian culture. No self-respecting girl would want to go out in the midday sun too long, for fear of becoming dark, less desirable, akin to the working classes. She'd always been aware of the prejudice hidden in homespun wisdom like that but never felt she had the choice to ignore it, to break from it, because everyone she knew in Bombay, where political correctness about skin tone was almost non-existent, followed it. She'd overheard many arguments about skin tone, caste, and religion at dinner parties that her parents hosted when some of the adults, after a few whiskies, would argue that they themselves didn't necessarily believe that a dark-skinned woman was lower class, or that Hindus and Muslims marrying was perfectly fine, but what would *people* say? What would *the neighbours* think? The blame was always put on others in society. No one at these dinner parties admitted that their reluctance, their lack of courage in standing up for what they truly believed to be right the next morning when they were sober, was part of the problem.

But now in London, surrounded by young people from diverse backgrounds, half a world away from her parents, the hypocrisy and prejudice in Indian culture was difficult to ignore.

Jyoti shook her head, trying to rationalize the dark skin thing to Gavin. She didn't know how to explain any of it. It would all seem so foolish to him, if not horribly antiquated. Wanting to change the subject, she sipped the wine and said, "Mmm, delicious." It was the first time she'd drunk alcohol but she didn't want to tell Gavin for fear of being thought a prude. The first couple of sips were acrid but eventually she grew accustomed to the taste.

Gavin teased, "So will you be getting one of those arranged marriages then? I suspect a fancy bird like you would be quite the catch."

She said, "No, not yet," but wondered if her mother had indeed begun. "I have a couple more years before I'm considered an old maid. My family is originally from the state of Gujarat, the state Gandhi was from, that borders Pakistan. There are so many different communities of Indians living in Bombay and most people get married within their own community, especially Gujaratis."

Gavin said, "I work with a couple of Pakistani blokes in the kitchen. Are they like Gujaratis?"

Jyoti laughed. "No. Pakistan and India have fought several wars." She explained how she was at first confused by the term *Paki*—a word that some British used to describe all brown people. "Most Indians would find the word abhorrent," she told him, "not only because it's derogatory, but also because to be compared to a Pakistani would be the greatest insult to most Hindu-Indians."

"So your parents don't like Pakistanis? What about Irish?"

She considered telling him how her mother would have a fit if she knew about the two of them seeing each other but decided instead to say, "Actually, my parents are reasonably open-minded," which was true, compared to most Gujaratis. "But there are levels of racism in Hindu-Indian culture." Jyoti smiled, hoping he wouldn't be repulsed by it, explaining, "The worse thing you could be is a Pakistani Muslim. But I suppose if you were filthy rich it might not matter."

They laughed, but Jyoti less so, knowing how much truth there was to the joke. "What's your family like?" she asked.

"My parents divorced when I was nine. Me da's in Yorkshire. See him once a year. Mum's in Dublin. I grew up with her. My parents were one of the first ones to get divorced on our Cath-a-holic street. We stopped going to church and became outcasts. But nowadays, only half the people from our street go to church, and just about as many are divorced."

"Do you go to church?"

"Only at Christmas with my mum. It's fantastically boring."

Jyoti told Gavin how her mother went to the temple every day, how she fasted on auspicious days throughout the year.

"Do you fast as well?" he asked.

"Not since I've been here. But I did back home." She realized it wasn't something she ever questioned, she just did as her mother did. "I'm not terribly religious but I kind of miss the temple. I took it for granted the incense, the bells, walking barefoot on the cool marble floor. I promised my mother I'd go to temple here every week but I've only gone a couple of times. It's just not the same as the one at home. Should I feel guilty?"

"No," Gavin said. "Catholics invented guilt."

He asked about arranged marriages again. She explained, "It's virtually every parent's dream to have a child with a fortunate kundali. They're even used in arranged marriages to see if the young couple might be a suitable match."

Gavin was fascinated. "So do you know yours?"

She'd never told anyone. Kundalis were as self-indulgent and gimmicky as the horoscopes she loved reading in the back of her Bollywood magazines.

"Come on, out with it," he said.

She said, "Well, I think he said something about being intelligent and that I would have a perfect marriage with my equal, my soulmate, and have at least one son. How sexist! He didn't even mention if I'd have any daughters."

The setting sun cast a brilliant wash of colours over the sky: bright oranges suffused with pinks and crimsons, creamy magentas melting into shades of azure blue, all beautifully reflected on the duck pond. From far off, faint sounds of celebration were heard: car horns honking and young people shouting with glee into the evening air. The city was no doubt celebrating the election results. Gavin held her hand as they watched the ducks in the pond.

GAVIN WALKED JYOTI home, holding hands. Were they officially a couple? She wasn't sure how these things worked. Jyoti reminded herself to ask her friend Carmen who'd noticed Gavin on campus recently and surreptitiously raised an eyebrow at Jyoti to indicate he was cute. They'd talked about it a bit after the movie they'd all went to but Jyoti had avoided the subject.

It doesn't matter what Carmen-Farmen thinks! You're here for your studies! Her mother's voice was reasonable this time. Soon, she'd be back home and Gavin would forget about her. *He's a cook, for god's sake!*

At the door to her flat, Gavin said, "Well, I suppose I should be getting along." They kissed.

Their tongues exploring each other's wine-stained mouths triggered something deep inside her—it felt a little like being on a Ferris wheel: just when you reached the apex and began the journey back down there was a slight moment of weightlessness, of uncertainty, a slight loss of equilibrium, and in that moment you were scared, a little unsure, but thrilled, because even though you knew the chances of plummeting to your death were infinitesimally small, it was possible, and not knowing with any certainty of what would happen next is what Gavin elicited in her, a type of vertigo that she'd become addicted to.

She said, "Stay," and closed the door behind him.

What if he's a rapist?

The new voice that spoke back to her mother shocked her and she let it grow.

What if I'm in love with him? What if he's the love of my life? The one that my kundali foresaw?

On the couch, she clambered on top of him and kissed him with reckless passion.

From underneath Jyoti, Gavin said, "Um, m-m-maybe we should slow down?"

She looked at him and saw in his eyes that like her, he was a bit afraid, a virgin. She let her desire lead her and kissed him deeply. They undressed each other while kissing and their bodies entwined.

- 23 -
1997

AFTER CLEANING THE ENTIRE FLAT, Jyoti repositioned a few knick-knacks on the mantel. She wanted everything to be perfect for her mother's visit. They hadn't seen each other in eight months. On the one hand, she missed her family, but she'd also gotten accustomed to living on her own, and was now a little anxious at the prospect of her mother staying with her for two weeks.

How ungrateful! We're spending a small fortune on you in London and this is how you think of your parents? The least she could do was show her mother around the city: museums, parks, a musical in the West End—maybe *Les Misérables*. Gavin had taken Jyoti to bohemian theatre, which was always in odd venues like at the back of pubs, outdoor parks, or abandoned car washes in the suburbs. Some of the shows were interesting, others baffling, but of course that kind of theatre would only perplex her mother, if not induce an arrhythmia from the language or nudity.

No, Jyoti reminded herself while rearranging some of Dr. Asli's tiny porcelain ballerinas on the mantel, I will not think about Gavin.

When Gavin had come by the LSE to pick her up a few days ago, she'd broken the news to him while hundreds of other students milled about. Rather then tell him of her mother coming, she'd simply said, "Sorry, I can't see you for a little while. I need to focus on my thesis in order to graduate." It wasn't exactly a lie. He was puzzled at the abruptness of it.

She felt terrible but couldn't risk him knowing of her mother being in London. He'd show up with a goofy smile and his messy hair, expecting the three of them to go for a picnic, totally unaware of the stroke his presence would cause. She'd thought about introducing him as a classmate, but the charade wouldn't last long. Her mother was nosy enough to figure out the truth. Jyoti hated being duplicitous with Gavin, but there was no alternative. She was only doing this to protect her mother, who had a history of blowing things out of proportion, and was on god-knows-what types of medication for her ulcer.

Jyoti was so steady in her resolve that day with Gavin that she didn't even give him a chance to respond (she hoped, without any malice, that he was at least somewhat heartbroken). She knew that if she'd let him, he would've convinced her to change her mind, so instead she quickly walked into the nearest campus building and left the poor boy standing with mouth slightly agape. As she walked up the stairs, it gutted her to think that he'd find some other girl soon. There were probably many cute girls at the restaurant where he worked who'd love to date him.

As she dusted the bookshelves now, she told herself that the time they'd spent together was special and she'd always remember him, but there was absolutely no use in carrying on further. Pretending otherwise was delusional. Their romance was a fling. They had next to nothing in common. And yet, there were many so things they still hadn't done that they'd talked about, like taking a coach to Oxford for an overnight trip, perhaps the Glastonbury music festival, where Radiohead were playing (at first she didn't see what the fuss was about—the lead singer sounded whiny, but after a few listens the CD had grown on her, the music and lyrics intelligent, nuanced yet evocative), and still she would've been happy to do none of those things and simply remain in London with him and carry on as they had with him sleeping over on weekends, watching *Simpsons* reruns on Sunday mornings with a full English breakfast cooked by Gavin, followed by a walk in the park with a newspaper that Jyoti read while Gavin sketched—he'd taken up drawing again (was that a sign that she'd stirred something in him, proving that they should be together?).

Oh my god, what is wrong with you? You can't even go two minutes without thinking of him! While sweeping the kitchen floor, she thought of Bombay, the warm sea air, the familiar smells of *khichdi* and *dhal dhokdi* cooking in the kitchen. She looked at a few of Kiran's wedding pictures Chaya had sent, but the beautiful saris and jewelry and henna didn't fill her with pangs of jealousy, of longing for home as they once had.

As she repositioned a little bronze bust of Wagner on the bookshelf (Dr. Asli was an opera fan), Jyoti thought of last

Sunday morning when she and Gavin had been eating their perfectly poached eggs, grilled tomatoes, beans, and toast, and he'd asked, "How many boyfriends does Dr. Asli have?"

There were a couple of photos of Dr. Asli on the beach with young men who Jyoti had always assumed were family members or platonic friends or younger colleagues. She'd never entertained the thought of Dr. Asli being gay.

As Gavin poked his poached eggs with a fork and the bright yellow liquid spread over his toast, several things ran through Jyoti's head quickly: how Gavin's hair, no matter how messy, always seemed perfect; how she'd lived in Dr. Asli's home all these months and not noticed he was gay; how Gavin's eyes in the morning sunlight were the most exquisite green; how it wasn't the fact that Dr. Asli was gay that shocked her, it was that she'd been oblivious to it all these months while Gavin recognized it in just three or four visits; how she'd always chalked up the prints of muscular Greek men on the living room walls to Dr. Asli's interest in the human body; how she lived a sheltered and boring life; how for a genius with a superb kundali and high IQ she was actually pretty stupid; how Gavin's poached eggs, unlike hers, were always perfect—not too runny, not too hard; how she wanted to be with him forever.

While cutting into her grilled tomato, Jyoti had let out a little laugh, as though she'd known all along Dr. Asli was gay. "Oh, I don't know. He probably has lovers all along the coast of Spain."

Now, as Jyoti finished cleaning for her mother's visit, she decided to hide a couple of the framed photos of the doctor on the beach with young men. Even though Jyoti doubted that her mother would be able to intuit the doctor's homosexuality from the photographs, she didn't wish to cause a scandal.

Normal, functioning gay men just didn't exist in her mother's world in India, and she wasn't sure how her mother would react to Jyoti living in a gay man's home. Since she was a little girl Jyoti's parents had always sheltered her from anything that could have possibly hurt or shocked her and now she felt compelled to shield them similarly. Jyoti wasn't sure why they treated her with such fragility. They let her brother take the local buses and trains but insisted that their driver take their Jyoti baby wherever she needed to go in the car. Having some time and distance from them made it clear that although they wanted to protect their only daughter, it was also very sexist to be treated as though she were a pretty canary in a cage. She wondered if she'd given them reason to handle her so delicately. She'd always been somewhat shy, but now she felt as though she'd come out of her shell. She wondered if eight months ago she might have been somewhat put off by the thought of living in a gay man's home. Of course she wouldn't have admitted it to Gavin or anyone in London, but she might have had private apprehensions about it since she'd never known any openly gay men in India. Now she felt more mature, more worldly than the wide-eyed girl who'd left home for the first time. Her parents had warned her not to go exploring around the city by herself, made her promise it. But as Gavin had begun to take her to concerts and art shows and films, the unknown in the world was no longer a nebulous thing to be afraid of, or judged. Gavin's easygoing effervescence and impulsiveness had rubbed off, and Jyoti wondered if her mother would notice the difference in her, be shocked by it, find it inappropriate, cavalier, whorish. Jyoti decided to hide a miniskirt she'd recently purchased at the bottom of her underwear drawer.

A wave of anxiety swelled and she found herself in the bathroom, smelling the deodorant that Gavin had left behind. She threw it in the rubbish along with his toothbrush. But the look on his face when she'd broken the news to him two days ago was still fresh in her mind. He'd been blindsided. And yet, she couldn't explain to him how it would break her mother's heart to know her only daughter, her little Jyoti baby, was going out with a cook! Of course Jyoti would never tell her mother of them having sex. (It had only happened three times—the first time, after the evening at St James's Park, was a strange jumble of things: pain, embarrassment, pleasure; the second and third times were much better. She had had no idea sex could make her feel so happy and confident, so tranquil, so connected to another person on a molecular level, and she yearned for more!) But she feared that her mother would find out no matter how much she denied it.

She didn't know how to explain to Gavin that her mother would literally have a heart attack knowing Jyoti was no longer a virgin. He'd laugh at the Victorian-ness of it—not out loud, of course—he'd keep a straight face, but she feared deep down he would be laughing. The fact that she couldn't explain it to him or the fact that he was incapable of understanding it proved that they were just not meant to be together.

She'd confided things to him that she'd never shared with anyone else. Like how her parents had a loveless marriage. They were more like roommates. The only reason they didn't get a divorce was because it would've been too scandalous for their friends and families. Before coming to London, Jyoti had never even considered how dysfunctional her parents' relationship was, but now she could see that they really only stayed together for pragmatic reasons and she couldn't help but wonder if they secretly would've been happier married to other people. After sex one night, when she and Gavin were lying together in the dark, she wondered if her arranged marriage would be like her parents' relationship, and while Gavin stroked her hair, she considered instead what life would be like if she remained in London: she could get a job in the city with an investment firm that paid handsomely, get her own place, be independent, go out for dinner on the weekends with friends, travel a bit, be happy. But what friends? She had no real friends here apart from perhaps Carmen and Gavin. Carmen would likely be heading back to Spain at the end of the term and although Gavin had a sympathetic ear, he'd probably take off to Timbuktu soon.

She checked the clock now, put on her coat, and took out the rubbish. The flight was due in an hour. She could picture her mother in her seat on the airplane, doing what she always did on long journeys, silently praying with a *mala* in her left hand, deftly moving each of the 108 sandalwood beads while the plane hurtled towards Heathrow. Jyoti felt the fluttering of butterflies in her stomach but she bolstered herself with the thought that she was no longer the little girl who had left Bombay. She was a woman. In some ways she knew more about the world than her mother did because her mother had most likely never experienced the kind of passion she had with Gavin. She wondered if it'd ever been different between her parents. Somehow she couldn't picture it. But she, on the other hand, had experienced something else. Was it love? Maybe it was just desire, ecstasy. Nevertheless, she'd acquired a certain amount of maturity, worldliness, and Jyoti took some solace in that as she headed out the door.

- 24 -

1997

JYOTI WOULD'VE PREFERRED TO WALK through St James's Park as it was a sunny spring afternoon, but her mother was waiting for her at home, and so she took the tube. At Temple Station, Jyoti fought her way onto a crowded train. She kept her head down, not wanting to run into *him*. She'd been going to school earlier in the mornings to avoid him, had successfully gone more than a week without seeing him—had not even uttered his name. Quit him altogether. Cold turkey. Almost. He still found his way into her thoughts while studying, walking, bathing. The nights were the worst.

As the train lurched into motion, she reminded herself her mother would return home in a week and Jyoti would be able to call him. Hopefully he'd still be in London.

At the next stop, more people boarded and passengers were shoulder to shoulder. When she'd first arrived in London, Jyoti was repulsed by the idea of being confined so tightly among strangers but had eventually become accustomed to it. While the train swayed, she expertly kept her textbook open with one hand and continued reading. With no nearby railing to clutch on to, she widened her stance and wedged herself tightly between other commuters and their bags to keep from falling.

Most people were overdressed as the day had begun deceptively cool, and the amalgamation of everyone's perspiration made Jyoti feel slightly ill in the cramped train compartment.

Ever since Jyoti's arrival, she'd been making a mental list of places in London that her mother would enjoy (Natural History Museum, Victoria and Albert Museum, Apothecary Garden of Chelsea, National Gallery), even bought a larger print version of the *London A-Z* for her, but her mother had not gone anywhere by herself, choosing instead to clean up after breakfast and watch television all day until Jyoti returned from school.

Even when the two of them went out, her mother generally complained about the weather or the food or the dishevelled people rather than appreciate the art or architecture.

Yesterday her mother said, "Wouldn't you be happier to come home and finish your thesis in Bombay? Your father and I miss our Jyoti baby so much."

Even though this had occurred to Jyoti a few months ago, she instantly said no. The idea of leaving London so abruptly made her heart skip and she knew it was because of him. She still wanted a summer with him in London after her mother returned home, and so she said, "I need to stay and use the library for research, seek guidance from my advisors for my thesis." It wasn't a lie exactly—she did use the library from time to time. What she didn't say was that she could've easily taken a few books home with her and posted them back, or called her thesis advisors from Bombay for help, and that several other international students were returning home to do just that.

The other day, while watching *Coronation Street*, her mother had said, "Well, everyone misses you back home." She'd become enthralled with the daytime soaps, catching Jyoti up daily on *Neighbours* or *EastEnders* (Jyoti didn't have the heart to tell her mother that she didn't like those shows), followed by a detailed prognosis of the weather. And no matter how mild the temperature was or was about to be, her mother was always incredulous of the forecaster's brightness on BBC One. "Eighteen degrees. Why is this fool celebrating? If the thermostat ever dipped that low in Bombay the street urchins would freeze to death."

Jyoti had thought about saying it *was* cause to celebrate after the dark and cold winter London had endured, but realized it wasn't worth the effort when her mother carried on: "How much money we're paying for your rent, and they're keeping the heat off?"

"It is on, Mama. They've turned it down because it's spring."

But her mother continued to grumble while watching *Coronation Street*. "The amount we're spending on your rent—most people in India don't even earn that much salary in ten years. We'll be begging in the streets by next year." At first, Jyoti had felt a pang of guilt but then dismissed it, knowing how her mother was given to hyperbole. Her father never complained about money. If they were really in any financial trouble, her mother would never have approved the

LSE. And now that her mother was homesick, she would say or do anything to retrieve her baby home. So Jyoti took it all in stride, reminding herself how she, too, detested London at first, how she cursed the damp air, the darkness at four in the afternoon, the loneliness.

Eight months ago, she didn't know how to operate a washing machine, had never cleaned dishes, cooked her own meals, or even made her own bed. But now these simple daily chores gave her a sense of self-reliance—something she'd never had before and she realized how sheltered her life in Bombay had been, how sheltered her mother's was. Perhaps, Jyoti thought, she ought not to judge her mother so harshly for not venturing out to museums on her own; after all, in Bombay the only place her mother went anywhere by herself was the temple, and even to that she was chauffeured by their driver. There were always plenty of friends or neighbours to chat with. She rarely did anything on her own, and Jyoti had never found it odd or questioned such norms. But now, after living in London, Jyoti wondered if she'd be able to readjust to India, if she'd miss feeling self-reliant.

It was funny how quickly a person could change without even realizing it. Jyoti remembered the morning when she'd finally screwed up enough courage to look at Gavin. How it was the most audacious thing she'd ever done. She nearly laughed out loud now at her naiveté.

Jyoti couldn't expect her mother to change in a week, to understand how it had taken her months to get to where she was, how she'd gone to rock concerts with Gavin, how on Sundays Gavin would insist she simply close her eyes and point blindly to a spot on the back of her *London A-Z* tube map and less than an hour later they'd be there, walking around the very spot her finger had been, navigating and exploring fruit and veg markets in working-class neighbourhoods, ducking into local pubs for a drink. The city was so dense and diverse—there was much to see. Some of her favourite places to walk were in the old city near where Gavin worked: the Square Mile, the financial district with the London Stock Exchange and the Bank of England that had been standing on Threadneedle Street since 1734. Jyoti loved the tiny, irregularly angled narrow streets and alleys that Gavin told her had been there since the Romans occupied the city two thousand years ago, when it was called Londonium. She'd never cared much for history, but Gavin talked about it so passionately that it became a little infectious. She was always amazed at his hunger for things like that, things that Jyoti had never thought about, like the light sources in seventeenth-century paintings, or how there had been a much taller church on the spot where St. Paul's Cathedral now stood, built nearly a thousand years ago.

As Jyoti walked down King's Road, towards her building, she realized she'd broken her rule about not thinking of Gavin by name and reminded herself: *I will not think of him. I will not think of him for one more week.*

In the drawing room, as Jyoti took off her shoes and jacket, she could hear her mother cooking in the kitchen. The fragrance of freshly chopped garlic and onions sautéing in oil was usually a welcome scent but it made her gag now. She wanted to open a window for fresh air. Had she been away from home for so long that the smell of Indian food was making her feel ill? But she and Gavin frequently went to Indian restaurants or got Indian takeout. She'd even made a couple of impromptu Indian dishes (both had turned out awful, but he didn't complain). She opened a window in the drawing room and stuck her head out, reminding herself not to think of him. At least by name. Easier said than done.

Her mother called her into the kitchen. Jyoti came and searched the fridge for orange juice. While adding mustard seeds to the sautéing onions and garlic, her mother complained, "No fresh ginger in this country—the stuff in the shop is all shrivelled and dried up. Oh, a boy named Gavin telephoned."

With her back to her mother, Jyoti froze stiff while looking in the fridge and her ears began to glow warm with blood.

"He's in my class," she said, more at a block of cheddar than to her mother. "In one of my group projects."

"Well, he said he wanted to come by to give you something," her mother said, adding turmeric, cardamom, coriander, and red chilli into the sizzling pan. The entire kitchen was all of a sudden suffused with the pungent tang of garlic and onions. Jyoti's stomach was doing flips. She sprang towards the kitchen window to open it but didn't make it in time and vomited all over the sink.

- 25 -

1997

As a child born during the end of the British Raj, Deepa Patik had grown up in a middle-upper-class family who emulated British customs as much as Indian ones and so a week ago, when Deepa arrived in London (her first trip to the UK), she had been excited, expected some civility, a little decorum, a touch of social grace. But on the underground train from Heathrow into the city, she noticed that nearly every single young person was slovenly, not to mention the tattoos and multiple earrings. Some of the adults weren't much better. People swilled beer from cans and munched loudly on snacks, leaving trails of crumbs on themselves, discarding refuse on the seat or floor. Things improved when they alighted at South Kensington Station but only slightly. Not that Deepa expected it to be full of ladies and gentlemen with tuxedos, white gloves, and evening gowns. She wasn't stupid. But they were in South Kensington. Nonetheless, money didn't ensure manners, she'd reminded herself as they walked to Jyoti's flat that grey afternoon, during which a light drizzle threatened to appear but never materialized (it'd been a week now and the sun had yet to show itself properly). It wasn't long before she realized she'd abandoned her little Jyoti baby to this ungodly squalor of a country. She'd never been keen on the idea of letting Jyoti go to the LSE. There were decent schools in Bombay, granted not as prestigious. But what did it really matter? Jyoti wouldn't be the bread winner (even though she'd likely be much smarter than her husband). She'd marry soon, work for a while, then have a family. It was Jyoti's father who'd put these ideas of the LSE into Jyoti's head, saying, "It'll broaden her mind and give her rich life experiences that will last a lifetime." The fool was obsessed with the idea that Jyoti should go to school in the UK because he never did. They fought over it. Eventually, Deepa relented when she realized that with a graduate degree from the LSE, Jyoti would have her pick of suitable boys.

But now in London, Deepa couldn't help but feel she'd failed in her duty as a mother to protect her Jyoti baby. She was furious with her husband because as far as she could tell, Jyoti was putting on a brave face, saying how much she'd grown to like the city, its architecture, and whatnot. The poor girl was clearly lying. She never talked about things like architecture or museums. Now she was obviously covering up the fact that deep down she was still as lonely as when she first arrived. Those early letters and phone calls had made Deepa weep. Over time, Jyoti had complained less, it seemed as though she was beginning to adjust to her new environment, and Deepa had taken some solace in that, but now she could see her Jyoti baby had just been brave over the months while she and her husband had conveniently convinced themselves that their daughter was adapting.

Every morning, after Jyoti left for school, Deepa prayed with her 108-sandalwood-bead mala on the floor next to the central heating duct. She prayed for forgiveness for letting her daughter ever leave home. She promised God that she would never abandon her little Jyoti baby again.

AFTER A WEEK, when Jyoti fell ill, Deepa was almost glad as it gave her something to do. She cleaned up Jyoti's vomit in the kitchen while Jyoti washed herself up. Poor thing probably had food poisoning from those dirty hippies who handed out free food at her school. Tucking Jyoti into bed, Deepa said, "It just proves how careless and unclean these white people are. Even their Hare Krishnas are incapable of preparing hygienic vegetarian food." Jyoti spent the rest of the day in bed while Deepa made her hot water bottles and tomato soup with toast.

The following morning, Jyoti insisted on going to school even though she wasn't feeling a hundred percent. Deepa kissed Jyoti on the head before she left. "My perfect student."

Later in the afternoon, while Deepa watched *Neighbours*, there was a knock at the door. She turned the volume down and peered through the peephole at a young man with green eyes holding a lovely little bouquet of daisies and irises. His hair wasn't kempt, but he looked somewhat more presentable than the young people she'd seen on the train that first day. She wasn't going to answer as it could've been a deranged criminal for all she knew, but then she remembered that there was a porter in the lobby downstairs. Whoever the young man was, he was approved of, so she opened the door, thinking he was most likely at the wrong flat.

"Oh, h-h-h-hello. I'm Gavin. Is Jyoti here?"

Deepa recognized his stutter and said, "No. Did you call yesterday?"

"Yes. I was j-just in the neighbourhood."

"Jyoti's at school. Didn't you see her in class?"

"What? I mean, excuse me?"

"Aren't you in her group project at school?"

They stood in an awkward silence for a moment, in which a number of thoughts raced through Deepa's mind. If he wasn't her schoolmate, then who was he? And why was he bringing her flowers? They were rather simple but pleasing, and she liked the colour scheme of white with purple. Part of her was still listening to Susan and Karl on *Neighbours* having a row; despite being childhood sweethearts, they were just not meant to be.

Taking the flowers, she said, "Thank you. I'll make sure she gets these," and shut the door.

There was a small card with the flowers that she carefully steamed open.

> Dear J,
> I'm sorry, I know you said not to come by but I can't stop thinking of you. I really don't understand what's going on. I thought everything was brill between us. Really really miss you (and Sunday breakfasts in bed & Simpsons reruns!)
> Please call. Or write. Or send smoke signals!
> Yours,
> G.
> xo

As Deepa read the note, an eerie presentiment came to mind—a mother's intuition from the farthest reaches of the universe arrived at such breakneck speed that it nearly toppled her over, and in that split second the earth seemed to spin off its axis as she instantly realized that Jyoti didn't have food poisoning but she was in fact pregnant. Pregnant with this dishevelled, stammering boy's child. At first, she nearly laughed out loud at the absurdity of it: Jyoti, pregnant. It was impossible. Her little Jyoti baby? But the more she kept trying to convince herself it couldn't be true, the more she knew it was. Deepa remembered how nauseous she had been during the first few months of both her pregnancies. How she couldn't stand the smell of food cooking. Especially onions or garlic or any kind of spice.

Did Jyoti know she was pregnant? Maybe that's why she'd been spending so much time in her bedroom after school. Deepa clutched her mala and started working through the beads. *Om tát savitúr várenyam bhárgo devásya dhīmahi dhíyo yó nah pracodáyāt Om.* God! Giver of life, Remover of all pain and sorrows, Bestower of Happiness, Creator of the Universe, Thou are most luminous. We meditate upon thee—from all who proceed, to whom all must return. May thou inspire, enlighten, and guide our intellect in the right direction.

She prayed to God with fervour that her intuition was wrong, that her little Jyoti baby had not been raped, and eventually the repetition of prayer relieved her anxiety somewhat. Jyoti was a bright girl. She would never have sexual relations with a boy before marriage, let alone unprotected sex with a grubby gora. Jyoti had worked too hard all these years to just throw it all away for a fling with some dirty white boy. She had such a bright future in front of her. All she had to do was return to Bombay with her degree from the LSE and she'd be able to marry nearly any Gujarati boy in the city. There had to be an explanation for it all. Jyoti must have some kind of stomach bug, the flu perhaps? And the reason she was feeling sick and spending so much time in her room alone was because she was stressed from all her schoolwork. It was the London School of Economics, after all, and her final semester—it wasn't meant to be easy. Deepa became paralyzed with a fear she'd never experienced, and with every breath she took she became more convinced that Jyoti was pregnant. Suddenly she had an overwhelming sensation in her stomach. Something was turning and twisting into knots. A torrent of emotions cycloned. She was angry that Jyoti would let herself get into this situation. Perhaps the boy was at fault. But, no, she thought, no matter how much he was to blame, Jyoti knew better. The girl's whole future was being flushed down the toilet. What would people say? How would she ever find a decent boy to marry? The shame. The stigma. It was the kind of thing that followed a girl for life. No one in the Gujarati community from an equal socio-economic background in Bombay would deem Jyoti worthy. She'd have to settle for a boy a tier or two below, far away in some small town with sporadic electricity. Deepa couldn't bear that. That had never even been in the realm of possibility. She'd always imagined Jyoti living in Bombay, near her in the city, not in the suburbs. But her world was no longer the same. The pain in her stomach suddenly turned to a sharp white-hot heat. She felt as though someone had cut open her belly and her intestines were falling out.

The mythical story of Vishnu transforming himself into Narasimha, a man-lion, came to mind. With his claws, Narasimha tore a demon's stomach open—a popular and ancient myth of good overcoming evil, depicted in stone sculptures and paint-ings. Hymns of it sung during *poojas* and *bhajans* at the temple always uplifted her spirit, but now she crumpled to the floor, feel-ing much like the disembowelled demon lying at Narasimha's feet, her life unraveling, spilling away from her.

O God, with your boundless glory, why have you forsaken me so?

- 26 -

1997

AS JYOTI WALKED DOWN KING'S Road, she tried not to fret about her period being two weeks late. After all, she kept reminding herself, it had skipped a month during times of stress—finals in college, or her first month in London. It was probably late because Jyoti was in a constant state of anxiety about keeping her mother from finding out about Gavin.

There was also her thesis. She'd never written anything so extensive. She was fine working with non-linear dynamics, stochastic processes, all of the multiple variables that influenced derivatives pricing; she could even adapt and create models to emerging markets, but writing a cohesive thesis about it all was so much more complicated.

Jyoti sighed as she unlocked her door, looking forward to a bath. The stench of perspiration on the chock-full tube still lingered vaguely in her nose. She was expecting her mother on the couch, recounting the day's television highlights, but instead found her sprawled on the floor next to some flowers.

Jyoti rushed to her side. "Mama!"

Her mother's eyes were swollen, fresh out of tears, and it seemed as though she'd aged ten years. Her mouth opened but no sound came out.

A heart attack, Jyoti thought. Then she noticed the dark maroon blotch of blood staining the back side of her mother's sari. It unhinged Jyoti slightly from her world, made her feel as though she was reeling, free-falling like skydivers who jump out of aeroplanes before they open their parachutes. She called for an ambulance as soon as she caught her breath.

The paramedics came surprisingly quickly. During the ambulance ride her mother couldn't speak as she had an oxygen mask on, but her eyes focused on Jyoti every now and then, as though she wanted to say something.

"Blood pressure dropping," a paramedic shouted to the driver. Jyoti teared up. The paramedic jostled Jyoti out of the way in order to administer an IV, and soon they were at the hospital, rolling her mother on a gurney, out of the ambulance, and down drab hospital corridors with fluorescent lights. Jyoti tried to keep up, wanting to glean something, anything, from the frantic medical talk between the paramedics and nurses, but before she had a chance they whisked her mother away. A nurse held Jyoti back, saying, "You'll have to remain here, dear."

Jyoti languished in the waiting area over the next two hours. Despite her pleas for information the nurses at the administration desk told her, "She's being treated. We'll inform you of any changes at once."

Jyoti thought about calling Gavin from the pay phone a hundred times. But what would she say? That her mother might be dying and her period was two weeks late? She thought about calling her father but decided not to until she had more information. What could he do half a world away besides worry?

She kept telling herself that she couldn't be pregnant, that she and Gavin always used protection. *Always?* Made her sound like the town whore. She'd only done it three times. But the last time, in the heat of the moment, Gavin was inside her for a minute—not even a minute—without a condom, but then they stopped and made sure to put one on like they always did. The orgasms she'd had that night were overwhelming; she'd had no idea it was possible to feel that amount of pleasure, euphoria, followed by deep calm.

If she could hear herself thinking this way a few months ago she'd never have believed it. The old Jyoti wouldn't have recognized the new mad-sexpot-possibly-pregnant Jyoti who couldn't think straight while her mother lay dying. The antiseptic smell of the hospital made her stomach feel queasy, and again she felt tipped over into a state of vertigo.

After two cups of tea, she finally called Gavin. When he picked up and said hello, she hung up.

After another hour and a third cup of tea, a female Indian doctor only a few years older than Jyoti came to speak with her.

"I'm Dr. Whiteman," she said. They shook hands. The doctor explained, "Your mother's condition is stable now."

Dr. Whiteman summarized: "Your mother had gastrointestinal bleeding, likely from a stomach ulcer, which made a perforation in her stomach. If she were to have come any later, the ulcer could easily have made the perforation rupture, possibly eroding a blood vessel, which would very likely have been catastrophic. She's lucky you called the ambulance in time. There was considerable blood loss so we'd like to administer a blood transfusion. We need your permission for that."

"Of course," Jyoti said, signing a form the doctor handed her.

"We'll need to keep your mother overnight, monitor her recovery, but with some medicine and good luck, she should be able to return home in a day or two."

Jyoti couldn't help but note the irony in Dr. Whiteman being neither white nor a man. Jyoti assumed Dr. Whiteman was married to an actual white man and wondered if they were happily married, if Dr. Whiteman's family had any objections to it, if she'd been disowned by them. It was unlikely. She seemed at ease, confident, and even though Jyoti had never been envious of coconuts like Dr. Whiteman, she now found herself coveting the doctor's independence, her impunity, because she grew up and lived in a country where every single neighbour didn't gossip and judge her, where people were free to do what they wanted, choose who they would marry, or at least a lot more than in India.

"Thank you," Jyoti said. "I'm a student and I have National Insurance but my mother doesn't."

Dr. Whiteman said, "Well, you'll have to fill out some paperwork with the nurses for the bill then. I suggest you fill this antibiotics prescription, make sure she takes them, and get her home as soon as she's well enough to travel to see a doctor."

"Of course. Thank you. Can I see her now?" Jyoti asked.

"Certainly," Dr. Whiteman said. She paused before adding, "While your mother was being given anesthesia, she said something about you being pregnant? She seemed very alarmed."

Jyoti shook her head and let out a little laugh. "It's nothing, she just worries about everything."

Dr. Whiteman said, "If you'd like to do a test, we can provide you with one. Your choice."

As Dr. Whiteman left, Jyoti stood immobile, wondering how in the world her mother had suspected pregnancy, how astronomical the bill for her mother's operation would be, how their lives might never be the same again.

Following the instructions on the pregnancy test, Jyoti urinated in a cup. A positive cross would appear if she was pregnant, a single horizontal negative line would appear if she wasn't. Out the window of the toilet she could see the Battersea Power Station. Its red bricks were glowing in the evening sunset. It was similar to the view she had from her bedroom. When she'd first arrived it had seemed like a cold and foreboding giant, with its four tall smoke stacks. But just a couple of weeks ago, very early one Sunday morning, when she and Gavin were coming home from Carmen's all-night birthday party, they'd looked at the sunrise over Battersea Park from her bedroom window and the power station seemed different then. Eerie, yet soothing, almost beautiful. It was on a famous Pink Floyd album cover, Gavin told her. He played her some of the album. She didn't care for the music at all. It was strange, nihilistic, but she could see why it was one of his favourite album cover designs.

As she stared out now at the power station, she wondered about her kundali. The whole idea of stars and planets being in certain positions predicting your fate seemed ridiculous. But hundreds of millions of people believed it. For the sake of her mother, who was so proud of Jyoti's kundali, Jyoti never said anything derisive about it. And yet, looking back on her life, it seemed as though her kundali had summed everything up to a T: she was shy, sensitive, excelled academically, and now she couldn't help but think of the bit about having at least one son and a very happy marriage with her soulmate. Was that Gavin? Was she carrying their child? She stopped herself from being so mawkish and prepared herself for the test result, but before she could even finish putting her pants back on a positive cross appeared on the stick. Her heart quickened. It had to be a mistake—a faulty stick. She had expected it to take at least a couple of minutes. The fact that it yielded a result so quickly proved that the test had expired or had been unwittingly tampered with. Perhaps being in a hospital around so many pregnant women and babies did that to pregnancy tests—all those hormones in the air. She headed straight for the nurses station.

"I'm sorry, but may I please have another test?" Jyoti asked. "This one didn't work."

The nurse stared at her for a moment before giving her another one.

Luckily, Jyoti had a little extra urine left in her bladder from all the tea. While she waited she thought of the flowers on the floor where she'd found her mother. Obviously from Gavin. She must have met him. What had he said to her? A small bunch of daisies and irises tied together with a simple piece of string— probably not from a High Street florist, and the thought of Gavin picking them from a garden or park for her was romantic.

He might have just nicked them off a table from the restaurant he worked at. There was something even more chivalrous in that.

She checked the test. Another positive cross. She expected to feel as though she were going to plunge again like a skydiver without a parachute, but instead felt a sense of exhilaration. She imagined herself as a mother, caring for an infant, and it didn't petrify her. In fact, it comforted her. She realized she'd longed for it without knowing it. Perhaps this was meant to be, perhaps Gavin was her soulmate. She had the sensation of flying, soaring.

But she was just twenty-three. And her parents would never allow it. It would kill her mother. Literally. Her poor mother. Jyoti had caused a nearly fatal bleeding ulcer. And that was just because her mother suspected she was pregnant. What would happen if her mother were to find out she wanted to have the baby with the grubby gora?

Was it even possible? Maybe she could stay in London and have the baby after all. The baby would automatically became a citizen. Would she eventually as well? Would she be disowned by her family? Never allowed to return home? Would Gavin abandon her and the baby to travel to Timbuktu? He probably wasn't ready to be a father. Would he want to marry her? Would she want to marry him? What kind of life would she have with him? He was a cook who made five pounds an hour. What would she do? There were recruiters who came to the LSE, offering jobs in the city at financial institutions and insurance companies. A few of her classmates like Carmen had gotten jobs and visas. Their grades were lower than Jyoti's so she might not have any trouble getting a job. She could work for a while, go on maternity leave, and then go back to work while Gavin cared for the baby. But even if that were possible, the shame would be too great for her mother to bear. What would her mother tell their family and neighbours? That her daughter was living in a run-down council estate flat with her half-breed baby and the father, a dropout-art-student-cook?

Jyoti told herself to stop dreaming. She'd only known Gavin for a couple of months. Did she really even know him? If he were to find out about her being pregnant he'd be scared out of his wits. He was only twenty-one. He'd most likely conceal his panic, tell her that he'd support her in every way, but hope for an abortion. They were too young. It was the kind of thing that ruined lives.

"Would you like to see your mother?" a nurse asked.

Jyoti nodded and was led to her mother, who was sleeping and hooked up to machines that beeped reassuringly. The nurse left them alone. Jyoti touched her mother's tepid hand. Would Jyoti ever be able to forgive herself?

How in the world had her mother intuited Jyoti's pregnancy? Would Jyoti have that kind of clairvoyance with her child one day?

Outside the window the gloaming sky was darkening. Jyoti scanned the horizon for the power station, but from that room it was nowhere to be seen.

- 27 -
1997

O N THEIR WAY TO THE women's clinic, seated on the top deck of the double-decker bus, Jyoti and her mother rode past verdant plane trees. Jyoti's stomach grumbled. As per the instructions on the pamphlet, she was to refrain from eating before the "procedure" (her mother refused to call it an abortion).

In the waiting room, while flipping through a magazine, Jyoti came across a serene photograph of a lovely English estate complete with ducks and a pond. It reminded her of the evening picnic at St James's Park—the night she'd lost her virginity. Was that the night the baby was conceived? It wasn't really a baby, Jyoti kept reminding herself. At this stage it was a tiny, microscopic sea monkey. A zygote. A blob of cells dividing and multiplying. She'd leafed through medical textbooks about prenatal development in the library. Her pregnancy was at week seven or eight. Complex cell division didn't begin till week eight or nine, which is when cells divided and grew a heart, a spine, lungs, and other major organs. Right now, it was just a blob. But didn't the blob have a soul? Contain the necessary DNA that would lead to life?

A few days ago, as soon as her mother had been released from hospital, she prayed a few malas at home, sitting cross-legged on the floor, and calmly asked Jyoti, "Is it true? You're with child?"

Unable to look her mother in the eye, Jyoti confessed. "Yes."

"We will take care of it. And never speak of it again."

Jyoti's mother refrained from reprimanding her. She barely spoke to Jyoti, who felt as though she was drowning in shame. Over the next few days, Jyoti did nothing but work on her thesis and sniff lemons to subdue her nausea.

When it was time to go into the operating room, Jyoti's mother followed her in. Jyoti wanted to go in alone, but feared that her mother would feel hurt, further betrayed, so Jyoti remained quiet.

The room was sterile. The bleached white sheets and shiny metal instruments made the room seem even more antiseptic. Naked under her gown, Jyoti lay on the bed and placed her feet in the stirrups. A kind nurse held her hand. The anaesthetic needle pierced sharply, making Jyoti wince. Her mother grasped Jyoti's other hand and began to mouth the gayatri mantra. The numbness followed quickly. She could faintly feel the doctor, a middle-aged man, broaden the entrance to her uterus, then begin scraping, and then the suction machine began. Jyoti stared at the empty white ceiling, willing herself not to cry. The post-card from Turkey that she'd received yesterday came to mind. Cobalt blue water, surrounding a lush green island with a white sandy beach all drenched with bright sun. On the back:

Dear J,

It's bloody brilliant here. Working on Jerry's uncle's boat is hard work, but fun in its own way. I tried to see you before I left to explain the last-minute excur-sion. I'll be back in a week or two. Can't wait to see you! Was that your mum I briefly met?!

Gavin. xo

PS: I got us 2 tix to Glastonbury! Radiohead are playing!! We can camp in a tent!

Jyoti had remained in the lobby for ten minutes, reading the postcard again and again, then ripped it up and threw it in the rub-bish bin before going up to her flat. There was no point in keeping it. If her mother were to find it, it might trigger another ulcer.

A few minutes later, the doctor was done and Jyoti was surprised the procedure was already complete. She wondered how the blob/baby was discarded. Did they incinerate it? Or just chuck it in the rubbish? She was about to ask but realized how morbid her curiosity would seem. Twenty minutes later, she was permitted to leave with her mother.

In the taxi on the way home, Jyoti's mother asked, "What can I get you, my baby? Anything. You name it. Chocolate pecan ice cream? I still have some *kaju-katri* that I brought from home." The silent treatment was over. Now that the bastard half-breed blob/baby was expelled, Jyoti was forgiven.

Jyoti was aware that she'd have to live with this secret forever. It wouldn't be difficult to keep hidden. No one else in India
would ever know. But she wondered if it would haunt her one
day. Would telling Gavin be the right thing to do? He was having
fun on boats and beaches with plenty of cute girls in bikinis. He'd
forget about Jyoti soon, if he hadn't already.

A few days later, her mother convinced Jyoti to finish her
thesis in Bombay. "Everybody at home is so excited to see you.
Chaya's wedding is in two weeks."

Dr. Whiteman had recommended her mother return home
soon so it wasn't a difficult choice for Jyoti to make. And ever
since the procedure, Jyoti had been glum, apathetic. When it
came time to pack their bags, Jyoti's mother was the happiest
she'd been while in London.

Walking towards the terminal at Heathrow from the underground station, Jyoti thought she saw someone who looked
like Gavin from the corner of her eye. There were dozens
of people, all busy with their bags, saying goodbye or hello,
looking at signage to guide them to or from the airport. As
she got closer to him she realized he was due to return from
Turkey around then. He didn't spot her in the crowd. She hadn't
seen him in nearly a month. His hair was a little longer. As
she kept walking with her mother, who was trying to figure
out where their airline kiosk was, Jyoti recognized one of his
friends with him. It was definitely Gavin. He looked different
with a tan—healthier. He was walking in her general direction.
The crowd was thick. He was busy laughing and talking to his
mates while carrying his luggage. He'd still not spotted her.
What were the chances of running into him at the airport like
this? Was it a sign that they were soulmates? Should she call to

him? His name was on the tip of her tongue. What would she say? *Hi, I just aborted our child. I'm going back to India. Have fun at Glastonbury and have a nice life!?*

"I found it. Air India—this way. Come," her mother said.

Jyoti continued walking with her mother into the terminal, grappling with the fact that she'd never see Gavin again.

PART III

VAROON
LUMINOUS BRILLIANCE

- 2 8 -

1964

WALKING ALONG WALKESHWAR ROAD, VAROON made his way to Wilson College, down Malabar Hill towards the beginning of Marine Drive, near the Chowpatty sea face. Unlike most of the other students from the affluent Malabar Hill area, who would either get driven by their fathers' drivers or take the bus, Varoon walked, along with servants, washerwomen, vegetable sellers, and the like, sharing the thin road with buses and cars and rickshaws that careened around corners. To be safe, the pedestrians had to stay on the inside of the road, the side that wasn't on the precipice of a cliff, which, depending where on Walkeshwar Road you were, dropped more than a hundred feet into the governor's verdant residence or the ocean.

Draped behind a lush grove of thick palm trees and

Sonneratia mangroves, the gothic stone structure of Wilson College stood more like an impenetrable fortress than a school. The monsoons, along with the new school year, had just begun, but a heavy downpour had not yet submerged the city. Instead, light showers drizzled, licking the dry grey stones of the college into a slick black sheen, and the faded red roof had turned into a dark shade of maroon in the saturated air.

Like many students at Wilson College, the twenty-one-year-old Varoon Sharma was enrolled as a bachelor of commerce student and would graduate in a year. Despite not having many friends, Varoon liked most of his classes. He enjoyed reading how Henry Ford created quality cars and sold them at an affordable price while paying workers a fair wage. It was the type of thing India needed. Varoon often came home from college with ideas of how to increase production and revenue at his family's small furniture shop, but his father insisted the few workers they employed do everything by hand, not machine. The old man had a penchant for antiques and didn't bother making newer styles of furniture. Over time they argued about it less.

Varoon's father, Praveen Sharma, said, "You can learn everything about business at the shop. After all, it's where you'll work after college. It makes sense to learn from experience rather than in a classroom from a teacher who has no real-world skills. Besides, it's not a secret that some of the teachers are bribed by the affluent students' families for top grades. You don't need an education like that."

But Varoon begged his father. Anything to avoid his fate at the furniture shop with its musty smells of lacquers and oils, where his father seemed detached from the world, losing himself in miniatures that he created by hand. When had the hobby turned into an obsession? Wasn't there a time when his father had been more engaged with the world? Varoon couldn't recall. Ever since they'd arrived in Bombay nearly seventeen years ago, his father had slowly let life crush him into a quiet surrender. Varoon couldn't help but think there was something cowardly about a man who'd given up so early. There were times when Varoon chided himself for judging his father. After all, he'd become a single parent early in life and had to raise his son alone. Varoon had been five years old at the time, too young to remember all the details of when he'd last seen his mother during Partition. Some of his memories of that time were missing. He wondered about all the things they'd left behind in their bungalow the night they fled. In Lahore, they'd been moderately wealthy, with land, a large bungalow, many servants, but now all they had was a dank furniture shop above which he and his father slept. It seemed an entirely unfair fate. Of everything left behind, Varoon wondered most about his kundali. He was certain his mother had said something to him about it, but what it was he couldn't remember.

As Varoon made his way into the courtyard of the college, a group of boys smoking under the shade of a large palm tree called out "*Ghati!*"—a derogatory term used to describe lower working classes. The boys snickered at this. They'd spotted him from their ambassador cars or the buses that raced past him as he walked down Walkeshwar Road along with some of their servants. Varoon often had to squeeze next to working-class servants, even untouchable toilet cleaners, to avoid being splashed when the buses went over potholes. He ignored the snickering of the rich Malabar Hill boys and climbed up the stairs to his first class of the day, maths.

Varoon had a knack with numbers. Over the years, he'd kept up with quadratic equations, algebra, calculus, and was near the top of his maths class. While most students worked out calculations on paper, Varoon was able to formulate some of the answers in his head. He had an exam to write. Along with sixty-five other students, Varoon filed into the classroom, walking past the girls who sat in the front half of the room, and found a seat in the back half, with the other boys. The classes at college were densely packed; students' desks were only inches apart.

Exam papers were on each desk and as students settled in, Mr. De Souza, the white-haired maths professor, said, "You may begin." Then he opened a paperback novel at his desk.

Before Varoon began his exam, he silently recited the gayatri mantra for good luck. It was a superstition he couldn't do without before beginning anything of consequence. *Om tát savitúr várenyam bhárgo devásya dhīmahi dhíyo yó nah pracodáyāt Om.*

But instead of focusing on his exam, he began to think of his mother, of her round, gentle face, the taste of her hot salty tears that night they were hiding under the gardener's carriage.

His father never spoke of her, and the one time Varoon had asked, years earlier, the old man had said, "She was lost that night, with many others." She was assumed dead, as hundreds of thousands were slaughtered by Hindu and Muslim mobs during Partition. There were stories of whole trains of murdered Hindus arriving in Amritsar and Muslims in Lahore, with blood on the floors, inches thick. However, a tiny part of Varoon believed his mother was somewhere, alive and well. But if she was, why hadn't she found him? It'd been seventeen years now. The subcontinent was vast, but a simple call to a Bombay telephone operator would have reunited them.

Before daydreaming further, Varoon took a deep breath and stopped himself; he only allowed himself to indulge this way at night, while lying in bed, when thoughts of his mother would make him wistful, angry, when he would cry silently, furious at life for taking her away from him.

A few minutes after Varoon started his exam, Shankar, a large and somewhat menacing student, took a seat next to him. Shankar was the only student at the school with a full beard and could be spotted with his friends smoking around the college grounds while classes were in session. He attended classes infrequently, and no one, including some of the teachers, dared to look him in the eye. Without even trying, with his permanent frown and hulk-like frame, Shankar was nothing less than a hazard, a bully, a mawali. When students saw him approaching they would move out of his way, much like the Red Sea parted for Charlton Heston in *The Ten Commandments*, Varoon thought.

As Varoon worked away on his exam, he caught a whiff of Shankar's perspiration. The stench was off-putting. He wondered if the parents in Shankar's building disciplined their young children simply by invoking the bully's name: *Eat your vegetables or I'll call Shankar from the third floor. Are you going to go to sleep or am I going to have to call Shankar to come and read you a bedtime story?*

In his peripheral vision, Varoon saw Shankar leaning towards his desk to copy his exam. Instinctively, Varoon turned away and covered his paper. They were near the back of the class and even if Mr. De Souza could see them, Varoon doubted that the old professor would do anything. Mr. De Souza had probably had to endure students like Shankar for years and had learned not to bother getting involved.

Reaching into his pants pocket, Shankar quietly produced a switchblade, flicked it open, and stabbed the sharp point of it into his wooden desk where it stuck. The black hilt of the blade shuddered slightly. For the briefest moment Varoon met Shankar's eyes, in which he caught a cold glint, and knew he had no choice but to concede. Just as he'd lost with the bus on Walkeshwar Road earlier that morning, stepping aside so it could pass, he lost again and let Shankar copy his exam.

Later on, while walking home, Varoon tried to summon memories of his mother in Lahore, of his kundali, but nothing came. All he could think of was how lousy his luck was. From living in a small mansion in Lahore to walking next to toilet cleaners in Bombay. As Varoon trudged uphill now on Walkeshwar Road, he made way for a rickshaw as it beeped at him. He felt useless for not standing up to Shankar, for letting him copy his exam. But he also wondered if the tiny gleam in Shankar's eye had taught him a lesson, or rather confirmed what he'd considered: that life was entirely unfair.

- 2 9 -

1965

FROM STREET LEVEL, THE DECREPIT Sharma Furniture Shop building seemed to only have two levels: the ground floor and the smaller floor above, where father and son lived in their modest flat. The two large godown floors were entirely subterranean and invisible from above.

Wiping the back of his neck with a handkerchief, Varoon inspected the besmirched cloth and winced at the filthy perspiration and sawdust. He was in the first of the two godown floors, where most of the sanding was done by the dozen workers he supervised. It was a dank room with concrete walls laden with dust from years of sanding and ripe with the fug of over a dozen workers perspiring in an ill-ventilated, damp room. A window that overlooked a dense grove of lush trees belonging to the governor's residence provided a bit of sunlight and a flicker of sea breeze. Leaning to one side of the window, one could admire a slice of the view across the crescent-shaped bay to the other side of Marine Drive, behind which lay the business hub of the city.

One of the workers bellowed, "We need a piece of ebony brought up from the lower godown." They were constructing a large almirah.

The workers argued over who would scurry down for this task. The second-level godown was only used as storage due to poor air circulation. Windowless, it housed huge stacks of walnut, sandalwood, ebony, deodar, rosewood, teak, mahogany, and shesham in various piles.

Chottu, the youngest, was picked. As he trundled below and flicked on a light switch, he yelped. The workers laughed.

One of the workers said, "A mouse or cockroach?"

"Chottu doesn't know the difference!" said another.

Good-natured and faithful, Chottu was born a Sudra. Most of his family cleaned toilets. He was also a little slow. It was rumoured by one of the sanders who came from the same village that Chottu had been dropped on his head as a toddler. Varoon had tried his best to discourage workers from spreading such gossip, but they didn't pay him the respect they did his father.

Varoon climbed up the stairs and went into the old man's office. "We should have the workers construct newer styles of furniture using inexpensive materials. Our margins will never increase otherwise."

This was not the first time Varoon had tried to talk to his father about this. The old man kept sanding away at an edge of a miniature rococo chair and without looking up finally said,

"I won't cut corners. We've always used quality hardwoods and joinery. Our workers here are highly skilled. That gives us distinction. You should be proud of that."

Varoon walked out for a cigarette—a pastime he'd picked up partly due to boredom. He saw an old matchmaker enter the shop and followed him in. Varoon remained outside his father's office, where he overheard him say to the matchmaker, "Varoon is of marrying age now. There's the Modis' daughter—sturdy and beautiful—she would bear plenty of children. Then there's the Dalals' daughter—fair, skin like milk, and the Jogias' daughter . . ."

A year ago Varoon would have jumped at the chance to choose. Like all the young men he knew in college, Varoon was a virgin and desired to know a woman's touch. He'd gone to see the seductive Asha Parekh in *Ziddi* five times at the cinema (an unusual heroine with beautiful eyes and yet tenacious enough to use a slingshot, even a shotgun, if needed). And although he wasn't rich like many of the students at Wilson College, there were plenty of families with less who'd be elated to have their daughters marry someone like Varoon Sharma, whose family owned a furniture shop in Walkeshwar. And like a prince picking his consort, Varoon was tempted now as he overheard the matchmaker say, "He's nearly twenty-three. He'll have to be married soon." But Varoon wondered if living above the dank furniture shop in the small flat with his father and bride was all that was to be in his life. Somehow it seemed unsubstantial. He could vaguely remember a time in Lahore when they had so much more—a bungalow, servants, some land. He was meant to have more. Wasn't he? Or was he just remembering the past with rose-coloured glasses?

His best friend, Manu Advani, was away in Delhi, climbing up the ranks of the military. But that was never an option for Varoon. Unlike Manu, Varoon did not have the fortune of coming from a military family, which would make substantial ascent through the ranks nearly an impossibility. Besides, he didn't like the idea of having orders barked at him.

Pacing around the office, Varoon caught a view of the city on the other side of the bay and then found himself outside. At the bus stop just up the road, the number 36 bus's diesel engine revved and exhaled a billow of black smoke as Varoon sprinted towards it, pumping his arms. A random hand from the crowded bus was offered. Varoon clasped it and leapt on board.

·The blistering sun prompted Varoon to cover his head with a discarded newspaper as he walked the streets. The newspaper's headlines said something about the threat of war looming. Pakistan had recently been trying to invade sections of the Indian state of Gujarat near the border. Manu had recently sent a letter to Varoon confirming the rumours about how the Pakistanis wanted to gain control of Kashmir, and the lengths they were willing to go to seize the tenuous state. *The Muslims,* Manu wrote, *are spreading lies and fear, and in some cases torturing and raping innocent Hindus. Outlying detachments of both armies have engaged in sporadic gunfire near the border . . .*

Every day now it seemed the papers were full of stories speculating on the imminent threat of a full-scale war. With memories of Partition less than two decades old, the country was more on edge every week.

But Varoon had more pressing things, such as marriage, on his mind. He weaved through the crowded side streets of the city, among the public and the hawkers with their carts of wares for sale. "New shipment! Brand-new bags from Singapore!" "Batteries from Hong Kong!"

Spotting a fresh fruit stand, he ordered a plate of pineapple, which the fruit walla sliced deftly with a sharp machete. It made Varoon think of the dhobi walla being stabbed, his wife screaming while Varoon and his mother hid under the gardener's carriage. He felt guilty for not being able to help. But what could he have done? As he ate the pineapple, Varoon told himself to snap out of it. The fruit was ripe and sweet, satiating his thirst, but the citric acid felt like tiny shards of glass in his mouth, inflicting a slight twinge of pain inside his cheeks.

As he paid the fruit walla, Varoon asked, "Do you know where the Port Authority office is?" He'd had the idea of applying for an import/export licence for a while now but had lacked the courage to follow through. With the rate that new technology and products were coming from overseas, he thought it might be a good business opportunity.

The fruit walla wiped his blade on his *lungi* and said, "Try down that road."

It was a busy place with men lined up in various queues, jostling and elbowing each other to get to the front. He realized the city had the largest port in the country, and that India had been exporting textiles and spices for centuries. With the recent influx of imports such as plastics and electrical machinery (Varoon had tried to convince the old man to order an electric sander from Singapore), he reasoned now that shipping was where the future lay. It was impossible for supplies to come by road. To the north lay the Himalayas—impassable; to the sides were East and West Pakistan, the latter with which India had fought a war, and another was likely imminent. And to the south,

India was surrounded by sea—the port of Bombay would have a considerable amount of traffic in the future.

If only he had the start-up capital or some way of getting into the game. If only his father had diversified some of the family money into other businesses rather than sinking their entire savings into a dusty old furniture shop. There were always too many *if only*s with his father. Would his old man lend him the money? It seemed so unfair to Varoon that despite the fact the family had once had wealth in Lahore, he now had to live in the scantiness of the middle class.

And even though his father never spoke of those times before Partition—before his wife, Varoon's mother, had been lost—Varoon often found himself wondering what his life might have been like if Partition hadn't happened, how he'd have stood to inherit much more than a dusty furniture shop. Not that he wanted things handed to him on a platter; he was happy to work and disliked the entitlement rampant among the wealthy, but he'd be a landowner who employed dozens and had the respect of the upper crust of society. Is that what his kundali had said? The one that was left behind that night they fled Lahore?

Varoon decided to keep his mind focused on the task at hand as he approached the front of the long queue of men applying for shipping licences. Could he accept that the rest of his life would be spent overseeing woodworkers in a damp and dingy godown? But why should he accept a life he loathed? Wasn't he better than that? Or did his kundali tell of a plain life? Is that why it was left behind?

As he checked his watch Varoon felt time pressing down on him, pinning him under its thumb. It wasn't only the shop that he felt burdened by, but also marriage to a young woman he'd never met.

When he finally reached the front, the man behind the wicket declined Varoon's request for an application and said, "Please come back when you have the necessary paperwork."

"But that's what I need from *you*," Varoon said, confused.

Men behind him became impatient and jostled him out of the way. One man explained, "Brother, you can't get anything done with empty pockets."

- 30 -

1965

VAROON GAZED OUT THE WINDOW at nothing in particular after the 36 bus departed Flora Fountain. Not having enough money to bribe the clerk at the Port Authority office, he was overcome with despondency, rendered immobile by the fact that the furniture shop was where his whole life would be spent.

"Where to?" A conductor rapped on the metal seat frame with his ticket puncher, irritated at Varoon for not having the fare ready.

But the bus was empty; there was no reason for the conductor to be in such a hurry. While searching his pockets for coins, Varoon mumbled, "Walkeshwar."

"What?" the conductor asked, annoyed.

Varoon repeated himself a little louder, glaring at the

conductor, who was shorter than him and twice his age. The conductor was wearing a Muslim *kufi*.

Among the small shrapnel of coins in Varoon's pockets, he could feel a fifty-paisa coin but he didn't want change from the Muslim conductor's filthy hands, so he continued to trawl his pockets for the serrated edges of ten-paisa coins. He needed three for exact fare. He found two and plunked them onto the conductor's open palm without touching him while continuing to search for the final coin with his other hand.

The conductor rapped on the steel seat frame with his metal ticket puncher again, louder this time. "Chal, chal! If you don't have enough you'll have to get off!" he barked, as though Varoon were no better than a servant wanting a free ride.

Why don't you go to Pakistan and live with your own filthy people, Varoon nearly said out loud, still searching his pockets and returning the conductor's glare. So lost in despair was he that he muttered the rest of his thought out loud, under his breath. "Why are you taking a job away from a Hindu? Bastard."

The conductor gave three hard yanks on the stop cord, signalling the driver to stop immediately so he could throw Varoon off the bus. However, the bus was unable to halt as they were in the middle of rounding Horniman Circle, which only annoyed the conductor, who began to pull at the cord again. Varoon became furious with the conductor for treating him so contemptuously. He stopped searching for the third ten-paisa coin and didn't even know he was standing on his feet in the aisle, inches away from the conductor's nose, when his face went red hot and all he saw were black spots in his vision, darting like shooting stars from one corner to the other. The heat that was glowing in his head quickly spread and overtook his universe. Only when he smelled the conductor's perspiration did Varoon realize they were in a brawl in the aisle. Varoon grasped the conductor by his collar, and as the bus shot out of Horniman Circle and onto the main road towards Customs House, Varoon used the motion of the bus to drive the conductor into one of vertical steel poles in the aisle. The conductor's ticket box, which was slung over one shoulder and hanging by his side, saved his body from smashing into the pole with full force, but Varoon drove the conductor's collar towards the pole once again and his head slammed into it before he was able to wrestle Varoon's hands free of his collar.

The conductor yelled to the driver, "Stop! Stop the bus!"

When the bus screeched to a halt, both Varoon and the conductor tumbled in the aisle as coins spilled out of the conductor's bag. Varoon quickly came to his senses and realized that it would take the driver only seconds to climb out from his seat and into the bus, and even if Varoon were able to fight off both of them, policemen weren't far away. In the Fort District there was one on every other street. The bus driver would naturally support the conductor and accuse Varoon of not only starting the fight but of also being a thief. So Varoon let himself be thrown off the back of the bus while the conductor yelled, "You have no respect for your elders! Your parents should beat some sense into you!"

The bus left Varoon on the side of the road as it chugged away, exhaling puffs of black diesel smoke in its wake. With his hair dishevelled, and shirt missing a few buttons, Varoon began making his way to the closest bus stop but realized that during the fight he'd lost all his money.

With empty pockets, Varoon stood on the pavement, wondering how he'd get back to the shop now. The summer heat was unrelenting, wilting the brilliant red blooms of the gulmohar trees in Horniman Circle.

Walking back to the other side of the bay and then up Malabar Hill would take nearly two hours—if he could bear the heat. He did have a few acquaintances from college who worked in the Fort District. He could go to one of their offices to borrow money, but how pathetic would that look? Borrowing thirty paisa for a bus ride? It was beyond embarrassing. Besides, he hadn't kept in touch with most of them. But maybe he could make up a story about being mugged; with his shirt dishevelled from the fight and two buttons missing, he wouldn't even need to play act much. However, he imagined his chums reacting with suspicion as they handed him the money, thinking: In broad daylight this happened to you? In the middle of the city?

His only true friend, Manu Advani, wasn't due home from the military academy until tomorrow. Varoon could telephone the Advani home and ask if one of the servants could take a bus and loan him the bus fare, but no, he had no money to place the call.

Perhaps he could try his luck with the next bus. But what if the conductor was another Muslim? The thought of having to beg for a free ride from a Muslim was too degrading. And yet, what other option did he have? He was already an hour late. How would he explain his absence? Luckily, his father took little interest in anything other than his miniatures. The old man probably thought his son was just up the road, dozing under the canopy of the large banyan tree next to the paan walla, listening to a cricket match. But Varoon had never been this late before. Maybe a walk was needed; it would give him enough time to come up with a solid excuse. Then he reminded himself he was doing nothing wrong; it wasn't as though he was some kind of truant. He was searching for a better job, doing something his father ought to have been proud of. Varoon was only trying to further himself, improve his lot in life. Was that not admirable enough in and of itself? Was it not noble to seek a better job? Especially one solely through his own merit, when so many other young men were handed cushy jobs through their families' wealth or connections?

But another part of him rallied: of course there were people who proclaimed such righteous creeds, a few who even believed them, but everyone knew the way things really worked in this country was through connections and money. A true meritocracy was as elusive as the end of a rainbow.

The heat was sucking the life from him as he trudged on. It was as though somebody was up there in the sky, pointing a magnifying glass directly at the crown of his head, as if he were an inconsequential ant.

After walking in the heat for what seemed like an eternity, Varoon telephoned his best friend, Manu Advani. The two of them had met at school when they were six years old and had been best friends since. It was only after high school that they saw less of each other, as Manu followed his father's footsteps into the military academy in Delhi. The Advanis had been in the military for generations. There were framed photographs of several men in uniform on the walls of their bungalow. Even though the Advanis were much wealthier than the Sharmas, it was a testament to the boys' friendship that Manu never behaved as though there was any difference between them.

Stepping into the shade of Manu's new ambassador car with its fine leather interior was a welcome respite from the sun. Manu slapped his old friend on the back while they embraced—a macho contest between men: whoever could withstand the harder backslap without wincing would win the exchange. Varoon, with little energy and in no mood for games, received the raucous backslapping and winced first. He was ashamed to be penniless and felt like a child in need of rescue.

As they drove, Varoon explained the episode on the bus with the Muslim conductor, but as he retold it, he became aware that he'd overreacted, even instigated it. It was difficult to explain how disdainful the conductor had been. Manu laughed and said, "You should've knocked some sense into the Muslim bastard, yaar. If the police had arrested you, I would've been happy to pay the bribe and collect you from the station." As they drove Marine Drive to the other end of the bay, Varoon told Manu about his efforts in applying for a shipping licence.

At a red light near Chowpatty Beach, Manu parked the car and got out.

"I have to get back to work, yaar," Varoon said, leaning out his window.

Manu said, "Come, have a drink" while sauntering to a lime juice vendor's cart.

Varoon refused, but Manu insisted, "Chal, yaar!" Manu's irritation conveyed that there was no humiliation in receiving a drink from a friend as well as a ride; friendship was not calculated on a ledger where both sides had to balance out.

Manu ordered. "One savoury, one sweet." They'd always ordered the same. Varoon finished his savoury lime drink in a flash and could easily have drunk three more. Manu said, "I have a business opportunity that might be right for you."

Varoon perked up a bit.

Manu said, "A truckload of goods has just arrived from Delhi and needs to be sold. On the black market. Quickly."

As Manu sipped his sweet lime drink and explained, something fell into place for Varoon: how the Advanis had amassed some of their wealth, how they'd probably used their influence in the military to get in on deals like this—stolen goods resold on the black market. Everyone knew it went on; police and politicians were paid to look the other way, sometimes they were the ones doing it.

Manu said, "It's being held in a container at the docks."

"What is it?" Varoon asked.

Manu looked at Varoon for a moment and then said, "All you have to do is take it to a place in *Chor bazaar*. I'll give you the address. Simple."

Varoon's mind raced as to what could be in the container. There were plenty of goods on the black market: imported electronics, cigarettes, booze. To be a part of an operation like this was something Varoon had never considered. His father would never approve. But then again, what did his father know about business? Two decades in Bombay and the shop had not made a significant profit. To hell with his father.

Varoon said, "You can count on me."

As they shook hands and slapped each other on the back, Varoon decided he didn't need to know what was in the container. Sometimes ignorance was bliss.

- 31 -

1965

THE CONTAINER VAROON PICKED UP at Victoria Docks for Manu was smaller than Varoon had anticipated—a reinforced steel box with a padlock, about the size of a crate of mangos. As instructed, he delivered it to a small shop in Chor bazaar. Varoon was about to ask how the man would open the steel box, but kept quiet when he got a glimpse of the back room through a door that opened for a moment. Inside, he saw half a dozen men working with soldering tools and flashes of gold. Varoon realized the box was most likely full of stolen jewelry about to be extricated and melted. His cut of the deal was fifteen hundred rupees—six months' salary at the shop. He walked away with a spring in his step. It was the easiest money he'd ever made, but guilt soon got the better of him. He met with Manu a few days later and Manu assured him. "Don't worry, yaar. These people in Delhi had it coming. They've done atrocious things. Even bought off a judge to stay out of jail. So just think of it as a bit of justice."

Varoon didn't press the matter as he knew Manu was somewhat on edge on account of the daily rumours of India and Pakistan fighting over territory in the Rann of Kutch and that Manu had just been called up to Gujarat, where the skirmishes were. With Partition still fresh in the minds of many, the entire country was a bit fretful.

Between sips of his lime drink near Chowpatty Beach, Manu whispered, "Mandatory blackouts are soon going to be implemented in Gujarati border towns so Pakistani bombers can't find their targets at night."

While Manu spoke, Varoon couldn't help but wonder how deeply Manu was linked with organized crime. In a country where nearly everything was mired in a jumble of bureaucratic chaos, maybe sometimes it was necessary to be like Manu, break the rules and take things into your own hands, be a maverick and make your own fortune.

Ever since picking up the box from Victoria Docks, Varoon had been spending more time there, amazed at the volume of containers. It had prompted him to start the application process for his import/export shipping licence, but for that he needed a hefty bribe. He explained to Manu, "The future of trade can only grow. The Americans have implemented containerization and it's only a matter of time until the entire world of shipping will adopt container technologies. India is desperate for imports. Heaps of money will be made." Then, as much as it galled him, Varoon continued, "I just need ten or twelve thousand to get started."

Manu said, "Brother, you know I'd give you the shirt off my back, but all my money is tied up with an ammunitions delivery contract. I can't really talk about it now. But I have about two thousand in savings—it's yours."

Varoon felt like a common beggar, but Manu slapped him on the back and ordered two more lime drinks.

During the following weeks, Varoon went to the Port Authority building every lunch hour where he had to jostle with dozen of men in various queues. Some days he'd finally get to the front, only to be told by a clerk he was in the wrong queue. When he got his hands on the correct paperwork, there were dozens of superfluous questions he had to write answers to and filling out the paperwork incorrectly meant you had to start all over again. It didn't help that there were no signs, that the queues changed daily, arbitrarily, leading to mass confusion. Prospective importers, exporters, suppliers, cargo providers, ship workers, tradesmen, all had to rely strictly on daily rumours to decipher where to queue up. Like the city police force, the civil servants who worked there earned so little that they relied on bribes, and each government worker seemed to have his own system—what was worth a ten-rupee bribe to one was only worth an eight-anna toasted vegetable sandwich to another. It was maddening that the primary duty of the government agency was to promote the flow of trade, and yet here they were, going out of their way to make it as difficult as possible for anyone to get a business going. If you were lucky, the government clerks were just incompetent, but some were downright deceitful, willfully misinforming applicants for no other reason than to quell their own malicious satisfaction or collect larger bribes.

While standing in a queue one day Varoon repeated the gayatri mantra silently—a habit he had developed to pass the time—but this time it brought memories of his mother, of his final night with her in Lahore, and so he abandoned it. When he got to the front, a new clerk approved his paperwork and granted him a meeting with a senior official for an import/export licence. Not wanting this meeting to be a failure, Varoon meticulously constructed a business plan. Since the containers were coming to Bombay full, he'd maximize revenue by sending them back full. He met with wholesalers of toys and fabric and spices—cheap goods to export. It wasn't a new idea, something the British East India Company had done for centuries. But now, after seventeen years of independence, the bureaucratic government India had inherited from the British, and perfected, now prevented the smooth flow of goods while encouraging the corruption that festered in every aspect of daily life. Seeing that it might be his last opportunity to get out of the godowns, Varoon was scrupulous in crafting his business plan. Every bit of cost was accounted for, researched, double and triple checked. It became an obsession. He frequented the city during lunch to keep in touch with the toy and fabric wholesalers he negotiated deals with. Through one of Manu's contacts, he reached an exporter in Singapore and spoke with him on the phone every week, discussing prices, inventory, etc. He talked with people at the docks and worked out transport fees, cargo space; all he needed was a healthy bribe for the senior official to approve a commercial import/export licence. Word was that the senior official would not approve a licence without a bribe of twelve thousand rupees, perhaps more. While working in the godowns, Varoon had his business plan always in hand. Instead of keeping a close eye on the sanders, the builders, the lacquerers, he added and subtracted and divided and multiplied numbers with his pencil and eraser. Even though his father wasn't business-minded or a risk taker, Varoon reasoned that the old man would have to see the sheer ingenuity of his plan: import machinery and electronic goods and then fill the same cargo space with toys and fabric and spices, all to maximize revenue. The rate at which the city was growing and imports were in demand, the business would inevitably grow.

The Sharmas didn't have much. Praveen Sharma had sunk all the family money into the furniture shop, but Varoon knew he had ten thousand tucked away for a rainy day. Even if Praveen didn't see why his son yearned for a different life, he would at the very least see this as an opportunity to invest the family savings and eventually get his money back with some interest.

It was seven in the evening and the workers began sweeping and closing shop while Praveen continued to work on his miniatures. Varoon bounded up the steps, three at a time, keen to show the old man his business plan.

In the office, Praveen was sanding a miniature Chippendale-style chair with a small piece of sandpaper tightly wrapped around his index finger.

"What is it, behta?" he asked without looking up. He was trying not to sand away the rococo-carved designs on the legs of the chair.

Varoon unfolded his papers on his father's desk, explaining the various contracts and costs and revenues, how profitable the business would be in a year, perhaps even six months, all he needed was ten thousand rupees for bribing the senior official at the Port Authority.

Praveen Sharma stopped sanding. "This business plan seems impressive, but I don't think you've thought it through."

Varoon was prepared for this. He spoke calmly. "But everything is in place. I could begin to repay you in a year. More docks are opening up soon, trade will only grow—it's just a matter of time."

But Praveen shook his head and said, "Haven't you heard? A war might start soon. It's no time to start a risky venture like this. Besides, once you start bribing these people it never ends. It will always be there with you. You'll never shake it loose. You're better than that."

Varoon was at a loss for words. The old man's antiquated homespun wisdom may have made sense a few decades ago but didn't the old man see that the world had changed? Hadn't he seen the ships at the dockyards eight, nine, ten stories high?

But of course he hadn't. The old man never went anywhere these days. He remained in Walkeshwar—the neighbourhood was a small peninsula, but it might as well have been a deserted island since he never left it. The old man had missed the evolution of business in the modern world, and his swift opinions of corrupt officials were smug, shortsighted. If a little grease was necessary to get the job done, than so be it. Varoon didn't like the fact that senior officials abused their authority by demanding large bribes, but times had changed. If you didn't keep up with life, it passed you by. There seemed to be no better example of that than the old man, who clung to his world of miniature antiques. Varoon swore to himself he'd never become like his father. But as he stood there, he realized he'd have to pay the price for his father's self-righteous pride. If Varoon wasn't able to get this licence, then some other fellow would elbow him out of the way for it, leaving Varoon in the godowns for eternity. The son would inherit the father's destiny—not that Varoon knew his father's destiny. He wasn't even sure if he believed in kundalis, but he didn't want to be manacled by his father's constellation of sad stars.

Praveen Sharma resumed sanding his miniature chair while saying, "Why don't you try to put even just half the effort you've put into this shipping-flipping business into the shop?"

Varoon wanted to overturn the table, smash every miniature, and yell: I can't stand it here any longer! I spend every minute of every day dreaming of being anywhere but in this musty-wood-rotting hell. I wish I were someone else's son. I wish it was you who had died instead of her all those years ago!

But all he could do was gather up his plan and go down the road to the paan walla under the banyan tree and exhale cigarette smoke at the orange evening sky.

- **3 2** -
1965

As the bus careened down Walkeshwar Road, towards Marine Drive, Varoon noticed the ocean on his right, usually sparkling under the sun, was now a subdued grey. The monsoon season had just begun. A leaden sky loomed above the bay, threatening to unleash a torrent of water onto the city. Even though he only had about a third of the twelve-thousand-rupee bribe gathered, Varoon was on his way to a meeting with the senior port official—it had taken months to secure so he had no choice but to go and hope that, miraculously, he'd be approved, perhaps be granted some time to come up with the extra money.

When he arrived, the Port Authority office wasn't busy—many people had likely not ventured out for fear of heavy rains.

However, Varoon was left waiting nearly four hours on a wooden bench, during which he became hungry, lost his appetite, and became hungry again.

Finally, a peon with greasy hair said, "The senior official will see you now."

Dressed in a traditional white kurta pyjama, much like the framed photograph of the late Prime Minister Nehru that hung on the wall, the senior official sat behind his desk eating his lunch. Tearing a roti with one hand and holding a *Times of India* newspaper with the other, the spectacled middle-aged senior official asked without taking his eyes off the newspaper, "What are you applying for?"

Varoon answered with a thick tongue: "Sir, I'm applying for a commercial import/export licence."

After clutching a bit of *palak aloo sabji* from a tiffin with his roti, the senior official popped it into his mouth and then gestured for the application. Varoon hesitated as the official's fingers were sullied with spinach and Varoon had gone to great lengths to keep the application in pristine condition. At all times it lived inside a thick brown paper envelope he'd purchased specially for it in the Fort District, and when he went to his suppliers and the bank for signatures, he was careful to not just let anyone handle the application for fear they might smudge something.

"Domestic goods foreign-bound for sale?" the senior official asked while chewing with his mouth open. Varoon noticed a birthmark on the man's right cheek about the size of a ten-paise coin. It sat there unceremoniously like an ink blot.

"Yes, sir," Varoon said, still standing as he hadn't yet been asked to sit.

"To where?"

"Singapore and Hong Kong, sir."

The senior official made a small grunt, indicating his satisfaction for the time being as he leafed through the eleven-page document while Varoon stood tense. Everything he'd worked tirelessly on the past few months was about to be approved or rejected. He'd heard several accounts of importers and exporters being rejected by the senior official for no valid reason. One man had been trying for nearly five years and hadn't gotten anywhere.

The senior official looked over the document while chewing his food. Varoon's stomach began to rumble and he felt nauseous. The thick humidity that hung in the air had him in a headlock. He wiped the perspiration off the back of his neck with a handkerchief. Out the window, a few cargo ships were berthed at the Indira docks. The cranes were immobile while the workers took their midday meal.

Looking over Varoon's application, the senior official said, "What do you have to offer?"

"I'm sorry, sir?" Varoon asked, pretending not to understand the question. Since he had very little money, he reasoned that this would be his best tactic, to plead ignorance and naiveté at first, and then offer his life savings—four thousand odd rupees. The senior official would hopefully take pity and grant him an extension. Varoon felt awkward standing there with his arms hanging by his sides and would have felt more comfortable sitting in the empty chair but he didn't want to be so presumptuous and run the risk of offending the senior official. After having to grovel with clerks over months to schedule this meeting, Varoon reasoned he'd lick this man's heels if it came to it.

The senior official glared at Varoon and said, "Have you ever been caught in the middle of a monsoon rain?"

"Sir? Yes, sir."

"Ever wonder how all that rain comes almost on the same day every year without fail?" the senior official asked, tearing into a roti with his right hand.

"No, sir. I mean yes—" Varoon was confused.

"Almost as soon as it comes, it goes back out into the ocean, up into the clouds, and then it all comes back again the next monsoon." The senior official paused to take a bite, and with his mouth full again, explained, "My point is that there's a circle in life. Things always flow back and forth. If I give you approval for your licence, what can you give me?"

Pulling the money out from his pants pocket, Varoon placed it on the official's desk and swallowed before speaking. "This is my life savings, sir—all I have."

The official let out a muted laugh while he chewed, then said, "Son, what I can give you is a downpour, a present from the heavens—and you're offering me a few beads of moisture." He laughed at the metaphor he'd so cleverly created and continued, "Only a parsimonious man goes to the temple with small offerings of sacrifice when he's aware of the rich returns that lie in his future."

"Sir, this is all I have. Every last penny," Varoon said, gesturing meekly towards the money on the desk.

The senior official leaned back in his chair to take a good look at Varoon and then said, "You wouldn't believe how many unworthy applicants have stood in my office over the years. What makes you so special, huh? Are you aware that we might be headed into a war?"

It was all that was on anyone's mind lately. Manu had still not returned from near the border in Gujarat. Varoon nodded and said, "Yes, of course, sir," while trying to figure out what that had to do with him getting a licence.

The senior official explained, "The eyes of the world will be on us. We have to show the world that we can trade on par with the best and for that to happen it's my responsibility to ensure that only the most qualified are given licences and not every halfwit that walks into my office. There is too much corruption in this country, sadly," he said while shooting the thin wad of bills on the table a contemptible look before focusing again on Varoon. "Bribes are eating this country from within, like maggots!"

Varoon had never felt so humiliated. His face and ears flushed hot. To be refused a licence was one thing—he'd half expected it—but then to be shamed like this was a kick to the balls.

After gathering his money, Varoon turned to leave. The senior official said, "Wait. Have a seat." Then, as Varoon did, the senior official asked, "You have a sister?"

"No, sir," Varoon said, confused more than ever, wondering where this analogy would go.

"Surely a cousin sister?"

"No extended family, sir."

The senior official asked, "Are you married?"

"No, sir."

The senior official's optimism disappeared. "How unfortunate." He clucked his tongue and muttered, "I could have used a pretty assistant," then returned his attention to the newspaper on his desk.

Varoon realized the insinuation and it instantly filled him with rage that the senior official had the audacity to intimate something so vulgar. He wanted to bash the steel tiffin into the man's face, stab the birthmark on his cheek with a pen, overturn the desk with all his might, but all he could do was sit there while the senior official read the newspaper. Varoon had kept the thought of being stuck in the godowns for the rest of his life at bay all this time, wanting to remain positive, calm, patient, because that's how you stayed in control, but anguish flooded him now. The truth of his destiny being one in which he was confined to a meagre life in the godowns was something he'd ignored for too long and it was now filling him with dread. His chest heaved, he felt as though he were drowning. Gasping for air, he got on his knees and with wet eyes, he managed to say, "Please, sir."

"I'm sorry I cannot approve your application at this time. I'm afraid it simply isn't in your stars, son," the senior official said without bothering to look at Varoon. Looking over the application one last time before handing it back to Varoon, he said, with some irritation, "Your application says you already have a decent job as a manager of a furniture shop. Be grateful. There are millions in this country who don't have that kind of opportunity. Count yourself lucky."

Varoon was ashamed when the senior official looked up from his newspaper to find him shuddering, trying to rein in his tears. He couldn't remember the last time he'd cried anywhere other than in his bed silently at night. It was one thing to have someone lecture you as though you were a common imbecile, and another for them to reject you, but it was absolutely degrading to let them see you blubbering.

Wiping his tears and blowing his nose with his handkerchief, Varoon went to leave.

"Well, I suppose there might be an alternative."

"Anything, sir, anything."

"I take a cut every month."

"How much?"

"Until you've repaid my generosity."

Knowing that the senior official would exact a large, unfair sum of money over the years, Varoon had little choice and agreed, "Of course, sir."

The senior official stamped the application and before handing it back to Varoon, he warned, "And don't even think of trying to cheat me. I know precisely what comes and goes from the docks." He motioned for Varoon to give him the four thousand from his pocket, and Varoon did as instructed.

"Yes, of course, sir," he said as he bowed several times and backed out of the office, adding, "Thank you, sir."

Despite seeing a cruel cunning in the senior official, Varoon considered himself lucky—he had his import/export licence. It was the first step out of the godowns.

On his way home, as the bus stopped at the foot of Marine Drive, unable to ascend Walkeshwar Road because of the heavy rains that people darted under shop awnings to escape, Varoon trudged up Malabar Hill in the warm tropical rain.

- 33 -
1965

AFTER SIGNING ALL THE NECESSARY paperwork, Varoon gave the dock foreman a box of sweets. His first shipment of toys from Singapore had just arrived. He was officially an importer/exporter. As he rode the double-decker bus home, he looked out the window from the top deck to the other end of the bay where the shop was and wondered if the old matchmaker was in the office again. At the shop, all was quiet these days as workers were on leave for the monsoon season. The rain that had fallen earlier that morning had now subsided but low-hanging clouds were threatening to unleash more.

"... A very decent family from Gujarat ... older sister's husband in Canada ..." Varoon had recently overheard the matchmaker say to his father, with whom Varoon had not spoken in nearly two months, ever since he'd asked for the bribe money for the Port Authority senior official.

Varoon was curious about the girls that the matchmaker had in mind. He'd fantasized about Bollywood heroines like Saira Banu and Sharmila Tagore. Their beautifully painted eyes and bosomy figures on the silver screen made him yearn for a woman's embrace.

It would've been somewhat easier to handle the match-making from elders he looked up to or was even a trifle inspired by, but it was annoying to have someone decide your fate who didn't know you, who wasn't aware of your capabilities, who couldn't understand your dreams, who in fact kept you from them. Although he was curious to meet with the girls and their families, he was also terrified. Would they be pretty? Fat? Thin? Ugly? Bosomy? Covered with warts? If he could only delay the meetings for six months, maybe a year, just until the shipping business was in full swing, then he might be in a better position to agree or disagree to any prospective match. Presently, he had no leverage. The bottom line was that the more money he made, the more executive power he'd have in the final decision.

He'd tried to talk about it with his father but the old man had said, "Having a job as a manager in the shop is respectable work. Nothing to be ashamed of." On the surface it seemed to any passerby a solid business. After all, it employed over a dozen workers who produced and refurbished vintage furniture. But the truth was the business was stagnating because Praveen Sharma refused to let it flourish.

Varoon had said, "There are ways to increase efficiency without having to compromise quality. The workers can be trained better, modern equipment could increase productivity, even ensure better quality."

But Praveen shook his head while continuing to work on his miniatures. "Electric sanders are for common lumber. We work with fine woods. An electric sander is incapable of feeling the grain of teak or ebony."

Varoon was both incensed and relieved that nobody knew that the shop barely kept afloat some months. The thought of getting married and living with his father above the shop in their tiny one-room flat was becoming less pleasant by the day. There was no privacy up there.

As the bus came to the north side of Marine Drive, traffic up ahead was being rerouted. There was confusion. Riders said to the conductor, "Arre, what's going on?" "Why are we not going down the normal bus route?" "I'll miss my stop . . ." People began to yell and shove, debating whether the driver should take a left or right, arguments erupted about where there would be less traffic. But Varoon refrained from joining the melee, content that his shipment had arrived and was on its way to the wholesaler. He couldn't erase the smile from his face as he sat by the window on the upper level of the bus. For the first time in his life he felt as though he might be in control of something.

Somewhere near Chowpatty Beach, instead of climbing up Walkeshwar Road, the bus unexpectedly veered to the right towards Opera House, swaying everyone on the bus to one side. Out the window Varoon saw a mob of angry people spilling out into the street from the beach. Some were carrying large signs: *Hindustan for Hindus Only!* Someone in the crowd yelled, "If you want to stay in our country, adopt our ways!" Several people in the crowd were in the midst of a fight. A man was holding a hand up to his bloodied face trying to stop the thick stream of crimson that was spilling onto his white kurta. The bus grew quiet all of a sudden as everyone took in the scene. But before long, the bus rounded the corner and the mob on the street was out of sight. It was clearly some kind of altercation between Hindus and Muslims, perhaps a political party was marching or a politician from Delhi was in town. Newspapers had been speculating that the fighting in Gujarat between Indian and Pakistani border police would soon escalate into war. In metropolitan cities like Bombay where there was a sizeable minority Muslim population, tensions between Hindus and Muslims were usually quelled without the need of police—level-headed citizens generally prevailed and the odd skirmish fizzled away. But all that had recently changed as the situation on the border became more unstable and both sides amassed more troops. Varoon wondered how Manu was doing. He hadn't heard from his friend in a while.

After seeing the man with the bloodied face, everyone on the bus had stopped arguing over the traffic. They were grateful the bus driver had avoided going into the heart of what could soon become a savage riot. Nearly everyone on the bus was old enough to remember the violent Partition nearly twenty years ago when millions fled from one newly created country to the other. Varoon's heart raced as the bus sped away and he tried his best not to think of the fateful night in Lahore when he'd last seen his mother but it all rushed to him now: the acrid smoke, the fires crackling in the distance, hiding under the carriage with his mother, the dhobi walla and his wife, his mother's salty tears, driving to the train station with his father, the night sky littered with stars, the train departing Lahore Station without his mother.

A part of him wanted to leap off the bus and join the turbulent mob, clutch Muslim throats with his hands and strangle the life out of them, rip and tear their limbs. Surprised at how quickly rage had filled him, he took a deep breath and remained on the bus, looking out his window.

The bus continued past Babulnath Temple, rounded Kemps Corner, and didn't make a stop until it went down Nepean Sea Road. After several minutes in the traffic jam the bus stopped near Priyadarshini Park. People leaned out the open back compartment of the double-decker, trying to look through the fog and traffic that snaked ahead.

A guava vendor boy pushed his cart through the traffic while announcing with his nasal voice, "One anna, one anna only for ripe guavas."

People on the bus stuck their heads out the windows and tried to negotiate with the boy. One lady said, "Shame on you for charging so much—just yesterday it was half-anna."

The guava boy said, "These are the best batch of the season."

"Forget the guavas," another man said, "ask him what's going on up the road."

A chorus of people agreed. "What if the whole city erupts into madness?" one man offered, although cooler heads shushed him to hear what the guava boy had to say.

But the boy refused to tell them anything until someone agreed to buy a guava, which someone reluctantly did. As the boy dipped his knife into a mixture of salt and red chilli powder before slicing into a ripe guava for his customer, he explained, "The street has flooded up ahead and is impassable." Word quickly spread and the bus emptied. People were relieved that there was no imminent danger of a mob.

Most travellers chose not to traverse the flooded street as they alighted the bus, hoping the sewers would clear up soon. There were a few paan walla stalls in the area and food shops where people were drinking chai, eating freshly fried *wada pauns*, listening to radios that hung on vendor carts, reading newspapers, and generally loitering. Some from the bus were still shaken from the mob they'd witnessed at Chowpatty Beach. As Varoon walked by them he overheard snippets of conversation: "How do you think the riot started?" "God only knows." "These politicians can whip the public into such a frenzy." "Has the situation at the border changed at all?"

If the water was only a few inches deep most people would have had little problem with hiking up their pants or saris and getting their feet wet, but depending on the amount of rainfall and how clear the storm drains were, Nepean Sea road flooded a couple of feet, sometimes more. As the rain fell on Malabar Hill it washed away earth and the water became turbid with all kinds of debris. Varoon remembered from when he was a schoolboy that tropical snakes and large bandicoot water rats would lurk in these murky waters, stealthily searching for toes and ankles to bite. It wasn't just a story parents scared their children with. Varoon had, on a couple of occasions, seen bite marks and little bits of flesh ripped away from people's toes and calves. As he disembarked the bus, Varoon contemplated having a cup of chai. Perhaps the flooded waters would soon ebb away, or then again, they might rise—there was no way of telling. But there was something banal in staying behind with everyone from the bus who'd gathered on either side of the road, smoking or sipping chai, speculating inanely for hours about the flood, the riot. His first shipment had come in, he'd just embarked on a new career, capitulating to a little rain now seemed inauspicious and so, with a newfound confidence, Varoon decided to wade into the caliginous water.

During this time of year, after a heavy downpour, in parts of the city where the storm drains became clogged the streets remained submerged for days. Most of Malabar Hill and Walkeshwar were high enough not to flood, but lower sections became waterlogged at times. On the eastern side, the lush tropical soil and trees in the governor's residence had little problem absorbing the water, but down the western side of Malabar Hill, the monsoon waters rose quickly on Nepean Sea Road, often trapping food vendor's carts, bicycles, rickshaws, even cars and buses.

Wading through the water on Nepean Sea Road, Varoon saw a half-submerged stalled rickshaw. The driver and an older gentleman were standing nearby, arguing. Varoon had no intention of getting involved, but as he approached the rickshaw he caught the eye of a pretty young woman sitting inside. As soon as their eyes met she looked away but then seemed to find the courage to look his way again. She was fair with long eyelashes and hazel eyes. Her mother was also in the rickshaw, busy gathering up the folds of her sari and petticoat to keep them from getting wet while keeping her legs perched upon the rickshaw seat. The mother stopped praying to instruct her daughter to do the same and the daughter smiled a tiny smile to Varoon that seemed to acknowledge the absurdity it, of trying not to get wet when they were surrounded by water. It wasn't until he got closer that Varoon could make out that the mother was quietly reciting the gayatri mantra. *Om tát savitúr várenyam bhárgo devásya dhīmahi dhíyo yó naḥ pracodáyāt Om.* She was obviously not a local and had never been in a Bombay monsoon. Her daughter tried to comfort her but it was no use. The mother, on the verge of tears, kept repeating the mantra.

Varoon spotted an old wooden fruit cart abandoned by the side of the road and found himself running towards it. He wasn't quite sure why, but the next thing he knew he was steering it through the knee-high water towards the rickshaw.

Up twenty yards ahead, the rickshaw driver and the gentleman were still arguing. The driver said, "People warned us the road might flood ahead but you insisted we keep going. And now my engine is waterlogged!"

They began haggling over a fair price. By the end of this exchange the gentleman was shocked to find that a young man was trying to kidnap his wife and daughter on a wooden cart, and to his utter dismay they were eager in accepting his help. He ran towards them as quickly as he could through the water while waving his hands in the air. "Take your hands off my wife and daughter!"

"Sir, I'm only helping—"

The daughter and mother, now somewhat composed and safely seated on the wooden fruit cart, came to Varoon's defence. "It's true." "He's helping us."

After the father calmed down, he apologized and pushed the cart with his wife and daughter up Nepean Sea Road alongside Varoon for nearly half an hour in silence.

Varoon, labouring with every step, stole furtive glances of the beautiful young woman. Her eyes seemed to smile at him. A cat and mouse game began. Every time they locked eyes, Varoon felt inexplicably drawn to her. It was if he was being pulled into her universe. An attraction he'd never experienced and could not explain. The water was now up to the men's thighs and both were breathing with more difficulty. Varoon noticed the girl's jade bangles and the chinks of milky white skin they concealed underneath. He'd never before considered a woman's wrist, how beautiful it could be.

The mother said, "I think the water is rising," and repeated the gayatri mantra.

There had been a handful of occurrences during monsoons throughout the past few decades where the storm drains backed up suddenly and some streets would flood ten feet. Two people and a cow had drowned at the bottom of the hill, on separate occasions, but Varoon assured the women, "We'll be fine." He wasn't sure if the mother believed him as she shut her eyes and silently prayed, moving only her lips.

The father asked Varoon quietly so that his wife couldn't hear, "Will the water get deeper?"

Through gritted teeth, Varoon kept pushing the cart and lied, "No, this is as bad as it gets." There was no reason to tell him otherwise. He wished now he hadn't stopped to help them.

The mother said to the father in a hushed tone, "This is a sign, an omen. Our *naseeb* is rotten here. Let's return home at once."

The man said to his wife, "I've told you—more importantly than bad luck or good luck, it's what you do with it that counts."

They continued on for some time pushing the cart uphill and then the man asked Varoon, "What do you think? You believe in luck?"

Varoon wasn't sure. Over the past year working at the shop, his life felt thoroughly devoid of any luck. But it occurred to him that after all these months of trying to get his business going, of trying to make a new life for himself out of the godowns, it might finally happen, and he reasoned that it was his hard work, his persistence, that made it happen, not his luck or kundali. Sure, he might have had friends like Manu help him along the way, but ultimately Varoon himself was the one responsible for seeing things through. Had other men with similar circumstances had to endure the same obstacles they might have quit and resigned themselves to be content with a life in the musty godowns making old furniture. Perhaps his old man was right never to have made a new kundali for his son after it was lost that night in Lahore. Luck had nothing to do with it. Maybe luck didn't even exist, and maybe destiny, while it supplied hope, only alleviated responsibility from the individual while lessening his character, his capabilities, mollifying him from standing up and fighting for himself.

"Sir, it's what you do with your circumstances. I believe in hard work," Varoon finally replied.

After more pushing, when they were nearly at the top of the hill, the father said, "This is an auspicious day. My daughter is getting married. We're going to meet our future son-in law."

Varoon's heart sank a little. He looked up at the young woman to catch another look but she didn't turn to him anymore. The flirtatious game they'd played with their eyes was over. The mention of her impending marriage had cast a gloom between them. The cart seemed heavier but eventually the murky water began to recede as they finished their ascent and came to a fork in the road. Between heaving breaths, Varoon asked, "Sir, which way?"

"Do you know the Sharma furniture shop in Walkeshwar?"

- 34 -

1965

VAROON DASHED OUT ON SUNDAY morning, eager to see Manu, who'd been in Delhi the past few months. They both had reason to celebrate: Varoon was engaged and Manu promoted to Captain.

Stopping at the Muslim *ghantia walla* up the road, Varoon said, "Half-kilo" and pointed a finger at the man. "Make sure they're fresh. Last time you threw stale ones in the middle." As the ghantia walla wrapped a freshly fried batch in newspaper, Varoon added, "and throw in a few green chillies. Last time there was only one in there." Varoon would have rather gone to the Hindu ghantia walla but the fellow was shut today. Hindus across the city were starting to frequent Muslim businesses less and vice versa as the situation between Pakistan and India worsened at the border. War seemed unavoidable.

"Two rupees, eight annas," the ghantia walla said. Even though the rupee had been decimalized into one hundred paisa for years now, the older generation still referred to change in annas.

"For frying up some chickpea flour—that's what you're charging now?!" Varoon asked, doing his best to act outraged.

"Sahib," the fat man said in a mock tone of respect, "you still owe me from the last two times, remember?"

Varoon silently cursed the ghantia walla while fishing for change in his pocket. Two toy shipments had arrived and been delivered to wholesalers, but after the senior official took his cut, Varoon was left with a shrapnel of coins. Unless he had more investment to increase volume, he was at his wits' end how to increase revenue. Going to his father now for money would only prove his old man right that the shipping business was a fool's dream. And even if he were to increase volume, there was the senior official's cut—the bulk of the profit margin. Maybe he'd made a huge mistake. Maybe he'd reached too far. Maybe he should forget about shipping and settle with the furniture shop. Maybe his kundali was terrible. Is that why it had been left behind and never redrawn?

"I'll give you the rest next time, I swear," Varoon said, placing a couple of coins on the counter and grabbing the package from the ghantia walla. A tug-of-war began but Varoon was younger, stronger, and managed to pry it from the man's fingers before fleeing up the road.

"You rascal! Come back here, I'll tell your father!" the ghantia walla shouted after Varoon, who tucked the warm package under his arm and walked away quickly, thinking, *Go to hell, you Muslim bastard*.

When he reached Manu's new address Varoon wasn't surprised to find that it was one of the new towers recently built on Malabar Hill. A lift boy took Varoon to the fifth floor. During the ride up, Varoon was struck with a pang of jealousy. The Advanis had always been well off, living in a little bungalow ever since Varoon had known Manu. But now, Manu had his own place in a brand-new building.

A servant opened the door for Varoon, who was let into a beautiful flat with marbled floors. It wasn't large but had a nice view of Priyadarshini Park and the sea that stretched out infinitely to the horizon. Manu Advani emerged from a room wearing his uniform. They embraced and laughed while slapping each other heartily on the back with resounding thuds. Varoon winced first.

"Congratulations, yaar! Can't wait for the wedding," Manu said, leading his friend to the balcony.

Varoon wanted to avoid talking about the wedding as it was going to be a much smaller affair then he would've liked. Surely not as grand as some of the weddings Manu had become accustomed to in Delhi. Now that Manu was climbing the ranks within the military he'd no doubt been to stately marriages of government ministers' sons and daughters.

Varoon said, "And congrats to you. At the rate you're being promoted you'll outrank your father and uncles in no time!" It wasn't an exaggerated compliment. Manu had always been astute, an effortless leader. Barely twenty-four, he already had a flat of his own that most men in the country could never even dream of.

There was a pleasant breeze on the balcony and they could see the ocean tide crashing silver froth on the black rocks as it waned. Varoon thought he'd consider himself lucky if he were to become one-tenth as successful as Manu. He was wondering if he should ask whether or not there was any more stolen jewelry from Delhi. It was reprehensible, of course, but his cut from the last deal was the easiest money he'd ever made. Besides, the jewelry was most likely stolen from those who had plenty.

"Tell me about the soon-to-be Mrs. Sharma," Manu said.

Varoon was thrilled to be marrying Anju. They'd barely spoken to one another during their formal meeting when the matchmaker and parents were present, but a connection was undeniable, the quick stolen glances charged with electricity.

"I'm a very lucky man," Varoon said. "Anju is lovely." Between all the surreptitious looks they'd exchanged during that first meeting, he'd sensed her intelligence, her bravery—she wasn't afraid to be his equal, his partner. The physical attraction was indisputable. But the fact that he was broke kept him awake at nights for hours on end. The idea of having to share the small flat above the shop with his father and Anju was distressing. They would have little privacy.

"I've missed these ghantias," Manu said, unwrapping the newspaper for a sniff. "Nowhere in Delhi can you get ghantias like these!"

Varoon imagined Anju and himself living in a beautiful new modern flat, one with a view of the sea. He knew that with her looks she could have gotten a more handsome and perhaps wealthier husband. Her marriage to him didn't seem entirely compulsory. Her parents weren't so draconian that they would force their daughter into a marriage she wasn't ready for. It seemed from that first and only meeting that her family had the upper hand. He could tell from the looks on their faces when they entered the shop that it wasn't quite what they'd had in mind. They could have politely refused and seen more suitable boys. When her parents had asked to see his kundali, the old man bluntly stated he didn't believe in astrological nonsense, at which Anju's mother was taken aback. But as her father paused and considered this non-traditional point of view, he glanced at his daughter, who seemed to beseech him with her eyes to overlook this minor detail. Anju had chosen him. And for that, Varoon would always be in her debt. But he worried if she didn't complain of living with his father in their tiny flat above the shop now, she would, over time, most likely come to loathe it, resent him.

As they started on the ghantias, Manu said, "Let's have some chai, yaar. It's not the same without the chai." Manu called his servant, who brought out the chai. It was piping hot, just the way Varoon liked it. The perfect Sunday afternoon snack. The sweetness of the chai perfectly balanced the heat of the green chillies, and the cardamom and cinnamon in the chai also countered the savoury ghantias. Varoon poured a portion of his chai onto his saucer to cool. It was a simple meal, but one that they'd often shared together on Sunday afternoons since they were teenagers. He couldn't help but feel like a failure sitting in his best friend's new flat, eating a meal that he'd gotten on credit, or stolen, depending on who you asked.

Finally Varoon screwed up enough courage. "Any chance of uh, another shipment of jewelry . . ." He was trying his best not to beg like a street dog for a bone, "I've started the shipping business, but it's small right now—"

"What can you ship?"

"Anything." Varoon shrugged. "Exports of textiles and spices are handled by the big companies, but so many new appliances and electronics are finding their way from America. I'm only able to afford toys at the moment. Despite the government's red tape everything can be bought and sold on the black market. Demand will only grow." He took a sip of his chai, but instead of sipping from the chai that was cooling in the saucer he drank from the cup, forgetting that it was piping hot. He immediately spat it out as it burned his mouth. Manu shouted for his servant. The young boy dashed from the kitchen and wiped up the mess.

"Ice water?" Manu asked.

Varoon was about to shake his head, not wanting to bring attention to his clumsiness, but he remembered seeing a brand-new refrigerator as he'd walked by the kitchen earlier. Of course Manu knew all about the black market. His contacts in Delhi were the ones who trafficked it. They were the ones he most likely got the new refrigerator from. "Maybe just a small glass of ice," he said to the boy, who darted back to the kitchen and reappeared moments later fulfilling Varoon's request.

After Varoon sucked on an ice cube and soothed his burn, Manu gave his servant some money to go down to the paanwalla to fetch a couple of paans and a pack of cigarettes.

Manu waited till the boy was gone before speaking in a whisper. "Something big is brewing in Gujarat, in Kashmir—with Pakistan."

"What's happening?"

"The military is prepared to attack but the government is sitting around with their thumbs up their asses. Those Pakistani *maadar chods* have come into Gujarat and Kashmir. We have to hit them hard."

The situation with Pakistan had escalated throughout the

monsoons. Newspaper reports were at times contradictory. Everyone knew both sides' media were biased. There was talk that secret infantry and armoured units were carrying out attacks all along Kashmir, around disputed border territories. It seemed as though every other day there were fresh rumours of Pakistani commandos infiltrating the border into Kashmir. The Indian newspapers and local leaders were repeatedly crying out for the central government and the prime minister in Delhi to take swift military action.

Manu explained, "A substantial attack from either side is imminent. We need to strike first. I have some connections in Gujarat at the Jamnagar port. We need supplies to be sent there soon. By the time the government decides to do something, it might be too late. We need a reliable source here at this end."

There was a slight pause in which Varoon crunched his ice cube. He'd never considered being involved with anything of this kind. Transporting army supplies—smuggling weapons? It all seemed out of his league. He just wanted another little box of stolen jewelry. But maybe this was an opportunity. This might be his chance to make some real money. Start a proper shipping business. Something that would get him out of the musty antique furniture shop for good.

Looking Manu squarely in the eye, Varoon said, "Yaar, you can trust me. I can secure containers for you at the Victoria Dock."

Manu paused and deliberated for a few moments before saying, "My uncle, the lieutenant general—is in charge of transporting weapons and ammunitions. We'll use your containers for transport. Don't worry, you'll be well compensated."

- 35 -

1967

"COME BACK TO BED SOON, jaan," Anju said, half asleep. "I will, jaan," Varoon said, getting dressed, thinking how beautiful she looked even in the middle of the night.

Manu had just come to town, unexpectedly, and as they only saw each other a few times a year nowadays, drinks were in order.

When Varoon reached the drawing room balcony, Manu was waiting there for him with an imported black market bottle of whisky. The two of them embraced and exchanged backslaps. Manu winced this time.

Varoon's servant, Chottu, brought out glasses with ice. Manu said, "This new flat of yours is amazing. Better view than mine."

"Thanks, yaar," Varoon said. A lot had changed in the two

years since he'd transported munitions for the army. Manu had made sure Varoon was handsomely compensated. The top port foreman was bribed to look the other way and had no idea of the contents of the shipment, ergo the senior official at the Port Authority office knew nothing so he couldn't exact his cut, leaving Varoon with a large profit, enough to buy an ocean-view flat on the top floor of a new building in Breach Candy named Sea Face Terraces.

The two men clinked glasses. Varoon asked, "How's everything?"

"First class, yaar. How's Anju? Your father?"

"She's well, thanks. But my father is losing his marbles."

Chottu, originally from the shop, but now employed as house servant, occasionally took food to the old man and reported on his condition, which was gradually deteriorating. Varoon explained how one day the old man would tell the workers to make one thing and the next day be furious at them for doing exactly what he'd instructed. Sales had pretty much dried up and Varoon was growing tired of paying the workers for doing little. "I think he'll soon have to come live with us here," Varoon said. Eager to change the subject, he added, "How's Delhi treating you?"

"Well, yaar. Very well."

Varoon sipped his whisky and couldn't help but relish the moment. He was happily married, lived in his own home, and was now supplying a number of wholesalers across the country, including Manu's connections in Delhi, with high-quality imported goods such as air conditioners, machinery, and electronics, worth much more than toys. But the greedy senior government official at the Port Authority was still taking a sizeable cut of Varoon's profits.

Varoon had a handful of employees and his mind was always churning on how to increase revenue, how to make more connections and supply more wholesalers. The supply chain was a problem: paying off truck company owners and their agents to earn their trust took time. It was also difficult to send things via rail as each city had its government bureaucrats, middlemen, and black market gangsters, not to mention a corrupt police force that also had to be kept happy. But Varoon had learned that where there was risk, opportunity also existed. It was a sophisticated juggling act that required constant attention. Someone, somewhere, was constantly needing more money. The wheels had to be greased. And as long as the senior government official was taking his cut, Varoon couldn't see how he would ever realize his full profit margin.

Luckily, Manu's connections in Delhi seemed trustworthy even though Varoon had never met them. He was curious but he also wanted to keep a distance because they moved his goods so quickly and paid him just as expeditiously that he knew they had deep pockets. And the way Manu talked about them, in hushed tones, suggested they were very powerful. Maybe even the Lal Nagas, the Red Snakes—one of the most infamous and violent gangs who ran the underworld black market in Delhi.

"Oh, I nearly forgot," Varoon said, raising his glass. "I hear congratulations are in order for you, Major!"

They clinked glasses again and drank. India had come out on top from the war and Manu had earned several medals, including a promotion in rank. But the Americans and the Soviets had spoiled an unequivocal Indian victory by negotiating a diplomatic cease fire via the UN. So even though the war was technically over, a small, contained conflict was still occurring.

Varoon asked, "Is it true what the say in the papers that a few dozen Pakistani soldiers have infiltrated the border and are in Indian territory?"

"A handful of Pakistani commandos paratrooped into an area my men and I were in charge of. We captured them."

"What did you do?" Varoon asked. All kinds of rumours were circulating. Some said that the captured soldiers were released for a price, while some were tortured, had their throats slit, and drowned in rivers with stones in their pockets.

Manu drained his drink and answered, "We did what we had to."

Varoon realized Manu didn't want to elaborate. And to his surprise, Varoon wasn't bothered by the fact that his friend had perhaps murdered Muslim soldiers. It made Varoon wonder if he would ever have the courage to take a life. He doubted it—even though a part of him still wanted to squeeze the life out of a Muslim. Memories of his mother and his time in Lahore as a young boy came to him in broken fragments but they were from so long ago that he couldn't trust their authenticity. Just recently he'd remembered his mother teaching him the call of the native birds, the chirps of the yellow bitterns and warblers, the repeated three-syllable call of the Lahore pond herons that sounded as though they were chanting *Va-roon, come!* Beseeching him to play by the river, where the dhobi walla and his wife washed clothes.

Manu said, "Still getting used to being called Major. Anyway, listen—I need a favour."

"Anything."

"Our friends in Delhi have been duped by a judge. Long story short is that they thought he was in their pockets but some bastard politician paid the judge more—anyways, the judge has been straightened out, but an arrest needs to be made now to appease the politician, the newspapers. Someone has to be thrown in jail."

"So what can I do?" Varoon asked, his heart skipping a beat. He didn't like where this was headed.

"The plan is that we give them someone, anyone, doesn't matter who. They just need to show the newspapers that someone has been thrown in jail for smuggling in the black market. Most likely the fellow will only be there for a few months. Do you have someone loyal you think would be willing to do this?"

Varoon was relieved he wasn't the one being asked to go to jail. But there was no one he could think of that would be willing to do something like that.

Manu said, "If you were to provide the Lal Nagas with a man willing to do this, they would be greatly indebted to you."

Varoon's suspicions had been right all along then. He shifted in his seat.

Manu said, "You OK?"

"Yeah, yeah, fine," Varoon said, reining in his anxiety. Where there was risk, opportunity also existed.

Draining his drink, Varoon called for Chottu, who came quickly from the kitchen. The boy refilled Varoon's glass with ice, smiling. He was so happy Varoon had taken him out of the godowns. Instead of inhaling musty sawdust every day the boy now enjoyed the ocean breeze. He was the worker in the shop some said had been dropped on his head as a child and was therefore a bit slow. No matter how much Varoon tried to disparage that kind of talk over the years, it never ceased, and when it came time to find a head servant, Chottu was a perfect choice.

The boy was loyal and did his work well. Now, as Varoon sipped his drink, he realized Chottu might be perfect for this task. The boy was likely not a day over sixteen, but being born in a village, he had no birth certificate. It wouldn't be difficult to say he was eighteen and could therefore be legally incarcerated. The boy would easily be appeased with a few years of extra salary for the time in jail. Even if he wanted a hundred years' salary it would be a pittance compared to what Varoon might gain.

"Suppose I do. Would I be able to ask for something in return?" Varoon asked.

"Of course."

"The senior government official at the Port Authority has been taking unfairly from me. I thought it would be only for a few months, but the bastard—"

Before Varoon could elaborate, Manu said, "Consider it already taken care of."

- 36 -

1973

ARRIVING HOME NEAR MIDNIGHT, VAROON unrolled the *pathari* on the drawing room floor where he slept most nights now that Anju and the baby were in the bedroom, waking several times a night for feedings. Varoon and Anju had been trying to have a baby for many years and had almost given up hope, but finally, by some miracle (Anju claimed it was all her praying), they'd been blessed with a beautiful baby boy that Anju named Anush, after a faint morning star above the Arabian Sea that she sometimes caught a glimpse of while praying at the Mahalakshmi Temple. The old man, who'd become quite senile, had moved in with them at Sea Face Terraces, and was in the spare bedroom. Some nights he woke as often as the baby and Varoon would have to calm him down and tuck him back into bed.

The shipping business was growing and Varoon was working fourteen-hour days, sometimes more. Despite being exhausted, he tiptoed into his bedroom to check in on Anju and Anush, who were in a deep sleep. They looked so peaceful, sleeping snug together on the bed. He noticed how Anush took two breaths for every one his mother did. Varoon was tempted to lie with them, but he knew Anush would wake in a couple of hours for a feeding and disturb his sleep, and so with a gentle kiss on each of their foreheads, he returned to the drawing room. He'd lie with them in the morning for a bit before leaving for work. Snuggling with the two of them in the warmth of their bed was his favourite part of the day.

Weary, Varoon was ready to dive into a deep sleep but just as his head hit the pillow, he heard a stirring in his father's room. He tried to ignore it but the old man kept mumbling, having incoherent conversations with himself. He hadn't been lucid in days and was given morphine daily. The two of them hadn't spoken to each other in years. Varoon finally went to his father. Quite often he just needed a glass of water and he'd fall back asleep. In the spare bedroom, Varoon, too tired to even stand, knelt on the floor by his father's bedside in the dark.

The old man's eyes were closed and he was mumbling, "The teak this season is dry . . . Check the mahogany, when first cut it should give a spicy tang . . ."

Varoon said, "Papa," but the old man was no longer himself. The doctor had said he'd fallen prey to dementia.

"Rosewood works well for joining, mortise it with black cherry . . ."

Varoon touched his father's hand and that seemed to calm him. It was the first time they'd touched each other in years.

In the dark room, the old man's breathing relaxed and he stopped mumbling. The waves outside crashed on the rocks. Varoon asked the question that had been at the back of his mind for over two decades: "Do you remember my kundali? It was lost the night we fled Lahore."

The old man, with eyes closed, didn't say anything for some time, and then blurted out, "Rosewood's grain grows more floral and dense at the core, so thick that it can dull blades . . . the deep reds and browns . . . tight growth rings overlap . . ."

Varoon shook his father and said again, "Tell me of the kundali." The old man was so weak and frail now that he weighed less than forty kilograms.

The old man opened his eyes and said, "Your kundali. We left it behind. Along with everything everything everything. Lost. Gone. Slipping through fingers. Impossible to keep it all. You you you were born in the middle of a monsoon storm. Even though it's customary to wait for seven days after birth to have a kundali made, your mother insisted I have it done right away."

Varoon couldn't believe what he was hearing. It was the most lucid his father had been in weeks.

The old man continued. "With sheets of rain flying sideways sideways sideways in my face, I went. At first, the panditji refused to believe the charts he'd rendered so he started again only to reach the same same conclusion. He sat me down, held my hand, and I'll never forget his words, he said: *This boy is extraordinary. I've never seen a kundali like this. The Sun firmly resides in his first house, indicating he will be a strong-willed leader. Neptune influences his Sun, making him even more courageous to overcome great odds. Mighty Saturn prevails in his tenth house, which represents his unbridled ambition. Nothing will stand in his way.*

But beware—this south node, where Pluto sits in his tenth house, marks ego or greed to be his downfall."

Something had changed in the old man. He hadn't spoken to Varoon so earnestly about anything other than the shop in years, and especially not about impractical matters like kundalis. A few moments of silence passed during which it seemed as though the old man had said all there was to say. The final secret had been imparted. An eerie calm imbued the room as he lay in his bed, staring up at the ceiling. It was almost as though he was another person now. The doctor had warned Varoon and Anju that with dementia, fragments of the personality can alter, changing the patient entirely.

Varoon asked, "Why didn't you tell me earlier? Why did you leave it behind?"

The old man continued to stare at the ceiling and beyond as he spoke, "Your mother believed in that nonsense. Not me. Left it. Left it. Left it all behind. No one knows exactly—Mr. Desai says it's the Muslim League, they have the police on their side. But there's a five-thirty train train train to Amritsar."

For a split second, Varoon was back under the gardener's carriage, hiding with his mother. She was shushing and kissing him. He could taste salt in her hot tears.

"The Desais will give us a ride to the station station station."

Varoon thought of the dhobi walla being stabbed and then his wife being stripped of her clothes. Her shrill shrieks fading away as the Jeep drove off. How he'd done nothing to help either of them.

"The train is leaving leaving leaving. Do you see her?" The old man remained lying on his bed but was in a state of panic now, shaking, perspiring.

Varoon could hear the sharp blast of the train whistle at Lahore Station while he and his father continued to search the platform. His father holding him tight, saying, *She'll be on the next train. She'll be on the next train.*

All these years that they'd avoided talking about that night had made it possible for Varoon to think that there was an infinitesimal chance that his mother had made it across the border and was somewhere safe. He'd never allowed the thought of his mother being set upon by a mob of Muslim men to fully play out in his mind. Whenever the thought had come, he'd suppressed it by thinking she'd been quickly killed along with many on the next train. But what if she'd been taken like the dhobi walla's wife, stripped of her clothes, raped by a number of men before being brutally tortured and murdered? Varoon's stomach churned. His universe went black and he felt as though he was lost in a vast expanse of nothing. His breathing became shallow and it felt as though there was an anvil on his chest. He couldn't take in a full breath. Finally, he managed to whisper, "We abandoned her. You abandoned her."

The old man continued staring at the ceiling and beyond, his body quivering.

Varoon went to the balcony for some fresh air. It was dark and there was no sound except for the waves crashing and the hum of air conditioners stuck in dark bedroom windows. As he gripped the railing, Varoon thought no amount of violence could quell his rage. He could shout and scream at the stars for an eternity and never be satisfied.

He heard the old man stir and returned inside.

The old man whispered, "Pani. I need water water water."

There was jug of water on the bedside table but Varoon

scooped up his father in his arms, walked to the balcony, and in one swift move cast him over. Varoon barely heard the quiet thud nine floors below. He walked into the bathroom, rinsed himself clean with soap and cool water. Soon, he was back on his pathari on the floor in the drawing room and fell into a deep sleep while the waves continued to crash on the black rocks.

- 3 7 -
1984

VAROON EXAMINED A BOTTLE OF Calmpose pills a
doctor had handed him two days ago, after Anju died.

The doctor had said, "They're mild tranquilizers, but habit-
forming—so use them sparingly."

Anju had been admitted into the hospital only two weeks
before after complaining of stomach pains. Varoon had told her
a dozen times to see a doctor but she refused, not wanting to
burden a doctor with what was probably cramps or a stomach
flu. After being admitted into the Breach Candy Hospital, they
decided not to worry Anush at Bharat Academy unnecessar-
ily. Varoon continued going to work but visited Anju every
evening, sometimes even sleeping on the floor of her hospital
room. During the first few rounds of tests the doctors were

confounded while Anju's condition deteriorated rapidly. The pains in her lower abdomen grew sharper and had to be dulled with morphine. Finally a senior doctor told Varoon that there was a possibility Anju had cervical cancer, that it had spread. Surgery was the only option. "She might only have a year or two if the cancer isn't removed."

Varoon paid the right hospital administrators so that Anju was placed at the top of the list. However, the day before she was scheduled to go into the operating room, while Varoon was at work, she died.

The autopsy revealed that the cancer had spread farther than anticipated: from the ovaries to the uterus to lymph nodes in the abdomen and even into the liver and pancreas.

It was difficult to comprehend. Two days ago she was alive, and now her body was cold, being prepared for cremation.

It was past midnight. After bidding a few distant family relatives goodbye at the door, Varoon sat in the balcony of his bedroom, looking out over the black and silvery sea. He listened to the sound of the waves rushing in and out among the rocks on the shore across the street, and as he stood in the dark, he was reminded of his father, of throwing him off the balcony all those years ago. Had he made the right decision or committed an unforgivable sin? He'd had this conversation with himself countless times, reassuring himself that his father's dementia had ravaged him to the point where he didn't know who or where he was. There had been no joy in his life, no purpose. If his father had been given the choice, when he was once lucid, he wouldn't have chosen to live out his days totally senile. And yet, it was still a life, with occasional moments of lucidity. A life Varoon had taken. Or thrown, like a piece of rubbish.

He also thought of how he should've taken Anju to the hospital earlier. Couldn't he have spent more time with her? Some evenings he only made a brief appearance at the hospital, as she kept insisting she was fine. He wondered how long she'd lied to him and put on a brave face. Had he spent less time at work and more at home he might have noticed her discomfort. If surgery had been performed earlier the cancer might have been eradicated. He'd failed in his duty to his family: his father, his wife, his son. His son—how was Anush going to cope with this? The boy was probably lying awake in his bedroom.

Varoon put his drink down and went to the mandir where Anju prayed daily and picked up her sandalwood mala. He rarely went to the temple these days, despite promising Anju he would, because work had become more demanding. He'd said, "I'm trying to reach more wholesalers—it takes time, jaan. Praying won't help." He loathed himself now for his hubris.

Varoon sat on the floor and lit a *devo*. Anju would make a month's supply at a time of the homemade cotton wicks dipped in *ghee*, and the little wooden box in which they lived was still nearly full. The flicker of light from the devo lit the Ganesha idol in the mandir. Lighting a stick of sandalwood incense, Varoon closed his eyes and began to pray with Anju's mala. *Om tát savitúr váreṇyaṃ bhárgo devásya dhīmahi dhíyo yó naḥ pracodáyāt Om*. In an instant, acrid smoke filled his nostrils and the spokes of the carriage wheel came into focus.

Varoon inhaled sharply and stopped the memory. He had no room in his heart to endure past loss; the present was enough.

Looking around the dark room now, he summoned a more pleasant memory, one from 1967, the day he and Anju moved into the flat. A priest had been hired to perform the *Griha*

Pravesh, a ceremony performed on the first entry into a new home. Anju had wanted to wait for another month to do the ceremony on *Uttarayanan*, an auspicious day when the sun begins its journey northward as a sign of coming summer, but Varoon didn't want to wait any longer to move out of his father's tiny flat above the shop. He'd worked tirelessly at growing his shipping business, meeting suppliers, distributors, manufacturers, struck friendships and bribed dozens people, secured cargo and containers with larger exporters and importers to make his business a success. He'd worked like a dog to get away from the shop and didn't see why he had to spend any more time there than necessary. Anju pleaded quietly at nights while they slept on the pathari, not far away from Varoon's father, "Please, jaan," she'd whispered, "let's wait till next month. It's bad luck not to wait till the auspicious day." But Varoon had feigned sleep and assuaged his guilt then by reassuring himself that she'd love the new luxurious flat, the incredible view of the Arabian Sea glimmering nine floors below, how there were two bedrooms, each with their own bathroom; even the servants' quarters had its own bathroom. How many people could boast of that?

The priest had been called and the ceremony went ahead at Sea Face Terraces as Varoon had arranged. They sat on the floor in the living room by the balcony while the priest chanted Sanskrit verses and poured dollops of ghee, handfuls of puffed rice, and other offerings into the bronze portable fire pit. Varoon and Anju were both garlanded with vermillion and white flowers, their foreheads marked with bright yellow turmeric. Anju's hair was in a bun, draped by her green and gold sari, and she wore a *mangalsutra* around her neck.

After the ceremony had finished and the guests left, the

two of them were finally alone. On the balcony in the master bedroom, the ocean glimmered before them, and Anju's eyes welled up.

"What's wrong?" Varoon asked.

She shook her head, wiped away her tears with the end of her sari, and said, "It's so big, so—empty."

He laughed, held her close, and said, "It's all for you. Look, the whole ocean is yours." They held each other. "It's so beautiful," she said. "Maybe we should've moved earlier." They laughed. He remembered that one of his importers had given him a gift, a new Nikon camera. With it, he took a few photos of Anju.

After putting the camera away he tugged at the end of her sari and began to unravel it from her body. She slowly turned in circles helping him, at first a little hesitant, then letting the centrifugal force quicken and unwind her. She giggled as she twirled, enjoying the feeling of being a little out of control. She usually wore her hair up in a loose bun so it remained out of her way while she was doing housework, and despite the bun having a haphazard quality to it, it never failed to arouse Varoon. During the ceremony, Varoon had noticed how the bun was sculpted and held together steadfastly with pins. Her exposed neck seemed so elegant, making her seem taller, more graceful than she already was. As soon as her sari was unravelled, they held each other in a tight embrace. He could smell the garland of vermillion flowers that had hung around her neck, and the faint scent of the coconut oil she combed her hair with every morning slowly burst into bloom as she let her hair down.

Varoon opened his eyes now in the dark, seated on the floor. Apart from his own rapid breathing everything was silent.

Guilt began to multiply in him. Was Anju's cancer somehow his karmic fault? Was his impatience, his refusal to observe the auspicious day all those years ago somehow responsible? Or was it something else he had done? Like sending Chottu, the most loyal of servants, to jail for the Lal Nagas? The boy was incarcerated for six months and even though Varoon had compensated Chottu handsomely for it and continued to send money to Chottu's family every year at Diwali, the boy never spoke of what happened to him, and Varoon never asked. But the boy returned from prison with a permanent scar on his forearm, probably as a warning from the Lal Nagas—what Varoon had asked of them in return for sending Chottu to jail was too much. The senior government official at the Port Authority had mysteriously disappeared soon after and his body was found in the sea, his throat slit, leaving Varoon to keep his profits. And then, of course, there was Varoon's father—was Anju dying from cancer a kind of karmic payback for killing his own father?

Putting Anju's mala down, he rushed for the Calmpose pills, popped two into his mouth, and swallowed them with a large peg of whisky.

If he was younger he would've argued with himself that one thing had nothing to do with the other, that it was foolish to be so superstitious, but he knew now life didn't work like that. You couldn't just pick and choose the things you were superstitious about. You couldn't waver on the things that were important. He was to blame. Perhaps if he'd kept going to the temple he would've made better choices, been more conscientious. But then again, he'd compensated Chottu well. And didn't the senior government official deserve his fate after suggesting Varoon pimp his wife to him and then by continuing to take an unfair portion of Varoon's profits? And anyway, Varoon hadn't asked for him to be murdered. As for the Lal Nagas, Varoon had slowly curbed his business with them. He'd done the best he could, always trying to be as fair as possible, rewarding meritocracy in the office rather than nepotism, unlike many in the country.

In his bedroom now, he looked at a framed photo of Anju he'd taken with the Nikon on the day of the Griha Pravesh ceremony and decided to commission a large portrait of the photo to be painted. He promised himself he'd go to the temple every morning till the day he died. It was the least he could do for Anju.

He could only hope God would forgive him. He took a certain pride in having achieved all he had by himself, but he could see now that abstaining from daily prayer had caused a lapse in judgment and given him a false sense of pride. He'd have to pray for forgiveness.

Sitting back down in front of the mandir, with the mala in hand again, he repeated the gayatri mantra and willed himself to not think of the memories that were intertwined with it, but even so he could smell the acrid smoke, hear the distant cries. Immediately he stopped and took another Calmpose pill. He wished he could erase that night from his mind. He hated how some nights, while lying in bed, that memory would come to him, like a fissure in the sky opening and swallowing him whole.

Poor Anush. He wondered how the boy was coping. Earlier that day, as they drove in silence towards the cremation site near Marine Lines station, Varoon had never seen the boy so well behaved. He thought Anush would be in tears, and so he'd readied himself to be strong. He refused to show any grief in front of the boy, giving Anush the opportunity to grieve, but the boy simply stared out his window, most likely overwhelmed.

When the car reached the cremation grounds, Varoon sensed his son's trepidation. Before opening the door, he wanted to say: *Your mother loved you more than anything. She wanted you to know that,* or *Life is sometimes unfair, cruel—you have to keep on going.* But he didn't say any of those things. They seemed condescending, trite, even for an eleven-year-old. Instead, he placed his hand on his son's head, hoping to bestow a kind of benediction. He'd never felt more useless. He realized Anju had been doing most of the parenting up till now and he had no idea how to deal with Anush.

After finishing his whisky, Varoon quietly let himself into Anush's bedroom and sat on the edge of his bed in the dark while waves crashed outside. Varoon whispered, "Anush," to see if he was awake. He was.

As Varoon sat there, the drugs began to take effect. His body relaxed and he felt as though he'd been submerged in a tub of warm water.

"You know, I lost my mother, your *dadima,* when I was young too."

Anush asked, "How was she lost?"

The dhobi walla being stabbed in the stomach flashed in his mind. His wife's cries echoed in Varoon's head. The men crowding around her, stripping her of her clothes and throwing her into the Jeep before driving away.

"Many people were lost that night. It was chaos. But your dadaji and I made it to Bombay. We stayed together and thrived. Just like you and I will."

Wanting to mitigate Anush's grief, Varoon began to lie. "Your mother and I were going to tell you something special when you were a bit older. Do you want to know what it is now?"

He wanted to protect his son from the times in his life when the fissures in his own sky would crack and want to swallow him whole. He wanted to make Anush feel as though he were someone special.

Anush sat up, nodding, intrigued.

"The next night after that dream she went into labour. A monsoon storm was beginning to gather offshore. The wind was tossing branches and spraying dust in all directions. We made it to the hospital just before the rains began. After you were born, I ran through the raging storm to the astrologer to find out your kundali, your destiny. Even though it's customary to wait for the seventh day after a child is born, I went—I was too excited. With sheets of rain flying sideways into my face I ran to the astrologer to find out your destiny . . ."

As he continued the story, he reminded himself to get rid of Anush's real kundali and have a new one made soon. It occurred to Varoon that a panditji might not be so easily swayed to concoct a kundali, but he knew that Manu's family had connections to an esteemed panditji. With enough money, nearly anything could be bought.

PART IV

INCANDESCENT CORUSCATION

- 38 -
DEEPA
1998

DEEPA PATIK'S SEARCH FOR THE ideal young man
for her Jyoti baby had begun the day after she returned
from London, more than six months ago. Once word got out
that Jyoti had finished her MBA from the LSE, inquiries began
to pour in, but one had to careful. In a city of twelve million,
God only knew how many unscrupulous families there were
just waiting to dupe you into marrying their no-good, deadbeat
nephews, sons, and cousins. It's how people were—snakes ready
to climb any ladder of opportunity. Her Jyoti baby was special.
Deepa had to be certain that the boy was equally exceptional,
his family as worthy; after all, this was Jyoti, her shining star. If
Deepa's ulcer flared up again, and God took her from this life,

her husband would be incompetent when it came to ensuring Jyoti a suitable match. The man was a capable geriatrician but useless in practical affairs. They'd be swindled out of the family wealth in weeks and Jyoti would be married off to a middle-class family in the suburbs. The onus of choosing the right boy fell squarely on her.

Over the months, through intermediaries, photos of boys and information about their families were presented, but they were either too plain, too ugly, too dark, too short, lived in cities too far away, from families too conservative or, too modern. A few non-Gujarati families also had the gall to approach her. To those, she didn't even respond.

There were an infinite number of things to consider not just about the prospective boy but what were the mother and father like? From where in Gujarat were they from originally? What caste? How religious were they? Did they observe auspicious days in the lunar calendar? Were they vegetarian? Where did they live? What kind of building was it? How many people in the household? How much square footage? The boy's age, his education, his job, his salary were all pertinent, as was estimating the family's net worth, and which private clubs, if any, did they belong to? There was much to consider. Over the months, a five-star rating method developed in her diary. There were plenty of twos and threes, a few fours, but never a five. Her search had uncovered a few decent families in the suburbs, but when it came down to it, Deepa didn't like the idea of Jyoti living so far away.

Then one day, she heard that a rich, handsome Gujarati man had just begun his search for a suitable daughter-in-law. Apart from Sharma Shipping, it was said that Varoon Sharma had other businesses, but the accuracy of such information was question-able, as it came filtered through a handful of gossipers at the temple. You couldn't believe everything people said these days. After digging around, Deepa was ecstatic to find that Sharma Shipping seemed as large and profitable as people had claimed. It was rumoured Varoon Sharma had his hands in construction, that he lived in Breach Candy—an affluent neighbourhood only a stone's throw away—in a palatial home on the top floor of a build-ing with an ocean view, and had only one heir, a handsome son with a terrific kundali. She refused to believe it all—it seemed too good to be true. A life lesson she'd long ago taught herself was not to be fooled into believing you were more special than you really were. So she didn't aim her hopes too high, knowing where hubris led, and buttressed herself accordingly, waiting for something objectionable or unpropitious about the Sharmas to surface.

The Patiks were introduced to Varoon Sharma by a common friend at the temple he went to nearby. A few cordial conversa-tions were had and it was Varoon who invited the Patiks for lunch.

It was unusual for a first arranged marriage meeting to be held at one of the families' residences. Customarily, it was held on neutral ground. Deepa and her husband would have preferred to go to one of the restaurants at the Taj or to Gallops Restaurant at the Mahalaxmi Race Course, but Varoon insisted they come to his home.

When Deepa took in the unobstructed view of the Arabian Sea glimmering nine floors below from the Sharma drawing room, she was speechless. At this time of the evening, the sun shimmered brilliantly over the sea like a million strewn dia-monds. The beautifully manicured gardens across the street were filled with people strolling among the violet petunias, crimson gulmohars, orange marigolds, and magenta morning glories—flowers that also grew in the finely manicured courtyard of the building that the Patiks resided at nearby in Malabar Hill. Just beyond the lush gardens at the Sharma residence the sea extended to the horizon as far as the eye could see.

"Welcome, welcome," Varoon said. After introductions, the five of them sat at an elegant teak dining table. Anush was a handsome young man with hazel eyes and a thick head of hair, like his father. Perhaps a bit short, but that wasn't a deal breaker.

Deepa appreciated that Varoon had chosen to serve traditional Gujarati food—a simple yet elegant choice. She'd heard that the Sharmas were new money and was relieved that Varoon hadn't tried to impress them by ordering pizza from one of the new Domino's restaurants that had popped up across the city—popular places with the incondite upwardly mobile.

Small talk was made over appetizers: the rapid growth of the city, the soaring real estate market, the official name change from Bombay to Mumbai.

Varoon said, "I just read today that at the current rate, prices will soon eclipse Tokyo and Manhattan. The building boom in our country has just begun. People don't believe it when I tell them our skyline will be changed soon with tall towers."

Her husband said, "Yes, I can't imagine Bombay with more traffic. But tell me, how do you think we'll do at the Cricket World Cup next year?"

Varoon said, "India will dominate. Tendulkar is going to beat Sir Donald Bradman's batting record."

It was a game, this arranged marriage business. They had to maintain the facade of not being aware of the possibility of all their lives changing forever when it was really all that was on everyone's mind.

Deepa wondered if Jyoti and Anush found each other attractive while they were all seated at the teak dining table. More importantly though, through the small talk, she tried to assess if relations between both families could truly be convivial. Of course one always treated their in-laws with exceeding goodwill at first, but if the families weren't a good match, relations became fraught with veils of kindness and cheer, quickly leading to bitter resentment and decades of antagonism. Deepa knew all about pretense. Fortunately, her in-laws lived in Gujarat and didn't visit often.

From the dining table at the centre of the flat, Deepa noticed a large oil painting in the drawing room of a pretty young woman dressed in a sari, who she assumed was the late Mrs. Sharma. She stole glances at the portrait, trying to glean anything of interest, but it offered little. It was a sober depiction of a young woman wearing a green and gold sari. Deepa had heard from people at the temple that Varoon Sharma was a widower. At first news of this last week, Deepa was secretly elated. The fact that the Sharmas had no matriarch meant that if there was to be a match, Jyoti would be the head matriarch of the family, not under the constant eye and judgment of a mother-in-law. There were so many cruel mothers-in-law willing to slowly torture their daughters-in-law by subjugating them, making them servants in the kitchen. Some, in the suburbs, slums, and villages, were less subtle, paying strangers to throw acid on their non-compliant daughters-in-law's faces, scarring, disfiguring them for life if they didn't obey. It wasn't just the uneducated lower class that inflicted this type of barbarity; the upper classes could be just as ruthless, and sometimes worse because they felt they lived with some impunity, which some did. What happened to the legions of poor girls whose faces were savaged by these types of attacks? It made one shudder. There were too few people in the world who knew mercy. But it was how the world worked. It was her duty to see to it that her daughter, her baby, was kept out of harm's way and out of the cycle of domestic violence. The lucky ones might not be physically abused, but there were countless girls who suffered daily hardships, who were told that their cooking or child-rearing was subpar, criticized every day in some small passive-aggressive way, humiliated little by little. Some mothers-in-law were so astute in this that they had the entire neighbourhood convinced they themselves were saints, that they were the most gracious and caring of women, while behind closed doors they inflicted emotional torture, and of course their perfect sons were never chastised. Also, if over the years a son was not produced, the daughters-in-law would somehow be blamed. Since divorce was out of the question as it blighted both families, these young women were sometimes driven to commit suicide, like her poor cousin in Gujarat had a few years ago. Those were the extreme cases, of course, but it was her duty to ensure that her Jyoti baby not be married into a family remotely like that.

Could Varoon Sharma be one of those types? He might be rich and powerful but was he actually crass and backward? He seemed confident in his traditional white kurta and pyjama and diamond-encrusted Rolex. His broad shoulders and thick salt-and-pepper hair suggested confidence, wisdom. He didn't seem desperate to please—there was something reassuring about that, but Deepa wasn't entirely convinced yet. It was her daughter's future, after all. She wasn't about to let good posture and expensive jewelry influence her judgment.

Varoon said, "The Australians have some fine pace bowlers this year . . ."

If there was to be a match between their families, she wondered if Varoon would ultimately be bold enough to ask for a dowry. Although Deepa abhorred how dowries devalued females, making them a liability to their parents, they were still a felicitous part of the ceremony and ritual of Hindu marriages. Instead of goats and chickens or money, nowadays among some of the more refined classes it was fine saris and jewelry that were given. Luckily, Patik women had a taste for fine jewelry and over the years Deepa had inherited a sizeable collection. In the vault there not only lay gold bars, but also fine artisanal jewelry made from diamonds and rubies, emeralds and sapphires, that would slacken Varoon Sharma's jaw. And, with no mother-in-law in the picture, the jewels would all be Jyoti's.

"Jyoti works with Citibank," Mrs. Patik beamed. "She finished her master's at the London School of Economics," quickly adding, "with distinction," and then tried to contain her smile, fearful of appearing crass, boastful. It was a fine balance this arranged marriage business, presenting yourself as the best qualified candidate while being modest.

Varoon seemed impressed but now Deepa felt a hot spell come on. She sipped some ice water. Had menopause already begun? She'd been getting these hot flashes ever since London. Or was that just the anxiety that someone might find out about the incident? Apart from her and Jyoti, no one knew. But Deepa was keenly aware of the minefield of gossips, countless housewives who lived for nothing other than to get together in the afternoons over tea, clucking their tongues at scandals and reprobates: "Did you see what the girl from the fifth floor was wearing?" "It's no surprise, I hear her second cousin ran off and eloped into a love marriage!" Of course when she hosted tea socials, Deepa didn't incite that type of talk herself, but she understood the purpose it served. It was gossip as much as it was intelligence. A community of women that kept each other informed was a strong one. And if it meant that they indirectly spread some fear and shame into their girls for behaving inappropriately, then it was of value because society would judge the young women for misbehaving, for the tiniest slip (but not the men—never the men!). This was how the world worked, and so in fact it was their duty, as mothers, to keep each other informed, to instill the right morals in their daughters.

Getting down to business, Deepa said, "You must hear Jyoti's kundali."

Varoon said, "Yes, of course. Please."

"It's quite simple really," she said, motioning her husband to unfurl the papers on the table, which he did while rolling his eyes ever so slightly. The professor was a closet atheist and didn't believe in kundalis. He was about to say something but Deepa shot him a look that made him keep quiet and sit back. She explained to Varoon, "The panditji said Jyoti would be a highly intelligent and successful girl through her whole life. Her ninth house is very robust, indicating success with higher education. And it's been quite accurate. Jyoti's always been at the top of her class. In her seventh house, where marriage and partnership are concerned, the Sun firmly sits, marking her marriage a great success." Deepa beamed, this time without restraint. She didn't care if she was being boastful, the arranged marriage game of peacocking had begun and she wanted the Sharmas to know that they should consider themselves lucky to have a girl like Jyoti sitting at their table.

Deepa continued, "He said all matters of Jyoti's life would be generally rewarding and prosperous: a long life with health and wealth. She will have a solid relationship with her soulmate and healthy children. At least one son."

Varoon said, "Obviously you've been blessed with a talented and beautiful daughter. I don't need a kundali to see that. And I hope to have as many granddaughters as grandsons."

It was the right thing to say. No one ever actually admitted it out loud these days that they preferred boys over girls, at least in their class of society, but Deepa kept her eyes on Varoon to see if he really meant it. His relaxed, genuine smile convinced her, for now, that he wasn't a misogynist.

"Would you like to hear Anush's kundali?" Varoon said.

"Of course, please do tell," Deepa said, shooting her husband a look to remind him to stay in his place. The custom of kundalis at arranged marriages was an ancient practice. She wasn't about to let his upstart passive-aggressive opinions sully venerable traditions.

"Right after Anush was born, I ran through a monsoon storm and knocked at the panditji's door in the middle of the night. Obviously, he was reluctant to make the chart right then. But I was so excited that I begged him. Eventually he relented, and when he made Anush's chart, his face went grave, he didn't say anything."

This piqued everyone's interest, including the doctor's.

Laying the astrological charts on the table for all to admire, Varoon explained, "The panditji sat me down, held my hand, and I'll never forget his words, he said, 'This boy is extraordinary. I've never seen a kundali like this. With the Sun in his first house, he is a natural-born leader. Courageous, he will overcome great odds through his own means. He will go on to do extraordinary things.'"

Deepa took a breath, doing her best not to think how for the first time in a while, luck was on their side.

- 3 9 -
VAROON
1998

"OH MY, FIVE DIFFERENT CHUTNEYS for the *pani puris*? Varoon bhai, you're spoiling us," Deepa Patik said.

Throughout the pleasantries, Varoon couldn't help but notice Anush's indifference, and even though it incensed him, he smiled through it.

A week ago, the BJP president had called about a photo in the newspaper of Anush and the Muslim woman. He warned Varoon, "I can't risk being associated with a mixed Hindu-Muslim relationship."

"I'll take care of it right away," Varoon assured the president. Varoon's future with the party and access to commercial and residential real estate deals worth mountains of money were on the line.

After informing Anush of the meeting with the Patiks, the boy was bold enough to contend, "How can I marry a girl I don't even know?"

"No one is forcing you to marry her. Just meet her and her family. Go out with her, get to know each other."

"What if I don't want to marry a Gujarati girl?"

Varoon had warned, "You won't get a rupee from me for the rest of your life. I've decided to sell the furniture shop and that building once and for all. Developers are offering a hefty sum of money. Once you're married to a respectable Gujarati girl, you will receive half of the money from the sale of the building and your monthly stipend from me will triple."

Anush had agreed, reluctantly, but the boy's rebellious streak was so healthy the fool was perhaps still seeing the Muslim girl. He was probably thinking of her right now while they sat at the table with the Patiks. The boy had absolutely no shame. Varoon wanted to reach over and smack Anush on the side of the head but he willed himself to stay put. It required a colossal amount of self-restraint.

"Were the chutneys for the pain puris made from scratch?" Deepa asked.

"Of course," Varoon replied as Chottu served the table.

Varoon had hoped to achieve two things by serving a Gujarati meal so perfectly prepared by his servants: the first was to let the Patiks see he was somewhat traditional—he didn't need to serve Western dishes to charm them—and at the same time he wanted them to understand that he wasn't too orthodox—he wasn't looking for a cook or head servant as a daughter-in-law. He was happy Jyoti was an educated young woman with a career. He wanted them to see he was unlike most Gujarati men, who proclaimed their modernity to society but really had antiquated notions of marriage and wanted their womenfolk to be nothing but lifetime housewives. By showing that the servants could easily prepare a magnificent multi-course meal without the supervision of a matriarch in the kitchen, he was hoping the Patiks would tacitly understand he was happy to let Jyoti work, and when she was ready to have children she would have skillful servants attend to her needs. If she wasn't interested in cooking, it would not be required of her.

As Chottu served the puris, Deepa said, "I've never seen puris like this in my life. They're all perfect."

Chottu and the other servants had been working for days to finish the menu and all of a sudden the amount of food on the table was teetering on overkill. Varoon hoped it wasn't perceived as desperate.

"Oh my god," Deepa said, tasting the pani, "this is incredible."

Varoon had had it special ordered from a pani puri walla who exclusively used Evian water. It cost a ridiculous sum of money, considering it was basically water with a handful of spices, mint, cilantro, cumin, lemon, and ginger, but the delight on the Patiks' faces was worth every paisa.

He could only pray that the Patiks had not seen the photo of Anush with the Muslim girl in the newspaper. Their arms around each other like drunk lovers—disgraceful.

"Did your servants make these puris? They're beautiful—like works of art," Deepa said.

"No, I had a puri maker come in and make them right in our kitchen this afternoon," Varoon said.

"I insist you give me his phone number. These are exquisite."

In the case that they'd seen the photo, Varoon wondered

if Anush would be able to manoeuvre the conversation, make up some story about how she was just a platonic college chum. But of course the ability to subtly take control of a conversation required a certain amount of competence, aptitude, and Varoon doubted Anush possessed these qualities. If they weren't innate in the boy, could they be acquired? Was one born with equanimity or was it a learned skill? The ability to remain calm under pressure was priceless and something Varoon felt he'd failed to instill in the boy. But maybe having dominion over one's wants and emotions was something that came with time, was finessed with experience while being in a role of leadership. Varoon had thought by now Anush would have cultivated some semblance of an adulthood but the boy lacked discipline; he was still too busy partying till the early mornings—the ingrate. He was barely even making an effort to be polite now, sitting slightly hunched over, staring at the table, as though there was something mesmerizing in the grain of the wood. All Varoon could hope for at this point was that Anush wouldn't excuse himself and nip into his bedroom for a drink, get tipsy, and say something impromptu and stupid, which he'd mistake for courage. The boy seemed to want to revolt against anything to do with his father. Varoon had some empathy, as he, too, had railed against his own father, but this was different. Anush was spoiled, entitled. A prosperous future with a good wife from a decent family was within grasp, right now, but that would change if Anush continued to see that Muslim girl. Would Anush be able to recognize the opportunity he had in front of him? Or would he throw it all away?

Varoon shifted in his chair. It was difficult loving your own children sometimes. He never thought it would turn out like this. He never thought he'd be capable of feeling so disappointed with his own flesh and blood. But perhaps it was his own fault. Perhaps if he'd been harder on the boy. Perhaps if he'd punished him more for doing so poorly in school; after all, Anush's behaviour wasn't exactly new. The boy had never excelled at anything. Never had the desire to work hard. Anush's original kundali told of a rather mediocre life, one in which there was wealth and health but nothing out of the ordinary. The boy was spoiled and Varoon, as the only parent, was the one to blame.

But there was no point in dwelling on the past now. It was time to focus on the task at hand: impress the Patiks and get Anush married to a decent Gujarati girl before the fool ruined his life by doing something stupid like running away and getting married to that Muslim girl.

"Mmm. These might be the best pani puris I've ever had," Deepa said.

"They're very good, but remember the *gol gappas* we had in Himachal Pradesh?" Dr. Patik said.

"Darling, there's no comparison. These are fantastic."

Hindu-Muslim marriages only worked well in romantic movies. Life was much more complex and nuanced. There was too much history between Hindus and Muslims for Anush ever to be happily married to a Muslim. Things might seem fine to the two of them now, partying in nightclubs every night, smugly proud of being so liberal and open-minded, but after a few years there would be little to hold them together. Society certainly wouldn't help their union, the public being overwhelmingly against mixed marriages.

Compared to arranged marriages, love marriages were far less successful. The divorce rate in Western countries was flagrant. Even President Clinton seemed to be heading towards divorce after his impeachment. Varoon could only pray the youth of India would be able to resist the temptation of becoming American. There was something inherently distasteful about a culture that espoused freedom and liberty without mentioning responsibility. For a while he'd hoped Anush would grow up and see this for himself, but perhaps the boy had succumbed to the lure of Western hedonism. Perhaps he was slow—not in the sense that he was stupid; Anush just thought about things too much. It made him incapable of making good choices.

"Aree, I'm just saying the gol gappas are quite different," Dr. Patik said. "The northerners use different ingredients and whatnot."

"Ha ha, bhai," Deepa argued. "They use *phalanoo* and *dhiknoo* kinds of things—God only knows what."

Varoon knew this meeting was somewhat like a card game and assured himself that he'd played cards with the best, sometimes for lakhs of rupees. A doctor and a housewife would be easy to read, flatter, defeat.

"You'll have to excuse my husband," Deepa said to Varoon. "He wouldn't know a proper authentic Gujarati dish if it slapped him in the face."

Beneath the playful barbs, there was real animosity between the Patiks. But Varoon sensed that he'd already begun to win over Deepa, the one who wore the pants.

It had crossed Varoon's mind that the Patiks might have the audacity to ask to take Anush's kundali and have it double checked by another pandit, upon which the forgery would be revealed. However, Varoon gave the Patiks no opportunity to doubt him. By presenting himself with confidence but without guile, he won their trust. Varoon wished he could mentor his son. Having built an empire from nearly nothing he understood people's weaknesses. He would tell him that reading people was an art. That listening to people and being a keen observer were skills that needed to be honed. That everyone deeply yearned for something, sometimes so deeply that they weren't even conscious of it, let alone able to express it. For example, the doctor wasn't able to stand up to his wife. Perhaps he didn't love her, perhaps he did, but he certainly didn't have her respect, and in the two hours that they'd been sitting here, Varoon could see that the doctor craved his wife's appreciation, or at least for her to show him some deference. And so, even though she made the decisions in their family, Varoon made sure to include her husband at every turn, making him feel as though he were steering the ship.

Once you figured out what it was that people wanted, you had to help them attain it, which earned their trust, their confidence. Once you had that, the sky was the limit.

Of course, it didn't always work on everyone. Anush, for example, was impossible to figure out. It was likely the boy was confused and didn't know what he wanted, which was at the root of his problem. Varoon nearly shook his head in disappointment before reminding himself of the task at hand, but not before wishing for a split second that he had another son, that to have his only child turn out this way could only be penance for his own unforgivable sins.

- 40 -
DEEPA
1998

EVEN THOUGH JYOTI AND ANUSH were the same age, Deepa hoped Varoon wasn't old-fashioned enough to think that the boy needed to be older. She knew how people talked about girls from decent families who weren't married after their mid-twenties—of course boys were always exempt from that type of judgment. When men remained bachelors into their thirties, they weren't regarded with the kind of pity or chastisement reserved for single women. Even if a girl was fiercely intelligent, beautiful, and charming, people would wonder why she hadn't been snapped up. "There must be something wrong with her," they'd whisper. A shady past, an illicit boyfriend—rumours were endless. There was the Nandani girl from their building—her family was filthy rich but the silly girl ran off and eloped with a young man from college who came from a lower socio-economic background. The two of them probably thought it was the most romantic thing on earth until they floated down to the real world six months later and ended up getting a divorce. With the blight of divorce permanently staining her, it was impossible to get the poor girl married to a decent family. She had to settle for a small cloth merchant in a paltry town in Northern Gujarat, living in a two-room flat with his parents where electricity and running water were sporadic. The mother of the poor girl put on her bravest face in public but she ventured out less and less, the shame too great to bear. *No thank you*, Deepa thought.

Anush was difficult to read, with his gaze lowered and slightly slumped in his seat. He seemed capable of being very handsome, heroic, if he'd just straighten up. But he didn't seem to take interest in conversation. Perhaps he just didn't like small talk. Was he obedient or just shy and withdrawn? Deepa couldn't tell. Did being capable of extraordinary things in his future mean he had to contain himself at present?

Deepa hoped that Jyoti's laconic answers hadn't come across as curt. Deepa was aware that at these first meetings there was pressure to be perfect. It wasn't an easy ordeal and a shy girl like Jyoti might find it overwhelming. But if anyone could impress anyone here it would be her perfect little Jyoti baby who finished her MBA at the London School of Economics, with distinction. It was Anush who would have to prove himself. Of course the Sharmas obviously had enough money. It was impossible to find a family with so much square footage in the city these days. Jyoti would be provided for, as would her children. Deepa knew Jyoti disliked it when her mother was so pragmatic, so old-fashioned, but Jyoti had the luxury of youth. When it was Jyoti's turn to find a suitable match for her son or daughter—after Jyoti had endured the hardships and overwhelming floods of love that accompany raising children, rendering her loyal to them to her last dying breath—Jyoti would feel the same way, of that Deepa was certain. It was up to her now to safeguard this most important decision for her daughter, which needed to be handled with competence, a dash of cleverness.

She wondered if Jyoti and Anush found each other attractive. Surely they must have been somewhat curious if not a trifle aroused by each other, since they were both young and handsome. But the two of them had hardly said a word, except chiming in every now and then to politely agree on how delicious the food was.

On the teak dining table, rivulets of condensation snaked their way down the bulbous silver water jug.

Her husband said, "Did I mention our son is studying at Stanford? He's a freshman, along with Chelsea Clinton."

Mrs. Sharma wanted to kick her husband. The boast about Rahul attending an Ivy League school with the daughter of the most powerful man in the world was too obvious, making them seem desperate. The bit about Chelsea Clinton could have come out later. The fool didn't know how to bridle his pride.

Varoon said, "Congratulations. I hear it's an excellent school. In my opinion, there are some good things about America, but most Americans have become morally bankrupt. President Clinton's illicit affair is just the tip of the iceberg."

Deepa hadn't kept up with all the goings-on of the affair in the news but she had no sympathy for the pasty-white saxophone-playing president with the big smile who had a fondness for cheeseburgers and young interns.

"Compared to Hindu values," Varoon said, "the Americans have nothing but fast food and fancy cars."

"I couldn't agree more," Deepa said. America was mired in a cesspool of selfish sex addicts. She not only approved of what Varoon said but also his forthrightness. The ability to voice challenging opinions confidently required a delicate balance. Many toppled over into cocky self-assuredness, which was arrogant, unbecoming, but Varoon was passionate without being self-righteous, and there was something else about him. Perhaps it was those broad shoulders that suggested he could be a bulldozer if need be. But at the moment he was a graceful Baryshnikov, not afraid to let his opinion be heard. A unique man, to be sure.

Deepa glanced over to both Jyoti and Anush, who remained frightfully shy and kept their focus on the table, as though the teakwood would come to life any minute.

"And did I mention that we have no Muslims in our building?" Varoon said, at which her husband nearly spat out a mouthful of his ice water. Varoon was pointing out that if Jyoti and Anush were to marry, Jyoti would be able to live in a Muslim-free building, but of course Deepa's politically correct husband was shocked by Varoon's audacity.

Even though many, including Deepa, might normally take offence at such a remark in mixed company, Deepa found herself thankful for his honesty. After all, at these first meetings parents went out of their way to fabricate or conceal so many things in order to seem flawless, impeccable. But the attempt to be infallible was vain, hypocritical, and so she was somewhat relieved that Varoon, even though maybe a bit prejudiced, was honest.

No Hindu Gujarati ever really wanted their son or daughter to marry a Muslim, no matter what they proclaimed to one another while drunk over whisky, competing over who was more liberal and open-minded. As far as Deepa was concerned, wealthier classes always professed their progressiveness and tolerance while looking down their noses at all those below. Always denouncing the poorer classes as racist fanatics whenever a race-riot breaks out in the slums, even though the wealthier classes knew that the biggest bigots, con-artists, and crooks walked among their own—yet this fact was ignored while those in power covered it up, even manipulated it to their own advantage. Politicians even created incentives for slum dwellers to start riots, or pay villagers to burn down Hindu or Muslim homes, whatever suited their agenda at the time to get elected. God only knew how many poor victims of callous, power-hungry men there were in the world. Varoon Sharma, however old-fashioned, wasn't conniving. He wasn't angling to hide his thoughts and opinions and had the courage to be honest.

She asked, "May I ask how you're able to keep a Muslim-free building?"

"Well, you see, all transfers of sales have to be approved by the building president." He smiled.

"And you're the building president." Her husband returned Varoon's smile. Deepa couldn't tell if her husband was repelled or fascinated by Varoon's uninhibited outspokenness.

Varoon continued, "You see, I have nothing against Muslims, but if we can live separately, then why not?"

"Absolutely," Deepa said. She'd rather be run over by a slow train than see her children marry Muslims. One did hear about the odd Hindu-Muslim marriage—young people madly in the throes of passion—but families always opposed it and cut relations with the couple. Children growing up without grand-parents, aunts, cousins. Not being able to celebrate holidays and birthdays together, being ostracized by the public or—even worse—by your own family. What kind of life was that?

Like her, her husband said he didn't believe Muslims were inherently beneath Hindus, in fact at a dinner party recently, the doctor had said, "I don't give a damn if my children marry Muslims, but what would *people* say? Society would make it too difficult for it to be feasible—too much water underneath that bridge." A convenient argument. *Liar!* she'd wanted to yell. It would kill him if Jyoti or Rahul were to marry a Muslim, and whether it was because of society's issues with it or his own, he would not be able to deal with it so easily as he made appear. He'd just wanted to come across as noble and high-minded to his friends. The truth was his open-minded liberalness had bounds. He liked to live in his make-believe world that only existed in the editorial pages of the newspapers that proclaimed equality for all and an end to communal bickering, but offered little in the way of implementing these ideals to a country whose very fabric was woven with enmity between Hindus and Muslims even before its inception. Of course we all wanted a world where everyone got along, but it was naive to think that hundreds of years of history could be erased. How would hundreds of millions of people be taught to break with age-old perceptions, doctrines, and customs? Who would teach them new notions of equality when there existed a caste system? Deepa knew a few Muslims, all of whom were pleasant people, but it was pointless to pretend that society would ever let their children be happily married. The few out of touch, educated men who lived in comfort and read the sanctimonious liberal editorials were disconnected from the realities that most people in the country faced every day. The fact that Varoon wasn't trying to pass himself off as one of those hypocritical intellectuals was a breath of fresh air. She only hoped her husband, who'd yet to voice any disagreement (but might when they got home—the coward!), would eventually see her point of view. He might not want an in-law as brash as Varoon, but for Jyoti's sake, Deepa would have to make him reconsider.

Now it was the boy who had to prove himself. He seemed shy. Was he really capable of being extraordinary? Her daughter's happiness was paramount. Let her be the final judge.

- 41 -
ANUSH
1998

AS THE FIRST MEETING WITH the Patiks was wrapping up, Anush became fidgety. He needed a smoke, a whisky, and to see Nasreen right away. This whole thing was preposterous. While they said goodbyes to the Patiks in the front hall, Anush could barely stand to look at the Plain Jane Jyoti any longer. She wasn't ugly by any means, but her long hair tied back into a ponytail made her look like a schoolgirl—virtuous and boring.

As soon as he could, Anush raced out of Sea Face Terraces in his Benz, sucking hard on a Marlboro. He put a Fugees CD in and turned the volume up so he could feel the thud of the bass in his chest. The idea of spending the rest of his life with Jyoti

Patik made him nauseous, not to mention that bitch of a mother, who veiled everything with a congenial decorum but was silently judging every fucking thing in sight. Bullshit sandwich. The worst thing was the entire time with them he'd lied and pretended to be amused, interested. It galled him to have to play that game. With Nasreen, he didn't have to be anything other than himself.

But why hadn't she returned any of his calls over the past few days? The last time he'd spoken to her, she said she was busy writing her first feature article for the *Times* and that she wouldn't be able to go out for a while. Every time he called her mobile after that she didn't pick up, and whenever he tried her home number the servants picked up to say Nasreen wasn't home. They hadn't seen each other since that night at Juhu Beach a week ago. He hadn't told her about the tirade the old man had unleashed on him after spotting the two of them in the paper, how the shop was being sold, and how he'd just had to endure a meeting with the Patik family to marry their nerdy daughter.

Anush sped along Marine Drive while taking a healthy swig of whisky despite knowing the moustached police officer might catch him again. This time Anush wouldn't get away so easily as there was no American cash to bribe him with. And yet Anush kept accelerating down the last stretch of Marine Drive and stopped at the paan walla stand near the Air India building, the one Nasreen had taken him to. He ordered two paans and raced towards Nasreen's building. Once there, he beeped his horn for the night watchman to let him in, but the watchman said, "Sorry, sahib, new policy. Only building residents can park in the compound."

Anush had parked his car there plenty of times in the past month. "Come on, there's lots of parking space."

"Sorry, sahib. I get the boot if I don't follow orders. I have a wife and three daughters to think about back in my village."

Anush had never been to the remote villages his workers talked about. The night watchman seemed too young to have three children, let alone be married. But then again, Reza from the shop had a wife and a daughter.

What would become of Reza? He'd been an excellent assistant to Anush. The old man had just let all the shop employees go, but Anush had kept Reza, paying him from his own pocket. What would happen to him once Anush went to work at Sharma Shipping? Maybe he could convince the old man to hire Reza as an assistant in the office. But what would Reza do there? Anush wasn't even sure if Reza could read or write much. Anush's stomach turned at the thought of having to work at Sharma Shipping and so he did what he'd done all week, which was avoid thinking of it. But he grew anxious now, knowing that he wouldn't be able to sidestep it forever. He needed to see Nasreen. She would help calm him. She would make him make sense of it, of what to do next.

Parked on the street, Anush could see that all the lights in Nasreen's flat were on. Maybe her parents had returned from their vacation in Alibag. He hadn't met them yet. Would they think it strange Anush turning up out of the blue? But he had to see her. Besides, she'd been working so hard over the past week, she'd welcome an interruption.

Earlier that evening at the dining table with the Patiks, Anush couldn't stop thinking of Nasreen, how making love to her was so blissful, how her neck smelled slightly of sweat and orange blossom from her perfume, how being inside of her felt like being home.

Jyoti Patik was nice enough, and maybe even somewhat pretty, in the most boring kind of way, but she was bland. Nasreen was a sensual woman. Apples and oranges. He wondered if he should tell Nasreen about his father forcing him to meet Jyoti Patik. Nasreen might be angry at him for even considering the meeting, but perhaps Nasreen's jealousy would finally spur her to commit to their relationship. Perhaps they could take off and elope somewhere. Or was that absurd? They'd never talked about anything like that. But they'd discussed a trip to Goa. A nice beach resort with a swim-up bar. No one ever planned on eloping. But maybe Goa would be perfect. And once they were officially married, his father would eventually have to capitulate. Nasreen was so charming, so intelligent, so driven, so ambitious. So like the daughter he never had. So like the son he wished he did.

With the paans in hand, Anush knocked on her door. He knew not to ring the doorbell. Only strangers did that, which upset Daisy, the senile Irish terrier who bit strangers. He could hear muffled sounds of people talking, laughing inside. He knocked louder on the wooden door, his knuckles having to squeeze through the outer steel grate that was just a couple of inches away from the inner door. Ever since the Hindu-Muslim riots of '93, in which people had been dragged from their homes and beaten, burned, even killed, many homes had added this level of enclosure for protection against vigilante justice.

From the muffled sounds of conversation and laughs inside, it sounded like a large dinner party. Maybe Nasreen was working in her room while her parents entertained guests. What would he say to them? His heart began to race. But no, there was no reason to get nervous. He would say he was Nasreen's friend who was stopping by to say hello, and the paans were a present.

He heard high heels clacking down the hall towards the door. Nasreen opened it, looking stunning in an evening dress. While keeping the outer steel enclosure shut, she closed the wooden door behind her as much as she could, keeping Anush from seeing inside. She whispered, "Anush—what are you doing here?"

"I thought you might want a paan," he said, trying to figure out why she was keeping the door shut behind her.

"Anush, not now," she whispered, unable to meet his eyes. "I'll call you tomorrow."

He'd never seen Nasreen nervous before. Even when she was uncertain, she was adept at hiding it. Something was wrong. Now he saw the diamond ring on Nasreen's finger. His heart began to pound.

"How's your feature for the *Times* going?" he asked.

At that point Daisy came to the door and pushed her nose out to see who it was. Anush called to her affectionately and stuck his hand out for her to sniff. As he reached to scratch behind her ear, she bit him.

The pain stung much more than he thought it would and he instantly recoiled. Nasreen berated Daisy, who was now barking loudly.

A man came to the door and shouted at Daisy with a booming voice, making Daisy scurry inside the flat. He opened the door and asked Nasreen, "What the bloody hell is going on?"

She turned to Anush and then quickly back to him, "It's a friend of Taran's. He just came because he thought Taran was here tonight."

The tall, broad-shouldered man said, "Well, let him in," and opened the steel grate for Anush. "Sorry, yaar. That dog is a total lunatic. I don't know why she hasn't been put down. I go to New York for a bit and the dog goes even more mad."

And just then as Anush got a good look at him, at the two of them standing together, he realized he'd seen the man before. At the club that first night when he met Nasreen. It was the man she'd been dancing with. He noticed the familiarity between Nasreen and this tall man now, how close he stood to her.

"Come in, yaar, come in. I'm Zafar. Is your hand OK?" he said, guiding Anush to a chair near the door. He ordered one of the servants to bring Anush some water.

As Anush sat, everything fell into place at lightning speed: how Nasreen hadn't returned any of his calls recently, how the night watchman suddenly refused to let him park on building grounds. It all seemed to make sense now, the night at Kulshand Malwani's party when Kulshand had playfully teased Anush for being Nasreen's boy toy. At the time Anush had thought nothing of it, but that's what Anush was to Nasreen, her boy toy. That's why Kulshand had kissed Anush on the lips that night, not just because he was drunk and horny but because he thought of Anush as some sort of gigolo. And all those evenings with Nasreen and Ameena and Taran, even though he couldn't keep up with their discussions about politics and philosophers, he'd fooled himself into believing that they genuinely enjoyed his company when they were most likely just putting up with him for Nasreen's sake, while Nasreen had fun with her boy toy.

People inside were beckoning Nasreen and Zafar back to the table. Someone said, "To the newly engaged couple!" and others echoed with merriment, "To the newly engaged couple!"

Zafar took the bag of paans from Anush's hand and said, "Thanks, yaar. I haven't had a *pukka* paan in ages. The *desis* in New Jersey make them, but it's rubbish," and went back into the flat.

Nasreen looked at Anush and whispered, "I'm so sorry—I didn't know. I should have told you about Zafar. We've been off and on for a long while." She sighed. "It's complicated. I'm sorry."

Anush felt as though he was drowning, with a slab of cement strapped to his chest.

Things that he hadn't paid attention to earlier became illuminated all of a sudden. He realized when they'd made love and she stood on the balcony, smoking, that she wasn't daydreaming of a life together with Anush as he'd done while pretending to be asleep on her bed, eyeing her beautiful figure in the moonlight. She was most likely thinking of Zafar. Any doubts he had about not being as smart as Nasreen and her friends, about not being able to quip as quickly as them, always feeling a little bit of an outsider, were all legitimate. He should've trusted his instincts. That night at the beach in the Benz, when it'd been Nasreen's turn to talk about the future, Anush could see now that she'd become taciturn and looked out her window not because she was thinking of him but because she was thinking of Zafar.

Anush could see she was somewhat remorseful yet determined not to let it show. She couldn't bring herself to look at him when she began to close the door.

He blurted out, "I never told you about my destiny." He knew it sounded ludicrous but continued. "I—I don't know how to explain it to you—"

"There's nothing to explain, Anush. I'm sorry, I really am.

I should've been more honest with you. I didn't know he was going to ask me. I really did have a great time with you. I'm sorry."

He wanted to say he loved her, that they belonged together, that without her he was nothing, that the past few weeks with her had been paradise, that with her he felt like a new person, with her he was capable of living his destiny.

"Zafar and I have been together a long time. I just needed some space from him. He was supposed to be gone for six months. We got engaged yesterday."

What really hurt was the fact that she wasn't the type of girl who was forced into anything. If she'd wanted to say no to Zafar, she easily could have.

"We're moving to New York, where Zafar works," Nasreen said. "I'm so sorry. I hope we can be friends. Please go to the doctor first thing tomorrow. I'm not sure if Daisy's had all her shots."

Anush got into his car and drove away while draining the quarter bottle of whisky from the glove compartment. A cover of the Bob Marley and the Wailers' "No Woman, No Cry" by the Fugees played on the car stereo. On Marine Drive a large wave broke over the breakwater. It must have been high tide as it sprayed water into the air, scattering large drops across the road. Some hit the Benz and sounded like little pebbles when they landed on the roof of the car. A street dog barked up the road, its sharp white teeth shining in the headlights. Without thinking about it, Anush steered the car towards the mutt. The Benz lurched onto the pavement and accelerated towards the barking dog who tried to dodge out of the way, but Anush hit it before smashing into the cobblestone wall.

- 42 -
JYOTI
1998

A FEW DAYS AFTER THE FIRST meeting, Jyoti met Kiran and Chaya for coffee.

They had many questions. "Is he tall? Handsome? Fair?"

"Mmm, a bit short. Not ugly. Huge penthouse with an ocean view."

"Wow." "Oh my god."

Jyoti said, "But I don't think there was any spark between us."

"How can there be the first time with parents and all sitting around?" said Kiran.

"As Vinay and I got to know each other, the sparks flew," Chaya, six months pregnant, said.

Although conventionally handsome, Anush wasn't really

her cup of tea. Jyoti wasn't taken with the designer watch, the perfectly sculpted hair, the expensive cologne—Anush was like every well-to-do young man in the city. He likely also had a brand-new cellphone, drank expensive whisky, and smoked Marlboro cigarettes exclusively. Indian men were so predictable.

Jyoti said, "I don't know. Is it just me or has Bombay changed?"

Kiran said, "Definitely changed, yaar."

Chaya said, "Changed, for sure. Have you noticed what the price of vegetables is these days?"

"Forget vegetables, look at real estate values," Kiran said.

"Stop talking real estate, freal estate. You sound like my husband," Chaya said.

"Have you played tennis on the new lawn at the Willingdon Club? Their papaya martini is to die for," Kiran said.

"No, but we were there the other night and so was that VJ from MTV, or is it channel V?" said Chaya and then whispered, "So handsome."

Jyoti felt a pang for London. She missed conversations and debates about things like whether Daft Punk was influenced by the Beach Boys or whether abstract videos of mundane things were worthy of winning the Turner visual arts prize (Gavin thought they were, but Jyoti didn't). She missed Gavin. As soon as his name came to mind, she willed herself to stop thinking of him, but it was impossible. His cute face, his tousled, sandy hair, his striking green eyes, the smell of Drum tobacco and Mountain Moss Speed Stick.

Snapping herself to reality, Jyoti said to Kiran and Chaya, "Well, we're going on a date tomorrow. But he's the one who had the accident on Marine Drive last week. With the dog."

"What?" "I didn't hear of it."

Didn't they read any of the newspapers at the various clubs they drank cocktails at? Or maybe they did and were exemplary liars, Jyoti couldn't tell. She'd read all the articles: BENZ DRIVER KILLS DOG. SON SLAUGHTERS STRAY PUP. WEALTHY BOY MURDERS MUTT. Animal rights groups were outraged. There was speculation that the driver was drunk, but no proof. Calls for justice abated, and the charges, along with the accused, were quickly forgotten, replaced by racier gossip, like the Lewinsky affair going to trial later that year.

"It's no big deal," Kiran said. "So maybe he had a couple of drinks. As long as it's not a recurring thing."

"I'm sure he's learned his lesson," Chaya said.

"No one is perfect," Kiran said.

"It's not like in the movies. You're not going to meet this perfect man and fall in love right away," Chaya said.

But I did in London, Jyoti nearly said.

"It takes time. Love doesn't magically happen right away. Just make sure he's fair to you," Kiran said.

"And not a liar," Chaya said, "about the important stuff."

"What do you mean?" Jyoti said.

Chaya explained, "For example, I know Vinay isn't really a vegetarian—when he's out for dinner with his friends or on business, he eats meat. I don't really care. His parents and grandparents do. I just want him to be honest with me about things that are important to me."

"Yeah," Kiran said, "like not going to those dancing bars some men do nowadays and have affairs with those dancing girls."

Chaya laughed, touching Jyoti's arm, and said, "Don't worry, we'll help you steer your way through this."

Jyoti resented her friends' condescension, their laughter, their assumptions about her being a naive virgin. She wanted to tell them about Gavin. How he was handsome, sensitive, funny, intelligent. How he made her appreciate paintings and architecture and history in a way she never imagined. How he made love to her in the morning and then brought her breakfast in bed. Did their husbands do that?

"I don't know if I can do this," said Jyoti.

"Why not?" "What have you got to lose?"

While Jyoti got ready for the date, her mother came into her room with a necklace and said, "Here, wear this." It was one of the more sober and elegant pieces from the family collection of jewels. As a young girl, Jyoti had looked forward to wearing the extravagant jewelry, but now when her mother placed the gold and diamond lavalliere around her neck it felt ostentatious. Her mother clasped it together and whispered, "I've combed the entire city and this is the best family available."

Her mother's medical bill from the hospital stay in London was costly and over the past few months she'd dropped hints to Jyoti of their financial difficulties. Before Jyoti left the house, her mother kissed her on the forehead and said, "All the best." It was what she always said to Jyoti before a big exam.

Her father said, "What's the rush? Sure the Sharmas are wealthy but Jyoti could have any boy in Bombay she wants."

Her mother snapped, "With Rahul's expenses at Stanford, my hospital bills, and your brilliant investments—" Taking a breath, she regained her composure and shot Jyoti a stealthy look that said if Anush Sharma was the least bit interested then Jyoti should consider herself lucky and close the deal as quickly as possible. If Anush was not a gentleman, or if she found him to be unpleasant in any way, she could say so and be relieved of pursuing the match, but in order for that to happen Jyoti would need proof of him being despicable. He would have to do something as horrible as she had. Good luck. There wasn't anyone she knew who'd gotten pregnant out of wedlock and then aborted their half-breed baby. Her duty to her parents now was to marry herself into a suitable family that would provide for her and her children without relying on her parents' dwindling savings. She also understood from her mother's slightly raised eyebrows whenever she talked about Anush Sharma that Jyoti didn't have many options, that Jyoti should consider herself lucky a boy like Anush Sharma was interested, and if someone were to find out about her incident in London, forget Anush Sharma—Jyoti would be left to marry some boy from in a petty town in Gujarat where she'd spend the rest of her life.

"What about the car accident?" Jyoti's father had asked a few days ago. "How do we know Anush's a good boy?"

Her mother had said, "We don't know all the details. Are you going to trust what the tabloids say? Besides, the police are so corrupt. They know the Sharmas have money. They'll say anything to milk more bribes. Varoon Sharma strikes me as a man of principle. He probably didn't pay them an exorbitant bribe and so now they make up these accusations of the liquor and the dog . . ."

JYOTI AND ANUSH sat in the back seat while the Patik family's driver drove. When they rounded Kemps Corner and headed towards Marine Drive, Anush, with a sling around his arm, said, "Let's take the inside road. Too much traffic on Marine Drive."

Jyoti said, "Traffic should be fine this time in the evening," but then suddenly remembered Marine Drive was where Anush's accident had happened, leaving him with a fractured collarbone. As curious as Jyoti was, she decided not to pry and said, "Oh no, you're right. The inside road is much faster." Jyoti hated lying and imagined people could see the jugular vein in her neck flutter ever so slightly whenever she lied, its pace quickening along with her heartbeat.

The driver veered them towards Opera House, then towards Regal Cinema, where the immensely popular American film *Titanic* was playing. Eager for the date to go well, Jyoti's mother had managed to get two good seats on the black market for triple price.

The cinema was packed. As the movie began, it struck Jyoti that Leonardo DiCaprio looked a lot like Gavin. She barely even paid attention to the story for the first half-hour because she was overwhelmed with memories of Gavin—memories she'd tried to dislodge over the past few months. Like the times he'd taken her to art house films at the Prince Charles Cinema in Leicester Square. She hadn't liked them all. Some were a bit pretentious, drab, but some were quirky, romantic.

During the intermission, Anush went outside for a cigarette. Jyoti couldn't help but think of Gavin and the smell of his hand-rolled cigarettes. If she and Anush were to marry, Jyoti wondered if Anush would ever brush his teeth after smoking, the way Gavin did, before making love to her. The thought of making love to Anush didn't excite her at all.

By the end of the movie, Jyoti couldn't help but be moved and was furtively wiping her tears away in the dark theatre. She was annoyed with herself for being so manipulated by a corny film, whose ending everybody knew, and she made sure by the time the lights came up that she'd dried her eyes. There was something too vulnerable and idiotic about crying at a sentimental movie on your first date.

On their way home, Anush asked, "Do you like paan?"

"I can't remember the last time I had it."

"I know the best paan walla in the city," Anush said, directing the driver.

They stepped outside and walked down to the south end of Marine Drive. The humid sea breeze felt lovely. Jyoti smiled nervously as she attempted to eat her paan whole as Anush did, trying not to make a mess of it, but bits of maroon juice let loose and came out from one side of her mouth, making her blush with embarrassment. Anush offered her a hanky that she quickly used. They tried not to laugh with their mouths full of paan, which only made Jyoti swallow a large chunk of hers. She'd only ever had *meetha* paans before, which she found cloyingly sweet with their dried cherry and fruit preserves, but this was a real paan with betel nut. She couldn't believe the tiny bursts of spices in her mouth. One by one she could taste them all as she chewed: cardamom, anise, coconut, lime, rose, jasmine, date, cinnamon, fennel, a hint of saffron.

They both smiled nervously as they chewed. She couldn't help but compare him to Gavin. Anush was a bit shorter, his hair was preened nicely, but he was vain, conventionally handsome, and of course had much more money. No, she would not compare the two. Maybe Kiran and Chaya were right—if Anush was courteous and honest, maybe that was enough to start with.

As waves broke over the breakwater she could feel light

ocean spray on her face. It relaxed her, and Bombay felt like Bombay again for the first time.

Anush said, "I crashed my car a little while ago down there. I didn't want to be reminded of that night; that's why I asked your driver to go another way earlier this evening."

"Oh, is that how you hurt your shoulder?" she said, pretending not to have heard of the accident.

"Yeah. A dog was accidentally killed," he said.

"Oh, I'm so sorry."

"Me too. But I'm over it. So, what did you think of the movie?"

"Uh, it was OK," Jyoti said.

"Yeah," he said. "Overrated. Mostly boring except near the end when the ship broke apart. The special effects were amazing."

She lied and agreed. "Yes, exactly."

Anush asked, "Do you like the Fugees?"

Jyoti lied again. "Yeah. Do you like Radiohead?"

Anush said, "Not really. It's their alternative image that people are into. Their music is mostly just noise."

"Yeah, I kind of liked them for a while. But maybe they're just being weird for the sake of being weird," she said. Lying wasn't so difficult. Why had she made it out to be such a big deal before?

"Exactly. My coconut cousin from Canada is really into that shit. Excuse my language."

"I don't mind." It bothered Jyoti that Anush had to apologize for swearing. It was an antiquated and sexist notion that women were too delicate to handle strong language, but one that all Indian men held. And she was annoyed at him for talking that way about Radiohead, Gavin's favourite band.

But her mother's words echoed in her head. *With Rahul's expenses at Stanford, your father's investments . . . Anush Sharma is a handsome boy. You'll have a large home to yourself with an ocean view. No mother-in-law, no grandmother-in-law, no grandfather-in-law . . .*

Jyoti thought about how she and Gavin had talked about going to Glastonbury last summer. She wondered if Gavin had gone with another girl to stand in a farmer's field to see Radiohead play. She wondered if they'd slept together in a tent under the stars like the two of them had talked about. Jyoti had been so excited to camp—she'd never done it before.

Now, as she stood next to Anush, Jyoti decided to throw out her Radiohead CD when she returned home.

"Well, would you like to go out again?" Anush asked.

"Sure."

- 43 -
ANUSH
1998

THE FIRST THING ANUSH DID after arriving home from the *Titanic* date with Jyoti was pour himself a tall glass of whisky, gulp it down, and then another.

After standing for a while at the large bay window in his room looking at the Arabian Sea, Anush wandered around the dark flat and found himself in the drawing room, staring at the portrait of his mother. He'd never allowed himself to look at the painting for this long. Even though it was dark, he knew the painting well as it'd been hanging in the drawing room for over a decade, and so his mind's eye filled in the bits that were too difficult to make out. He stood for a long time, taking in her kind brown eyes, her fair, smooth skin, her perfectly sized nose and chin. He stood in the dark as random memories of her permeated him: her striding from her bedroom to answer the door while drying her long wet hair with a towel, holding her hand and hearing her bangles jingle as they crossed the street to get ice cream, her slicing vegetables in the kitchen on a hot day, stopping frequently to wipe her forehead with the end of her plain cotton sari, how she made her everyday saris seem elegant with her stride, her graceful gait, her thin arms. At formal events she wore fancier saris with jewelry that made her smile sparkle. He remembered hearing her laughter at dinner parties they hosted, when he was supposed to be asleep in his room. Her mellifluous voice playfully arguing with someone. Her singing to him quietly in his bed at night:

Kabhi kabhi, mere dil mein, khayaal aata hai . . .
Sometimes, in my heart a feeling emanates
As though you've been created just for me;
Before this, you existed among the stars somewhere,
And now, you've been called down to earth only
for me.

It had been nearly fifteen years since her death. He'd tried to not think about her so many times while at boarding school that he'd actually become reasonably good at it. But at times, fragments of her, or memories of her, would come racing into his consciousness from afar—sometimes, it seemed, at breakneck speed from the farthest reaches of the universe; other times, imperceptibly, like daybreak spreading across the sky, leaving him uncertain of their authenticity. He wondered if his memories had begun to take on a verisimilitude, an appearance of the real thing, a close copy, leaving him feeling uncertain, lost at sea.

He would've liked to have gone for a drive but the Benz was totalled. If he married Jyoti, the old man would buy him a better car.

Anush went back to his room for another whisky and turned on the TV. On Discovery an astrophysicist was talking about the universe, intercut with computer-generated visuals: "Who are we? How did we get here? What are we made from? The stars can reveal all. All stars have the same destiny. All matter in the universe came from stars. Atoms are the building blocks of life and all atoms come from stars. Stars were born in nebulas— nurseries in space where new stars burst into life. All matter in the universe comes from these stars. Our own sun's destiny is the same as every other star that has ever existed and will ever exist. One day, it will run out of hydrogen and helium, become unable to produce nuclear fusion, and expand to hundreds of times its size. This is the red giant phase where its surface will burn hot while its core cools, and at its core, where all the ingredients of life are—atoms of hydrogen, oxygen, and so on—the star will battle against gravity, in a fight of futility, protons and neutrons will struggle, atoms will be formed, they will desperately try not to collapse in on themselves but eventually they will succumb to their fate. And as the core collapses, hydrogen and helium and carbon and oxygen and magnesium and iron and other elements that make up all life will be created, and then with a large bang, the star will burst, distributing these elements through space. This is the destiny of all stars. It has happened billions of times and will continue to happen countless more."

Anush turned off the TV. The house was quiet. Chottu

and the other servants were sleeping in the garage downstairs because the ceiling fan in the servants' quarters was broken. Anush found himself pacing the dark flat. There was something strangely unsettling about all the stars collapsing in on themselves, buckling to the laws of the universe, succumbing to their fate. Is that what we all had to do in the end? Yield? Capitulate? Cave in?

The shop had just been sold for well below asking price and the paperwork was with lawyers. Any contracts Anush had with hotels to provide furniture would be winding down. What would happen to Reza and his family? Would they be thrown out onto the streets? The old man had no idea anyone was even living in the flat above the shop. Anush could see his future in fast forward: working at Sharma Shipping, drawing a decent salary, never making furniture again, being married to Jyoti Patik, and living out a mediocre life. The alternative was unthinkable—to be cut off financially. Jyoti was pleasant, intelligent, and sort of pretty, in a regular, boring kind of way. They were cordial to each other and Anush could see the two of them being a couple. Going out for dinners, entertaining friends, having children, taking family vacations, growing old, eventually submitting to life's tedious monotony. The children would supply some joy, but would the happiness last? Would he be able to shake that sense of having lost the chance to really live? The chance to be with someone special? The chance to be someone special? He'd have to recalibrate, convince everyone he was content, including himself. It wouldn't be easy. Being with Jyoti wasn't even comparable to what he felt like being with Nasreen. But then again, Nasreen didn't feel the same about him. Thinking of her and Zafar gutted him. After guzzling another glass of whisky, Anush found himself knocking at his father's bedroom door. The old man was most likely in a deep sleep after his usual dose of Blue Label Reserve and Calmpose pills. Anush banged on the door with his fists and feet. He was shaking and had no idea what he was going to say or do but something in him had come unhinged.

Finally the door opened. Standing bleary-eyed in his rumpled white kurta, the old man was still half asleep. "What? What is it?"

"I'm not marrying Jyoti Patik, and I'm not going to work with you," Anush blurted out and barged into the room. He hadn't been in there in years. It felt foreign, but also eerily familiar. When his mother had been alive, he often ran in there to jump on the king-sized bed and stick his head under the air conditioner. The decor in the room hadn't changed much. The bed was still the same, as were the almirahs. Everything was in the same spot as it had always been, there were just fewer things: his mother's makeup was no longer on the dresser; her bedside table, usually strewn with bangles and earrings and creams, was now bare.

The old man scratched his head and yawned. Anush continued to the end of the room, towards the balcony. The old man, baffled, said, "Are you drunk?"

"I'm not going to marry Jyoti Patik and I'm not working with you," he said once more. It felt liberating saying the words out loud again. Maybe the more he said it, the easier it would come true. He should've done this a long time ago. He wasn't a puppet. He could decide for himself who he was going to marry and where he'd work for a living. It was time he stood up for himself.

The old man shuffled towards his almirah, from which he took out a bottle of whisky, poured a glass, and drank it as though he were dying of thirst before wiping his mouth with a sleeve to say, "Listen to me. You will marry Jyoti Patik and stop fooling around with your silly daydreams."

Anush shook his head. "No. And I won't come to work with you. I want the shop. I don't need an inheritance from you, just the shop."

"You ungrateful bastard!" The old man's voice cracked, his pride injured. "Do you have any idea how hard it was for me to convince the police commissioner not to press charges against you when you killed that dog and crashed the car? It was just like when you were in college—I had to pay your professors to pass you."

"Maybe you should've let them fail me."

"And then what would you've done? And what the hell will you do with the shop? Make some strange chairs and fuck Muslim sluts there?"

"You take that back!"

"I will take nothing back!" the old man said, his nostrils flaring.

There was an altogether different look in the old man's eyes. Anush wondered how drunk or high on Calmpose he was, if he'd even remember all this the next morning.

The old man swayed while he waited for a reply, but Anush couldn't think of what to say. The old man continued, "Sometimes I can't believe you're my son."

"I wish I wasn't," Anush said and lunged at the old man, clutching his throat. The old man dropped his glass and the two of them were face to face, grabbing at each other's throats. As much as Anush wanted to punch, stab, and kick his father, he also wanted the same wrath on himself—he wanted to be punched, kicked, and beaten, to be obliterated and disappear into nothing, to cease to exist. Anush could see the broken blood vessels in his father's eyes and smell the whisky on his breath, which for some reason reminded him of the sweet-smelling orchids and jacarandas he'd laid on his mother's funeral pyre. The two of them fumbled onto the balcony, awkwardly jostling back and forth. They were near the balcony railing when it occurred to Anush that this was his opportunity to get rid of the old man. All the other windows were dark. No one would know. But because of Anush's broken collar bone, the old man was able to overpower his son and drove him into the balcony railing. Anush's back hit the railing with a dull thump and every bit of balance and stability he lost was taken up by the old man, and Anush realized if the old man didn't relent they'd both end up toppling over the balcony and plummet nine floors to their deaths. Anush tried to speak but the old man was choking him, and he had a look on his face Anush had never seen, a demented, tortured glaze.

What if this was the end? What if the two of them died just like their mad grandfather? There was no way to survive the fall. Would he die and be burned on a pile of wood? Who would burn him? Would his soul cease to exist while his body converted into hydrogen atoms in the atmosphere? Or would he join his mother up there in the sky somewhere? Or would he be reborn in some other part of the world with no knowledge of this life? Or would he defy gravity on his way down like the eagles? Would he suddenly grow wings and unfurl them at the last split second? If he truly had an extraordinary destiny, something would save him.

Nasreen came to him, her perfect face, her full lips, her big brown eyes that he could swim in for an eternity. But of course she didn't feel the same about him, she'd lied to him, made a cuckold of him, and was moving to New York with Zafar. The hollow pit in his stomach would never be filled. Maybe it was better to be burned on a pile of wood than to live with the humiliation of unrequited love.

But then there was his destiny. He'd not even come close to doing anything extraordinary. How could he quit now? Maybe surrendering to his father and being thrown off the balcony would be the one extraordinary thing he'd do. Yield. Capitulate. Cave in.

The thought of stars dying, losing their light, turning black and collapsing, then exploding with a blinding flash of light inspired him. Anush stopped struggling and went limp. He rolled his eyes as though he were losing consciousness. The old man relented and that's when Anush suddenly sprang back to life and mustered a knee into the old man's groin. In one deft move, Anush switched places with the old man and now had him over the balcony railing.

With his hands around his father's neck, Anush was shaking and crying. Through the tears streaming down his face, Anush managed to say the thing that he'd kept in his heart for so long. "I wish it was you who'd died all those years ago instead of her."

The old man gasped for air and Anush loosened his grip just enough to let him speak. There was a wild look in the old man's eyes. He seemed to smirk while sputtering, "I guess this is only fair. Like father, like son. Come on, do it! For once in your life, do something extraordinary!"

Anush tightened his grip on the old man as a cool waft of sea breeze blew in, and with it a small epiphany: it was the old man who'd pushed his own father over the balcony all those years ago. It made sense. The old man's aversion to the furniture shop. Maybe he blamed his father for what happened to his mother all those years ago when she was lost during Partition. Maybe Anush and his old man weren't that different. Like father, like son.

With one heave Anush could easily push his father over the railing now. He realized it would be a sort of justice for his grandfather. No one would know. Anush would inherit everything. Buy back the furniture shop. Buy a hundred furniture shops. He wouldn't have to answer to anyone. He wouldn't feel like a stranger in his own home. Everyone knew the old man enjoyed his whisky. And there were the Calmpose pills. There'd be enough empty containers of those around to convince the police if foul play was suspected. Like father, like son, everyone would assume. The old man was depressed, Anush would say, addicted to the pills. He must have jumped. It would be the extraordinary thing Anush was destined to do. Like father, like son.

- 44 -
ANUSH
1998

"CONGRATS," PARRY SAID, PUMPING ANUSH'S hand and slapping him on the back. "Kuttay, Kaminay!"

The wedding reception was well underway at the Taj Hotel ballroom where hundreds of guests were mingling among dozens of wait staff serving hors d'oeuvres and drinks. The majority of the guests were business associates and friends of the old man. The rest were friends and family of the Patiks. Anush had a few friends in attendance, mostly acquaintances. Parry had just returned from his travels and was standing by Anush's side now in the receiving line while Jyoti's parents and the old man mingled among the crowd.

Before Anush could introduce Jyoti to Parry, Parry did it

himself. "You're more beautiful than I remember," he said, shaking her hand.

Anush was as perplexed as Jyoti, until Anush realized Parry had Jyoti mixed up with Nasreen. Parry's first and only night in town was the night they'd gone to the nightclub, the first time Anush had met Nasreen.

"No, uh, my cousin Parry's a little confused. He's been travelling for four months—the heat's obviously baked his brain," Anush said.

Parry corrected Anush. "It's Paresh. And yes, I've been travelling quite a bit, just got off the train this morning."

Anush was glad Paresh was using his Indian name but still wondered if he was a confused coconut. Paresh kept talking. "Goa, Kerala, Rajasthan, Dharamsala, Varnasi, Nepal—it was incredible. Soul nourishing. I never once travelled first class. It's amazing—so many people with so few things, and yet they seem so content. It really makes you think." He went on at length, forgetting to ask Jyoti about herself.

Anush tried not to let Paresh's narcissism irk him too much. He'd be flying back to Canada soon and no matter how many times he travelled third class or what he changed his name to, he didn't live here. He'd be back in Canada skating on a frozen lake and India would always be a fondly remembered vacation. He'd frame exotic photos of his travels on his walls of his dorm room, speak of his time in India as soul nourishing, life changing. Bullshit sandwich. Countless people had come and gone and done the same, seeking some sort of enlightenment, feeling blessed to be able to see that there was beauty in poverty, that it was somehow noble to have so little, but that was so reductive, patronizing, lacking nuance and complexity. The truth was more elusive. Of course the people in the slums and villages were resilient, ingenious, but there was little nobility or grace in having to endure hardship and suffering. Anush had accompanied Reza to his village not long ago to help his family move to Bombay, to the flat above the shop. The shame of treating Reza any differently in the past still clung to Anush, and he knew no amount of money would be able to forgive his previous conceit. But for Reza's whole family to not live in squalor, the chance for his daughter to go to a good school, was something real, a change that Anush was happy to be able to provide.

Now at the reception, Jyoti turned her attention away from Paresh to receive guests. Anush was thankful she was as kind and patient as she was, but she kept a part of herself hidden. Maybe he did too. It would get easier as they got to know each other. At least that's what everyone kept saying.

As Paresh chased after a waiter who was walking around with a tray of champagne, Anush rolled his eyes at Jyoti, apologizing for Paresh. Jyoti smiled and squeezed his hand while whispering, "It's OK. I have some annoying cousins too."

The two of them had been standing for nearly two hours and so far had only received half the guests. At this rate, it would be an eternity till Anush was able to have a drink as it was disrespectful of the bride or groom to be drinking alcohol in front of their elders—it being a Gujarati marriage reception. Trust the Gujus to take the fun out of everything. Maybe he'd nip to the toilet and get Paresh to sneak him a quick whisky.

While guests congratulated them and shook hands, he wondered what Jyoti was thinking. It was difficult to see her whole face with the jewelry and Gujarati-style sari that draped her head. Over the past couple of months they'd been on a number of dates, and each had gone slightly better than the last. There were no sparks or fireworks. In fact, they'd only kissed once. It was barely a peck. No passion, no yearning, no tongue, but they got along well enough. They even talked about it, admitting how strange it felt to be considering marrying the other. Jyoti had said, "My friends confessed that getting along is what's required at first. Maybe the rest will evolve naturally?"

Anush had admitted, "Yeah, I hear that too. And arranged marriages have a much better track record than Western marriages, half of which end in divorce."

Even though that first kiss was more like a handshake, it was a good start. It felt like an honest beginning. Something he had never had with Nasreen.

In between guests now, Anush leaned towards Jyoti and whispered, "Do your cheeks hurt from smiling as much as mine?"

"Absolutely. And I don't even know most of these people."

Mrs. Patik arrived with a couple of drinks, a pineapple juice for Jyoti and a Coke for Anush. Anush was so parched he took a large gulp only to find his glass half full of whisky. Mrs. Patik shot him a stealthy wink before she disappeared back into the crowd.

Maybe the old lady wasn't as uptight as she appeared. Breathing a little easier, Anush caught a glimpse of the old man celebrating among a crowd of his friends with the colonel and some BJP men. They were so boisterous that they seemed more like a group of college chums. The old man was smiling wide and embracing people with an enthusiasm Anush had never seen.

He wondered how much of their fight on the balcony the old man remembered. It was difficult to tell. They would never speak of it—that was certain. The old man had been in such a haze that night when Anush pulled him up over the railing and put him back into his bed that he fell asleep almost immediately and was snoring by the time Anush left his bedroom.

The following morning, for the first time in years, Anush had sat down for breakfast with his old man. He agreed to marry Jyoti but insisted on keeping the furniture shop. The old man conceded. It was the first time Anush had stood up to him and won. Anush got to keep the shop and in return, he had to marry Jyoti, for which he received a hefty monthly stipend from Sharma Shipping. It kept Reza employed as his assistant and Reza's family continued to live above the shop.

Even though that night now seemed as unreal as a strange dream, Anush kept wondering what would've happened if he hadn't been able to knee his father in the groin to get the upper hand. Would the old man have thrown him over? Like he did his own father? Is that what had really happened? Isn't that what he'd suggested?

Anush smiled and shook hands now with guests while keeping an eye on the old man across the room, who was happier than he'd been in years. More guests gave their felicitations to the new bride and groom, telling them they made a perfect couple. Anush wondered what sex with Jyoti would be like. As good as it was with Nasreen? He wondered when the comparisons would stop. Even though he'd done his best to forget about Nasreen she still hijacked his thoughts now and then.

Clusters of people in the ballroom broke out cheering, leaving Anush and Jyoti perplexed. The old man stood up on a chair, clinked his glass with a fork until the crowd shushed itself silent. It was entirely inappropriate behaviour for someone to be standing on a chair in the Taj ballroom, and some of the older guests gasped at the old man's audacity. Anush's heart skipped a beat. He had no idea what the old man would say or do.

"Ladies and gentlemen, my son's kundali says that he will have an extraordinary destiny and I think it's being realized today as he begins his life with the equally exceptional Jyoti Patik! Let's all raise a glass to their future. And to our country!"

As the entire room raised their glasses, Anush was puzzled by the remark about the country. Jyoti smiled at him in a way that suggested a wedding reception wasn't complete without a proud, drunken groom's father.

Everyone in the room soon resumed chatting while Anush drained his drink.

Paresh returned, all of a sudden nervous, and said to Anush, "Glad I'm leaving the country soon. Did you hear?"

"What?"

"Everyone's talking about it—India just tested its first nuke!"

- 45 -
JYOTI
1998

IT DIDN'T TAKE LONG FOR Jyoti to learn that the Sharmas were a taciturn family who rarely ate meals together. Varoon Sharma, or Papa, as Jyoti called him now, was an early riser long gone to his office by the time Jyoti or Anush were even awake. Varoon took his breakfast at the dining table at six thirty, then Jyoti would eat at seven thirty, followed by Anush, who would sleep until eight or nine o'clock. Dinner was similarly conducted. Jyoti tried to dine with Varoon a few times but he ate dinner much too early and Anush came home so late. It was as though there were a covert agreement between father and son not to get in each other's way, which Jyoti found strange at first but quickly grew accustomed to and became a part of.

The three of them only dined together when company was over, which was rare.

She was relieved her father-in-law wasn't old-fashioned. Many Gujarati wives were still expected to cook and serve meals along with the servants of the household. Jyoti had little time for that anyhow as she worked full-time, but it wasn't always easy working from home—Chottu was always asking her about the following day's menu, what vegetables to buy from the vegetable walla who showed up at the door every morning at different times, how much milk to order from the milk walla every Monday and Friday, how much ghee and yogurt to prepare, weather to use glass bottles for grain and lentil storage or stainless steel containers—the disruptions were endless. Being the lady of the house was tedious and Jyoti sought solace in her job. She enjoyed getting lost in the minutiae of the numbers on her laptop while keeping tuned to CNBC on satellite TV for the latest news and info on markets and business. The hours and days slipped by. Once a month she got together with Kiran and Chaya, both of whom were full-time housewives without careers, and were starting to become as gossipy as their mothers, eager to show off the new trinkets their husbands had bought them. At their last meeting, Jyoti had caught herself showing off a new diamond bracelet Anush had bought her. She hated herself for becoming so bourgeois and couldn't help but wonder what Gavin would have thought of her life—comfortably married to a man whom she neither loved nor hated.

Anush was a decent husband, when he was home, which was not often. He worked six days a week, and days would go by where the two of them would only see each other for a few minutes a day. Usually Anush was at the shop during the day, then out for dinner with business associates and didn't get home till Jyoti was nearly asleep. She'd gotten used to his side of the bed smelling faintly of whisky and a scent that she could only surmise was of animal flesh. She knew Anush wasn't a vegetarian even though he'd claimed to be one when they dated. She didn't entirely blame him as there was plenty of pressure on both of them to be nothing other than perfect during those first few weeks of courtship. In the big scheme of things she told herself not to be bothered by his meat-eating. After all, her secret was much worse. She was thankful that at least he respected her enough not to eat meat in front of her. They'd gone out for dinner a few times at some fine restaurants, but had little to talk about. It wasn't that they didn't get along. They were both agreeable and considerate with each other, but their conversations were almost always about practical matters: what sort of air conditioner they should replace the old one with, what sort of leave they should give the servants to see their families in the village. They made love once a month, always around the time she was ovulating. The sex was mediocre at best and had a detached quality to it—neither of them ever did it with their eyes open like she and Gavin had. Even the first time they made love on their wedding night it'd been uninspiring. Jyoti had noticed her mother inconspicuously plying Anush with whisky and Cokes at the reception, which puzzled Jyoti at first, but after the party, when they were in the honeymoon suite, she realized her mother's intentions of getting Anush drunk enough so he wouldn't notice her lack of virginity. And he didn't. After being inside her for a few moments that first night, he apologized for losing his erection and soon passed out.

AN EXTRAORDINARY DESTINY   363

Jyoti's parents and Varoon Sharma had recently begun to ask under the guise of cheerful teasing when they'd be expecting a grandchild. Chaya had a baby and Kiran was trying for one. The two of them were coming over to Sea Face Terraces for chai later that day.

Jyoti worked through the morning on her laptop, unable to focus. Something had been nagging at her lately. Perhaps it was the letter she'd received a couple of months ago from Carmen, her Spanish friend from the LSE. After graduating, Carmen had found a job in London working with the Children's Education Ministry as an economist and policy analyst. Carmen enthusiastically explained how the data she gathered and formulated eventually had an impact on public policy, how her recommendations went up the ladder and were implemented to make a real difference in children's lives. By comparison, Jyoti felt like a cog in a gigantic faceless machine. She wondered how many hundreds of hours she'd spent tracking price fluctuations on derivatives and crunching numbers through algorithms to provide her investment bank with. The bank had hundreds of employees like her crunching numbers, pricing commodities, stocks, and options, but apart from making rich people richer, what good did it do in the world? What difference was she making? Besides, wasn't it the kind of job that would one day be taken over by a computer? What would become of her then?

This morning, she caught herself playing out a daydream she often indulged in where she'd stayed in London with Gavin and the two of them had their baby in a one-bedroom council estate flat without central heating, living among working-class Londoners. It was a tough go at first, but they were happy.

She eventually got a job with an investment firm (the one she worked for currently paid her a quarter of what people earned in London), or even a better job—something like what Carmen did that helped make a difference in people's lives, something she could feel proud of. After the baby was a few years old, Gavin went back to art college, and then they bought a nice little place in the not-too-far suburbs of London with a small yard for their child to run around in . . .

She'd been to London once since being married. A quick business trip, just three days. When she wasn't in meetings, she stayed mostly in her hotel room, afraid to go to museums or even walk down the street for fear of bumping into him. Anush had called and told her to stay for a few days longer. "Catch up with some of your friends," he'd suggested. But she'd lied. "It's cold and miserable. I don't like London."

Now, Jyoti stared at her laptop screen blinking with numbers in different colours. She heard her mother's voice: *There's no sense in agonizing over the past. Best to move on and make the best of what you have.* It was the last thing her mother had whispered to her in private before her marriage. And when it'd come time at the end of the ceremony, when the daughter bids goodbye to her parents before officially becoming part of her husband's family, her mother had nodded and kissed Jyoti on the forehead, reminding Jyoti of those words.

The doorbell rang and Jyoti shut down her computer. Kiran and Chaya were let in by Chottu, who served them chai and *nasta*.

The two of them were both beaming. Kiran said, "Guess what?"

It was obvious from her ecstatic smile that Kiran was finally pregnant but Jyoti pretended not to catch on. Ignoring the pang in her own womb, she asked, "What?"

"I'm pregnant!" Kiran yelped, and the three of them embraced each other, jumping up and down.

While Kiran and Chaya talked of breastfeeding, of diapers, of baby wipes, of teething, of the best places to buy cute baby outfits, of all the jewelry to be designed for the baby, Jyoti did her best to appear enthusiastic. A part of her was genuinely happy for both of them, but she also couldn't help but think how frivolous they were being, how juvenile, how conventional. Perhaps she was just jealous. Or perhaps it was Gavin who'd burrowed deep inside her mind and was making her think these things. Perhaps he was the one to blame. She was angry all of a sudden that he was able to infiltrate her thoughts this way. She wished she could delete him from her life as she did to the numbers on her laptop screen.

The doorbell rang again and Chottu answered. It was the postman with a tube-like package that required Jyoti's signature. Jyoti was happy to excuse herself. After signing for it she noticed the familiar handwriting on the package. It was his.

Kiran and Chaya went on about babies and didn't notice Jyoti slinking into her bedroom, where she closed the door and opened the package. She wondered how he'd gotten her address. Probably Carmen. Inside the tube was a carefully wrapped three-foot-by-four-foot canvas rolled up. Jyoti delicately unfurled it and lay it out on her bed.

It was an acrylic painting of the duck pond at St James's Park where they'd picnicked. The sunset sky was a brilliant shade of tangerine and coral with flecks of magenta and amethyst as vibrant as the spring crocuses, daffodils, and rhododendrons underneath. The overall look of the painting wasn't entirely realistic, but rather a meditation on light. The balance of light and dark was subtle, leading the eye from one thing to the next: the luminous sunset to the wispy clouds in the sky to the tree tops to the lush plants and flowers to the few little ducks in the corner. It was the most perfect thing she'd ever seen. She couldn't help but smile because it was the happiest she'd felt in months. Perhaps ever.

On the tube package, he'd written his return London address.

- 46 -
ANUSH
1999

THE RESTAURANTS AND CLUBS THESE days were full of entrepreneurs, investors, hotel owners, industrialists. It was a social network that Anush enjoyed being a part of. They drank the best whisky, ate the most succulent fish pompfret masala fry, and exchanged business cards over steak tartar, and stock tips over sushi.

Tonight, Anush was at a club, having drinks with business associates in a private room. On the TV, a cute American reporter on CNN International was doing a story on India: "The Asian financial crisis of 1997 is long gone, tech stocks are making spectacular gains, the writing is on the wall. China and India will soon be calling the shots. And India has just emerged from the

Kargil War with Pakistan as a clear victor. Two weeks after India tested their nuclear weapons last year, Pakistan tested their own, eventually leading to an armed conflict in Kashmir. After two months of fighting, the Indian army eventually regained control of the lost ground, the Pakistanis were defeated, and India was reborn in its victory. Patriotism is at an all-time high. The stock markets in Mumbai are soaring. Indians are buoyant, self-aware, and for the first time they feel as though the world is beginning to recognize them as a major player . . ."

A year ago Anush had never imagined owning stocks, but now he checked the numbers several times a week. Part of the wedding present money from the old man and all the guests was invested in the stock market and doing very well. It was one of the few things he and Jyoti talked about with genuine enthusiasm.

The old man was happier than he'd been in years and was frequently out of town on business as he'd become an investor in real estate developments in Bangalore, Chennai, and elsewhere. The two of them even shared a drink and laughs once in a while over stock tips. The old man had bought him a Rolex like his. Now that Anush had won his father's approval, something he'd craved his whole life, he expected to be happy, and yet he felt unfulfilled. There was something missing.

Anush had become a supplier of furniture to new hotels. To his own surprise, he found he had a knack for business. The shop was busier than ever, Sharma Shipping and the old man's real estate holdings continued to do well, from which Anush recieved a healthy monthly stipend. Between the two incomes, Anush lacked little. He spent most of the day at the shop, in the newly refurbished office where he kept promising himself he'd get back to designing and making furniture. But a year had passed and he'd not made a single thing. Meanwhile, Reza had been promoted to shop manager and was busier than ever, in charge of three dozen new employees in the godowns who made furniture for the new hotels. He seemed much happier now that he had a baby daughter and was living with his family in the flat above the shop.

Occasionally the men Anush drank with would go to discreet clubs like this in the suburbs where beautiful girls danced. The men would start the night in a private room, away from the dancing girls, where they could dine, talk business for a while, and then go into the main dance hall to enjoy the women. There was no nudity, but the men could pay for a dance with the girls on stage, showering them with small bills in front of the crowd. At first Anush didn't like these clubs. There was something off-putting about married men lusting after young girls who'd come to the city from villages in search for work. These desperate girls were the lucky few who hadn't been sold by their families at a younger age into prostitution, and no matter how gentlemanly the men were it seemed lecherous. But in order to satisfy his growing number of business associates, Anush went along and drank whisky and laughed at their shenanigans until a girl who bore an uncanny resemblance to Nasreen danced one night, and Anush couldn't help but stare. Luckily it was the sort of place where he could do exactly that without shame. She looked younger than Nasreen, but she had Nasreen's deep brown eyes and full lips, even her neck was thin and elegant and her hips and breasts held the same full, taut curves. Anush tried to catch her eye but had no luck as he was sitting in a booth near the back. The next time he saw her he considered paying for a dance. The men had all wanted Anush to do this for months but he'd refused.

Tonight, after some play-act deliberating, he finally danced with her. Anush swore she livened up more with him than any of the others. After all he was closer to her age than many of the men in the club. She pirouetted around him and halfway through the song they made eyes at each other while dancing and flirting like a lustful Bollywood couple. As she twirled for him, he caught wafts of her perfume mixed with her perspiration. The scent was alluring. She even gyrated her hips into his crotch—a move usually reserved for men who'd paid for two or three dances. The crowd cheered. Surprisingly, Anush didn't feel dirty afterwards. In fact, he was exhilarated and felt more alive than he could remember. She smiled at him before collecting her bills off the floor. He wondered if it was just a courtesy smile, thanking him from not having to dance with a paunchy older man for once, but when they left the stage and were out of the lights, she smiled at him again. Of course it did occur to Anush that she might be stringing him along—some of these girls had admirers who bought them gifts, made them their concubines—but there was something private in her smile that seemed to say she wanted nothing more from him except to thank him for the dance. He smiled back, letting her know it was he who was grateful.

At the end of the night, Anush bid the men he came with good night and they all drove home, slightly sloshed. Jyoti was in London for a full week on business so Anush didn't have to be home. She'd been going more frequently, and Anush didn't mind—it meant he could stay out later. They still made love, about every other month or so, but it was never exciting. Tonight, halfway home, Anush turned the car around and headed back to Santa Cruz.

As he pulled up to the club, the dancing girl was about to hop into a rickshaw. He beeped his horn, rolled down the window of his Benz, and said, "Let me give you a ride home."

"OK," she said.

Her name was Priya. She was nineteen, new to the city, and was dancing to save enough money to go to college next year. Priya was shy, respectful, guileless. Nothing like Nasreen and yet the physical resemblance was remarkable. He couldn't stop wondering what she looked like naked, but then felt guilty. He was a married man. Although he didn't yearn for Jyoti, he wasn't about to betray her. He'd just have a drink or two, flirt for a bit. No harm in that. He worked hard and deserved to have a little fun.

Soon they were alone at her place, a tiny flat in Andheri. Her flatmate was working late and wouldn't be home till morning. After talking and smoking cigarettes for nearly an hour she began massaging his shoulders. He asked her to trace circles on his back while he lay on his stomach. When Anush closed his eyes he could almost smell the coconut oil in his mother's hair, hear her singing:

Kabhi kabhi, mere dil mein, khayaal aata hai . . .

After a while, Priya excused herself to the bathroom.

Anush turned on the TV. It was a news channel with footage of the '93 Bombay riots. The presenter said, "Charges might be brought against the BJP and the Shiv Sena for inciting sectarian violence. There is little proof but some speculation. Did the BJP filter money to local politicians to distribute among poor Hindus to foment this violence? Is this why poor Muslim tenements were burned down? Or was it also because the property was worth a lot more razed? Did real estate investors have a part to play in this?"

Anush considered if the old man was partly responsible.

"Unfortunately, there is little chance any of this can be proven in court."

Anush still wondered if what the old man had blurted out that night on the balcony was true, about killing his own father all those years ago. Had the old man just said that, knowing it would confuse Anush enough to not throw him over? And yet the more Anush tried to convince himself of this, the less sure he was.

The picture on the TV went out all of a sudden. Satellite channel disturbance. Snowy fuzz filled the screen, making Anush think of the Canadian prairies. Thank god he didn't live there. Paresh's parents had called recently, saying they were concerned about their son. The idiot had dropped out of his MBA program and wanted to write a novel about India.

The satellite signal returned. On CNN, a news anchor reported, "In minutes now, we should know the results of the Senate vote on President Clinton. Will he be acquitted on impeachment charges?"

Priya emerged from the bathroom in a sheer black bra and skimpy panties. She was statuesque. Anush turned the TV off and tossed the remote aside. Priya got on all fours and prowled towards him like a jungle cat. They kissed and Anush's hands travelled all over her smooth bronze skin, caressing her supple curves. Despite the whisky earlier, he got a rock-hard erection and asked her to put her hair up, the way Nasreen wore it.

ACKNOWLEDGEMENTS

I wish to thank the following for their advice, assistance, and support: my wife, first-reader and inspiration, Paula Ayer; my publisher, who saw the potential in this manuscript, Taryn Boyd; my story editors for their invaluable insights, Colin Thomas and Pam Robertson; Kate Kennedy; Andrew Riley; my entire family in India with whom I lived for a year, especially Chika and Chiki, whose generous hospitality knows no bounds; and my mother, Bharti Paleja, who helped me with Sanskrit, Hindi, Urdu, and Punjabi translations of poems and songs over various drafts, and for her endless love and support.

The following sources were helpful with my understanding of modern Indian politics: *Warriors in Politics: Hindu Nationalism, Violence, and the Shiv Sena in India* by Sikata Banerjee; *Snakes and Ladders* by Gita Mehta; and the BBC2 four-part documentary *Wonders of the Universe* by Brian Cox, which illuminated my understanding of the cosmos.

SHEKHAR PALEJA graduated from the University of Calgary with his BFA in Theatre, and has many film and theatre credits to his name. A resident of Vancouver, he has also published two children's books, *Native Americans: A Visual Exploration* and *PowerUp! An Extraordinary Destiny* is his debut novel.